TROIKA

TROIKA

Clive Egleton

HODDER AND STOUGHTON
LONDON SYDNEY AUCKLAND TORONTO

British Library Cataloguing in Publication Data
Egleton, Clive
    Troika.
    I. Title.
    823'.914[F]   PR6055.G55

    ISBN 0 340 36108 5

Hodder and Stoughton Editorial Office: 47 Bedford Square, London WC1B 3DP.

Jenny—for the roses

CHAPTER I

The authorities had called him John Doe because he was thought to be an American and he'd refused to disclose his real identity. He was a tall man, around six foot three inches, but his body had wasted away to less than 130 pounds and the hospital fatigues swamped his skeletal frame. His right leg had been amputated well above the kneecap, which Kirov found puzzling, for the preliminary medical examination had referred to a gunshot wound in the ankle. In the absence of any official explanation, he could only assume that gangrene had already set in by the time the American had reached the casualty clearing station at Kabul.

"My name is Georgi." Kirov looked up from the medical dossier and smiled encouragingly. "What do I call you?"

The American ignored him and continued to stare at the snowcapped mountain range in the distance. A small frown creased the pallid skin between the dull gray eyes as if he were thinking that the far-off peaks looked familiar but he couldn't place them. It was a futile exercise; the American had been brought to this isolated GRU interrogation center near the Afghanistan border at Pata Kasai in an Mi-24 helicopter, strapped into a litter, blindfolded from the moment he'd been carried out of the army base hospital.

"You're in the Soviet Republic of Uzbekistan," Kirov informed him, "and a very long way from home."

"So what? You think I don't know that?"

His voice sounded weary, but there was a note of defiance in it that was truly amazing considering that more than four months had elapsed since he had been taken prisoner.

"Then I assume you know why you are here?" Kirov asked quietly.

"You want a confession from me. Right?"

"Who said anything about a confession?" Kirov leaned back in his chair, elbows resting on the arms, his fingertips

7

pressed together and leveled at the American. "I'm just looking for a little cooperation from you. For instance, it would enable us to arrange for your repatriation if we knew your serial number, rank, and name."

"I'm a press photographer, not a soldier."

"Really? Well, one would have thought your editor would have been sufficiently alarmed by now to get in touch with the U.S. State Department."

"I don't work for any particular newspaper. I'm a free lance; I go where the action is, take a few pictures and sell them to the highest bidder." A faint smile appeared on the American's colorless lips. "Private enterprise, that's what the capitalist system is all about."

"You must be one of its failures then," Kirov said dryly. "Tell me, how did you manage to take any photographs without a camera?"

"We're not going over that same old ground again, are we? Jesus, your intelligence people in Kabul already know what happened to my equipment. If I told them once, I must have told them at least a hundred times. It's all there in that other green folder on your desk."

"I'd like to hear it from you. These field interrogation reports usually make dull reading, and they're not always accurate."

"I never thought I'd hear a Soviet officer admit to that."

"I'm only voicing my opinion," Kirov said mildly. "It's something I've always done."

"You couldn't afford to do that unless you had influential connections." The American eyed him speculatively. "On the other hand, they must be on the fringe of the inner circle, otherwise you'd never have ended up in this hellhole, a hundred miles from nowhere. What happened? Did you step out of line once too often?"

The jibe struck a nerve; the American was right on all three counts. His father was General Fedor Fedorovich Kirov, a Hero of the Soviet Union twice over and a contemporary of Comrade Nikita Krushchev, a man whose star had burned out along with the former Chairman of the Council of Ministers and Party Secretary's. And it was also true that his secondment to this GRU outpost was directly

8

attributable to the awkward questions he'd raised after Tania had died, Tania who had been very special to him. None of these factors was, however, relevant in the present context.

"You're the one who's stepping out of line, John Doe," he said curtly. "I asked you a simple question and I'm still waiting for an answer."

"You can drop the J.D. My name is Russell Moorcroft and I walked into Afghanistan with two cameras and enough film to last me a couple of months. If you want to know what happened to my equipment, you'd better ask the soldiers who took me prisoner. They stole everything I had."

Moorcroft's story had a ring of truth to it, but the "after action" report was even more convincing. Kirov placed the medical dossier to one side and opened the security file at the appropriate folio.

"You were captured in the Kinjan valley, approximately eight miles from the village of Doshi on the seventh of June. The terrorists under your command . . ."

"Resistance fighters," Moorcroft said, correcting him swiftly. "And they weren't under my command. As a matter of fact, they considered me a pain in the ass. If I hadn't had a letter of introduction from Daoud Khan, who controls the whole area around Paghman, they would have slit my throat from ear to ear, and the guide who came with me all the way from Kurram in Pakistan."

"You may call them what you like," Kirov snapped. "As far as I'm concerned, they're terrorists." He opened the center drawer in the desk, took out a glossy photograph and slapped it down in front of Moorcroft. "Major Anatole Molodony," he said. "His vehicle was ambushed on the road to Charikar. The driver and escort were killed instantly but he merely sustained a broken leg and was concussed. It would have been better for him had he died with the others. Your so-called resistance fighters staked him out on the ground and proceeded to strip the flesh from his right arm from wrist to elbow. When presumably Molodony had told them everything he knew, they cut off his penis and sewed it up in his mouth."

"I never said I approved of the way they treat their

9

prisoners, but then they've never heard of the Geneva Conventions."

"Are you implying that we don't observe them?"

"I'm not making any accusations," Moorcroft said carefully.

"I should think not."

Kirov rubbed his forehead as if seeking to relieve a severe headache. The interrogation had lost direction because Moorcroft had deliberately set out to provoke him, and he'd fallen for it, something that would not go unnoticed. There were eavesdroppers next door recording every word of their conversation. The fact that he was the only English-speaking linguist on the post was immaterial; in due course, the tapes would be dispatched to GRU Headquarters in Moscow for detailed analysis, and his handling of the inter-rogation would be subjected to an in-depth examination. If his superiors wanted him to fail, as he suspected they did, then he was certainly going about it the right way. The remedy, however, was simple enough; from here on he would stick to the facts and wouldn't allow himself to be sidetracked by the American.

"Do you know how many casualties we suffered in that ambush on the seventh of June, Mr. Moorcroft?"

"I haven't the faintest idea. I was too busy keeping my head down."

"Nineteen," Kirov said angrily. "Eight dead, eleven wounded. Of course, deciding just when and where to lay an ambush is never a problem for the terrorists. They have their spies and informers among the local population, and in this instance they knew that a mobile patrol consisting of two T62 tanks and two BTR 60p armored personnel carriers checks out the road to Doshi every day. They also knew that it was customary for the patrol to be covered by a helicopter gunship with two others on call. However, although their prebattle intelligence is generally very good, a complete absence of discipline and a profound lack of sophisticated hardware usually ensures that an ambush is rarely successful."

The ambush Moorcroft had witnessed had been different. It had been sprung at exactly the right moment, several radio-controlled demolition charges cratering the road and causing a rockfall from the overhanging cliff face a split second before the lead tank was hit by an 84mm Carl Gustav. The hollow charge had struck the driver's compartment, ruptured the reserve fuel tanks, and ignited the gas. As the flames began to envelop the tank, the rear T62 had been immobilized by two 84mm rounds, one of which had shattered the offside driving sprocket while the other had bored into the turret ring and destroyed the traverse mechanism. With the main armament jammed in the nine o'clock position, the crew commander had quickly realized that only the heavy machine gun on the external mount could be swung around to engage the enemy on the hillside above the narrow unpaved road. Reacting instinctively, he had opened the hatch and stood up, thus exposing the upper half of his body to a withering hail of small-arms fire that had virtually cut him in two.

The armored personnel carriers had been trapped in the middle, unable to move in any direction, a sitting target for every terrorist armed with a rocket launcher. Knowing this, the patrol commander had radioed for assistance, then fired the multiple phosphorus smoke dischargers on his vehicle to screen the infantrymen while they dismounted to take cover in the monsoon ditch beside the road. It was a standard operational drill, one that somebody familiar with Soviet infantry tactics had anticipated.

"The ditch had been sown with antipersonnel mines, and the surviving members of the platoon had to shelter behind the blazing BTR 60s. They were still crouching there when the helicopter gunship arrived over the target area and was promptly shot down by a man-portable surface-to-air missile."

Kirov opened the center drawer again and took out a packet of Lucky Strikes. Slowly and very deliberately, he stripped off the cellophane wrapper, tapped out a cigarette, and lit up. It didn't matter whether Moorcroft indulged in the habit or not; the cigarettes were intended to remind him of home, and he could see that they had.

"You should have gotten out while you were still ahead," Kirov said idly.

"What?"

"I'm referring to the ambush. Hit and run, that's how a guerrilla force should operate, but your bunch of terrorists were too elated to observe that maxim. No doubt you realized that the helicopter pilot would have sent a situation report as he approached the target area?"

"How the hell would I know that? I'm just a press photographer." Moorcroft squirmed in the chair and pressed his thighs together. "You got a bathroom around here?" he asked abruptly.

"There's a lavatory at the end of this office block."

"Can I use it?"

"Later."

"You don't understand; I need to go now."

"Then you'll just have to control your bladder until I've finished." Kirov paused to tap his cigarette over the ashtray, then said, "Back in Kabul we had four MiG fighter ground-attack planes at instant readiness, and they were already airborne before the gunship was shot down. Also available at five minutes' notice to move was a company-strength rapid deployment force, which, fortunately for us, happened to be less than twenty-five miles from the contact area. We were therefore able to mount a counterattack much sooner than you had probably anticipated. The MiGs were supposed to keep your group pinned to the ground while the heliborne infantry force deployed, but the enveloping movement was largely unsuccessful, thanks to you. One has to admire the way you extricated the terrorists from a difficult situation but, in your shoes, I would have appointed someone else to command the rear guard."

"I'm getting tired of saying this, but I really am just a press photographer."

"And I'm getting tired of hearing that feeble story. If you were genuine, then, free lance or not, somebody, some-where, would have reported the fact that you were missing." Kirov stared at his wife's photograph on the desk and wondered if the American had someone like Tania waiting for him back home. "How old are you, Mr. Moorcroft?" he asked softly.

"Twenty-eight."

12

Tania would have been twenty-eight next month. But she was cold in the ground, put there eighteen long months ago by some unknown drunken driver while Kirov was serving in Blagoveshchensk on the Sino-Soviet border.

"Somebody would have missed you," Kirov said, picking up from where he'd left off. "A man like you just doesn't suddenly disappear without a trace. Sooner or later, your State Department would have been asked to look into the matter. Their deafening silence can only mean that either you're a CIA agent or a mercenary."

"In Soviet eyes that amounts to the same thing, doesn't it?"

"That's only propaganda for the masses. The way our colleagues in the KGB see it, a CIA agent can always be exchanged for one of ours should the necessity arise, whereas a mercenary is good only for target practice."

"And you're a long time dead," Moorcroft said in a flat voice.

"Precisely." Kirov stood up and adjusted his tunic, tugging the skirt until the ruck disappeared above the leather belt around his waist. "You've got two hours to think about it," he said, then repeated the statement in Russian for the benefit of the eavesdroppers next door.

Lunch was being served in the mess hall but Kirov didn't feel like eating. Wheeling left outside the office block, he headed toward the officers' quarters on the far side of the compound. There were ten officers on post, and of the three wooden huts, one was allocated to Colonel Leonid Paskar while the other two were subdivided to accommodate the rest. Junior lieutenants were allotted a room not much bigger than a cell; as a senior captain, Kirov's was scarcely palatial but it was furnished on a slightly more generous scale. This meant that in addition to the usual single bed, upright wooden chair, combination closet and chest of drawers, the army also provided him with a trestle table and a bedside locker in which he kept a bottle of brandy and a small tumbler.

He poured himself a drink and downed it in one gulp. Soviet brandy, Tania had once observed, was good for lighting fires and dulling the senses, and there was a lot of truth in that. He was tempted to have another but resisted the idea, knowing that the second would lead to a third, and he didn't want to finish up in a drunken stupor ever again.

Kirov put the bottle away, undid the leather belt around his waist and, removing his tunic, hung it up in the closet. An angular face with sad-looking eyes under a crown of dark brown hair stared back at him from the mirror on the reverse side of the door. He was thirty-two, four years older than the American and at least forty pounds heavier, but they did have one thing in common: both of them appeared a good deal older than they were.

Kirov closed the closet door, set the alarm on the cheap clock he'd purchased from the GUM stores in Moscow, and then lay down on the bed to dream about the slender blonde lounging on the beach at Sochi who had once been his wife.

The alarm woke him promptly at 2:15.

*   *   *

Moorcroft was still perched on the uncomfortable, slatted wooden chair, both hands clutching the lower of two horizontal rungs behind his back to ensure he didn't slide off onto the floor. Nobody had fed the American in his absence, but Kirov knew the guards had forced him to drink a lot of water and then refused to take him to the lavatory. The proof was there in the puddle of urine on the linoleum and in the wide, damp patch around the crotch of his hospital fatigues. That he felt humiliated as a result was also evident from the way Moorcroft avoided his gaze.

"I've been doing some hard thinking." Moorcroft hesitated as though uncertain how to broach the subject, then said, "Suppose I did cooperate? What's in it for me?"

"It would depend on who you are and what you are," Kirov told him. "As I said before we broke for lunch, a mercenary is only good for target practice. On the other hand, a CIA agent might be regarded as a valuable acquisition, the kind we could trade on a one-for-one basis should the occasion arise."

"And that could happen any day. Right?"

"Your guess is as good as mine," Kirov said, poker-faced.

But the American wasn't guessing; he knew an exchange was in the cards, and he wasn't referring to the Soviet warrant officer whom the South Africans had captured in southern Angola either. The details of that affair had been widely reported outside the USSR before Moorcroft had been taken prisoner, as had the arrangements for the NCO's eventual repatriation. However, two Soviet airmen, Nikolai Molayev and Ivan Chernitski, had recently fallen into the hands of the Unita rebels operating within Angola. This was still classified Top Secret, though, and while the U.S. State Department might well be aware of the situation, the world press certainly wasn't. If Kirov's hunch was correct and Moorcroft was in the know, then some highly placed officer in either the KGB or the GRU must have deliberately leaked the information to him. With this thought in mind, Kirov took out a fountain pen and scratch pad and wrote a brief memo to himself that read: "Re disclosure from Moorcroft—send breach of security report to HQ GRU stating culprit unknown."

"I do have one other question," Moorcroft said tentatively.

"Yes?"

"If I did confess, would there be a show trial?"

"I doubt it. For what it's worth, I think you'll be held in solitary confinement until we're ready to make a deal."

"Then you'll be interested to know that I'm a graduate of the Virginia Military Institute and a regular officer in the United States Army. My serial number is JA 614003. I was commissioned into the infantry in September 1976 and joined the Green Berets a little over twenty-one months ago in the rank of captain."

"Hold it a minute."

Kirov uncapped his fountain pen again and jotted the facts down on the scratch pad, using a form of shorthand that was entirely his own invention. With the room wired for sound, there was no need to record anything in writing but he wanted to squeeze Moorcroft dry, and the notes would be a useful aide-mémoire.

"My control was a guy called George Lamar," Moorcroft said when Kirov looked up. "He operates out of Miram Shah in the Waziristan Province of Pakistan."

"Lamar is probably a cover name."

"Probably," Moorcroft agreed. "But I daresay the KGB will know of him. He's an itty-bitty fella, about five foot six, fat as a barrel and in his mid-forties. He has a clipped way of talking and his instructions to me were pretty brief and to the point; I was to link up with the Paghman group in the Khinjan Valley and create as much mayhem as I could."

"You keep saying 'I' when common sense tells me you weren't alone." Kirov smiled and shook his head as though mildly disappointed that the American should take him for a fool. "It's standard practice for the CIA to send in a team of three, and I don't believe an Afghan tribesman is capable of handling a sophisticated weapon system like a surface-to-air missile."

"My Afghans were."

"Then somebody trained them, and it wasn't you."

"I had two noncom assistants," Moorcroft said reluctantly, "Sergeants Henry Silverman from Chicago, Illinois, and Jerry Opalko from Omaha, Nebraska. I don't know their serial numbers, Georgi. It's not the sort of information you need to carry around in your head."

It was always the same, Kirov thought. A prisoner would hold out for just so long, then suddenly he would divulge an item of information, and from there on it was as though a sluice gate had been opened. The use of his first name was also an indication of the rapport now growing between them.

"Maybe we ought to have a few more personal details for the record," he said warmly. "Starting with your date and place of birth, Russell."

"Sure." Moorcroft nodded eagerly. "Well, now, let's see; I was born on the twenty-fifth of January 1954 in Bendix, New Jersey. Then when I was about three or four, the whole family upped and moved to Staten Island to a house on Page Street."

"Any brothers or sisters?" Kirov asked.

"Two sisters; one older than me, one younger."

Question and answer, question and answer; the interrogation had settled into a familiar pattern, except that Kirov conducted it as if they were two old acquaintances who hadn't met in a long while and had a lot of catching up to do. Halfway through the afternoon, he had the guards bring them a platter of cold meats and some goat's cheese from the mess hall, which they washed down with lemon tea laced with vodka. When, later on, Moorcroft asked if he might use the lavatory, Kirov pretended to notice the American's urine-stained fatigues for the first time and summoned the guards again to upbraid them for their callousness.

Question and answer, question and answer; the tapes silently revolving in the room next door, the evening shadows steadily drawing across the compound. Question and answer, question and answer; Kirov kept the dialogue going until he had squeezed the American dry and knew everything there was to know about his personal life. At 1800 hours he turned Moorcroft over to the duty officer and instructed him to arrange suitable accommodation for the night. Then he rang Colonel Paskar, gave him a brief résumé of the interrogation, and returned to his quarters. Less than half an hour later, the colonel's orderly arrived with a formal invitation requesting the pleasure of his company at dinner that evening.

★　　★　　★

Despite the Order of Glory Second Class and the Medal for Battle Merit, Colonel Leonid Paskar had few admirers among the officers under his command. A short, barrel-chested Ukrainian with coarse features and an equally uncouth manner, he had come up through the ranks, winning his commission on the battlefield in October 1944 at the age of twenty. Though undoubtedly a brave and competent infantryman, he had precious little aptitude for intelligence work and virtually no language qualifications apart from a reasonably good knowledge of German, which he spoke with an execrable accent. Few people could understand how he had reached the rank of colonel; this was because they failed to recognize his uncanny ability to gauge the wind's direction and bend with it. Although aware that Kirov was out of favor with the high command, he'd nevertheless handled him with kid gloves from the day the younger man had joined his unit. Experience had taught Paskar that outcasts were often rehabilitated, nor did he overlook the fact that although no longer on the active list, General Kirov was still close to the center of power.

It was apparent that the general was uppermost in Paskar's thoughts that evening as Kirov listened patiently to one anecdote after another about his father, most of which were certainly hearsay. When the five armies comprising the First Belorussian Front had liberated Warsaw, Paskar had been a junior lieutenant; when they seized Berlin, he was still only commanding a rifle company in the Third Shock Army. Throughout the same campaign, Fedor Fedorovich Kirov had been a major general of artillery on Marshal Zhukov's staff, and it was extremely unlikely that their paths had ever crossed, but the way Paskar told it, they'd been bosom companions.

"A brilliant tactician, your father." Paskar drained a goblet of wine, the fourth since they had sat down to dinner, and then gave a loud, satisfied burp. "You should have seen the barrage he laid on for us when we crossed the Oder. A gun to every ten yards, eight thousand artillery pieces over the whole front, and that's not counting the multiple rocket launchers. I tell you, the Comrade General altered the landscape with that orchestra."

"It must have been very impressive," Kirov said and cupped a hand over his mouth to hide a yawn.

"The Fascists were definitely impressed." Paskar picked up the wine bottle, saw that it was empty and fetched another from the private stock he kept locked up in a cupboard. "They didn't know whether they were coming or going."

Kirov watched him uncork the bottle and wished he could think of a plausible excuse to leave. A little of Paskar went a very long way, and he couldn't recall an evening that had passed quite so slowly.

"Like father, like son." Paskar filled his goblet and raised it, saluting him. "You did a fine job on the American, Georgi."

"He was very malleable."

"Because you succeeded in winning his confidence, a

prerequisite that must have defeated every other intelligence officer who tried to interrogate him."

The colonel was only echoing Kirov's own thoughts but on a much more superficial plane. Moorcroft had been in Soviet hands for more than four months and, even allowing for a period of hospitalization, there had been ample opportunity for a whole army of interrogators to question him.

"Believe me, Georgi," Paskar said in a slurred voice, "Moscow will sit up and take notice of you when they hear those tapes."

"I've only scratched the surface so far. There's still a gold mine of information waiting to be tapped—the names of all his contemporaries, the officers and men he met on his Ranger course."

"Quite."

"With your permission, Comrade Colonel, I'd like to question him again the day after tomorrow."

"Seems a good idea, provided you're still with us then." Paskar wiped his mouth, removed a piece of red cabbage that had been obstinately clinging to the lower lip and flicked it onto his plate. "It wouldn't surprise me if you were recalled to Moscow. A lot of people will be interested to learn how you broke the American."

In four months, Moorcroft had been reduced to an emaciated skeleton and had lost most of his right leg, allegedly as a result of a gunshot wound in the ankle. If the malnutrition was hard to accept, the surgery was even more difficult to explain. Kirov found himself wondering how many operations the American had endured and whether any of them was medically necessary.

He didn't have to ask himself who would be capable of perpetrating such a barbaric atrocity. The KGB was responsible for the state security, and those in charge could be utterly ruthless in the execution of that duty. And when things started to go wrong, it would also be typical of them to unload Moorcroft onto the GRU so that Military Intelligence ended up holding the shitty end of the stick. The KGB was always trying to exert its authority over the GRU, and when you came right down to it, Kirov thought, it wasn't surprising there was no love lost between the two intelligence agencies.

"If I am recalled to Moscow," Kirov said, voicing his doubts aloud, "I hope they will tell me how I broke the American."

Chapter II

A popular figure with those Westerners who'd met him at various social functions in Moscow, Aleksei Ivanovich Vatutin was a slender, average-size man in his mid-fifties. The Professor of Political Studies at the Patrice Lumumba University, he was held in high esteem by the non-communist diplomatic community, who regarded him as the least prejudiced and most open-minded of Soviet academics they'd encountered. Widely read, interested in the arts, especially ballet and opera, he had enlivened many a dull cocktail party with his gentle humor, persuasive charm, and ability to speak fluent English and French.

Vatutin's scholarly appearance, emphasized by receding light brown hair, a somewhat prominent forehead, and rimless spectacles, was such that nobody suspected that the university appointment was merely a "legend" to conceal his real occupation. A major general in the KGB, he was the senior deputy controller of the First Chief Directorate and had special responsibility for the ultrasensitive Executive Action Department. His office was on the fourth floor of a vast, half-moon-shaped office block that had been custom-built for the directorate when the ornate rococo building on Dzerzhinsky Square had finally proved inadequate for their needs, despite a nine-story extension added during World War II. Located north-northeast of Moscow and set well back from the twelve-lane outer-ring motorway, the building's first six floors were totally obscured by a thick belt of fir trees. In consequence, the view from Vatutin's office was limited to a wide expanse of dull gray sky. However, taking everything into consideration, he preferred to gaze at this blank vista rather than look at his visitor.

The man seated across the desk from him was Lieutenant Colonel Dmitri Nikishev of the GRU. Young, ambitious, and self-seeking, he reminded Vatutin of a sleek and well-fed cat, with the same easy loyalties. Officially, Nikishev was the chief instructor at the GRU Training School on Militia Street; unofficially, he was a prime source of information for the KGB's Third Directorate, which was charged with monitoring the armed forces. Vatutin thought it was one of life's rich ironies that for the duration of this particular operation, Nikishev would be working hand in glove with the KGB with the full knowledge and consent of his superiors for the first and only time. That this upstart lieutenant colonel and the entire Headquarters Directorate of the GRU were being led around by the nose was another pleasing thought, one that Vatutin dwelt on with pleasure while Nikishev rambled on.

"I assume there are no problems, then?" Vatutin said, finally cutting through the monologue. "Captain Kirov will arrive on Aeroflot flight 265 and will be met at the airport by a staff car from Moscow Military District Headquarters. When he reports in, the duty staff officer will inform him that he is to attend a special briefing early tomorrow morning but that, unfortunately, the army is unable to accommodate him overnight. However, arrangements have been made for another staff car to pick him up from his father's residence on Kalinina Prospekt at 0630 hours. Then he will hand Kirov a sealed envelope and congratulate him on his forthcoming promotion to major."

"Yes."

"You sound doubtful?" Vatutin turned to face him, his eyes bleak and cold as a glacier.

"There could be one slight difficulty, Comrade General." Nikishev swallowed nervously. "It seems Kirov has submitted a Breach of Security report, alleging that the American prisoner, Moorcroft, was aware of certain facts that could have come only from a Soviet intelligence officer. To be specific, he knew that we've agreed to an exchange for the two Soviet airmen held by the Unita terrorists in Angola."

21

Vatutin was aware of everything that had passed between the American and Kirov during the first interrogation and the four subsequent follow-ups the GRU officer had been allowed to conduct before being recalled to Moscow. In fact, the KGB had broken Moorcroft long before he had been handed over to Kirov, and the American had been told exactly what information he was to disclose, but the Breach of Security report was a new and unexpected development.

"It's odd that Kirov didn't question him about the supposed leak when he had every opportunity to do so."

"Yes." Nikishev cleared his throat. "That's the one disturbing thing about the whole business."

The way Vatutin saw it, the American had departed from his script for one of two reasons; either he was looking for confirmation that he would indeed be repatriated, or else he'd decided the KGB intended to renege on their agreement and, out of revenge, had attempted to sabotage the forthcoming operation by alerting Kirov to the fact that he was probably being set up. Kirov's motive in filing the Breach of Security report was harder to fathom. It would be nice to think that he'd figured it wasn't his job to discover which intelligence officer had been responsible for the leak and had merely filed the report to cover himself, but the stakes were far too high to leave anything to chance. Kirov would have to be watched, his every move noted and checked out from the time he arrived in Moscow until the GRU had him safely under wraps at their safe house near Mozhaysk.

"I'm wondering if we shouldn't question Moorcroft about the leak, Comrade General?"

Vatutin was tempted to ask him whom he meant by "we," but refrained from doing so because Nikishev knew damned well the American had been returned to the KGB's tender care several days before Kirov had been recalled to Moscow. "I don't think that's a very good idea." He smiled fleetingly, then said, his voice almost purring, "After all, why should we give Moorcroft the opportunity to sow dissension within our ranks?"

"The same thought had occurred to me."

"Then, no doubt, so has the obvious solution."

The emphatic nod didn't fool him. Nikishev hadn't the

faintest idea what he was driving at. The man was a dull, plodding workhorse who had been promoted above his ceiling and had to rely on bluff to get by. That made him easy to manipulate and was the reason Vatutin had arranged for him to become the GRU case officer.

"The American was captured on the seventh of June," Vatutin continued, "and today is Wednesday the twenty-seventh of October. He has therefore been in our hands for close to five months. It shouldn't be too difficult for the GRU to trace every officer who questioned him before Kirov saw him, and by a process of elimination arrive at those officers who know about the exchange deal with Unita. Naturally, the KGB will do the same."

"And Kirov, Comrade General? What do we do about him?"

"He only submitted the report. It's no concern of his how the matter is investigated."

"I'm told he did have a reputation for being difficult."

"Did is the correct word," Vatutin said firmly. "There's nothing wrong with his attitude now."

Tania Abalakinova Kirov, elder daughter of Yuri Nikolaevich Abalakin, program controller for Moscow State Radio, aged twenty-six, height five foot six inches, weight 119 pounds, hair blonde, eyes gray, killed night 8/9 April 1981, victim of an unidentified hit-and-run driver on Samolocny Lane. No witnesses. Those were the only details listed in the police record, but the KGB had carried out its own investigation and a duplicate copy of the report was lodged in Vatutin's safe. It named the senior GRU officer who had arranged for Kirov to be posted to Blagoveshchensk on the Sino-Soviet border on completion of his English language course, and the ageing Deputy Minister of Defense who'd lusted after Tania and had wanted her husband out of the way.

"I wouldn't like the Comrade General to think I had any reservations about Kirov. He's an outstanding young officer, the best in the class of '71 at the Frunze Military Academy."

"Quite so. I imagine that was one of the factors your superiors took into account when they selected him for this assignment."

Vatutin thought any further explanation was unnecessary.

Nikishev knew the forthcoming operation had been sanctioned at the highest level and that the final choice of agent had been approved by certain interested parties in the Politburo.

"Are there any other points you wish to make, Dmitri?" Vatutin asked pleasantly.

Nikishev shook his head, stood up ramrod straight and requested the general's permission to leave. Then he saluted, turned about and marched out of the office.

Tania Abalakinova Kirov, a wide-eyed innocent who'd been flattered by the attentions of the Deputy Minister and had been naïve enough to believe that, as one of General Kirov's oldest friends, he was simply taking a fatherly interest in her. Incredibly, she'd convinced herself that the invitations to official receptions and private dinner parties were merely his way of ensuring that she wasn't left out of things while her husband was serving in Blagoveshchensk. That curious illusion had been destroyed on the night 8/9 April 1981 when the Deputy Minister had tried to rape her and, half-naked, she had run out of the house on Samolocny Lane and straight into the path of an oncoming taxi.

It had been the kind of incident with political repercussions that the police were only too anxious to hand over to the KGB. The taxi driver had been exonerated, then sent back to his native village in the Ukraine on the pretext that his Moscow resident permit was no longer valid. As had been envisaged from the start, no charges had been brought against either the senior GRU officer or the Deputy Minister, but the two men were aware that the KGB would have an inexorable hold on them for the rest of time. It was this latent threat of exposure that had enabled Vatutin to make sure they selected the right man for the job. Kirov's apparent success in breaking the American when so many others had allegedly tried and failed was the ultimate subterfuge to ensure that he was recognized as the outstanding officer on the short list. Vatutin also knew that this same subterfuge would protect the senior GRU officer and the Deputy Minister in the unlikely event that they were subsequently accused of showing undue bias.

★   ★   ★

Kirov paid off the taxi outside number 54 Platovskij Thoroughfare, picked up his canvas suitcase, and walked into the gray apartment block, uncertain whether he would find anybody at home. He'd rung the Smolenskaja Hospital from Moscow Military District Headquarters, learned that his half sister wasn't on duty, and had then tried her private number, only to be told by the exchange operator that the phone appeared to be out of order. So also were the two elevators in the entrance hall, but there was nothing unusual about that. They hadn't been working when he'd said goodbye to Irena before he was posted to Paskar's GRU unit back in April '81.

Transferring the suitcase to his left hand, he started up the staircase toward her tiny four-room apartment on the eighth floor. Halfway there, Kirov found himself wishing he hadn't bothered to call on his half sister because it was no joke lugging a bag that weighed forty-five pounds up one steep flight after another. He let go of the handrail, switched the suitcase to the other hand and continued on up, counting off the steps. By the time Kirov reached the seventh floor, even that mindless diversion had worn thin. Out of breath, he finally made it to the eighth, walked down the dimly lit corridor, and rang the bell to her apartment.

The welcome he received was worth all the effort. Irena's eyes widened with surprise, then her face lit up and she flung both arms around his neck and hugged him. The questions came thick and fast; what was he doing in Moscow, when had he gotten in, how long was he staying?

"The signal didn't explain why I'd been recalled," Kirov told her between affectionate embraces. "I arrived a couple of hours ago and I'm still none the wiser, but that's how it is in the army, all hurry up and wait."

"Well, whatever the reason, it's marvelous to see you again, Georgi." Irena steered him into the living room, helped him out of his light topcoat, then walked over to the television set and switched it off, silencing the newscaster in mid-sentence. "Now let me look at you properly." She stepped back a pace and examined him with a professional eye.

Good old Irena, he thought, doctor and surrogate mother,

25

the latter a role she had adopted when his natural mother had died of a cerebral hemorrhage shortly before his eighth birthday. Irena had been nineteen then, and, with the wisdom of hindsight, he supposed her compassion had been aroused by the knowledge that she too had suffered a similar loss but at a much earlier age and in entirely different circumstances. There had been nothing clean or quick about the way Natasha Kirov, the general's first wife, had met her death; she had been gunned down with hundreds of other innocent civilians when a pair of marauding ME 109s had strafed a column of refugees on the road out of Bialystok in the summer of '41. How the two-year-old Irena had survived the attack was a miracle; how she came to be in the orphanage for war foundlings where the general had eventually found her five years later was an even greater one. All the authorities had been able to tell him was that, throughout the long journey from Bialystok to Moscow by way of Smolensk, she had most certainly been passed from one stranger to another and that they had managed to identify Irena from the engraved bracelet she was wearing on her left wrist.

"Well, little sister," Kirov said. "What's the verdict?"

"You've lost weight, Georgi."

"So have you."

"Flatterer." Irena pushed a hand through her short gray hair and laughed. "Look at me, my thighs are too heavy, my waist is too thick."

"Nonsense. You won't hear Igor complaining. By the way where is that husband of yours?"

"He's still at the university, attending a meeting of the faculty."

They both knew he was more likely to be dallying with one of his students. Igor Gusovsky had always had an eye for a pretty girl and oddly enough they seemed to find him attractive too, something that puzzled Kirov since his brother-in-law was no Greek god.

"Well, I shall be sorry to have missed him," Kirov said, trying to sound as though he meant it. "Perhaps we'll have better luck next time."

"Can't you stay the night, Georgi? We haven't got a spare room but I can easily make up a bed for you on the couch."

26

"I know you could. Trouble is, the army's sending a car to pick me up from Kalinina Prospekt at the crack of dawn tomorrow."

"Why can't you come straight out with it, Georgi? Why can't you just say that you are spending the night with our esteemed father?"

"Because I didn't want to hurt your feelings. I know how things are between you two."

The conflict between father and daughter was not of Irena's choosing. The love-hate relationship was entirely one-sided and there was no logical explanation for it. In his blacker moments, General Fedor Fedorovich would tell her point blank that she was not his daughter, that the real Irena had been killed with her mother on the road to Smolensk. He knew that because she bore no resemblance to his first wife. As for the bracelet the authorities had found around her wrist, well, that didn't prove anything. Some looter had obviously stolen it and passed it on to his own child before he died.

"Have you eaten?" Irena asked him, breaking an awkward silence.

"I had something on the plane." He smiled. "I'd like a cup of tea, though, if you're making one."

"I managed to get a jar of instant coffee from the commissariat."

"That would be even nicer." Kirov followed her into the tiny kitchen and sat down at the table while she filled a kettle and put it on the gas. "How are you getting on at the hospital?" he asked. "Have they made you chief of surgery yet?"

"You know they haven't." Irena broke the spent match in half and dropped it into the wastebasket, then faced him, arms folded across her chest, her eyes narrowing thoughtfully. "What prompted that question, Georgi?"

"Nothing in particular," he said evasively. "I'm just interested in your career."

"Hmmm."

"What does that mean?"

"It means I know there's something on your mind."

"I never could hide anything from you, could I?" Kirov

27

lit two cigarettes and gave one to Irena. "Actually, I wanted your professional opinion about the sort of treatment a friend of mine has been receiving."

"I see." Irena drew on her cigarette and blew a smoke ring toward the ceiling. "I have a feeling this particular friend is seated at my kitchen table. You haven't contracted a social disease, have you, Georgi?"

"Me?" Kirov laughed, then almost choked on a lungful of cigarette smoke. "Me?" he spluttered. "Where I was stationed there was no opportunity for any social intercourse."

"I'm glad to hear it."

"This friend exists, Irena. He was wounded in action, had his right ankle shattered."

"This happened in Afghanistan?"

Kirov nodded. "The surgeons had to amputate the right leg a good four inches above the kneecap."

"I don't think I want to hear any more, Georgi. What you're about to ask me is highly unethical."

"Please, it's important."

"No." She shook her head. "No, I won't pass judgment on a fellow surgeon purely on hearsay evidence."

"Listen, I'll make it easy for you. How soon can gangrene set in?"

"That depends on so many things; the time it took to get your friend to a field hospital, whether the wound was already infected before he received expert medical attention, and so on." Irena found an ashtray, stubbed out her cigarette, then pushed the dish toward him. "Only you can answer those questions, Georgi."

He could certainly answer one of them. Eleven soldiers had been wounded in the Khinjan Valley ambush and the "after action" report stated that they had been rapidly evacuated by helicopter to the casualty clearing station at Kabul. There was no reason to suppose Moorcroft would have been treated any differently; even the most stupid of dunderheads would have realized that he was a very important prisoner and there would be hell to pay if he bled to death before anybody had a chance to interrogate him. It was therefore highly improbable that his shattered ankle

28

had turned gangrenous before the medics saw him, and that meant the subsequent amputation of the limb had been a deliberate and calculated act. No army surgeon would have performed such an inhuman operation, but the KGB was far less inhibited and had few scruples. You didn't have to be an admirer of Solzhenitsyn to suspect that most of the dissident intellectuals locked up in mental hospitals were as sane as the psychiatrists who had committed them.

"Your cup of coffee, Georgi." Irena placed a steaming mug in front of him and removed the cigarette stub that had burned down between his fingers without his being aware of it.

"I think they cut him up a piece at a time until he was ready to cooperate."

"What on earth are you talking about?"

Kirov looked up. "My friend—they chopped him up to break his spirit, then they handed him over to me."

"For heaven's sake, Georgi. Have you taken leave of your senses? You can't go around saying things like that."

"Only to you, little sister."

"Then keep it that way. I know what you've been through; others don't, and they won't make any allowances.

"You're alluding to Tania?"

"You haven't been yourself since she was killed, and your judgment is not what it was."

It was a careful way of saying that there were times when he lost touch with reality and allowed his imagination to take over. The disturbing thing about the Moorcroft interrogation was the possibility that Irena could be right. He didn't have one shred of evidence that the American had been tortured by the KGB interrogators, but that hadn't stopped him from building a solid case against them in his mind.

"You always did give me sound advice," Kirov said quietly.

"Which you habitually ignore."

"Well, this time I promise I'll act on it."

He had said the right thing, knew it by the way Irena sighed and visibly relaxed. It was as though a great weight had been lifted from her shoulders, and she reacted accordingly, turning their conversation around to talk of everyday matters—Igor's hopes of being invited to head the Agronomics Department at the university, her work at the hospital. When finally he made an excuse to leave, she embraced him warmly, asked him to give her love to Lydia Kirov, Fedor Fedorovich's third wife, then stood there in the doorway of her apartment waving goodbye and blowing kisses until he reached the end of the corridor and started on down the staircase.

It was past seven, there were no taxis about in Platovskij, and a chill wind cut right through his light topcoat and made him shiver. Turning right outside the apartment house, Kirov made his way to the Kijevskaja metro station. Deep in thought, he wasn't aware that he was being followed, but then neither had he noticed the succession of unmarked Lada saloons that had shadowed him all the way from Moscow Military District Headquarters to Platovskij Thoroughfare.

★   ★   ★

The two men who waited in the forest clearing were not professional gravediggers. Well before dusk that afternoon, they had left the KGB training center near Kartino, about fifteen miles southwest of Moscow, to make their way via the outer-ring road to the Leningrad Highway. Leaving the twelve-lane motorway at the interchange, they had driven northeast to Molzaninovka where they had turned off onto one of the many dirt roads leading to the forests, lakes, and marshlands of the Sestra basin. Some forty minutes later, the headlights of their car had illuminated the small signpost they had been told to look out for and, taking the right-hand fork, they had trundled on down a narrow track through the forest until it finally petered out beside a log cabin.

The journey had taken longer than they'd anticipated, and the first hard frost of winter had made the ground that much tougher to dig. With less than two hours' leeway before the body was delivered for burial, their task had been further complicated by a tangled web of tree roots they'd encountered after the surface layer had been removed. Given any latitude, they would have chosen another site and started again, but the orders they'd received had been very specific; the corpse was to be interred alongside the woodpile directly behind the dacha belonging to General F. F. Kirov.

To have finished digging the grave on time had been quite an achievement under the circumstances, but their satisfaction had rapidly evaporated when the truck had failed to appear at 1930 hours. Numb with cold, the sweat of exertion rapidly cooling on their bodies, they had retreated to their car where they were now sitting it out and mentally cursing the factory inspector who'd allowed a Moskvitch saloon to leave the assembly line with a defective heater.

Finally, after what seemed an eternity, a pair of headlights appeared in their rearview mirror, and a few moments later a Zil truck lumbered into the clearing and drew up beside them. Thoroughly disgruntled, both KGB men waited until the driver had climbed down from his cab before they deigned to get out and meet him.

The driver was dressed in army uniform, his greatcoat adorned with the green shoulder boards and the single wide black stripe of a sergeant major in the medical and veterinary services.

"Which of you is Lavrenti Litvinov?" he demanded.

"I am." The taller KGB officer moved a pace nearer the NCO and jerked a thumb at his companion. "He's Bukharin, Nikolai Bukharin."

"Right." The sergeant major reached into his pocket and dug out a small pad of receipt vouchers. "Here," he said tersely. "Sign on the dotted line; one body male Caucasian identity unknown, sixteen feet of hessian sacking in lieu of regulation issue pine coffin, and one bag of quicklime."

"Yeah? What's your name, soldier?" Litvinov asked, his voice dangerously quiet.

"It's best you don't know."

"You hear that, Nikolai?" Litvinov shook his head. "I think this pig has ideas above his station."

"I don't like his attitude either," Bukharin growled.

"Don't let the uniform fool you, comrades," the NCO told them. "We're all employed by the same firm."

"Well, fuck me, wouldn't you just know it." Litvinov

31

snatched the receipt vouchers from his hand and signaled the NCO to turn around and make a back for him. Grubbing through his pockets, he found a stubby pencil and signed his name with a flourish, aided by the beam from the flashlight that Bukharin obligingly trained over his shoulder. "Lavrenti Litvinov," he announced and slapped the receipt vouchers into the NCO's hand, "and I'm a *Mladshii Komandnyi Sostav*. It's as well to set the record straight. I don't want you thinking that you outrank me."

"The thought never crossed my mind, Comrade Warrant Officer."

"Obviously a man who knows his place in life," Bukharin said dryly.

Litvinov walked around to the back of the Zil, removed both cotter pins, and dropped the tailgate. The corpse had been dumped lengthwise inside the truck, its head pointing toward the cab up front. Sewn up in a gray-coloured piece of hessian, it looked just like a log of wood.

"What was the cause of death?" Litvinov asked idly.

"A brain tumor," the NCO said, "the Makarov kind."

"Sudden, was it?"

"You could say he never knew what hit him."

Litvinov chuckled, made to grab hold of the corpse, then froze. "This man has only one leg," he said in a plaintive voice.

"Yes, he's deficient of a limb." The NCO rubbed his jaw. "Tell you what I'll do," he said, poker-faced. "If you're that worried, I'll alter the receipt voucher to read 'one body incomplete.'"

CHAPTER III

The apartment house where Kirov had spent the first ten years of his life stood on the corner of Arbatskaja Square and Kalinina Prospekt, almost directly opposite the Praga restaurant. Within a radius of half a mile there were five large department stores, four museums, three restaurants, two theaters, a post office, and innumerable monuments. Lydia Kirov, the general's third wife, had visited all the museums in the neighborhood and had been bored to distraction in the process, but a stranger meeting her briefly at an official reception could be forgiven for thinking she was the chief curator of any one of them. Her cultural knowledge had been gleaned from guidebooks she'd studied and committed to memory in her desire to create the impression that she was much older and wiser than her tender years would suggest.

The general had been sixty-two when Lydia married him, and she had always been very conscious that he was old enough to be her father. Even more embarrassing was the fact that people who didn't know the family naturally assumed that Georgi and Irena were her elder brother and sister. Presenting her husband with twin daughters in 1977 had led to further confusion, with strangers then thinking the general must be their grandfather. This in turn had undermined Lydia's confidence to the point where she had become positively neurotic about her still youthful appearance. Unlike most women, she was determined to look older than she was, and instead of dieting, had become something of a glutton, with the result that she was now a rather plain and dumpy woman of thirty.

Kirov had never been at ease with his stepmother, nor she with him. Under the circumstances, it was hardly surprising that he was greeted with much less affection than Irena had shown, Lydia merely offering a cheek instead of embracing him. His father, however, was even less cordial, treating him like an errant young officer who was late on parade and demanding to know where he'd been. Predictably, Kirov's explanation in no way abated the old man's anger.

"What the hell did you want to see Irena for?"

"Because she's my sister and I'm very fond of her," Kirov told him, then added, "She asked me to give both of you her love."

"Rubbish. She hates me and dislikes Lydia. So does that fat husband of hers, the bootlicking tutor."

"I'm sure he means well, Fedor Fedorovich," Lydia said diplomatically.

33

"He's an asshole in anybody's language. That's why he's a KGB nark."

"You don't know that, dear."

"Of course I do. All university tutors are narks; spying on people is part of their job." The general rounded on his son again, jabbing a stubby finger into his chest. "And while we're still on the subject of those miserable Gusovskys, why didn't you phone and let us know you were going to be late?"

"I'm sorry, Lydia," Kirov said contritely, "I didn't mean to be discourteous."

"Of course you didn't, Georgi."

"It's just that Irena's phone is out of order."

"Ah, well, that explains everything," Lydia said and flashed him a nervous smile.

"It most certainly doesn't. He could have rung us from GRU Headquarters."

"They don't like you making private phone calls over the military network," Kirov said.

"It didn't stop them making use of us when it suited them. I don't know what the army's coming to. We looked after our own in my day. If one of our soldiers needed a bed for the night, we didn't have to shop around to find him one." Fedor Fedorovich paused for breath, then glared at his wife and said, "Well? How much longer are we going to stand around out here? I'm starving, woman."

"I'm sure you must be." Lydia wrung her hands as though washing them under a tap and flashed Kirov another brittle smile. "If you're ready, Georgi . . .?"

Kirov removed his light topcoat, hung it on the clothes rack in the hall, and followed the general through the lounge into the dining room, Lydia half running to draw ahead of them both.

The round table was practically groaning under the amount of food she had prepared. There was a choice of hors d'oeuvres, a sakusska of salmon, sturgeon, and crab or a caviar pancake. A tureen of goulash simmered on the hot plate along with a pyramid of mince balls on a salver. For dessert there were apple pelettes with sour cream, cakes, and Plombir ice cream, which Kirov knew the twins adored.

"So where are the girls, Lydia?" he asked.

"In bed, where they ought to be," Fedor Fedorovich said before she had a chance to answer.

"They wanted to see you, Georgi, really they did." Lydia kept her eyes downcast, her cheeks flushing. "And we allowed them to stay up long past their bedtime but, in the end, they could hardly stay awake."

"They were fretful, bloody fretful." Fedor Fedorovich moved to the sideboard, uncorked a bottle of Zinadali white wine, and filled their glasses while Lydia served the hors d'oeuvres. "Now suppose you tell me why you've been recalled to Moscow," he said abruptly.

"I wish I knew," Kirov said.

"You're not in trouble again, are you?"

"No, as a matter of fact, it seems I'm being promoted to major with two years' seniority."

"Incredible."

It wasn't quite the reaction Kirov had expected, even though he knew his father rarely praised him. Bemused, he watched the general return to the sideboard and pour himself a very large vodka before taking his place at the table.

"When's the effective date?"

"I've got the temporary rank already but it will be confirmed in the annual Red Army Day list on the thirteenth of February next year."

"Don't bank on it," the general growled. "The annual list has to be approved by the Politburo, and they may be preoccupied with more important matters."

"You mean the war in Afghanistan?" Kirov shook his head. "I know it's still dragging on but we have the situation under control."

"I'm talking about the leadership problem. Leonid Brezhnev is a sick man; he has a heart condition, and I doubt he'll live through this winter."

There had been no reports in the newspapers that Brezhnev was ill, nor did Kirov recall hearing anything about it on the radio. But that didn't surprise him; unless the Politburo put out an official statement, a news item like that would never get past the censors. "Who's likely to succeed him?" he asked diffidently.

35

"Any one of the thirteen members of the Politburo. Chernenko, Mikhail Gorbachev, the Minister for Agriculture, Foreign Minister Gromyko, Marshal Ustinov, Andrei Kirilenko, and Yuri Andropov must be the front-runners, and they're all in there with a chance."

His father was wrong there, Kirov thought. Andrei Kirilenko was out of the reckoning; he was too old at seventy-three, and there were persistent rumors that his son had defected to the West.

"I'll give you a piece of advice." Fedor Fedorovich knocked back the glass of vodka, wiped his mouth, then said, "Keep your head well down until the leadership question is settled and don't speak out of turn. If anyone tries to draw you into a political discussion, just smile and walk away. Be smart for once in your life and act dumb, otherwise you could end up in Siberia or Uzbekistan again."

"This is 1982 and Stalin's been dead for nineteen years," Kirov said reasonably. "I don't see how a power struggle within the Kremlin can possibly affect me."

"Then you can't see the end of your nose." Fedor Fedorovich clenched a fist and slammed the table. The crockery rattled and the wine spilled over their glasses to form two separate but ever-widening puddles. "Fuck it, boy, even you can't be that stupid."

"Fedor Fedorovich." Lydia drew in her breath with a sharp hiss and looked up, deeply shocked. "Do please watch your language."

"What's the matter with you, woman? You're an army brat, not a wilting flower. This is my house and I'll say what I like to whom I like."

My father is afraid for me, Kirov thought. He thinks I am in some kind of danger and his anger is born of frustration because it's just a gut feeling and he can't be specific.

"I wish you wouldn't take on so, Fedor Fedorovich," his wife said anxiously. "It's bad for your blood pressure, and you'll only wake the children shouting like that."

"Don't you dare speak to me like that."

The reprimand was delivered in a parade ground voice that in days gone by had reduced enlisted men and most commissioned officers to quivering jellies. The soldiers used to refer to him as "the bull" behind his back, and Kirov thought it was an apt description of his father. The general had the barrel chest, broad shoulders, and thick neck of an ox. He was also quick-tempered and tended to snort like an enraged bull when angry. On this occasion, the stentorian bellow had an even more unnerving effect on his young family, for one of the twins woke up and began whimpering. Lydia left the table in tears to comfort the child, and although any other wife and mother would have done exactly the same, Fedor Fedorovich appeared to find her reaction absolutely incomprehensible.

"I can't think what's come over Lydia," he grumbled. "She never used to be temperamental. If I didn't know how old she is, I'd put it down to the change of life."

"The fault lies with you," Kirov told him calmly. "Instead of mellowing with the years, you've become more irascible."

"When I want your opinion, I'll ask for it. Now, where was I before we were so rudely interrupted?" His voice had taken on the plaintive whine of a spoiled child used to having his every whim indulged.

"You were saying I was stupid because I couldn't see why a power struggle within the Kremlin should affect me."

"Well, so you are. Lenin, Stalin, Malenkov, Khrushchev, and Brezhnev; they wouldn't have amounted to anything but for the Red Army. We made them and then they turned on us."

He was talking about himself, and it was an old familiar story. In 1962, Fedor Fedorovich had been the youngest colonel general in the Red Army and had looked all set to become a Marshal of Arm if not of the Soviet Union. He'd been chief of the Operations Directorate in those days, and on Krushchev's orders had studied the feasibility of positioning medium-range surface-to-surface missiles in Cuba. By the time he'd considered all the relevant factors and completed his appreciation, Fedor Fedorovich had been convinced that Kennedy would never let them get away with it and had said so forcibly. Khrushchev had ignored his advice and told him to get on with it. The rest was history; the Americans had reacted in exactly the way Kirov had predicted, Khrushchev had found himself boxed in a tight corner, and the army had been obliged to dismantle the missile bases at San Cristobal, Guanajay, and Bahia Honda. It had been a national humiliation, which America's willingness to remove her obsolete Jupiter missile bases in Turkey had in no way redressed. It had been a national humiliation that had demanded more than one scapegoat. Khrushchev had been removed from power in 1964 and Fedor Fedorovich had been shunted from one minor post to another until he was finally retired in May 1972 at the age of sixty with the honorary rank of general. Kirov had often wondered if Igor Gusovsky would have been quite so ardent in his pursuit of Irena had he known his prospective father-in-law was under a cloud.

"Zhukov is another example of what I mean," Fedor Fedorovich continued. "He saved Stalin's hide when the Fascists were knocking on the gates of Moscow and went on to become the architect of victory at Stalingrad, Kursk, and Berlin. And how did Stalin reward him when it was all over? By appointing him to command the Odessa Military District. You might have thought that was the end of the story but not a bit of it."

Of course it wasn't. His father would now go on to recount how Zhukov had made it possible for Malenkov to succeed Stalin when he died in 1953. Nor would he forget to mention that Khrushchev and the rest of the Kremlin gang would never have had the balls to liquidate Lavrenti Beria if it hadn't been for Zhukov.

"He got the tanks out on the streets and made sure the KGB stayed inside their barracks."

"MGB," Kirov said, gently correcting him. "They were known as the MGB in those days."

"You must forgive an old man; I didn't have the benefit of your education." Fedor Fedorovich helped himself to another large vodka, then said, "Did they also teach you that Zhukov saved Khrushchev when his associates in the Politburo were plotting to overthrow him in June 1957? Did they tell you that he put air force planes at Khrushchev's disposal so that he could fly his supporters on the Central Committee into Moscow and so win the crucial vote? And did these erudite men who taught you remember to point

38

out that later on it occurred to Khrushchev that if Zhukov had enabled him to stay in power, the Marshal could just as easily remove him from office whenever it suited him?"

Kirov nodded. "They said Khrushchev was always an opportunist, which is why he decided to act first and had Zhukov arrested when he returned from an official visit to Albania in October of '57."

"Well, at least they've got the right version in the history books for once. That certainly wasn't the case when I was your age, Georgi."

The observation stirred a distant, seemingly unrelated memory, and he began to talk about the outbreak of war when he was commanding a field artillery battery in the Tenth Army. He was lucid and recalled with absolute clarity every detail of that fateful Sunday morning in June, the way old men do when they hark back to the past that for them is more vivid, more real than the present and far more certain than the future.

★　　★　　★

Igor Gusovsky left the metro station at Puskinskaja just beyond the Hotel Minsk and turned left into the first of two approach roads leading to the Rossija Kino. A modern, somewhat grandiose movie theater that resembled a slab of fruitcake, the Rossija was perched on stilts so that it was necessary to climb a long and overly steep flight of concrete steps in order to reach the foyer. The building was also fronted by an oblong-shaped lawn large enough to be considered a small park in any other city.

The evening had begun well enough for Gusovsky with a phone call toward midafternoon from a man he knew only as Boris, who'd told him that instead of returning home at his usual hour, he was to stay on at the university until he heard from him again. Far from being displeased, he'd immediately called Irena at the hospital to inform her that he was obliged to attend a faculty meeting that evening and couldn't say when it was likely to end. Then he'd sent a message to Zinaida Shuvakin to remind her that her grades had been disappointing of late and hinting they would

39

almost certainly improve with further private tutoring and would six o'clock be convenient?

It was a ploy that had never failed before and at exactly six o'clock, Zinaida had knocked on the door and walked into his room at the university armed with a briefcase filled to bursting with assorted textbooks and reference papers from the library. The briefcase was entirely for the benefit of the other students and provided the necessary camouflage for their more amorous activities which occurred at some stage during every private tutorial. On this occasion, however, a second telephone call from Boris had brought their love-making to an untimely and thoroughly unsatisfactory end.

Gusovsky felt cheated and was angry with Boris for interrupting him at such an inopportune moment. Zinaida was a very attractive girl with the sort of Junoesque figure he admired and, unlike many of his students, was always neatly dressed and well groomed. Tonight, for instance, she had backcombed her dark hair, arranging it in a beehive, and had been wearing a navy two-piece over a white blouse. The navy costume had been purchased from the GUM stores in Red Square, but the ice-blue nylon underwear trimmed with lace was English and bore the Marks and Spencer label. They had indulged in the usual petting, he gently caressing her ample breasts while she groped inside his trousers to stimulate an erection. Then, just as he'd positioned Zinaida comfortably in the armchair and was about to mount her, the incessant jangle of the telephone had ruined everything.

Preoccupied with his own thoughts, Gusovsky didn't notice the Lada saloon moving slowly toward him from the direction of the Kino and was startled when it suddenly halted beside him and the rear door nearest the curb was flung open. Boris hadn't said anything about meeting him with a car and it was impossible to make out just who was sitting in the back, but there was no mistaking the voice.

"You're late," Boris growled. "Who were you screwing this time? Another of your receptive students?"

"I was in the middle of a tutorial," Gusovsky said and vented his anger on the door, slamming it shut as he got in beside the KGB officer.

"It's a good thing I know you," Boris told him, "otherwise I might get the idea you were having second thoughts about our meeting."

"Don't be ridiculous."

"My word, we are touchy tonight, aren't we? What's the matter; did my phone call wreck your chances?"

"Of course it didn't." Gusovsky tried to keep his distance from the other man, but the driver let the clutch out so fiercely that they ended up rubbing shoulders. "How many more times do I have to tell you that I was holding a tutorial?" he said coldly.

"That depends. The question is, who was there?"

"Zinaida Shuvakin."

"Ah, yes." Boris sucked on his teeth. "Her father is a senior captain with Aeroflot. Correct?"

"You know very well he is."

Aeroflot was frequently called upon to reinforce the transport fleet of the Soviet Air Force. In consequence, the flight crews, technicians, and certain key administrative personnel were subjected to the same kind of scrutiny the KGB applied to the armed forces. The day he was appointed as a tutor in the Agronomics department of the university, Gusovsky had learned that apart from his normal academic duties, he was also required to assess the political reliability of his students, especially those whose parents were in a professional occupation or were members of the armed forces. Gusovsky saw nothing wrong in this; in fact he considered it the duty of every Soviet citizen to protect the state from subversive reactionaries, but there were times when he could have wished for a more agreeable link officer than the coarse and uncouth Boris.

"Any problems with that family, Igor?"

Zinaida was more than likely to cause a few problems because she had ambitions that exceeded her talents. She had her eyes on a post in the planning department of the Ministry of Agriculture and needed a first-class honors degree. Unfortunately, Zinaida was only an average student and was honest enough to recognize it. Her trouble lay in thinking that she could improve her chances by lying back in his armchair with her legs spread wide apart. Never one to look a gift horse in the mouth, he was prepared to fudge her grades in recompense for services rendered, but there was nothing he could do about the final examination and that was undoubtedly the one dangerous factor about the whole business. If Zinaida failed to get the results she wanted, he fancied there could well be hell to pay. Boris, however, was not interested in his problems; he was concerned only with facts.

"Shuvakin's about to be switched to a domestic route: Moscow–Omsk–Vladivostok."

"Too bad."

Zinaida had said much the same thing to him. There would be no more flights to London and, more importantly from mother and daughter's point of view, no further opportunities to purchase attractive items of clothing from the Oxford Street branch of Marks and Spencer.

"Your brother-in-law's been recalled to Moscow," Boris informed him abruptly.

Gusovsky avoided his speculative gaze and looked straight ahead. The driver of their car had followed Gorky Street into town, then turned left on Marx Prospekt, taking them past the Little Theater. Right now, they were approaching Dzerzhinsky Square, headquarters of the KGB and, behind it, the notorious Lubyanka prison.

"You got any more good news to tell me?" he growled.

"Don't you two get along, Igor?"

"There's no love lost between us," Gusovsky said grimly.

There never had been, not since the day he'd introduced himself to Irena at the ice rink in Gorky Park where she'd gone skating with her kid brother. Georgi had been about twelve years old then and had seemed to think that being a cadet at the Suvorov Military Academy made him the absolute cat's whiskers. It was nauseating to recall now how he'd tried to suck up to the snotty-nosed little brat, praising him for his natural ability on the ice, the confident way he'd executed a series of double axels and toe loops. Any other kid would have lapped it up, but not Georgi; instead, he'd taken the rise out of him, mimicking his provincial accent, which Irena had found amusing. Her laughter had added to his humiliation and he'd wanted to turn his back on the pair of them and walk away, but a wiser counsel had prevailed. He'd seen her at the ice rink before, and while she was only moderately attractive, she had been better-dressed than most of the other girls, which he'd thought significant. As soon as he'd learned who she was, Gusovsky had decided there and then that he was going to make Irena his wife. Love had nothing to do with it; he was in his last year at the university and dreaded the prospect of having to return to his native village in the middle of nowhere. In those days, his ambition in life was to be a lecturer at the University of Moscow, a goal he quickly realized would be that much easier to attain for a man whose father-in-law happened to be a general.

"Hooray for nepotism."

"What?"

"Nothing," Gusovsky said hastily. "I was just thinking out loud."

"A dangerous habit," Boris observed laconically.

"Yes, so I'm beginning to discover."

Gusovsky noticed they had skirted Dzerzhinsky Square and were now heading roughly southwest on Novaja, the huge GUM store in Red Square clearly visible on their right. He assumed Boris intended to follow the inner-ring road all the way back to their starting point, until the driver signaled that he was about to turn right into Kitajskii, which would take them past the Rossija Hotel and on down to the river.

"Is Georgi in trouble again?" he asked presently.

"Not as far as I know, Igor."

He supposed he should be grateful for small mercies but it didn't change his feelings toward Georgi. He could never forgive him for the way he'd behaved after Tania had been killed, the wild allegations he'd made about the police investigation. No matter how patiently he'd argued with him, Georgi had refused to believe their version of events and had persisted with his demands for an independent judicial inquiry. Gusovsky had tried to enlist Irena's support in a final effort to make Georgi see reason but she had taken her brother's part, with the inevitable result that in the end the whole family had suffered. As far as Gusovsky was concerned, the fact that he was unlikely to progress any farther in his academic career was entirely due to his brother-in-law.

"He called on your wife earlier this evening, Igor."

"That doesn't surprise me."

There was an unnatural bond between Irena and Georgi that went far deeper than the usual brother and sister relationship. In his opinion, their love for each other bordered on the incestuous.

"Kirov refused the offer of a staff car to take him from GRU Headquarters to his father's residence on Kalinina Prospekt. Instead, he made a detour to see your wife, and we'd like to know why. In view of the way you feel about him, I imagine you must share our curiosity?"

Gusovsky felt his stomach drop. The KGB was asking him to interrogate Irena. No, that wasn't quite correct; the KGB was ordering him to do so. Appalled by the idea, he gazed at Boris, silently pleading with his eyes to be let off the hook, but there was no response from the link officer.

"All right," he said wearily. "How do I go about it? I mean, supposing my wife doesn't tell me that Georgi has been to see her?"

"You'll think of something, Igor."

"And if I run into a wall of silence?"

"Then we'll assume that she must have something to hide."

The driver had turned right at the T-junction to head north on Kremlovskaja Quay, the Moskva River on one side, the Kremlin walls on the other. There was, Gusovsky thought, something very symbolic about the route they were now taking; it was as if the KGB wanted him to realize that he was boxed in and had no room to maneuver.

"I wouldn't like you to get the wrong impression about Irena and me," Gusovsky said, choosing his words with care. "Despite everything I may have implied, there are no secrets between us."

"Aren't you forgetting Zinaida?"

It was a subtle reminder that Boris knew him better than Irena did. Furthermore, there had been a succession of Zinaidas over the years, and no doubt some jealous faculty member had made it his or her business to inform the authorities of his various peccadilloes, both real and imagined. The men of the KGB were avaricious task-masters, and every informer knew it was useless telling them that he had nothing to report. There was a norm to be met and what you didn't know you invented. If he didn't come up with the information Boris wanted, then the KGB would give Irena all the evidence she needed for a divorce and he would probably be removed from his university appointment. At the end of the day, that was the implicit threat behind the snide observation.

"Phone me tomorrow morning," Gusovsky said abruptly. "I'll have all the information you want by then."

"Good," Boris nudged him in the ribs. "I knew I could rely on you, Igor."

Nothing more was said. Five minutes later, they dropped Gusovsky off near the Kalininskaja metro station and left him to make his own way home on the Blue Line.

★　　　★　　　★

The two men emerged from a side door and walked unsteadily toward the wooden posts that had been erected in the courtyard a few yards out from a high wall protected by a triple row of sandbags. Both men were dressed in army uniform, but there were no buttons on their tunics and the shoulder boards had been hacked off, together with the insignia of rank.

"General Dmitri Pavlov, commander in chief Western Front; Major General Klimovskii, his chief of staff."

Kirov heard his father whisper their names and watched the escorts bind them to the posts, their elbows and wrists lashed behind them, thick ropes around their waists to hold them upright in case they should buckle at the knees. Two men about to die on a clear June morning. Two scapegoats for the disasters that had befallen the Third and Tenth armies at Bialystok and Grodno. Two scapegoats who had lost three hundred thousand men in six days because Stalin had refused to believe that the Fascists were about to attack the Soviet Union and had forbidden them to mobilize their troops and deploy them to their battle positions in time.

45

"Fominyi was the third member of the command troika," Fedor Fedorovich murmured, "but he was the political commissar and one of Stalin's cronies, so they didn't try him."

There was an aiming mark fixed above their hearts now, and Pavlov was tossing his head from side to side, as though trying to shake the blindfold loose from his eyes. A dark stain had appeared around the crotch of Klimovskii's breeches and his lips were moving, but his final words were drowned by the harsh voice of the officer in charge of the firing squad. Twenty men moved as one to open and close the bolts on their Mossim Nagent rifles. The volley, when it came, was less certain and more like a ragged clap of thunder. Then the dance of death began and Kirov woke up sweating.

He lay there in the darkness, uncertain about where he was. Common sense told him that only a few hours ago he had dined with Lydia and Fedor Fedorovich, but the dream was so real, still so vivid in his mind that he needed to reassure himself that the room he was sleeping in was not a tiny cell in the Lubyanka. Unable to find the light switch, he rolled out of bed, groped his way toward the windows, and drew back the curtains.

The streetlights were still burning in Arbatskaja Square, but the Praga restaurant across the way had long since closed for the night. A Lada saloon was parked outside, and he assumed that it belonged to the proprietor; then he saw a tiny pinpoint of light that was obviously the glowing ember of a cigarette and realized that somebody was sitting inside the car and watching the house.

Chapter IV

Although Kirov had set the alarm for 5:30, his father woke him ten minutes earlier with a glass of tea that was steaming hot and had a slice of lemon floating on top. There was also a lump of sugar to pop into his mouth so that he could drink the brew in the traditional Russian manner.

"I'd make a good orderly, wouldn't I?" Fedor Fedorovich said jovially.

"Better than I deserve." Kirov swung his feet out onto the floor and sat up on the edge of the bed, yawning. "I don't know how you do it, Papa," he said.

"Do what?"

"Manage to be so cheerful at this unearthly hour of the morning. I feel half-dead."

"You look it. What's the matter, suffering from a hangover?"

"Something like that." It was easier to fall in with the suggestion than to admit he'd had a nightmare, which would only provoke a contemptuous reaction and a lot of tiresome questions. "I know I woke up in the middle of the night with a splitting headache and needed a breath of fresh air."

"And forgot to draw the curtains afterward?"

"Yes." Kirov dropped the lump of sugar into the glass of tea, waited until it had dissolved, and then took a sip. "The proprietor of the Praga must be doing well," he said casually. "I noticed there was a new Lada saloon parked outside the restaurant last night."

"Really?" Fedor Fedorovich walked over to the window and looked out. "Well, it isn't there now."

"Maybe the militia towed it away."

"Why should they do that? Residents are allowed to park their cars in the square."

"In that case, it must have been a courting couple."

"I suppose there's always that possibility." Fedor Fedorovich drew the curtains and slowly turned around. "On the other hand, it could be that somebody's keeping you under surveillance."

"I'm not in anybody's black books."

"So you assured me last night. And you're also up for accelerated promotion."

"Yes."

"Why?"

Kirov hesitated, wondered just how much he should tell his father about the Moorcroft interrogation. Retired generals weren't entitled to receive classified information, which meant that even the briefest disclosure would be

47

regarded as a serious breach of security. There was also another equally important consideration; although his father had always been tight-lipped and was most unlikely to pass anything on to his cronies, the apartment itself might be bugged. Fedor Fedorovich had a reputation for being out-spoken and he'd been one of Marshal Zhukov's protégés—two reasons the KGB might still take an interest in him.

"You can't tell me. Is that it?"

"More or less," Kirov said. "What I can say is that I did something that other people had tried to do and failed. Colonel Leonid Paskar, my former commanding officer, thinks I've been recalled to Moscow in order to give the GRU Headquarters staff a complete rundown on the technique I used."

"So what happens after you've said your piece? Will they send you back to Uzbekistan?"

"No." Kirov shook his head. "No, the rumor is I'll be posted to one of the training schools as an instructor."

The movement order had been vague, merely informing him that his baggage allowance for the flight to Moscow would be restricted to forty-four pounds and that the rest of his kit would be sent on by rail under arrangements made by the Military Communications Service. Nothing had been said about his next appointment other than that a staff car would collect him from the airport and that he was to report to the duty staff officer at GRU Headquarters in Znamensky Street.

"Of course the grapevine is notoriously inaccurate, but it would be nice if there was some truth in the rumor for once. Should my next appointment be somewhere in the Moscow area, we could spend the occasional weekend at the dacha, take a punt out on the lake, and bag ourselves a few wild duck."

"I'd like that, Georgi. I haven't been near the lodge in two years. Lydia doesn't care for the place, thinks it's too isolated, especially in the autumn when the forest is at its best, and the children prefer Gorky Park or picnicking by the river when the weather is fine enough."

"Why don't you invite some of your friends to go shoot-ing with you instead?"

"They're getting past it."

But not Fedor Fedorovich. The years hadn't caught up with him, or so he liked to pretend. "I'm the picture of health," he was fond of saying, but he had high blood pressure and came down with bronchitis every winter. The doctors could talk to him until they were blue in the face and it didn't make a damn bit of difference; he still went on drinking more than was good for him and smoked far too many Pamirs. One day he would drop dead and, despite all his faults, the world would be a poorer and smaller place without him.

"I suppose I could always ask Marshal Ustinov," Fedor Fedorovich said thoughtfully. "I still see him occasionally, but the Defense Minister is a very busy man. What little free time he has, he prefers to spend with his family."

Kirov had been told that they'd gotten to know one another at the General Staff Academy, when Ustinov had been one of the 150 students on the course and his father had been a member of the directing staff. Friendship had grown out of mutual respect and had lasted over the years.

"Why not invite his wife and family as well? I hear she's done a bit of clay pigeon shooting."

"It's an idea," Fedor Fedorovich said, without showing too much enthusiasm.

Kirov swallowed the last of the tea and set the glass down on the small bedside table. "I'd better get on, otherwise I'm going to be late."

"We can't have that, Georgi. But no soldier ever marched very far on an empty stomach. I'll get you something to eat—white bread, honey, cheese. Will that do you?"

"Fine, just fine."

Kirov went into the bathroom, ran the tap until the hot water came through the pipe, then filled the basin, honed the cutthroat razor on a leather strap, and lathered his face. He shaved mechanically, his mind on other things. His father was a lonely old man, the more so now because he had nothing in common with Lydia. Kirov knew that, in his own way, Fedor Fedorovich loved both him and Irena and if, in one of his black moods, he sometimes lashed out with a savage tongue, it was understandable. He had loved two

49

women, both of whom had died young and under harrowing circumstances. Through no fault of his own, he had seen very little of his children in their formative years, and his bitterness stemmed from a belief that in growing up they had also grown away from him. And there was another factor that had to be taken into account when making allowances for Fedor Fedorovich: the black moods were attributable to severe attacks of migraine occasioned by the steel plate in his head, a souvenir from Kursk.

Kirov wiped the razor clean, washed his hands and face and dried them on a clean white towel. He should have told his father about Moorcroft and asked him whether he thought the Americans had any justification for meddling with the internal affairs of Afghanistan. And the British too; if you were prepared to believe Moorcroft, they had an SAS team operating with one of the terrorist groups in the Kandahar region. It would have meant a lot to Fedor Fedorovich had he taken him into his confidence. Technically speaking, it would have been a breach of security, but that was really applying the rules to the extreme. If you couldn't trust a man who'd been a general in the Red Army and was a Hero of the Soviet Union twice over to respect a confidence, whom could you trust? And did anybody seriously believe that when they met socially, Fedor Fedorovich and Marshal Ustinov confined their conversation entirely to mundane topics?

Marshal Ustinov, Defense Minister, a member of the Politburo and one of the men tipped to succeed Leonid Brezhnev. Kirov stared at his reflection in the mirror. What was it his father had said to him last night? Keep your head well down until the leadership question is settled? He wondered if his father had been talking about himself and was trying to warn him that the apartment was bugged.

He looked up at the ceiling and instantly dismissed the idea. Electronic surveillance had developed to such an extent in recent years that, unless he was exceptionally lucky, the chances of an amateur locating one of the latest devices were zero. Magnetized transmitters that could be spotted with the human eye, provided the occupant was observant enough, were a thing of the past. Nowadays, even a sophisticated radio emission detector was next to useless. Powered by four long-life batteries, the latest transmitter was insulated within a polythene tube remote from an ultrasensitive microphone that itself was no thicker than a strand of wire and, as a result, virtually invisible. Inserting several of these transmitters in the ceilings, walls, and skirt boards of the flat would have been unlikely to give the KGB too many headaches. There were apartments above, below, and adjoining from which they could have mounted an attack on the Kirov household after they'd persuaded the neighbors to let them in on some pretext or other.

"On the other hand, it could be that somebody's keeping you under surveillance." Those had been his father's words only a few minutes ago and, come to think of it, his tone of voice had been pretty sarcastic. Maybe Fedor Fedorovich had thought he was developing a persecution complex again and believed the family was about to witness a repeat performance of his behavior after Tania had been killed, when he'd convinced himself that everyone was against him? If his father was right, there was a very simple remedy; he could anesthetize his mind and cease looking for an ulterior motive every time he was given an order.

Kirov returned to the bedroom, changed into uniform, and repacked his suitcase, then joined his father in the kitchen for a bite to eat. The white bread, each slice the size of a doorstop, was visible proof that Lydia was still fast asleep in bed.

"I was never very domesticated," Fedor Fedorovich said apologetically.

"Never mind," Kirov told him, "it's the thought that counts."

He ate standing up, a slice of bread and honey in one hand, a second glass of lemon tea in the other. Between mouthfuls, he made desultory conversation with his father, promising to write as soon as he knew what GRU Headquarters proposed to do with him. Then he embraced Fedor Fedorovich, asked him to give his love to Lydia and the twins, and left. As he emerged from the apartment house, a winterized GAZ jeep pulled up outside the entrance.

51

The driver was no ordinary private from the motor pool. His uniform was immaculate, tailor-made to fit him perfectly. Observing the twin stars of a lieutenant colonel on the shoulder boards of his greatcoat in the light from a streetlamp, Kirov grounded his suitcase, snapped to attention, and saluted him.

"Major Kirov," he said, formally introducing himself.

"And I'm Lieutenant Colonel Nikishev. Dump your suitcase in the back and get in."

The jeep was fitted with a heater but the atmosphere inside was decidedly chilly. That Nikishev resented having to chauffeur a junior officer around town was all too evident from his tight-lipped expression and the way he slammed the gear lever into first. Turning left on Kalinina Prospekt, they headed toward the 31-story-high Headquarters of *Comecon*, the Council of Mutual Economic Assistance, at the far end of the avenue, and then crossed the river onto Kutusov Boulevard. The Ukraina Hotel loomed up in the gray light of early morning, one of seven look-alike buildings with towering cathedral spires that had been erected in the late forties when Stalin was busily transforming the Moscow skyline. Still continuing on down the wide boulevard, they drove past the Borodino Panorama Museum and on through a green belt area to the intersection with Republic Highway, where they turned right and made their way into the outer suburb of Kuncevo.

"Where exactly are we going, Comrade Colonel?" Kirov asked him politely.

"Mozhaysk."

":I don't think I know it."

"It's a small town on the road to Minsk about seventy miles from here." Nikishev glanced at him and smiled fleetingly with all the warmth of a Siberian winter. "We've taken over an old hunting lodge on the outskirts of town that used to belong to Count Rostov in the days of the Czar. It's quite a mansion, comes in handy for all sorts of things."

"Like seminars?" Kirov suggested.

"Yes."

"Is that what I'm going to attend—a seminar?"

"Something like that," Nikishev said.

The colonel was positively a gold mine of information, Kirov thought, full of rich seams he couldn't tap.

★   ★   ★

Within the First Chief Directorate there were ten geographic departments, all of which were responsible for operations in a specific area of the globe. Numbered in chronological order, the First Department covering the United States and Canada was the largest, while the Tenth, which looked after the French-speaking nations of Africa, was the smallest. At one time, the departments had been arranged in descending order of importance, but this was no longer the case. The Fourth had now outgrown the Third, largely because the KGB had some five thousand illegals planted within the Federal Republic of West Germany, a figure that was several times greater than the combined total the Third controlled in the United Kingdom, Australia, New Zealand, and Scandinavia. Political developments, some of which were unforeseen, could also suddenly promote the relative importance of a department within the general scheme of things. The Eighth, whose fiefdom included the Arab republics, Yugoslavia, Turkey, Greece, and Iran, had come very much to the fore following the overthrow of the Shah, Soviet involvement in Afghanistan, and the Israeli invasion of Lebanon.

Whatever their respective importance, standing orders required each department to have one officer of field rank on duty in silent hours, Moscow time. They also laid down that all communications received during the night should be decoded and placed in a folder for perusal by the senior deputy controller of the First Chief Directorate when he arrived in the office at 0700 hours. The in-tray awaiting Vatutin that Thursday morning was piled no higher than usual, but with a lecture scheduled for ten o'clock at the Patrice Lumumba University, preceded by a special briefing for Colonel General Vitaly Fedorchuk, the newly appointed chairman of the KGB, he had precious little time to spare. A man noted for being methodical, Vatutin tackled the folders belonging to the less active geographic areas first, then

53

concentrated on the information received by the First, Third, Fourth, and Eighth departments.

Despite the advent of sophisticated communication satellites, the basic rules of security remained the same. Any dispatch containing highly classified material of a long-term nature was never transmitted by radio, because the enemy had the capacity to monitor simultaneously every frequency on the wave band, and the cipher had yet to be invented that a computer could not in time unscramble. The majority of reports therefore were sent through the diplomatic bag or by special couriers who were then debriefed on arrival by the appropriate duty staff officer. As an additional safeguard, a message was sometimes couched in such innocuous terms that only the originator and the recipient knew what it meant.

Among the routine intelligence reports, there were two such messages for Vatutin, one in writing from London, the other by word of mouth from Washington. The latter merely informed him that "The fruit has ripened in the orchard and may be plucked at any time," an oblique reference to the present whereabouts of a Soviet defector named Vera Berggolts, while the message from London stated that, in accordance with previous instructions, a routine security check had been carried out and all classified documents had been accounted for. Translated, this meant that the Top Secret card index belonging to the GRU cell at 13 Kensington Palace Gardens had been secretly photographed by the KGB.

Vatutin initialed both folders, placed them on top of the pile in his out-tray, and then turned his attention to the folder prepared by the duty staff officer of the Fourth Department. Much to his satisfaction, he saw that the resident KGB officer in Bonn had submitted a brief that read like a catalogue from the GUM store, except that the video games, train sets, and powered model aircraft were virtually unobtainable in the Soviet Union and the items listed showed the wholesale price rather than the retailer's. What was bound to be equally puzzling to the uninitiated were the annexures attached to the main body of the report that compared the freight on-board charges to New York quoted by various shipping agencies against those supplied by Pan Am and TWA. The annexures did, however, make sense to him, because they provided exactly the sort of information an importer of manufactured goods would need to have at his fingertips. Uncapping his fountain pen, Vatutin wrote a brief memo to his personal assistant instructing her to make one unattributable copy of the document for onward dispatch to Lieutenant Colonel Dmitri Nikishev.

The last folder contained a depressing analysis of the current political and military situation in Afghanistan. It was yet another vindication of the original assessment made by the First Chief Directorate, which the Politburo had seen fit to reject on the advice of the GRU. The sharp division of opinion that had existed between the two intelligence agencies at the time could be summarized in two sentences. For their part, the advisers at the KGB had been convinced that it would be a huge and costly mistake to install Babrak Karmal as head of a puppet regime in Kabul when all their evidence showed that he enjoyed precious little support in the rest of the country. The counterargument by the GRU had stressed the unsettling effect a fundamentalist Islamic regime in Afghanistan would have on the neighboring Soviet republics of Turkmenistan, Uzbekistan, and Kirghizia and had grossly overestimated the ability of their Spetsnaz commando units and the Red Army to pacify the country. Now, thanks to the idiots on Znamensky Street, the Soviet Union had created its own Vietnam and was embroiled in a guerrilla war it could neither win nor afford to lose.

The Party had spawned the Revolution and the army had accomplished it, but without the KGB the whole edifice would have crumbled long ago. Yet it was the army that had made Malenkov, Khrushchev and Brezhnev, and had subsequently extracted a crippling Danegeld that continued to stretch the whole economy to the breaking point. Fortunately, there were some members of the Politburo who were determined that the Red Army would have no hand in choosing Brezhnev's successor. It had often been said that where there was a will there was a way, and Vatutin believed he'd found the means to implement it.

55

In recent years, the army had come to depend on the GRU as its eyes and ears. Render the GRU impotent, and the high command would be hamstrung. Provided no unforeseen difficulties arose, two unsuspecting men, Lieutenant Colonel Dmitri Nikishev and Major Georgi Kirov, would accomplish that mission for him without either one ever realizing it.

Chapter V

The house was still referred to as "the Rostov place" even though the entire family had been liquidated in 1919 during the civil war. A good seven miles from Mozhaysk, the hunting lodge had been designed by an architect called Joachim Rohm and was typically Germanic in appearance, which meant it was Gothic, solid, and very conservative. The ground floor was dominated by a large square hall with oak-paneled walls, an ornate stone fireplace, and a crystal chandelier that was suspended from the dome roof two stories above. The library, the music salon, and the drawing room lay directly opposite with the kitchen, pantry, servants' hall, and estate office forming the third side of the hollow square. Between the estate office and the servants' hall, a staircase spiraled up to the first-floor gallery where there were eight bedrooms and four bathrooms. In the northeast corner of the gallery, a concealed door opened onto a narrow flight of wooden steps leading to the servants' quarters in the attic. The outdoor staff had lived above the stable block, an ugly-looking building with a clock tower on the west side of the lodge that now housed the drivers and general duty men.

Kirov had been allocated a room above the main entrance, overlooking the approach road. The lodge itself was situated in a shallow depression surrounded by fir trees, which restricted the view from his window to about 100 yards. Midway between the house and the tree line, there was a

56

high protective fence of barbed wire and the second of two checkpoints manned by an NCO covered by a sentry armed with a Kalashnikov. The first checkpoint was on the access road at the far side of the wood, and, on the way in, he'd noticed that the whole of the outer area was patrolled by guard dogs.

Nikishev had led him to believe that the lodge was used for various seminars that the GRU organized from time to time, but the security arrangements seemed more in keeping with a prison camp than a study center. There were, however, no bars on the windows, and the absence of a spy hole in the door was also reassuring. Told to wait in his room until he was sent for, Kirov was catnapping on the bed when an orderly arrived to inform him that his presence was required in the library.

He got up, rinsed his face with cold water to freshen himself, and went downstairs. The main hall was still deserted, the permanent staff conspicuous by their absence, and there was no sign of his guide and mentor, Lieutenant Colonel Nikishev. He crossed the hall, tapped on the door, and entered the library a split second before a languid voice told him to come in.

The library was twice the size of Irena's apartment, a great barn of a room with bookshelves from floor to ceiling, all of which were empty and gathering dust. The only items of furniture were a long, low coffee table standing on a rug and two leather-upholstered armchairs arranged to face each other on either side of the fireplace. As he moved toward the log fire burning in the grate, a tall, slim figure dressed in civilian clothes rose from one of the armchairs to greet him.

"My name is Nikolai Tudin," he said, offering a hand. "And you must be Georgi Kirov."

"Yes."

Tudin was wearing a white polo-neck sweater under a tweed sports jacket with leather patches on the elbows and a pair of dark green corduroy slacks that hung in folds above his brown suede shoes. His hair, parted on the left side, was silver-gray and needed cutting. He had a long, angular face that could only be described as craggy, and piercing blue

57

eyes. Despite the languid voice and appearance, he had a grip of iron that left Kirov with numbed fingers.

"Do sit down and make yourself comfortable." Tudin sank into his own armchair and crossed one leg over the other. "I've been reading the Moorcroft dossier," he said. "In my opinion, you did a marvelous job."

"It's very flattering of you to say so."

"What's a little praise? It's no more than you deserve." Tudin smiled, his eyes creasing as though something had secretly amused him, then said, "Tell me, what did you think of the American? Was he a sympathetic character?"

Kirov thought it a loaded question and wondered how best he could answer it. To admit to a sneaking regard for Moorcroft could be dangerous, yet to claim he'd despised him would be equally foolhardy. Tudin would know that once the American had started to talk, he would have gone out of his way to establish a friendly rapport.

"I considered him naïve," Kirov said finally. "I told him that within eighteen months to two years he would be exchanged for one of our people, and he believed me."

"Really?" Tudin dipped into the pockets of his jacket and brought out a tin of tobacco and a pipe, which he proceeded to fill in a leisurely manner. "I think that from now on, we'll conduct our conversation in English."

Kirov nodded. His tutor had said much the same thing to him at the end of his first term at the Moscow Institute of Foreign Languages. He supposed it was only natural that Tudin should wish to test his fluency, especially as he'd spoken very little English since the graduation ceremony in December 1980. But that was the army all over; they spent thousands of rubles training you to become a first-class interpreter, then posted you to Blagoveshchensk. Except, of course, that he and Moorcroft hadn't conversed in Russian and the whole interrogation was on tape.

"And while we're at it, we'll anglicize our first names. I'll call you George and I'm Nick. All right?"

"I'm easy," Kirov said. "Whatever pleases you is okay by me."

"You're a very amiable fellow, George."

"You think so?"

"Oh, yes, it's part of your technique. You size people up, discover their Achilles' heel, then tell them what they want to hear. That's how you got to Moorcroft."

"I wondered why I'd succeeded where others had failed. I hadn't realized the explanation was that simple."

"You were only doing what came naturally. You're blessed with an engaging personality, George, and you're also highly intelligent, shrewd, and very quick thinking. You must know that; after all, these qualities have been stressed time and again in your annual confidential reports. You're everything the army could wish for, but of course they've had years in which to fashion you to their liking. How old were you when you first put on a uniform, George?"

"Ten," Kirov said.

"Seven years at one of the Suvorov schools, four at the Frunze Military Academy; eleven years of instruction. It's no wonder certain attributes are second-nature; you've been programmed to behave in a specific way."

"You make me sound like a computer, Nick."

"You're wrong there. If a computer has been correctly programmed, it doesn't throw the kind of wingding you did after your wife was killed in a traffic accident."

Suddenly, Kirov thought he knew why Nikishev had brought him to this house, and he felt his blood run cold. The people at the GRU weren't interested in learning how he'd broken Moorcroft; they wanted to know if he still harbored a grudge. Could it be that Tania's admirer was a member of the Politburo and one of the men tipped to succeed Brezhnev? It seemed highly unlikely, but some underling could have been involved, some faceless official closely connected with the Kremlin.

"I loved Tania," Kirov said quietly. "When she died, a part of me died with her."

"You were grief-stricken?"

"Yes."

"In fact, so grief-stricken that you weren't responsible for your actions? You didn't mean half the things you said; it was just that you had an irresistible compulsion to lash out?"

Damn right he had. Everybody else had been running scared and had been only too eager to accept the police version of the accident. The way his father had told it, Tania had been playing fast and loose in his absence, behaving more like an amateur whore than a loving wife. And it was questionable who'd had the most to drink that fateful night, the drunken taxi driver or the victim lying dead in the road. Even the Abalakins had appeared to accept that their elder daughter was somehow to blame and had seen fit to apologize to him for her errant behavior—the Judas kiss that still made him want to throw up every time he thought about it. But Tudin was putting words into his mouth, and in a way that suggested he wasn't prepared to accept such a feeble excuse.

"It happens to be true, Nick."

"Oh, I believe you, George. But some people might think it was the sort of pragmatic explanation they could expect from a man like you."

"I can't help that. They can believe what they choose to believe."

"Like your American friend."

"Exactly."

It was impossible to follow Tudin's thought process or understand his tactics. A moment ago he'd had him pinned in a corner, hanging on the ropes and wide open, then, for some quite inexplicable reason, he'd decided to back off.

"You and Moorcroft obviously had a lot in common, George. Your careers have followed a similar pattern: the Frunze Military Academy and the Virginia Military Institute, commissioned into the same arm of the service, then four years at regimental duty before secondment to Special Forces. Of course, it's a very superficial comparison; you were the top cadet in the class of '71 while Moorcroft was well down in the order of merit when he graduated. One can understand why he thought his future lay in the infantry, but your choice seems very perverse to me. Why didn't you go into the artillery?"

"Because too much would have been expected of me," Kirov told him.

Fedor Fedorovich had become a legend in his own lifetime. He was the man who'd led his battery out of the encirclement at Bialystok, heading first northeast toward the Lithuanian border, then east to Vilna and on across the Dvina River. By day, they'd gone to ground in the forests; by night, they'd marched cross-country, tagging along behind the panzer spearhead of Von Leeb's Army Group. Along the way, Fedor Fedorovich had collected an army of stragglers from every unit under the sun—riflemen, engineers, cavalrymen, drivers, and signalmen who'd boosted the numbers under his command from seventy to more than three thousand. Two hundred and fifty miles and twelve days later, he'd smashed his way out of the ring, decimating a battalion of the Third Motorized Division and capturing 129 men in the process. The Great Patriotic War of the Fatherland had been going badly, and the Soviet people had been desperately in need of a hero. They'd gotten one in Captain Fedor Fedorovich Kirov. When asked by an earnest war correspondent to give a brief account of his spectacular escape, he was alleged to have retorted, "Who said we were trying to avoid the enemy? Fuck it, boy, you want to get your facts straight—we launched an offensive from the rear."

"Joining the infantry didn't make a scrap of difference to you in the end, did it, George? You still felt you had to prove yourself."

It was only natural that he should try to emulate his father and make a success of his career in the army. A string of outstanding reports earned during four years at regimental duty had not gone unnoticed by the high command, which had transferred him to the GRU in January 1976, having apparently decided that his talents were unlikely to be fully exploited in the mechanized infantry. His brief secondment to Special Forces had occurred in a similar manner. After Kirov had been placed first at the end of course examination, the chief instructor of the intelligence school had indicated that he was the sort of officer any Spetsnaz unit would be glad to have. He'd volunteered because the hint had been more in the nature of a direct order than a friendly suggestion, and in those days he'd been concerned about keeping his nose clean and getting ahead.

"Of course, it's always difficult for a son to live in the shadow of a famous father," Tudin said, philosophizing.

"And in your case it must be twice as hard, knowing that General Fedor Fedorovich is on first-name terms with some of those gangsters in the Kremlin."

"Gangsters?" Kirov echoed. "Who the hell are you talking about?"

"The Politburo. What have they ever been if not a bunch of hoodlums? Capone liquidated his rivals, so did Stalin, but on an infinitely larger scale."

"I'm not listening to this."

"Whyever not, George? I'm only paraphrasing what Khrushchev said to the Twentieth Party Congress. Mind you, Comrade Nikita was a fine one to talk; his hands weren't exactly lily-white. But at least while he was in charge a lot of people slept easier in their beds." Tudin leaned toward the low coffee table, knocked his pipe against the ashtray, then cleaned it out with a small penknife. Presently he looked up and gazed thoughtfully at Kirov, a faint smile hovering on his lips. "Do I shock you, George?"

"I think you've taken leave of your senses." Fear and anger turned his voice into a harsh croak.

"Capone, Moran, and O'Banion represented the un-acceptable face of prohibition and it's arguable that they did more than anybody else to get the Volstead Act repealed. Wiser criminals took note of this and decided the Mafia wouldn't make the same mistakes. Surely you can see the connection?"

Kirov shook his head vehemently. The connection was only too obvious, but he wasn't about to admit it.

"I can't believe that, George, you're far too intelligent. Why don't you go away and write me a paper on coercion, with particular reference to the methods employed by the Politburo and the Mafia?"

"*Net*." They had set a trap for him and he said *net* over and over again, reverting to his native tongue in a desperate attempt to establish his innocence. Then, for the benefit of any hidden microphone, he declared in an even louder voice that the Soviet Union had the most democratic system of government in the entire world.

"English, George, say it in English."

"Fuck your mother."

62

"If you must swear, use an Anglo-Saxon epithet."

"Goddamn it," Kirov shouted, "I've had enough of this. Every time you open your mouth I hear a pack of lies."

"Are you going to report me for seditious talk, George?"

"You bet your sweet ass I am."

"Good," Tudin murmured, "very good. The way you express yourself in the vernacular couldn't be better, but we've got to work on your accent."

"My accent?"

"North American," Tudin said. "Or to be more precise, a Canadian who has been living in the United States for the past ten years."

They were going to send him across. There could be no other explanation, though just why Tudin had thought it necessary to scare the living daylights out of him was completely beyond his comprehension.

"I think it's time we broke for lunch, George." Tudin got to his feet and moved toward the door. As he opened it, he glanced over his shoulder and said, "We'll start again at three o'clock. Okay?"

Kirov nodded, waited for him to close the door, then tried to unwind. Long after Tudin had left, he was still sitting there by the log fire, gazing at the fir trees beyond the strip of lawn and at the snow falling from a lead-colored sky.

★   ★   ★

Igor Gusovsky scuttled into the Universitet metro station, fed a five-kopek coin into the turnstile, then passed through the automatic barrier into the great marble hall resplendent with ornate chandeliers and murals on the walls depicting the heroic achievements of the Soviet proletariat. In a thoroughly disgruntled frame of mind, he rode the escalator down to the platforms, silently cursing Boris for dragging him away from the university in the middle of the afternoon. He could easily have passed the information Boris had asked for over the telephone, but that was too simple for the KGB; with their cloak-and-dagger mentality, they just had to make a big production out of everything. If the weather had been better, he wouldn't have minded quite so much, but he was developing a cold and now his socks were damp from trudging through the wet snow to the metro.

Gusovsky stepped off the escalator and followed the signs for Frunzenskaja, unaware that he was being followed until Boris clapped him on the shoulder.

"Well, if it isn't old Igor," the KGB man said jovially. "Fancy meeting you here."

"Yes, it's a small world."

"How's Irena?"

"She's fine—busy, of course." Gusovsky turned left and walked to the far end of the platform.

"And that brother-in-law of yours in the army?"

"The same as ever, except he's lost a little weight. Irena thinks he's been working too hard." Gusovsky wondered why the KGB officer thought it necessary to continue with the charade when there wasn't another person within earshot.

"You've seen Georgi then?" Boris inquired politely.

"No, I'm merely repeating what Irena told me. He dropped by to see her yesterday while I was out." A draft of cold air gusted down the platform, making Gusovsky shiver. He glanced to his left, saw that the signal was on green, then looked expectantly in the opposite direction. A few moments later, a train rumbled out of the tunnel and drew into the platform. "About time," he muttered.

"What?"

"Nothing, I was just talking to myself."

The doors opened with a pneumatic hiss. Entering the coach ahead of his companion, Gusovsky chose a seat remote from the other passengers and slumped down. Boris joined him and gazed at the roof panel above the opposite window, pretending to study the route map while he waited for the train to pull out of the station. When finally it did, he came straight to the point and asked why Kirov had called on Irena.

"He wanted to know how he stood with his father," Gusovsky told him. "They hadn't parted the best of friends when he was posted to Uzbekistan and he was anxious to know if Fedor Fedorovich had forgiven him for the way he'd behaved after Tania had been killed. Naturally, Irena couldn't advise him one way or the other because we haven't been on speaking terms with the general for months."

"I see." Boris clucked his tongue. "What else did they talk about?"

"Nothing in particular. Georgi did tell her that he was being promoted but he didn't say why."

"So how long did he stay?"

"Twenty minutes to half an hour. Irena made him a cup of coffee."

"You're quite sure nothing else was said?"

"Absolutely. I'd know if my wife was keeping something from me." He said it with total conviction, even though the claim had little validity. When the mood took her, Irena could be as secretive as any KGB agent, but he wasn't going to admit that to Boris.

"I'm glad to hear it, Igor." Boris eyed him thoughtfully, then said, "You might as well get off at the next stop."

"The next stop?" Gusovsky pushed his fingers under the band of his fur hat and rubbed his temples. "If that's all you wanted from me," he said, "why couldn't we have discussed it on the telephone?"

"Because only your eyes would tell me whether or not you were lying through your teeth. Incidentally, why are you sweating, Igor?"

"I've got a terrible cold," Gusovsky said and sneezed all over him as if to prove it.

★   ★   ★

The safe in the estate office was the only surviving piece of furniture that had once belonged to the Rostovs. Made by Chubb of London around the turn of the century, it had been used for a variety of purposes over the years. Before the Revolution it had contained the estate records and the Rostov silver, which had always been kept under lock and key when the family was not in residence. The silver and the estate records had vanished during the civil war, when the house had been taken over by the local Soviet, then the NKVD. The NKVD had used the hunting lodge as a detention center, and a large number of their interrogation reports had still been lodged in the safe when the Forty-seventh

65

Panzer Corps had overrun the area in July 1941. Two years later, the house was in Russian hands again, miraculously intact despite the heavy fighting at Mozhaysk.

By the time the GRU had acquired the property in 1952, the safe had been bricked in and fitted with a combination lock, which was the reason Lieutenant Colonel Nikishev had commandeered the estate office and ordered the camp commandant to remove his unclassified files. Security regulations permitted Nikishev to hold Top Secret material in the modified Chubb safe, and while the can of 16mm film and Kirov's personal documents, which he'd brought with him in a locked briefcase, did not appear to fall into that category, Nikishev firmly believed that they did. The catalogue of video games, radio-controlled model aircraft and O gage train sets manufactured by Marklin, which had been delivered by a dispatch rider from the First Chief Directorate late that afternoon, was also too sensitive to be seen by unauthorized eyes. And, as far as Nikishev was concerned, that included Nikolai Tudin.

Nikolai Tudin had been born Norman Tellacott in Scranton, Pennsylvania, on the first of May, 1930, and was the eldest of six children. His father had been a steelworker and had been one of the first to be laid off during the Depression because he was a strong union man and a member of the Communist Party. He'd also been a bitter opponent of fascism and had been killed in action at Guadalajara while serving with the Lincoln battalion of the International Brigade in Spain. Unlike his father, Tellacott had been a reluctant soldier. Drafted in 1948, he had been posted to the U.S. Twenty-fourth Infantry Division stationed in Japan and had had just over a month to serve before his discharge when the Korean War had broken out. Instead of returning home, he'd boarded a C123 for a one-way flight to Pusan. Pitchforked into battle, Tellacott, along with most of his platoon, had been cut off from the rest of the battalion at Taejon and had been taken prisoner. One month later, after a long forced march to the north, he'd ended up in PW Camp 18 near the Yalu River.

Although the camp had been administered by the North Korean Army, a GRU officer had been responsible for advising the political commissar on the methods and techniques of compulsory indoctrination. Because of his family background, Tellacott had proved more susceptible to brainwashing than any other Allied prisoner of war in the camp. In fact, he'd become a genuine convert to the Marxist-Leninist cause and, following the cessation of hostilities, had been the only man to apply for political asylum in the Soviet Union. His request granted, he had been allowed to settle in Moscow where, thanks to the GRU officer from Camp 18, work had been found for him as a translator in a major publishing house. Within five years he'd become a Soviet citizen, had changed his name to Nikolai Tudin by deed poll, and had married the only daughter of the literary director.

Although life may have seemed cosy to Tudin then, the GRU had not forgotten him. From the moment he'd arrived in Moscow, they'd kept a discreet eye on him and had noted with approval his complete identification with the Soviet way of life. In their opinion, his bilingual talents were being wasted in the publishing house and, following an informal approach in 1965, he was offered the post of language counselor in the GRU training organization, an appointment he'd readily accepted.

In the short time they had been working together, Nikishev had rapidly come to the conclusion that the GRU had made a bad mistake when they'd taken Tudin on. Although he would never admit it even to himself, his judgment was founded on a clash of personalities. In his view, the language counselor was arrogant, conceited, and quite insufferable. Furthermore, if there was one thing calculated to make his hackles rise, it was Tudin's habit of talking down to him whenever he asked a question.

"I don't want a lecture," Nikishev told him, "just a straight answer to a straight question. How good is Kirov? Can he pass himself off as a Canadian?"

"That's two for the price of one." Tired of standing up while Nikishev occupied the only chair in his office, Tudin perched himself on the edge of the desk, one leg planted on the floor, the other swinging slowly back and forth. "Well, like I said, Georgi is pretty fluent, which is no mean

67

achievement considering how little practice he's had in the past two years, but are you sure you've picked the right man?"

"Kirov is a very high-grade officer."

"He's not so hot under pressure. Scare him enough and he'll start jabbering away in Russian." Tudin grinned. "Of course, I really hit him below the belt with all that seditious crap about Stalin, Khrushchev, and Co."

"Yes, I've been warned that sometimes you're apt to go too far."

"I was only trying to see what he's made of."

"Do you have any other observations?" Nikishev asked him icily.

"Georgi tends to be a little stilted at times."

"You mean he doesn't sound natural?"

"Uh huh. Still, that's something we can put right, given time. By the way, how much time have we got?"

"A week, perhaps ten days, if we're lucky."

"I won't ask why all the hurry."

"I wouldn't tell you anyway," Nikishev said.

"That figures." Tudin took a slip of paper from his jacket pocket and passed it across the desk. "I'm going to need a few training aids—*Ordinary People, Kramer vs. Kramer, E.T., some others.*"

"Are you mad?" Nikishev looked up, jaw sagging. "This is a list of films."

"Movies," Tudin said, correcting him. "And I'm not crazy, merely practical. I haven't been near the States in over thirty years and it shows. I want Georgi to hear the new idiomatic expressions, and that's something only the latest movies can give him."

"And what exactly will he get from *E.T.*?"

"Nothing. But it's the biggest box office draw in history and he ought to see it, otherwise some busybody might just wonder if he's from outer space too. Besides, I wouldn't mind seeing *E.T.* myself."

"You're asking for the impossible."

"Don't give me that bullshit," Tudin drawled. "All you've got to do is ask our people in London or Washington to purchase the video cassettes, and they'll be here in the next diplomatic bag." Tudin pushed himself off the desk, walked toward the door, then turned around, snapping his fingers as though a last-minute thought had just occurred to him. "And while you're at it, get on to *Pravda* and ask for their microfilm copies of the *New York Times* and the *Washington Post* going all the way back to Watergate. Give me a week and Georgi will know more about the political scene in the States than most Americans do."

"You appear to think that Kirov will be entirely at your disposal."

"Won't he?"

Nikishev shook his head. "There are other areas that need honing—his skill at arms, physical fitness, and so on."

"You're aiming to make a gladiator out of him, and that's stupid. If Georgi is going to survive for any length of time among the enemy, he must be able to blend in with the background."

"Who said he was going in deep?"

"I don't know." Tudin shrugged. "I just assumed he was."

"Then you couldn't be more wrong. This operation will depend on speed, not stealth."

"It's beginning to sound like a 'wet' job."

"We're not planning an assassination," Nikishev said guardedly, "but there's no telling how the situation may develop."

CHAPTER VI

The field was a quagmire, his feet disappearing ankle deep into the glutinous mud at every stride. Both legs were lead weights that held him back, his chest felt as though it was being compressed by a steel band, and the old familiar gagging sensation in the throat was back again. The T34 tank mounted on a concrete plinth in front of the belt of fir

69

trees in the valley below was Kirov's inspiration, the only thing that kept him going. There were hundreds of identical war memorials all over Belorussia and the Ukraine, but this one was special because it marked the home stretch. When he reached it, Kirov knew that he would have less than a mile to push.

Nikishev had drawn up a tough fitness training program for him that would have taxed an Olympic-class athlete. Every morning before sunrise, a sergeant from Special Forces accompanied him on a 10,000-meter cross-country run that was supposed to loosen him up, although more often than not in the four days they'd been at it, the punishing routine had had the opposite effect. The first time out, Kirov had blown up at the halfway point and had been as sick as a dog when he'd finally staggered into the house. The following morning, he'd slipped on a patch of ice on the drive about two hundred yards from the inner barrier and had fallen awkwardly, skinning both kneecaps and the palm of one hand on the asphalt. But yesterday he'd turned in his best performance to date and had kept up with the sergeant all the way around the circuit, including the lung-bursting sprint to the finish line that had ended in a dead heat. The ground had been firm then and although carpeted with a thin layer of snow, the going had been relatively easy, but now it was a vastly different story. Around noon yesterday, the temperature had risen above the freezing point and the warm front had been accompanied by heavy rain that had turned the whole circuit into a huge bog, so that every stride demanded a superhuman effort.

"Keep going, Major, you're doing fine."

Kirov had lost count of the number of times the sergeant had said that to him. It was the kind of hearty, banal exhortation he found particularly irritating because they both knew it wasn't true. He was gasping for breath, his calves were two lumps of iron, and his heart felt as though it would burst at any moment.

"Not much farther now."

Not much farther now? Shit, who was the sergeant kidding? They hadn't reached the T34 tank yet and the bloody house was light-years away.

70

"Wrangel Island was never this easy, was it, Major?"

Another stupid remark, but then what could you expect from an NCO who was all muscle and locomotive power and had space to rent between his ears? Of course Wrangel Island was never this easy; Wrangel Island was the frozen asshole of the world, at 73° 25′ north latitude, 81° 9′ east longitude, and 250 miles from the nearest point of civilization at Pevek, and that was just a tiny settlement in northern Siberia. Wrangel Island was one vast training area for Special Forces, the place where the GRU put the finishing touches to a Spetsnaz agent and separated the men from the boys in the process. The instructors were all gladiators, men who'd been selected for their determination, physical prowess, and field craft, but some of them hadn't been exactly over-subscribed with brains. The major in charge of Kirov's course had been a real moron, the kind of dedicated fanatic who would charge a brick wall head first if he thought that was the quickest way to negotiate the obstacle. It was the same major who'd ignored the advice of his assistants and had decided that the para drop would take place on schedule despite a thirty-knot wind. Twelve men had jumped from the Illyushin but only three had walked away from the drop zone, and the major hadn't been one of them. Neither had Kirov; landing heavily, he'd broken his ankle and right leg in two places.

The accident had been a blessing in disguise. Sent to Moscow after discharge from the hospital, the GRU had taken one look at his medical case notes and decided there was no point in back-squadding him to a later course. Instead, they'd sent him to the language institute to learn English and, knowing he would be settled in one place for at least two years, Kirov had proposed to Tania Abalakinova, whom he'd first met in 1976.

"We're on the home stretch, Major. Race you to the barrier."

Kirov raised his head and saw that the sergeant was right. He didn't recall passing the war memorial or entering the belt of fir trees, but they were on the asphalt road now and there were the sentries, a bare two hundred yards ahead. Chest out, legs pumping as fast as he could drive them,

71

Kirov responded to the challenge and crossed the finish line less than a hand's span behind the noncom.

"Nice try, Major," the sergeant told him.

"Thanks."

"Same time tomorrow?"

"Yes," Kirov said, wanting to add, "unfortunately."

"See you then."

Kirov watched the NCO break into a gallop and head toward the stable block and wondered where the devil he got all his energy from. Then, still out of breath, he shuffled into the house to find Nikishev waiting for him in the hall.

"Ah, Kirov." Nikishev flashed him a brief, perfunctory smile. "I've had to make a slight change in the program because it seems we need a few snapshots of you in civilian clothes, which is a bit of a nuisance. However, you'll find a shirt and tie on your bed, so as soon as you've showered and changed, I want you to report to the photographer in the dining room. All right?"

"Whatever you say, Colonel."

"Good. Tudin's been warned that you'll be ten minutes late for the next period."

Kirov nodded, went upstairs to his room and stripped. The shirt was brand new and still in its cellophane wrapper. Like the tie with the Saks label, it had obviously been purchased in New York. The way Kirov saw it, the skeleton wardrobe was yet another pointer to his ultimate destination, which he'd already guessed from the nature of the political briefings he'd been getting from Tudin. The land of the free? Well, he'd know whether that was true soon enough. Whistling tunelessly to himself, he went into the bathroom next door and turned on the shower; adjusting the temperature to his liking, he stepped under the spray.

★   ★   ★

The photographer was in her late twenties, had shoulder-length auburn hair, a lot of freckles, and a provocative figure. She was wearing a white silk blouse, a green skirt that had been tailored to fit just a little too snugly, and a pair of black patent leather shoes with low heels that were definitely not regulation issue.

"You must be Major Kirov?" She advanced toward him smiling, her right hand extended to shake his. "My name is Alexandra Podgorny. I'm here to take your photograph."

Her voice was a painful echo from the past, reminding him of Tania. There was a similar vibrancy with its hint of suppressed laughter, and he noticed too that Alexandra had the same perpetual half-smile on her lips, as though she were enjoying a very private joke.

"Would you like to step over here, Major?"

Alexandra took his arm and steered him toward the upright chair in the center of a makeshift studio that consisted of three hardboard screens arranged in an open-sided square.

"Are you photogenic, Major?" she asked.

"Far from it." Kirov sat down. "You should see the mug shot on my ID card. I look like an escaped convict."

"You were probably startled by the flashbulb." She placed a hand under his chin and gently raised his head. "We don't want your face in shadow."

"No, that wouldn't do at all," Kirov said, his voice suddenly hoarse.

Alexandra had long tapering fingers and a gentle caressing touch that had an unnerving effect on him. The top two buttons on her blouse were undone and he found himself staring at her bosom, mesmerized by the deep cleavage. Tits, knockers, boobs; for some reason he didn't even begin to understand, every Anglo-Saxon slang expression for a woman's mammary glands sprang readily to mind. Unable to take his eyes off her, he watched Alexandra walk toward the Pentax camera mounted on a tripod, his gaze drawn to the exaggerated pelvic motion and the sight of her well-rounded buttocks, which the snug-fitting skirt did nothing to conceal. He hadn't looked at another woman since Tania had died and he'd been equally celibate during the three months prior to her death when they had been forcibly separated while he was serving in Blagoveshchensk. Now suddenly this stranger had reactivated a libido that had lain dormant for so long.

"Try to relax, Major; you're looking very tense at the moment."

Kirov gave her a weak smile, wondered how the hell he could relax when his penis was as erect as a flagpole. In a futile attempt to hide the prominent bulge in his pants, he hastily crossed one leg over the other. "How's that?"

"Better. Your face is a little red though. Perhaps I'd better open a window; it's very stuffy in here."

She knew he had a hard-on and was getting her kicks from teasing him about it. He felt embarrassed and ashamed of his lack of self-control. Then, too, he was angry that Alexandra Podgorny should have succeeded in making him feel humiliated.

"Of course I'm hot and look flustered," he snapped. "So would you be if you'd just completed a grueling ten thousand meters."

"My apologies, Major. I didn't mean to sound critical."

The half-smile was still there on her lips, but now it betrayed a certain nervousness.

"And I don't want to appear rude," Kirov said, "but why don't you get on with what you're supposed to be doing? I've got a very full schedule and I can't afford to waste time making idle chitchat."

The smile vanished and she reared back as though he'd struck her. Oh, well done, Kirov, he admonished himself. First you put Alexandra Podgorny in her place for over-stepping the mark, then after she has apologized, you slap her down again for good measure. He racked his brains trying to think of some way he could make it up to her without appearing venal, and was still frowning when the flashbulb popped.

"You caught me on the hop," he said and grinned at her like an errant schoolboy.

"My fault," Alexandra told him. "I should have told you to watch the birdie."

"I'm the one who's to blame," Kirov insisted. "I had my mind on other things."

"Are you ready now?"

"Yes." He wiped the grin from his mouth and faced the camera, steeling himself not to blink at the flash.

"I'm afraid your eyes look as though they're about to pop out of your head, Major."

"Sorry." Kirov shifted his gaze so that he was no longer staring directly into the lens. "Is that okay?" he asked.

"Much better." Alexandra tripped the shutter, then took another exposure to be absolutely sure.

"Are we finished?" Kirov asked.

"I hope so."

Her tone of voice left him in no doubt that she would be glad to see the back of him. Somewhat crestfallen, he got to his feet and left the dining room.

Crossing the hall, he entered the library to find Nikolai Tudin settled in his favorite armchair by the fire.

"You enjoy quiz games, Georgi?" he asked without looking around.

"Not particularly." Kirov sat down in the spare armchair and made himself comfortable.

"Tough luck. This one's a test of your general knowledge, except you'll have to look for the question and decide what sort of answer I'm hoping for. You get the idea?"

"I think so, Nick."

"Good. Let's start with Haldeman, Dean, and Ehrlichman."

"Bob Haldeman was the White House chief of staff," Kirov told him. "John Dean succeeded John D. Ehrlichman as legal counselor when he was appointed Nixon's domestic affairs adviser. Dean later wrote a book describing his involvement in the Watergate affair and called it *Blind Ambition*. Ehrlichman wrote a novel entitled *The Company* that eventually became the TV movie *Washington behind—*"

Tudin raised a hand, silencing him in mid-sentence. "Very impressive, George," he drawled, "but you sound like a walking encyclopedia, and that could be dangerous. You can't afford to draw attention to yourself in a hostile environment, so the rule is, never give out with more than you have to when conversing with a stranger."

"Point taken."

"Okay. Here's another. Nobody drowned at Watergate."

"That was a clever but distasteful slur on Edward Kennedy dreamed up by his political enemies when there was some talk of the Senator from Massachusetts running for the Democratic nomination. It refers to an accident he had when his car went off a bridge on Chappaquiddick Island and a young woman called Mary Jo Kopechne was drowned."

"The Green Bay Packers?"

Kirov did a quick double take, then said, "American football doesn't appeal to me. I'm an ice hockey fan."

"Yeah? So how do you rate the Montreal Canadiens' chances this season, George?"

★   ★   ★

Nikishev leafed through Kirov's security file again, looking for some chance remark by one of his former superior officers that might indicate a character defect. "Drinks in moderation and then only on social occasions." That would have been a reassuring statement, Nikishev thought, had it not been written by Colonel Leonid Paskar, the well-known bottle-a-day man who regarded anyone who drank less than he did as being unnaturally abstemious. "The marriage seems to be happy and stable; his wife is a delightful young woman who takes a proper interest in her husband's career." "Kirov is often depressed and singularly uncommunicative. So far, these undesirable traits have not affected his work and I am assured by the psychiatrist that his present behavior is only a temporary aberration, but I have my doubts."

That two senior officers could hold such diverse opinions of the subject was of little significance in Nikishev's view. The former assessment had been made before Tania Abalakinova had been killed, while the latter had been submitted by the lieutenant general commanding Uzbekistan Military District some three months after her funeral.

"Manages his financial affairs sensibly. Definitely not a womanizer but no evidence of homosexual tendencies either." Another report from Paskar and the reason Nikishev was going through the security file again, on the ground that whatever the colonel said was almost bound to be the exact opposite of the truth.

A discreet tap on the door told Nikishev that Corporal Alexandra Podgorny, had arrived. Locking Kirov's security dossier in the Chubb safe, he placed the folding chair he'd borrowed from the camp commandant in front of the desk and then loudly told her to come in.

From the moment she entered his office, it was very evident to Nikishev that Corporal Podgorny hadn't been near a parade ground since recruit training and he suspected that even then the drill sergeant had probably given her up as a bad job. Although her shoulders weren't slumped, she walked rather than marched into the room, and the way she came to a halt bore no relation whatever to the movement set out in the drill manual.

"You sent for me, sir?" she inquired politely.

"I most certainly did." Nikishev moved past her, closed the door, then pointed to the chair and told her to sit down.

"Yes, sir."

Corporal Podgorny glanced at the chair, saw the film of dust on it and wrinkled her nose. Completely taken aback, Nikishev watched her produce a handkerchief from her shoulder bag and wipe the seat before she condescended to sit down. Her impertinence angered him and at the same time made it that much easier for him to handle the situation.

"I want to talk to you about a matter of state security." He paused for effect, then said, "Concerning Major Kirov."

"Major Kirov?"

Her voice was a small echo of his and he didn't like the way she gazed at him, all wide-eyed and innocent.

"Are you deaf, Corporal?"

"No, sir."

"Insolent, perhaps?"

"No, sir, just surprised that you should wish to consult an NCO about a commissioned officer."

"I've just told you that this is a matter of state security. It so happens that Major Kirov has been provisionally selected for a delicate assignment, and we have to satisfy ourselves that he has no character defects before we brief him. Do you understand what I'm getting at?"

"I think so."

"Good." Nikishev leaned forward, elbows on the desk. "So what are your impressions of the major? Was he friendly toward you?"

"Friendly?" she repeated.

"You're an attractive young woman, Corporal," Nikishev said impatiently. "Any normal man could hardly fail to be aware of that. The point is, did Major Kirov take any notice of you?"

The question demanded more than a simple yes or no, and her reluctance to answer it was obvious from the way she was frowning.

"I caught him looking at me rather furtively a couple of times," Alexandra Podgorny said at last.

"And?"

"Well, Major Kirov got very annoyed and told me to get on with my job, said he wasn't prepared to waste valuable time on idle chitchat. I think he was embarrassed."

"What about?"

"Do I have to answer that, sir?"

"This interview is confidential," Nikishev informed her. "Whatever you tell me is privileged information and you can rest assured that not a word will ever be repeated to Major Kirov. Does that set your mind at rest, Corporal?"

"A little."

"Then you'd better answer the question."

"He had an erection," Alexandra murmured. "I couldn't help noticing it."

Nikishev smiled. So Kirov wasn't a stone man after all. He could be reached and turned on by a voluptuous woman. There had never been any indication of homosexual tendencies before or after Tania Abalakinova had been killed, but apart from confirming the supposition, this revelation also opened up new possibilities. For personal reasons, Nikishev considered it essential to ascertain exactly why Kirov had submitted a Breach of Security report, and it seemed to him that perhaps the one person likely to discover this was the auburn-haired corporal sitting opposite him.

"We're all rather worried about Major Kirov," Nikishev said, feeling his way. "He seems preoccupied, as though he has something on his mind. We think it's some personal problem connected with his late wife. Naturally we have done our best to persuade him to discuss the matter with us but we're not getting anywhere."

"And you think I may be able to help?"

"Yes."

"How?"

"By drawing him out of his shell, by being nice to him."

"Nice?" she repeated. "What precisely does that mean, sir?"

"Don't be coy with me, Corporal," Nikishev told her angrily. "I've seen your personal security dossier."

It wasn't necessary to recite the details; he could tell by the resigned expression on her face that she had a pretty good idea of its contents. "Alexandra Podgorny, age 27, Party membership number L1477A234. Enlisted Military Transportation Corps 1973, married Sergeant Anatoli Zubko linguist special intelligence on 23 June 1975, transferred to GRU in an administrative capacity and subsequently employed as a unit photographer grade 1. Reverted to maiden name following divorce on ground of incompatibility promulgated on 17 May 1978. Updated psycho–profile 10 February 1980: normal, conventional outlook on life, no evidence political/reactionary aberrations; intelligent, pleasant manner, stable personality, definitely heterosexual but with higher than average libido. Subject confessed she was frustrated by husband's lack of enthusiasm for sexual intercourse and this was probably root cause of divorce. Suitable for entrapment purposes." Extract from debrief Operation RHEIMS: "Corporal Podgorny succeeded in compromising Major Claude Bastin, Assistant Military Attaché to His Excellency the French Ambassador Extraordinary and Plenipotentiary, Moscow. This NCO was extremely cooperative throughout and indicated she would be prepared to undertake further assignments of this nature if required."

"I'm a good photographer, but that's not the reason you asked for me, is it, sir?"

Nikishev saw little point in denying it. In his opinion, Kirov was unpredictable, like weeping gelignite, and if there was a premature explosion, Nikishev would catch most of the blast. He wanted to make sure the substance was safe to handle and had suspected that only a certain kind of woman could get close enough to Kirov to ascertain that. The computer at GRU Headquarters had come up with

Corporal Alexandra Podgorny; the fact that she was also a grade 1 photographer was merely a bonus.

"My unit is expecting me back late this afternoon."

"No problem, Corporal," Nikishev said calmly. "I'll inform your commanding officer that you're to be temporarily attached to my establishment."

"And the negatives, sir?"

"The duty driver can take them back to the lab for processing this afternoon. Since you weren't to know that you'd be staying on with us, he can also collect whatever extra clothing you require at the same time." Nikishev smiled. "Do you have any other questions, Corporal?"

"Only one. When do I renew my acquaintance with Major Kirov?"

"Tonight at the movies. We're showing *Kramer vs. Kramer*, you can join the very select audience and take it from there."

★   ★   ★

The sworn deposition submitted by Captain Viktor Petrovich Ignatchenko, officer commanding 26 Counterintelligence and Interrogation Team, had been dictated by the head of Department 15 of the First Chief Directorate in accordance with the guidelines verbally expressed by Vatutin. Graded Secret and dated 31 October 1982, it read:

> Alleged Breach of Security
> *Reported by Major G. Kirov, GRU*
> Reference "A"; your inquiry of 28 October 1982.

1. On Tuesday 6 July 1982, I was instructed to collect a male Caucasian prisoner from the detention wing of 785 Base Hospital, Moscow Military District. I was further informed that the Caucasian had been captured on Monday 7 June, having been wounded during the course of a terrorist ambush on a Soviet army patrol in the Khinjan Valley, and that I was to interrogate him with a view to establishing his identity, nationality and status.

2. The interrogation was carried out in accordance with the procedures laid down in standing orders I/SO/D15 dated 1 May 1980 and was conducted by myself, assisted by Warrant Officer Mikhail Dishukin and Staff Sergeant

Venyamin Antipin. The prisoner remained in our custody until Saturday 16 October, when as a result of our failure to obtain the desired information, he was handed over to Headquarters GRU in accordance with orders received from higher authority.

3. While every inducement was offered to secure the prisoner's cooperation, we did not give him reason to hope that he would be exchanged for one of our agents held in custody by a foreign power. Furthermore, an examination of our files will show that this unit was not aware that the Ministry of Foreign Affairs was negotiating with the Unita rebels to secure the release of airmen Nikolai Molayev and Ivan Chernitski.

Captain Viktor Ignatchenko had knowingly signed a false deposition because he'd been told to do so by the head of Department 15, and a captain was not in the habit of disobeying a direct order from a full colonel in the KGB. The rest, Vatutin knew, was up to him. Reaching for the tape recorder on his desk, he plugged in the mike and depressed the play button.

He said, "This letter is to be graded Confidential and is to be addressed Personal for General Petr Ivanovich Ivashutin, general officer commanding the Glavnoe Razvedyvatelnoe Upravlenie. Subject heading is alleged breach of security reported by Captain, now Major G. Kirov.

"Paragraph one. Your liaison officer, Lieutenant Colonel Nikishev, acquainted me with the nature of the above-quoted report and as a result, I undertook to investigate the matter.

"Paragraph two. The KGB officer in charge of the interrogation team who questioned Moorcroft has been interviewed at length and has made a statement categorically denying that his team was responsible for the leakage of information. Furthermore, a detailed examination of departmental and unit files has shown that Twenty-six Counterintelligence and Interrogation Team was not aware of any negotiations with the Unita terrorists.

"Paragraph three. The American was, however, aware of these negotiations because they had been widely reported in the capitalist press before he was taken prisoner. Unless your own investigations have proved more fruitful, one can only conclude that Moorcroft was attempting to sow dissension between our respective agencies.

"Paragraph four. I suggest therefore that we take no further action on this matter. You could ask Moorcroft to name the officer responsible for the breach of security but, in my view, this would only afford him another opportunity to create further mischief."

Vatutin switched off the tape recorder, rewound the cassette, and placed it in his out-tray. He thought the final sentence was the real clincher, because it implied that the GRU still had Moorcroft in their custody. As a result of the measures Department 15 had already taken, they would have a hard time proving he wasn't.

★   ★   ★

Kirov removed his tie, undid the buttons of his shirt, and was about to shuck it off when he heard somebody tap on the door. Then, without waiting for an invitation, Alexandra Podgorny walked into his room and closed the door behind her. When she turned about, he noticed that she was holding a cigarette between the thumb and index finger of her left hand.

"I'm sorry to bother you at this time of night, Major, but I'm dying for a smoke and I've run out of matches." She smiled and moved nearer, her other hand fumbling with the catch on her shoulder bag. "I don't suppose you could oblige me with a light, could you?"

"I think so."

Kirov opened a drawer in the built-in desk unit, found a box of matches, and struck one. As he looked up, he saw that Alexandra was showing him a scrap of paper. Written on it in block capitals was a brief message that read: "I'M HERE UNDER ORDERS FROM LIEUTENANT COLONEL NIKISHEV. PLEASE TRUST ME AND DON'T ASK ANY QUESTIONS." The request didn't appeal to him one bit, but her eyes were searching his face looking for some kind of response, and he nodded to show that at least he understood the message.

"Thank you, Major." Alexandra held the slip of paper

82

over the flame, waited until it was well alight, then left it to burn in the ashtray. "Bother, it seems I spoke too soon. The wretched cigarette has gone out."

The match hadn't, though, and the flame was licking his finger and thumb. Somehow Kirov managed to restrain the four-letter word that sprang instantly to mind. "What are you smoking?" he asked manfully.

"Pamir."

"Yes, well, they're nearly always packed too loosely." Kirov struck another match. "One moment the flame is singeing your eyebrows, then before you know it half the tobacco has spilled out and you're left with a dead cigarette."

"So what's your favorite brand?"

"I don't have one now; I've given up smoking." Kirov thumped his chest. "It doesn't do the old lungs any good, or so my athletics coach tells me every time we go running together."

"How often is that?"

"Far too often for my liking."

It wasn't all that funny, but Alexandra forced a laugh, then sat down in the only armchair. "What are they trying to do? Make an Olympic champion out of you?"

"Some hope."

Their conversation was stilted and Kirov knew he sounded wooden. Although he couldn't lip-read, it wasn't difficult to guess that Alexandra Podgorny thought so too by the way she was mouthing at him. Finally, in sheer desperation, she dipped into her shoulder bag, took out a small notebook and frantically scribbled another message with a propelling pencil, then held it up for him to see. It urged him to "SAY SOMETHING CHATTY."

"What did you think of the movie?" he asked weakly, and thought a moron could have done better.

"I didn't understand most of it. What little I did struck me as sad. Of course, I know only a few words of English, so it was difficult for me to follow the story." Alexandra frowned. "Did the woman leave her husband?"

"Yes."

"Why?"

"Because he was an advertising executive and she thought

83

he was putting his job first and neglecting her. For all the notice he took of her, she could have been part of the furniture, like the Frigidaire or the dishwasher.''

"And that's why she left him?"

"Well, the lady also felt she owed it to herself to prove that she could earn a living."

"But that's stupid," Alexandra said indignantly. "In our country, a woman can be a wife and mother and still have a career. What was her problem? Surely the babushkas could have looked after the boy while she was out at work?"

"I don't remember the grandparents being mentioned."

"That doesn't surprise me. Everybody knows that family ties are much stronger here than they are in America." Alexandra studied him thoughtfully for some moments, then said, "The film depressed you, didn't it? I couldn't help noticing how sad you looked."

Neat, Kirov thought, very neat. Although he'd provided the opening Alexandra Podgorny had needed, it was she who'd skillfully maneuvered their conversation around to Tania. Evidently, Nikishev and Tudin weren't satisfied with his explanations and the GRU still had misgivings about the way he'd behaved after her funeral.

"The leading lady reminded me of my wife," he said in a flat voice. "She and Meryl Streep could have been sisters."

"Yes. From what Colonel Nikishev said, I gathered she must have been quite beautiful."

"He told you about Tania?"

"Only because I asked him if you were married." Alexandra got up and moved across the room to stub out what was left of her cigarette in the ashtray on the bedside table. Then, very coolly, she sat down on the divan, tucked her left leg under her rump, and leaned one shoulder against the far wall. "I suppose it was rather forward of me, but I liked the look of you."

"You're very direct."

"Honest might be a more accurate word."

"Yes, I think it might."

"Do you still miss Tania?"

"I try not to," Kirov said, "but every day seems empty without her."

"She must have been a wonderful person. I wish my former husband had been half so devoted to me."

Suddenly Alexandra Podgorny was off and running on a different track, telling him the whole of her life history in a series of anecdotes that were often amusing. Her infectious laughter, her sometimes husky voice, and the way she occasionally reached out to touch his hand, once again had a disturbing effect on him. Nothing would ever make him forget Tania, but she was cold in the ground; Alexandra Podgorny was alive, vibrant, and his for the taking.

"Eighteen months is a long time, Georgi."

"Yes."

She had read his thoughts and he didn't like it, but the nearness of her, as she leaned toward him, finally suppressed his inhibitions. Her open mouth closed over his, her tongue probing, her arms enclosing his neck. Kirov unbuttoned her blouse, slipped both hands inside, and fumbled with the shoulder straps of the slip and bra, trying to work them down over her arms.

"It would be a lot easier if I got undressed," she murmured.

There was little doubt that Alexandra was simply following orders but all the same, there was nothing mechanical or reluctant about the way she took off her clothes, then helped him out of his, her hands caressing his body with a touch that was featherlight. And the way she trembled and moaned with pleasure at his response was genuine and not the faked reaction of a whore performing a hundred-ruble trick.

He matched her eagerness, pulling the blankets and sheets aside so that she could scramble into bed and lie flat on her back, her legs spread wide apart to receive him. As he entered her, she raised her hips and scissored her legs behind his back to lock him in.

"Yes . . . yes . . ." Her eyes narrowed to slits and she bit her bottom lip. "Oh, yes."

He could feel himself coming and wanted to hold back but Alexandra egged him on and he thrust deeper and deeper, pumping and grinding toward a climax. She writhed beneath him, her fingernails raking his back; then suddenly she arched and in the same instant he exploded. Totally spent, he lay there for a while, then, very gently, he withdrew and rolled over onto his left side.

"You know what I'm going to tell Nikishev?" Alexandra whispered after a lengthy silence.

"I haven't the faintest idea." He tried to sound casual and devil-may-care, but there was a slight edge of anxiety in his voice.

"You've no reason to be alarmed, Georgi. I shall tell that sleek pussycat that any man who's as good as you are in bed can't possibly have any hang-ups."

"I doubt if that will satisfy him," Kirov said dryly.

"Well, I'm satisfied." Alexandra turned over onto her right hip and snuggled closer. "At least I am for the time being," she murmured.

CHAPTER VII

The phone call had roused Vatutin at 6:21, and it was still dark when he parked his car in the alleyway between the KGB Headquarters on Dzerzhinsky Square and the Lubyanka prison. After showing his pass to the militia man guarding the rear entrance, he entered the building and took the elevator up to the ninth floor.

Until May '82, when Yuri Andropov had become the Secretary to the Communist Party Central Committee, the chairman's office had always been at the front of the building overlooking the statue of Feliks Dzerzhinsky, the founder of the Cheka in 1917 and hence the KGB. Colonel General Vitaly Fedorchuk had broken that tradition; the day after he'd taken over from his predecessor, the chairman's office had been transferred to a room with a view of the Lubyanka. The new arrangement had only one advantage that Vatutin could see; it enabled senior officers to come and go without being observed by agents of a hostile intelligence service.

It had taken Colonel General Vitaly Fedorchuk forty-one years to reach the top of the tree. A career officer, he had made his name in the Ukraine, where he'd crushed nationalist dissent and stamped out the growth of religion by suppressing the Baptist and Uniate churches with ruthless efficiency. He was a stolid man with a round face, fleshy cheeks, a double chin, and a fat neck that bulged over his collar. His dark hair, streaked with gray, was combed straight back in a style favored by Hollywood actors in the late thirties. Beneath a broad forehead, the left eyebrow was half an inch longer than the right and included a quizzical kink above the pupil, which gave him a lopsided appearance. Fedorchuk was sixty-four and looked his age for once. Observing his drooping eyelids, dark jowls, and the rumpled suit he was wearing, Vatutin concluded that the KGB chairman had been up all night. It also became rapidly evident that he was in one of his surlier-than-usual moods.

"The Vera Berggolts syndrome," Fedorchuk growled, and waved him to a chair. "How soon can we bring it into play?"

Long ago, Vatutin had learned that the simple questions were nearly always the most difficult to answer. This one was no exception because Fedorchuk would have phrased it differently had he really understood the mechanics of the projected operation. It was not politic, however, to point that out to the colonel general. A more subtle approach was called for when dealing with a man like the chairman.

"Technically speaking, it's a GRU operation," Vatutin said cautiously. "Of course, if it was absolutely essential, we could give them a nudge."

"The question is, Vatutin, are we ready?"

"London is all set, and that's really the essential prerequisite."

"And you're confident that our people can pull it off?"

The fact that Fedorchuk had asked him virtually the same question at the special briefing five days ago was an indication that he was looking for something more than a simple yes. On the other hand, Vatutin was not prepared to give the chairman the 100 percent guarantee he so obviously wanted. No matter how well an operation had been planned and rehearsed in advance, came the day and there was always a chance it could founder on a stroke of pure bad luck.

"I have every confidence in Natalia Rubanskaya, Comrade General," Vatutin said, feeling his way. "She has already accomplished the most difficult part of her assignment and I believe she is a good enough actress to carry off the rest."

Natalia Rubanskaya was the assistant chief archivist for the GRU staff of the Soviet Embassy in London. A pleasant, not unattractive widow in her early forties, she had held a similar post in Athens from 1974 to 1976 and was highly regarded by her present superiors, who had no reason to suspect that she was a KGB plant. With a vetting status that allowed her constant access to Top Secret material, it had simply been a question of waiting for a suitable opportunity to photocopy the card index of GRU agents in the UK.

"This Aleko Denisenko," Fedorchuk said abruptly. "Does he have a reputation for being a womanizer?"

"I doubt it. After all, he's the man Kirov will be contacting in London, and the GRU would never have selected him as a go-between if he hadn't been whiter than white. Not that that will make a jot of difference; the beauty of this frame lies in the fact that it can be made to fit anybody."

When Denisenko failed to report for duty after meeting Kirov, a tearful Natalia Rubanskaya would confess that she had been having an affair with him. Then, after the investigators had found a mass of incriminating evidence at his residence, she would make a further statement alleging that although Denisenko had told her he was going to defect, she'd refused to take him seriously. And Denisenko wouldn't be able to contradict her because he would be lying on his back in the mortuary of a London hospital, a suicide who'd chosen a grisly way out.

"I know how it starts, I know how it ends." Fedorchuk stared at him, eyes cold as a fish. "What about the middle bit?"

"We'll lift Denisenko after he's seen Kirov. Naturally, I haven't asked Nikishev how they will make contact because that would only arouse his suspicion. However, we've had

Denisenko under physical and electronic surveillance ever since he was picked for the job, and we're pretty sure we know where they will rendezvous." Vatutin smiled fleetingly. "Comrade Denisenko has been familiarizing himself with the London Underground."

The surveillance team consisted of KGB personnel drawn from the Aeroflot and Intourist offices, the Tass news agency, and the Moscow Narodny Bank in King William Street. Security was preserved in both directions; Denisenko had never come into contact with any of the men who were shadowing him and the KGB officers had not been told why he had been put under surveillance.

"We're planning to keep a close watch on Kirov while he's in transit," Vatutin continued. "As soon as we know his flight number and estimated time of arrival in England, we'll double the surveillance on Denisenko and put the hit team on full alert. As you might expect, they'll be in contact with the surveillance detail."

"I see." Fedorchuk rubbed his jaw and looked pensive. "Refresh my memory," he said presently. "What are their names again?"

"Konstantin Fomin and Mikhail Izveko. Both men are known to Denisenko, especially Fomin, who's the chief personnel security officer at the embassy. That's why he won't be alarmed when they lift him. You also have my word that it will be done very discreetly."

"Then, from our point of view, there's no reason the operation shouldn't be put into immediate effect?"

"None at all." Vatutin cleared his throat nervously before sounding a warning note. "However, as I said before, technically speaking this is a GRU operation, and I know Lieutenant Colonel Nikishev is under the distinct impression that he'd have a week to ten days in which to prepare Kirov."

The glacial stare told him that Fedorchuk was not impressed with his argument, and Vatutin wondered how he could persuade him to leave the GRU alone and allow them to get on with the job in their own good time.

"We'll need a very convincing excuse if Nikishev is to curtail his training program." It sounded feeble even to his ears. Cold irrefutable logic was required to move Fedorchuk, and what had he come up with? A whining plea that did his case no good at all.

"Comrade Leonid Brezhnev had a heart attack during the early hours of this morning," Fedorchuk said in a harsh, grating voice. "He survived the coronary without any apparent physical deterioration but the prognosis isn't good. The physicians say the next attack will probably be fatal. I need hardly add that that's for your ears only."

Vatutin could now understand why the chairman was so anxious to set the wheels in motion. Even so, it wasn't going to be easy; he could hardly pick up the phone, talk to his opposite number, and urge him to get moving. The ground would have to be prepared and the right kind of information fed into the system, intelligence data that would make the GRU sit up and take notice. Moreover, it would have to be subtly done and in such a way that the military intelligence organization believed that the reports had come from their own sources. That would take time and time was one thing he didn't have.

"Don't let me detain you, Lyosha."

Vatutin looked up, startled by the use of his nickname and the implication that Fedorchuk assumed that, having discussed the problem, they had somehow arrived at a satisfactory solution.

"It may take me up to twenty-four hours to induce the desired reaction from the GRU," he said tentatively.

"You won't have to do anything."

"I won't?" Vatutin felt his jaw sag and hastily closed his mouth.

"Don't tell me you've forgotten whom they're backing for the leadership and how easy it was to interest them in Vera Berggolts and her lover, the prodigal son?"

"You mean my opposite number knows that Brezhnev has had a heart attack?" Vatutin said slowly.

"Exactly that. Foreign Minister Gromyko was on the phone to General Petr Ivanovich Ivashutin before I left the Kremlin." A grimace that passed for a smile twitched Fedorchuk's lips. "You know something, Lyosha?" he said

90

dreamily. "That idiot actually believes he has Gromyko in his pocket."

★   ★   ★

The mist was a portent of the grim winter to come. It hung motionless, a ghostly shroud that obscured the treetops and reduced visibility to a few yards. The temperature had fallen to minus 10 degrees centigrade during the night and the ground was rock hard under foot. Later on in the morning, the ground mist would disperse and there would be a partial thaw when a weak sun like a blood-red orange finally broke through the overcast. But the days were getting shorter and the time was rapidly approaching when 10 below would seem mild compared with the harsh climate of mid-January.

Kirov, however, drew little comfort from the knowledge that the weather could have been a whole lot worse. The sports jacket provided by the quartermaster's department offered little protection against the cold and, despite several nips of vodka, he couldn't stop shivering. Under the watchful eye of the weapon-training NCO, he walked over to the trestle table that had been erected on the firing point and picked up the Colt .38 Police Positive. Holding the revolver in his right hand with the barrel pointed downward to the ground, he disengaged the cylinder from the frame and proceeded to load all six chambers with the ammunition nestling in a small cardboard box. That done, he snapped the cylinder home, unbuttoned the sports jacket, and tucked the revolver into the shoulder holster under his left armpit with the butt facing outward.

The weapon-training NCO retired to the wooden hut behind the firing point where the electric target console was housed. As soon as Kirov began to move off down the narrow but steep-sided gully, television cameras hidden in the fir trees on either bank would monitor his progress onto a display screen above the console. By this means, the range-control NCO was able to activate the remote-controlled figure targets at exactly the right moment to achieve maximum surprise.

"Ready whenever you are, Major," the NCO called out.

Kirov waved his left arm, then went down into the gully.

He assumed that the red danger flags had already been hoisted on either flank and at the farthest point of the range directly ahead, but in the prevailing mist it was impossible to tell. In such adverse conditions, hearing was more important than seeing, but there was no way he could move through the shin-high frozen grass in the gully bottom without making a racket. Instinct was the only other sense he could rely on, and instinct told him that the weapon-training staff would have concealed the pop-up targets among the bushes dotted here and there on both forward slopes. He also figured that they would be spaced well apart.

Both assumptions were disproved seconds after Kirov came around a sharp bend in the culvert. Sixteen yards ahead and slightly to the right, a plywood figure of a man in a crouching position suddenly reared up from the grass. Kirov reacted just as swiftly; drawing the Colt .38 revolver from its shoulder holster, he swiveled around and squeezed off two shots in rapid succession, the whole movement conducted in one fluid motion. The first round plowed into the earth in front of the target; the second hit dead center and bowled the plywood figure over. Above the reverberating echo of gunfire, he heard the crack and thump of a bullet cleaving the air above his head and almost in the same instant saw a small column of dirt thrown up by an electrically detonated charge a bare yard ahead. A second bullet from a high-velocity weapon firing on a fixed line whiplashed past him, this time from a slightly different direction. Two Kalashnikovs, he thought, both set for repetition instead of automatic; then the head and shoulders of three targets at five-yard intervals appeared in a rough arc to his left and a submachine gun started chattering.

The strike of shot was uncomfortably close and he dived forward, hit the ground, and rolled over twice in a desperate attempt to get out of the beaten zone. Although the instructors at Wrangel Island had been known to bend the safety regulations in their eagerness to achieve the maximum degree of realism, Kirov thought Nikishev's weapon-training NCO had stretched them beyond the acceptable limit. It was also evident that the idiot had rigged up an old PPSh with a seventy-one-round drum to fire a series of short bursts while traversing. Still lying prone, he spread his elbows, gripped the wrist of his right hand and, taking a deliberate aim, fired at the nearest target, knocking it flat with a hit just below the neck.

The submachine gun had been traversing from right to left, but having reached the predetermined maximum arc, it now began to swing the other way. Watching the strike of shot, Kirov calculated that the PPSh was firing a burst of three to four rounds at five-second intervals. He waited for the next burst, saw that the beaten zone was less than a yard from him, and started rolling frantically to the left. Exactly five seconds later, there was another staccato rattle, but this time the impact area was at a much safer distance to his right, and he breathed again.

Three rounds left, two figure targets to go; the odds hadn't changed but he needed a cool head to see it through. Kirov moistened his lips, aimed at the middle plywood man, and saw it go down a split second after he'd squeezed the trigger. The last one was going to be a real bastard, however, because from where he was lying, he could see only the right side of the head. Even worse, the foresight blade on the Colt totally obscured the visible mass when he brought the revolver up into the aim again. "Cover from view is not necessarily cover from fire." Recalling that old maxim, he took dead center in the confident knowledge that the evergreen bush couldn't possibly deflect a .38-caliber bullet.

One shot was enough, but although the target went down, it didn't produce the effect Kirov had anticipated. He'd assumed the two Kalashnikovs and the PPSh had been activated when the targets had been raised and that the converse would happen when they were no longer standing. That comforting theory had certainly applied to the Kalashnikovs, but the submachine gun was still hammering away. It was also traversing much faster and the interval between each burst had now been reduced to around three seconds.

A burst hit close enough to spatter dirt into his face, and he immediately rolled over to his right. A seventy-one-round drum was good enough for seventeen, maybe eighteen, squirts but that calculation didn't get him very far because he'd been too busy to keep a running total in his head. "Shit." He screamed the word aloud, crazy with fear because now it seemed that the arc of fire had diminished and the PPSh was swinging his way again and accelerating fast. He threw himself to the left, praying for his life to a deity that the State had taught him did not exist.

The gun changed direction for the fifth time and he rolled the other way, mouthing obscenities as his bladder opened. Somewhere among the fir trees on the banks above him, hidden television cameras were tracking his every move and the weapon-training NCO was doing his level best to kill him. There could be no other explanation, although just why the GRU had decided to execute him and had chosen such a bizarre method was beyond Kirov's comprehension. Nor was he inclined to give it much thought because right now his only concern was to stay alive, and he thrashed, rolled, twisted this way and that in a frantic bid to do so. Then suddenly the submachine gun ceased firing with a dull clunk as the working parts went forward for the last time, riding above an empty magazine.

Kirov lay there, his limbs trembling, the sweat running down his face to mingle with the blood oozing from a dozen cuts inflicted by the long grass that the frost had made razor sharp and tough as wheat stubble. Miraculously, he was still holding the Colt revolver in his right hand.

"Major Kirov." Nikishev's voice boomed at him through a bullhorn. "Can you hear me, Major Kirov?"

There was no way he was going to answer that question. If Nikishev wanted him, he would have to come and get him.

"Are you all right, Georgi?"

It was Georgi now, was it? Well, if he was okay, it was no thanks to that sadistic half-colonel and his misbegotten weapon-training NCO. Slowly and very cautiously, Kirov raised his head and looked around; when nobody attempted to shoot him, he stood up and moved toward the group of figure targets. Nikishev was still calling to him on the bullhorn, demanding to know why he didn't answer in a voice that managed to sound both anxious and plaintive at the same time.

Kirov went up on the left-hand bank and examined the targets. He raised the nearest one, saw that there was a small metal plate fixed on the wooden batten to which the plywood figure was nailed and realized that it obviously made contact with the solenoid partially buried in the ground behind. When the target was raised by an electric impulse to the winding gear attached to the underside, the associated weapon was activated. When it was knocked down, the metal plate came into contact with the solenoid, the circuit was broken, and the Kalashnikov or PPSh ceased firing.

He scoured the crestline and discovered the PPSh positioned in a small depression between the fir trees. It was mounted on a tripod, clamped fore and aft on spindles, the butt elevated so that the barrel pointed downward into the gully. Two stops on the traverse ring marked the left and right of arc. Motive power was supplied by a small electric motor attached to the forward spindle that drove a rotating cog splined into the traverse ring. Two metal rods extended rearward from the forward spindle to a T bar inside the trigger guard that exerted sufficient pressure on the trigger mechanism to release the bolt, while the rate of fire was regulated by an interrupter gear also driven by the electric motor. The system wasn't entirely automated; before the range practice began, somebody had to slap a drum magazine on the submachine gun and cock the weapon.

"Where are you, Major Kirov?"

Kirov glanced round, spotted Nikishev and the weapon-training NCO as they rounded the first sharp bend in the gully and took cover in the depression. Both men were unarmed and had their heads well down searching the ground directly to their front as though they expected to come across his body in the long grass. Their action suggested that the TV cameras had only a limited scan and had failed to keep track of him after he'd gone to ground.

"Major Kirov."

Nikishev sounded alarmed, but it was nothing to the way he was going to feel a few seconds from now. Cold with anger, Kirov waited for the two men to move beyond his position, then he stood up, locked both hands around the butt of the Colt revolver, took a deliberate aim, and squeezed the trigger. The bullet hit less than two inches behind Nikishev and scared the wits out of him.

"That was a close shave, Colonel," Kirov said casually. "Almost as close as I had." He climbed down the bank and strolled toward them, his face expressionless. "Somebody ought to take a look at the submachine gun. Among other faults, it has a defective trigger mechanism."

"Yes, well, no doubt you'll be submitting a report." Nikishev glared at him. "You're very good at that sort of thing."

It was some moments before Kirov made the connection, and even then he found it hard to believe that Nikishev was referring to the Breach of Security report. He wondered how the report could possibly have affected the colonel, unless of course Nikishev had been responsible for the leakage of information in the first place. If he'd been hauled over the coals for it, he'd have reason to be sore with him, but the rest didn't make sense to Kirov. Nikishev was his case officer, and the training he'd been receiving was geared toward something big. That being the case, the GRU would hardly entrust such a sensitive job to an officer who'd previously demonstrated a lack of security awareness.

"It's a wonder you don't suffer from writer's cramp."

Another reference to the Breach of Security report and a more obvious one this time. Kirov just wished to hell Nikishev would come clean and tell him exactly what it was that he found so disturbing about it. Unfortunately, the trouble with Nikishev was that he was so damned secretive; he couldn't even bring himself to give Alexandra Podgorny a proper briefing before he dispatched her to Kirov's bed.

"I do things by the book, Colonel," Kirov told him evenly. "When something is wrong, I report it in writing, the way I'm supposed to."

"I'm glad to hear it," Nikishev said tersely. "Now turn your weapon in. Orders have come through that your course of instruction is to be terminated forthwith."

Kirov broke the revolver open, ejected the spent cartridge cases from the cylinder, then handed the Colt .38 to the weapon-training NCO, butt first. The noncom avoided his gaze, looked everywhere but at him, his face ashen, his hand shaking. He was, Kirov thought, an unlikely assassin and had probably been as unnerved by the incident as he had.

"All right, Staff Sergeant, you know what to do." Nikishev jerked a thumb over his shoulder in the general direction of the figure targets. "Take that PPSh to the armorer and tell him I want a detailed examination report on my desk by 1600 hours. Then get hold of the electronics artificer and have him check out the whole circuit."

"Yes, sir."

The staff sergeant looked down in the mouth and not without reason. His day had gotten off to a bad start the moment he'd discovered that the console had gone haywire. And there were no prizes for guessing who'd end up holding the bag.

"Are you coming with me, Georgi?" Nikishev asked.

Despite the use of his first name again and a mild tone of voice, Kirov was left in no doubt that it was an order, not a friendly suggestion. Together, yet apart, they walked back to the firing point and then on to the stable block with its incongruous clock tower.

"About the training program?" Kirov said, breaking the silence between them. "What happens to me now that it's been canceled? Do I go back to Moscow?"

"Only to catch a train."

Where to, he wondered and waited for Nikishev to elaborate. If you departed from the wrong station and traveled southeast out of Moscow, you could find yourself on the spur line from Potma to one of the labor camps around Barashevo.

"You're going for a 'swim,' Georgi."

Kirov digested the news in silence as they walked through the stable block, heels clumping in unison on the cobblestones. Although it was something of a relief to know that they were going to send him abroad, he thought Nikishev's choice of expression was unusual. Every intelligence agency had its own jargon, and going for a "swim" was definitely a KGB slang term.

"When do I leave?" he asked in a neutral voice.

"Late tomorrow afternoon." Nikishev opened the back

door to the old servants' hall and ushered him inside. "And we've got a lot of ground to cover before then."

"I presume I'll have time to change out of these things?"

Nikishev eyed him, nose wrinkling in disgust at the sight of his urine-stained trousers. "You've got ten minutes," he snapped, "then I want to see you in the dining room."

Kirov nodded curtly, then went on up the spiral staircase to his room above the front entrance. Closing the door behind him, he stripped, dumped the sodden clothing into the linen basket, and wrapped a bath towel around his waist. Soap, face cloth, talcum powder: he checked the contents of his wash bag and was about to go into the bathroom next door when he heard the sound of footsteps and a low murmur of voices in the courtyard below. Moving to the window, he looked down and caught a final glimpse of Nikolai Tudin and Alexandra Podgorny as they climbed into a GAZ jeep.

Kirov tapped on the window to attract her attention but she didn't hear him and, moments later, the jeep moved off down the drive, a plume of white smoke trailing from the exhaust. He was still standing there long after the vehicle had disappeared from sight, saddened by the thought that he might never see Alexandra Podgorny again.

Chapter VIII

Kirov opened the door and walked into the dining room to find that it had been converted into a makeshift theater again. While he'd been taking a shower, a fatigue party had moved the furniture out of the way, drawn the curtains, and erected a portable screen in front of the serving hatch from the kitchen. Unlike the previous evening when Nikolai Tudin and Alexandra Podgorny had been present, it seemed that this particular movie show was going to be entirely for his benefit. There was another difference: last night the projectionist had been a qualified operator, this morning

Lieutenant Colonel Dmitri Nikishev had taken that job upon himself and was making a real hash of threading the film through the gate.

"Vera Berggolts," Nikishev said, his back still toward him. "Does the name mean anything to you?"

"No, never heard of the woman," Kirov told him.

"I thought you were interested in athletics?"

"So I am."

"Then you must have heard of her. She was a small, petite brunette with a turned-up nose and a hairstyle that looked like it had been cut around a pudding basin, with a fringe above her eyes."

"What was she noted for, track or field events?"

"Track," Nikishev said. "Four and eight hundred meters. She once made the national relay team in the four hundred meters."

"Vera Berggolts?" Kirov repeated the name, then shook his head. "I can't say I remember her."

"Well, she never really made the headlines." Nikishev closed the gate and wound the film onto the lower spool, then walked over to the light switch. "Better sit down, Georgi, while you can still see the chair."

Kirov thought his air of bonhomie was overdone. Despite his seemingly relaxed manner, Nikishev was on edge, which was hardly surprising when less than an hour ago he had tried to kill him.

"You're going to see a montage of video tapes. I shall be doing the commentary, and we start with an athletics meeting at Leningrad that took place in June 1975, when Vera Berggolts was eighteen." Nikishev quietly locked the door, plunged the room into darkness, and returned to the projector, using a small flashlight to find his way. Moments later, the camera started running and the frame numbers were projected onto the screen. Five, four, three, two, one; the camera panned the crowded stands, then came down to the track. "It's the four-hundred-meter event," he announced, "eight competitors, four local girls, two Poles, a Czech, and a Bulgarian. Vera Berggolts has drawn the outside lane and her main threat is Maria Jankowski, the blonde Polish girl in lane two."

Vera Berggolts was the smallest in the field of eight and looked very tense. It showed in the way she fidgeted with her running shorts, first hiking them right up into her crotch, then easing them down until the waistband was just about sitting on her hips. When finally she had adjusted them to her satisfaction, she began to fiddle with her jersey, as though the shoulder straps were chafing her skin. Eventually, she strolled toward the starting blocks, wrists flapping, legs kicking in some kind of loosening-up exercise. As if bored with her antics, the camera suddenly moved away from Vera Berggolts and zoomed in on Maria Jankowski. The tall, loose-limbed Polish girl was completely relaxed and very businesslike. Without any histrionics, she crouched down, eased her feet into the starting blocks and got set, her whole body coiled like a powerful spring under tension. With some reluctance, or so it seemed, the camera returned to Vera Berggolts, who was now also set, her head up, deep worry lines etched into her forehead, her bottom lip drawn in.

One of the officials appeared as an inset in the top right-hand corner of the picture, his right arm raised aloft. Kirov saw a small puff of smoke from the starting pistol, then the inset vanished and was replaced by a clear but oblique view of the track from an elevated position. Despite her nervousness, Berggolts had gotten off to a good start and was going well, her spikes fairly eating up the track. When the field entered the back stretch, she was still holding the lead she'd enjoyed from the staggered start, but the blond Polish girl was closing fast and was now lying a comfortable third behind the Czech girl. On the final bend, she moved effortlessly into second place and was nicely poised to attack Berggolts. As they came off the bend into the final straight, the Russian girl glanced over her left shoulder, saw Jankowski bearing down on her like an express train, and desperately kicked for home. For a while it looked as though Berggolts was going to beat off the challenge, but with less than fifty meters to go, she began to tie up, her legs suddenly lumps of iron, her head lolling from side to side. Jankowski sailed past her and was followed by the Czech; then right on the line, the Bulgarian girl dipped lower to nudge Vera Berggolts out of third place. The camera showed a final glimpse of her as she left the track and made her way to the changing room with tears in her eyes and a mortified expression on her face. Then the scene changed to a different stadium under a blue and cloudless sky.

"Moscow, the tenth of May 1976," Nikishev intoned. "The women's eight-hundred-meter event at the intervarsity meeting among Leningrad, Moscow, the Patrice Lumumba, and Kiev. The Leningrad team is in white shorts, blue jerseys."

Vera Berggolts had drawn lane three and Kirov noticed that once again she'd gotten off to a good start. On the second lap, when the stagger unwound and the field broke for the inside track, she put on a spurt to make sure she wasn't boxed in. Lying fifth down the back stretch, she began to pour it on and moved up to second place but was still a good three meters behind the leader when they came off the final bend. Kirov thought Berggolts had waited too long, but she proved him wrong. By sheer guts and determination, she overhauled the girl in front to cross the finish line half a stride in front. Then, completely exhausted, she jackknifed at the waist and remained bent in two until she regained her breath. When Berggolts finally straightened up, she turned to face the main stand and waved to the crowd. The smile was slow to appear but when it did, it was worth waiting for.

"She looks really happy," Kirov observed.

"Berggolts had every reason to be overjoyed," Nikishev told him. "The girl who came in second had just been selected for the Montreal Olympics."

"But even so, Vera didn't make the team?"

"No."

"I bet that pleased her," Kirov said dryly.

But it didn't seem to make any difference. At a meeting in Kiev later that summer, there was the same radiant expression after she'd won the 400 meters. And losing didn't appear to bother her now. At Leipzig in May 1977, when the East German veteran, Juta Solf, left her standing, she had waved and smiled at the crowd as though the race had been her greatest triumph.

101

"Warsaw, July 1977, the East European Games," Nikishev announced as the scene changed yet again. "Berggolts went there as a reserve for the four-by-four-hundred relay team and made the squad by default when one of the girls came down with a nasal virus the day of the finals. For a number of complicated reasons, she ended up running the anchor leg."

The Soviet team was in second place when Berggolts received the baton, but she was a good five meters behind the blonde Polish girl, who was much taller and had a longer stride. The odds against her seemed insuperable, but somehow she found the reserves of strength and willpower to overhaul the other girl and nip her at the finish line.

"She ran that lap in fifty-two point one seconds," Nikishev said. "Her best performance ever."

The same hand wave and a smile to the crowd, but Kirov thought it significant that the radiant expression was missing, which was strange, because the girl she had just beaten was Maria Jankowski. At Moscow, Kiev, and Leipzig somebody very special to her must have been there in the crowd; at Warsaw he or she had been absent. Another change of scene, this time to an indoor stadium with a foreshortened track and exaggerated banking on either end of the stretch.

"Cosford, England, February 1979," Nikishev informed him. "Not a full international but her first visit to a capitalist country."

The 400 meters was an easy win for Berggolts and produced exactly the same kind of reaction to the crowd she'd previously displayed in Warsaw. In Kirov's opinion, her lack of enthusiasm confirmed his theory about a boy or girl friend.

"Dortmund, West Germany, seventeenth of May 1979."

An aerial view of the athletics stadium and the town, then a quick fade-out to a blank illuminated screen as the last frame passed through the gate.

"That's where she defected, Georgi," Nikishev said and put the overhead lights on.

"Yes? Who with?"

"Nobody. She did it all by herself."

Bullshit, Kirov thought, bullshit from beginning to end. There had to be more to it than that, otherwise Nikishev wouldn't have gotten rid of Nikolai Tudin and Alexandra Podgorny in such a hurry.

"So why are we interested in her?" he asked in a neutral tone of voice.

"Her father's in shipping; before that, he was a merchant navy captain."

The before and after were relevant only in the light of what he was doing now. The merchant fleet was part of the Red Navy, just as Aeroflot was an adjunct of the Soviet Air Force. There was therefore a good chance that Berggolts was a member of the GRU.

"Her father is a Leningrader born and bred," Nikishev continued. "He grew up during the siege, lost his entire family—grandparents, mother, father, two sisters, younger brother. Can you imagine what it must have been like, what it did to him?"

Kirov shook his head. Nobody could who hadn't been there and lived through the siege. Even Fedor Fedorovich, who'd spent most of the first winter there, had often said that he still found it hard to imagine what life must have been like for the civilian population. After their initial attempt to cross the Neva River had failed, the Fascists had abandoned the idea of storming Leningrad. Instead, they'd decided to cut the road and rail links to the outside world and starve the city into submission. Their bombers had set the Bedayev warehouses alight with incendiaries and all the entire food reserves had gone up in smoke. Every truck that had four wheels had been commandeered and the Red Army, together with a horde of civilian volunteers, had brought in what supplies they could using the ice road over the Lake Lagoda, but it hadn't been nearly enough. By January 1942 there had been no light, heat, or power in the city and the bakeries had been reduced to making bread out of sawdust and the sweepings from the flour mills. By January 1942 the basic bread ration had been cut to 500 grams a day for everybody except the factory workers and front-line soldiers, and people had begun to strip their wallpaper in order to eat the paste on the back. Ration cards were issued from week to week and if you lost yours or had it stolen, you'd almost certainly die of starvation before you were able to collect the next one. To stay warm, you had to wear all your clothes, day and night; when you wanted a drink, you had to carry a pail to one of the ice holes in the Neva, provided, of course, you had the strength. A black market had flourished, cannibalism had not been unknown, and everywhere there had been special vigilante squads who'd executed rumormongers on the spot. One million people had died in the siege but the city had held.

"When spring finally came, they found fourteen-year-old Pavel Berggolts all alone in the apartment except for the bodies of his mother and two sisters in one of the adjoining rooms, and they'd been partially eaten by rats." Nikishev paused to light a cigarette, then said, "He was too weak, you see, to load each corpse onto a sledge and drag it to the nearest cemetery. Not that it would have made any difference if he had; the gravediggers were either at the front or dead."

"Why are you telling me all this?" Kirov asked.

"Because I want you to understand Pavel Berggolts and why he vowed that his children would never want for anything. As it happened, his wife couldn't have another child after Vera was born, which is probably another reason he spoiled her to death. Vera had only to ask for something and it was hers. The most damning thing you could say about Pavel Berggolts is that he turned his daughter into a selfish, greedy little parasite."

"And when she went to England, she saw an abundance of luxury goods that weren't available in the Soviet Union and decided to defect at the first opportunity?"

"There's more to it than that, Georgi."

"I should think there is," Kirov said tersely. "Who was the friend she waved to in the stands?"

"He was a scientist specializing in metallurgy. He used to be in charge of a research team at the Izhorsk factory in Leningrad that was developing a new type of armor plate for the next generation of the main battle tank."

It wasn't difficult for Kirov to guess how Vera had met her scientist. He and Pavel Berggolts had obviously become friendly while they were serving with the GRU cell at

Leningrad Military District. Nikishev's use of the past tense also told him that he too had defected.

"This scientist," he said, "does he have a name?"

"Matthew Willets."

"And before he changed it?"

"That needn't concern you. As of now, Willets is living in America, and that's the name he's using over there." Nikishev collected an ashtray from the dining table and stubbed out his cigarette. "Mr. and Mrs. Matthew Willets, 566 Constitution Avenue, New Haven, Connecticut. What does that tell you, Georgi?"

"That we have a source who's very close to him."

"He's more of a confidant than a source. In fact, Willets has told him that he would like to come home."

"Really? So where's the problem?"

"Vera Berggolts. She's not keen on the idea."

"I'm not surprised. America is supposed to be the consumer's paradise; unless they're short of money, she must be having the time of her life. If all you say about her is true, Vera will never come back."

"She will if she knows that her father-in-law will become the First Secretary of the Communist Party when Brezhnev dies."

Kirov folded his arms, leaned forward in the chair, and rested both elbows on his knees. Suddenly there was a chill in the air as though a window had been opened and all the warmth had gone out of the room. "Keep your head well down until the leadership question is settled"; well-meaning advice from Fedor Fedorovich but wholly impracticable. Nikishev and his fellow conspirators needed an emissary to convey the news to Vera Berggolts, and what better messenger than the son of the general who was a Hero of the Soviet Union twice over? They hadn't asked him to volunteer for the job because they knew he couldn't refuse. If he did object, they would crush him as they would an insect; he could end up in a mental hospital, meet with a fatal accident, or succumb to some mysterious but highly contagious disease. The power they enjoyed was limitless and even with Fedor Fedorovich lurking in the wings, there was no way he could stand up to them and survive.

105

"I doubt if Vera Berggolts will take my word for it," Kirov said.

"She will when you show her this."

Nikishev dipped into his pocket and produced a heavy gold ring with three small rubies set in a triangle on the flat upper surface. While barely large enough to fit his little finger, Kirov thought the ring was too big for a woman. Fedor Fedorovich had mentioned Andrei Kirilenko as a possible successor to Brezhnev and rumor had it that his son had recently defected. But Kirilenko was seventy-three and on that basis, his son was likely to be in his early forties. Although there was no fool like a man hopelessly in love, especially if there was an age gap of twelve to fifteen years between husband and wife, he had a hunch that Willets was not Kirilenko's son.

"The ring is only a part of it. You will also tell Vera Berggolts to phone the Inter-Continental Hotel in Helsinki on Thursday, the eleventh of November, between the hours of two and three P.M. eastern standard time, and ask for Mr. Willetowski."

Andrei Kirilenko was definitely out of the running then. Whoever this Willetowski was, and the Russianizing of the Anglo-Saxon name was almost laughingly inept, he had to be someone whose presence in Finland would be considered unremarkable. That seemed to indicate Grigory Romanov, the Party boss in Leningrad. Romanov was fifty-nine, the right age if they wanted a younger man to succeed Brezhnev. There had been no rumors circulating about his son either, and that was another plus factor because there wouldn't be any speculation when he and Vera Berggolts surfaced inside the USSR again. Romanov did have two handicaps, though; his name and the fact that he was a Leningrader. His political opponents might put it about that he was in some way related to the Czar, and Moscow had always distrusted Leningrad. The city may have spawned the Revolution, but its population was too nonconformist for the Kremlin's liking.

"You will also impress upon her that she is not to make the call from her home."

"Because the FBI will have a tap on her line?"

"I'd be surprised if they haven't," Nikishev said.

"And after she has made the phone call?"

"Your job is finished and you come home." Nikishev picked up the large brown envelope lying on the dining chair next to the projector and handed it to Kirov. "This is to be studied in private; your new identity, family background, what you do for a living. Given your photographic memory, it shouldn't take you long to learn it by heart."

Kirov weighed the envelope in his hand and thought Nikishev was an optimist. The "legend" felt heavy and thick enough for the opening chapter of a long-winded biography.

"I suggest we meet again in my office at three o'clock. All right?"

"I have a couple of questions."

"I'm sure you have, but they can wait until after the final briefing." Nikishev turned his back on him and began to remove the spools from the projector. "Until then, the contents of that envelope come first, and that's an order."

"It would be."

Kirov left the room without further comment, went upstairs to his room, and opened the envelope. The biography on the first page told him that he was George Kershaw, a Canadian citizen born in Vancouver on the twenty-first of May 1950. The mimeographed price list attached to the "legend" indicated that Kershaw sold toys for a living.

★   ★   ★

Aleko Denisenko was forty-four years old, overweight for his height, and going bald. A graduate of the Volgagrad Institute of Technology, he was listed as Third Undersecretary of Commerce, a post he'd previously held during his first overseas posting when accredited to the Soviet Embassy in New Delhi. Throughout that tour he had been loaned out as a technical adviser to the Ministry of Agriculture in furtherance of a mutual aid agreement that, among other facets, envisaged the manufacture under license of the latest KV tractor by the Indian government. No intelligence officer could have asked for a better cover, and while determining

107

which factories were best suited to the program, he had been able to assess their future potential for tank production in time of war.

Having made such a success of his initial foreign posting, it was now a matter of some concern to Denisenko that he was not doing nearly so well in England. The disappointing performance was hardly his fault; Anglo-Soviet trade had been at a virtual standstill since a Conservative government had been returned to power and, as a result, the opportunities for intelligence gathering had been drastically curtailed. Unfortunately, GRU Headquarters in Moscow didn't seem to appreciate his difficulties, and Denisenko also had an uncomfortable feeling that his assessment of the British reaction to the Falklands crisis had not been received with any marked degree of enthusiasm. He had reported only what he'd seen and heard, and again it was scarcely his fault that the British people had displayed a resolution that had surprised friend and foe alike, as well as most of their own media pundits. Although anybody who'd witnessed the speed with which the British had fitted helicopter pads to the *Canberra* and the *QE2* couldn't have helped being impressed by their efficiency, he'd deliberately kept his reports neutral and had studiously avoided any phrase that smacked of admiration. However, judging by the icy questions he'd subsequently received from Moscow, his superiors had evidently thought otherwise.

Under the circumstances, Denisenko was only too relieved that GRU Headquarters had decided to involve him in what was obviously a Top Secret operation. The fact that he had been cast in the role of a cutout, a job that could easily have been done by one of the embassy's leg men, was irrelevant. So far as Denisenko was concerned, it was a sign that he was back in favor again. His only worry was that the operation might be canceled at the last moment, thus denying him the opportunity to redeem himself. This perpetual nagging fear was finally dispelled by an internal telephone call from Natalia Rubanskaya, the assistant chief archivist, who informed him that a Top Secret signal addressed for his eyes only had just arrived from Moscow. A stickler for observing standing orders, Denisenko locked the door of his office and then walked down the corridor to the GRU registry.

Although Natalia Rubanskaya was only eighteen months younger than he, her youthful-looking face suggested that there was an age gap of at least five years between them. She was always well groomed, and he suspected that most of her salary went to clothes. This morning, for instance, she was wearing a bottle-green skirt and bolero jacket over a white frilly blouse, and the whole effect was definitely eye-catching. Lately, she had taken to painting her nails and using perfume; lately, she had also gotten into the habit of greeting him with a warm smile as though delighted to see him.

"I believe you have a signal for me, Comrade Rubanskaya," Denisenko said pompously.

"Yes, indeed, Op Immediate and TS." She flashed him another smile, brighter and warmer than the November sun outside, and indicated the small receipt book on her desk. "I'm afraid you'll have to sign for it first, Aleko."

The sudden and unexpected use of his pet nickname excited him. The fragrance of her perfume and her dark silky hair brushing his face as she half rose from her chair when he leaned forward to sign the docket gave him a thrill and set his pulse racing. His signature, never completely legible at the best of times, looked as though he were suffering from palsy.

"I hope I've signed in the right place," he said in a voice that sounded breathless.

"I hope so too." She chuckled as though they were enjoying an intimate joke and somehow managed to stroke his wrist in the process of handing the signal to him.

When Denisenko looked up, he found the chief archivist staring at him, his thick black eyebrows drawn together in a disapproving frown. He glared back, then left the registry with as much dignity as he could muster.

Denisenko unlocked his office, opened the combination safe, and took out the cipher book. The signal had an Op Immediate precedence that claimed his undivided attention, but he couldn't stop thinking about Natalia. Comparisons were always invidious, but she was infinitely more attractive

109

than his wife, Raya, who was running to fat, scorned all beauty aids, and dressed like the frump she was. His three small daughters were already younger versions of their mother, and a visual recollection of their pudding faces, which he'd seen across the breakfast table earlier that morning, made him shudder.

With a determined effort, he pushed all thoughts of Natalia aside and concentrated on the classified signal. To avoid leaving any impressions on the blotting pad, he rested the blank flimsy on a sheet of glass before deciphering the message, a task that took him less than ten minutes to accomplish. The message simply told him that the freight would arrive Saturday afternoon, 6th November, but it was the single word "destruct" after the full stop that really claimed his attention. Security regulations stipulated that an independent witness had to be present when he destroyed the original enciphered message together with the clear text, and he wondered if he dared ask Natalia Rubanskaya. Caution and a natural fear of being rebuffed led him to check the neighboring offices first.

The naval attaché, Captain Anatoli Zotov, was out; so too was his assistant. The army and air force attachés were located in the transverse corridor, and he quickly persuaded himself that it was pointless to waste any more time looking for a witness when the registry was so much nearer. Hesitating no longer, Denisenko returned to his office and called Natalia Rubanskaya on the internal phone. When she told him she would be only too delighted to do as he asked, his pulse quickened again and he waited impatiently for the sound of her footsteps. When she walked into the room a few moments later, he was as tongue-tied as a teen-ager on his first date.

"It's good of you to drop everything to help me," he said lamely.

"It's a pleasure," Natalia told him.

"Anyway, destroying this message won't take a minute."

"That's all right, Aleko, I'm not in a hurry."

The innuendo wasn't lost on him and he couldn't believe his luck. Denisenko just wished he could close the door for a little privacy, but security regulations insisted it was to be

110

left open when the office was occupied, and orders were orders. Still, the secret-waste destructor was in the near left-hand corner of the room and partially screened from the corridor by the retaining wall. He switched on the power and set the machine running.

"Originator's number Center 30, date time group 020955 November plus clear copy." Denisenko showed her the enciphered message and the flimsy before dropping them both into the secret-waste destructor.

"It always fascinates me the way the revolving plates shred papers into strips no thicker than a strand of hair," she said.

"Yes."

He felt Natalia's thigh press against his and turned toward her. Her mouth was just a few inches away, the lips parted invitingly. The temptation was too much for him and he kissed her hungrily. There was nothing demure about Natalia's response; her tongue forced its way into his mouth and she moved against him. As he tentatively clasped her buttocks, she pressed the palm of one hand into his crotch and began to massage him gently.

"Natalia Rubanskaya?"

The familiar voice sounded querulous and the heavy footsteps in the corridor conveyed impatience and a growing annoyance. Natalia froze, then hastily stepped back one pace, a second before the chief archivist poked his head around the door.

"Ah, there you are," he said, and advanced into the room. "I was wondering where you'd gotten to."

"I needed a witness." Denisenko pointed to the secret-waste destructor and gave him a sickly smile. His mouth was smeared with lipstick and there was no way he could hide his erection. "Perhaps I should have asked your permission first," he added lamely.

"Quite." The chief archivist glared at Natalia, then turned around and stalked out of the office.

"Don't take any notice of him, Aleko," Natalia murmured. "He's only jealous."

"Yes." Denisenko licked his lips, then used his fingers to rub away all traces of lipstick.

"There's nothing to worry about, really there isn't. Just leave everything to me. I can handle him."

"Yes."

Denisenko just hoped she could. Stomach fluttering like a butterfly, he returned to his desk and sat down. Usually, a cigarette steadied his nerves, but for once it had no effect whatever, and it was some considerable time before he felt calm enough to get on with his routine work.

Had Vatutin been present to witness the byplay between Denisenko and Natalia Rubanskaya, he would have had every reason to be delighted. Although the incident had been neither planned nor rehearsed, it had strengthened the impression the KGB was striving to create. In capitalizing on an unforeseen situation, Natalia Rubanskaya had shown great presence of mind, which was to be expected from a very experienced intelligence officer.

★   ★   ★

The final briefing session was being conducted in a way Kirov had least expected. He'd assumed Nikishev would want to satisfy himself that he knew everything there was to know about the fictitious George Kershaw, but after questioning him for roughly twenty minutes, he had suddenly announced that they were going for a stroll in the grounds. Kirov supposed he thought that it was safer to conduct the rest of the briefing in the open air, where it would be extremely difficult for any eavesdroppers to overhear them. It was also a fact that within a very short space of time nobody would be able to see them. Although it was only 3:25 P.M., the weak sun was already disappearing below the horizon and night was drawing in fast.

Hands deep in the pockets of his light topcoat, he followed Nikishev down a flight of steps that led from the neglected rose garden outside the dining room to a large ornamental pond that had been equally untended. Long ago, the water had seeped away through a myriad of cracks in the concrete basin and the silted bottom had become a jungle of weeds and nettles. Where a gazebo had once stood, there was now only a pile of rotting timbers, but the sundial in front of it was still recognizable even though the copper hour-face was green with verdigris.

"You'll fly to Lvov in the Ukraine early tomorrow morning, then catch the two o'clock train to Budapest," Nikishev said abruptly. "When you arrive at the West Station, take a taxi to the Duma Hotel where a single room has been reserved for you in your own name. Later in the evening, one of our officers from the embassy will drop in on you to deliver a Canadian passport for George Kershaw and sufficient cash to tide you over in Vienna. He'll collect your Soviet passport and identity papers at the same time."

"That figures. How long do I stay in Vienna?"

"Just the one night." Nikishev turned around and began to circle the ornamental pond in a counterclockwise direction. "Kershaw has been booked into the Bristol on the Opera Ring by one of his Austrian business associates, and you'll find there are a couple of letters waiting for him. One will have been posted in the Twelfth District of Vienna some time this afternoon; the other will have allegedly been redirected from the Hilton Hotel where Kershaw was staying before he went to Budapest."

Both letters were intended to flesh out the "legend" that had been created for George Kershaw. The one posted in the Twelfth District contained a receipted hotel bill from the Hilton and sundry others from various restaurants around town, while the airmail letter that had been redirected was supposed to be from the current girl friend in New York. Yet another package containing further supportive evidence would be waiting for him when he checked into the Steigenberger in Bonn late on Friday afternoon. Several phone calls, a working dinner that same evening, and a telex from the New York office would help foster the illusion that Kershaw was a successful businessman.

"The telex will instruct you to drop everything in order to attend a sales meeting in London the following morning. It will involve a last-minute change of plan and you'll have to make your own arrangements. Get the reception staff at the Steigenberger to help you because that's what any normal businessman would do."

In London, Kirov was to make two phone calls; the first to a subscriber living in the Highgate area; the second, exactly three-quarters of an hour later, to a number in the west central postal district. As they walked around and around the pond in the gathering darkness, Nikishev made him repeat both numbers over and over again until he was satisfied that Kirov had committed them to memory.

"You're to stay on in London until the evening of Monday the eighth of November; then, unless the embassy link officer gets in touch with you again, you're to catch a night flight to New York."

The stopover meant that the GRU would have two days in which to check him out and make sure he was still clean. After that, he was on his own until such time as he returned to Vienna.

"Longest way out, shortest way back," Nikishev said in a flat voice. "Once the Berggolts woman has spoken to her father-in-law in Helsinki, you can catch a plane to Rome. From there you'll go by train to Vienna and walk straight into the embassy."

"Just like that?"

"What are you expecting? A military band and a guard of honor to greet you? Or are you thinking of copying Vera Berggolts and her husband?"

"I've no reason to defect," Kirov said angrily. "If you've read my dossier you should know that as well as anybody. Anyway, it's a little late in the day to be having second thoughts about me, isn't it?"

"I've always had them, right from the moment I was told that you'd been selected for the assignment. There are too many shades of gray in your background for my liking."

For the first time since they'd known one another, Nikishev had lowered his guard and disclosed some of his nagging doubts. With a bit of leading, there was a good chance he would really unburden himself.

"You're referring to Tania?" Kirov suggested quietly.

"Well, it's on record that you refused to accept the conclusions drawn by the police and alleged that the investigation had been one big cover-up."

"I paid for that mistake. Remember?"

"That's right, they posted you to Uzbekistan. All the same, there are some people who think you got away with it." Nikishev laughed softly. "Still, if a general who's a Hero of the Soviet Union twice over can't pull a few strings for his son, who can? Or was it those very influential friends your wife acquired while you were serving in Blagoveshchensk who didn't want to make too much trouble for you because they had something to hide?"

"Why ask me? Your guess is as good as mine."

"Then I can't help wondering if it was these same influential people who got you this assignment?"

To hear Nikishev talk, one would have thought Kirov had just been given a plum job in preference to others who were equally if not more deserving. But there was more than a grain of truth in what he'd said; somebody had pulled a lot of strings to make sure Kirov was chosen.

"Guess who'll be the main scapegoat if you mess things up, Georgi?"

"You."

"That's right," Nikishev said bitterly. "I'm a nobody, a career officer without influential connections in the Kremlin."

It was out in the open now. Nikishev had done everything he could to have somebody else appointed, because deep down he suspected that some people were determined that the operation should fail and that the GRU should be discredited in the process. Nikishev knew a purge would surely follow and was certain that he would be one of its first victims. When all his lobbying had come to nothing, he'd resorted to more desperate measures, concocting a training program for Kirov that was largely irrelevant. The cross-country runs, the workouts in the gym, were merely designed to prepare him mentally so that he would accept the small-arms training on the electric target range without question and would go quiet as a lamb to a rendezvous with death.

"I want you to know that we're on the same side," Kirov told him quietly.

"Are we? Then who's the enemy?"

"The KGB. They set this whole thing up beginning with the American, Russell Moorcroft."

115

"Ridiculous. I'll remind you that our present chief, General Petr Ivanovich Ivashutin, was a former member of the KGB."

"Well, there's your answer."

"I don't think so," Nikishev said curtly. "No matter where his former allegiance may have lain, Ivashutin is a realist. He knows that even if he agreed to destroy the GRU, his enemies would ensure that he went down with us."

Kirov waited, hoping that Nikishev would enlarge upon his theory, but he was not forthcoming. "Somebody else then?" Kirov suggested tentatively. "The chairman of the KGB or one of his deputies? Do you think they're behind the conspiracy?"

"I think it's time you started packing. You've got an early start in the morning and no doubt you'll have some letters to write."

"I'd like Irena to know that everything's okay, and I ought to drop my father a line. I assume you'll want to read them?"

"How right you are," Nikishev said dryly.

CHAPTER IX

The corner room was on the twelfth floor of the Steigenberger directly above the New Zealand Embassy and overlooking the parking lot and railroad tracks behind the hotel. Beyond the up and down lines, a neat patchwork of garden allotments fronted a well-designed and prosperous-looking housing estate set against the backdrop of the Venusberg hills. From the other window, Kirov could see the Reuter Strasse flyover and the Adenauer Allee, the main thoroughfare leading to the town center of Bonn.

Although he'd spent only one night in Vienna, Kirov had already acquired a taste for luxury and thought the Steigenberger compared very favorably with the Bristol Hotel on

116

the Opera Ring. The room with bath *en suite* that had been reserved for him was spacious, well furnished, and spotlessly clean. Moreover, there were no defective electric light bulbs, and the radio, color TV, refrigerator, and telephone were all in working order, which, from personal experience, he knew couldn't be said for most of the hotels in Moscow. There was little danger of getting stuck in any of the silent and smooth-running elevators either, something that had once happened to him at the Ukraina.

Kirov opened the mini-bar, fixed himself a brandy and ginger ale, and then sat down in an armchair to read the mail that had been waiting for him when he'd checked into the hotel. In all, there were three messages and one large, bulky brown envelope that had been delivered by hand. Of the telephone messages received from the desk clerk, two were from the sales directors of firms with business addresses in Frankfurt and Munich, while the third was from a Joachim Abbetz, who described himself as a tax consultant and requested that Mr. Kershaw call him at 99-8011 anytime before 6:00 P.M.

The large brown envelope contained an assortment of receipted bills that in date sequence indicated that George Kershaw had visited Frankfurt, Munich, and Stuttgart between the eighteenth and twenty-fourth of October before moving on to Vienna and Budapest. There was also a brief memo wrapped around a slim appointments diary roughly six inches long by three wide. Embossed on the front cover in gold leaf was the legend "Nestor's Toy Emporiums, Boston, New York, and Philadelphia." The memo, written in longhand, was from Joachim Abbetz, who said that Kershaw had left the diary behind when he'd visited him at his office in Bonn a few days back. It seemed the diary was not the only thing Kershaw had left behind; attached to the memo with a paper clip were fifteen 100-Deutschmark notes.

The diary was the real surprise. There was a used look about it, with the pages well thumbed and a series of cryptic entries from Friday the first of January right through to Tuesday the second of November. The notes had been made with a ballpoint pen, the individual pages subsequently

117

treated with a chemical solution and then exposed to varying degrees of ultraviolet light in order to age them. It was, Kirov had to admit, a brilliant forgery. Like as not, the penman had obtained one of the essays he'd been required to write in English when a student at the Moscow Institute of Foreign Languages in 1978 and had then spent hour after hour practicing every characteristic. The end result was such that Kirov could have sworn the handwriting was his.

It was not the kind of job that could have been accomplished while Nikishev was putting him through his paces at Mozhaysk. The perfect forgery demanded infinite patience as well as skill, and although it was difficult to estimate precisely how long the penman had spent on the task, Kirov thought it must have taken him at least a month. That meant that somebody had decided he would handle the negotiations with Vera Berggolts long before he'd started to interrogate Moorcroft. Dmitri Nikishev had assured him that it was a GRU-sponsored operation, but the scale of the logistic and financial support it had been allocated suggested that the KGB was actively involved, and he could think of no good reason they should be eager to assist Military Intelligence.

Kirov glanced at the messages again and decided he could ignore the sales directors in Frankfurt and Munich. Nikishev had made it clear that the GRU would check him out along the route to make sure he was clean; if one of their local agents wanted to run his eye over him, he'd pick a rendezvous somewhere in Bonn. On that premise, Joachim Abbetz was the obvious contact. Leaving his brandy and ginger ale on the occasional table, Kirov walked over to the phone, obtained an outside line, then dialed 99-8011.

The woman who answered the call seemed pleasant, cheerful, and efficient. In appalling German, Kirov said, "*Guten Tag, mein name ist Kershaw, George Kershaw. Ist Herr Abbetz zu sprechen, bitte?*"

The request produced a curious gurgle that sounded like suppressed laughter, then he understood her to say that she was putting him through. Moments later, a hearty voice came on the line.

"Good afternoon, Mr. Kershaw. I trust you had a comfortable journey and that you found everything to your satisfaction at the Steigenberger?"

Abbetz spoke perfect English but with a guttural accent. It was also evident that he was inclined to be pompous and overbearing.

"I did," Kirov told him.

"Good. While you've been in Vienna and Budapest, I've had time to examine in some detail your proposal to open a branch of Nestor's Toy Emporiums in Frankfurt. Of course, I have to say here and now that there is no avoiding state and federal taxes in the first year of trading. However, I believe there are a number of ways and means by which the parent company in New York can minimize the assessment for corporation tax on profits. Naturally, these recommendations will be set out in the report I'll be submitting to your head office, but I think it would be helpful if you and I were to discuss them before they are typed up."

"Seems a good idea," Kirov said noncommittally.

"Well, now, are you free this evening, Mr. Kershaw?"

"I don't have anything planned."

"Excellent. I'll get my secretary to book us a table at the Zur Lese restaurant. Shall we say seven-fifteen?"

"That suits me. How do I get there?"

"The top end of Adenauer Allee near the Kennedy Bridge." Abbetz laughed. "You won't have any trouble finding the restaurant, Mr. Kershaw; every taxi driver in town knows where it is."

Kirov said it would be just his luck to flag down the one cabdriver who didn't, thanked Abbetz for inviting him to dinner, then said *Auf Wiedersehen* and put the phone down.

Collecting the executive briefcase from the closet, Kirov returned to the armchair and filed the latest batch of receipts in date order. From the eighteenth of October through the fourth of November, he now had all the proof he needed to account for Kershaw's every move; the only thing missing was an airline ticket that would show where and when the Canadian sales director had arrived in West Germany. The apparent omission didn't worry him; if the GRU, with a little help from their opposite numbers, could provide him with a complete wardrobe at twenty-four hours' notice, it was highly unlikely that they would overlook such an important detail. Chances were he would find the airline ticket inside the report Herr Joachim Abbetz claimed he'd drafted.

Kirov took out the Falk street plan he'd purchased from a kiosk at the Hauptbahnhof, opened it up and located the approximate position of the Zur Lese. He thought it was somewhere in the area of the university library, at a point where the main road into town almost converged with Rathenau Weg, which ran alongside the Rhine. According to the map scale, the restaurant was roughly a mile and a quarter from the hotel, which meant that it would take him about twenty minutes to get there on foot. He studied the map again and chose a route that would enable the GRU to make several random checks on him.

Kirov looked at his watch, saw that it was only a quarter past three, and decided to stretch out on the bed. Before doing so, he buzzed reception and asked the girl at the desk to give him a call at six o'clock.

★   ★   ★

Nikishev stared at the red light above the communicating door and wondered just how much longer Major General Vatutin would leave him to cool his heels in the personal assistant's office. Five minutes past three, and he'd been told quite categorically that he was to report at two-thirty. He kept reminding himself that it wasn't unusual; Vatutin nearly always kept him waiting until he was wound up like a clock and was gripped by nameless fears.

Only, this time, they weren't so nameless. Could it be that the general had heard about the episode on the electric target range the day before Kirov had departed? No, that was impossible; the weapon-training NCO would be too frightened to open his mouth because he knew the authorities would blame him for what had happened. He was the man who'd slapped the drum magazine on the PPSh submachine gun and cocked the trigger mechanism. The fact that the accident had been caused by a defective interrupter gear was immaterial. He had failed to notice that the elevating spindle had been tampered with, and a court of inquiry would have his balls for that. The electronics artificer then? He'd examined the console and reported a defective circuit, but was astute enough to realize that some of the mud would cling to him if he made an issue of it. At the end of the day, he was responsible for servicing the equipment and knew that since the officers always stuck together, the court would be anxious to protect Nikishev and would conclude that he must have goofed off.

There was always Kirov, of course; the bastard loved submitting reports, but he'd only had time to write a couple of letters, one to his half sister Irena, the other to General Fedor Fedorovich, and neither had contained even so much as a veiled hint about the close shave he'd had. The Breach of Security report on the Moorcroft affair? Nikishev frowned. If the KGB had discovered the officer responsible for the leak, he was in the clear; on the other hand, he wouldn't be exactly fireproof should Vatutin want to know why Kirov had filed the damned thing. According to friend Georgi, he always did everything by the book, and that stupid bitch, Alexandra Podgorny, had supported his story. But then she would, Nikishev thought savagely; her brains were located below her navel and Kirov had that knack of bringing out the mothering instinct in women.

The light above the communicating door suddenly changed from red to green; behind him, Vatutin's personal assistant said, "The general will see you now, Comrade Colonel."

Nikishev licked his lips, opened the door, and marched into the office on legs that felt as though they were made of rubber. As usual, Vatutin was dressed in civilian clothes, but Nikishev threw up a salute, believing that it was the politic thing to do. At the same time, his eyes swept the desk and noted the empty in-tray, empty pending, and the mound of files in the out-tray. He hoped he'd been kept waiting because the general considered that the files had overriding priority.

"Good afternoon, Dmitri." Vatutin smiled as though genuinely pleased to see him. His manner was so courteous that for a while he really was the cultured Professor of

Political Studies at the Patrice Lumumba whom the diplomatic community knew. "How's everything?" he added.

An innocent enough question on the surface, but there was no telling what lay beneath it. Put a man at his ease, then hit him when his guard was down; that was one of the better-known ploys used by the general.

"Absolutely fine," Nikishev said, playing it safe.

"Kirov arrives in Bonn today, doesn't he?"

"Yes." Nikishev cleared his throat. "As a matter of fact, he should have checked into the Steigenberger by now."

"Good. I'll arrange for New York to send him a telex. If the cable is dispatched around five o'clock their time, he'll receive it late this evening. I assume you agree that will convey an appropriate sense of urgency?"

"Yes, indeed."

"Excellent." Vatutin rewarded him with another friendly smile, then said, "Thank you, Dmitri, that will be all."

All? Nikishev saluted and walked out of the office in a daze, happy in the knowledge that he'd obviously misread the situation. There was nothing sinister about this operation; the KGB was involved in its execution only to the extent of strengthening the "legend" that had been composed for George Kershaw. The fact that Vatutin had waited to summon him until now, some forty-eight hours after Nikishev had returned to Moscow from the Rostov lodge at Mozhaysk, was of no significance whatever. Vatutin was aware of the timetable and had merely wished to satisfy himself that the operation was proceeding on schedule before initiating the telex. A euphoric feeling that everything was all right lasted as far as the parking lot behind the building, when it suddenly evaporated, as all the nagging doubts returned.

*   *   *

The phone woke Kirov from a light sleep. When he answered it, the girl at the reception desk told him it was six o'clock. Thanking her politely, he hung up, rolled off the bed, and stripped. Twenty minutes later, having showered and changed into a dark blue pinstripe, he took the elevator down to the lobby, left his room key with the desk clerk, and walked out of the hotel.

A Mercedes was parked in the narrow covered drive outside the front entrance blocking the one-way circuit even though its offside wheels were on the far pavement. There was no sign of the driver, and the silver-green two-door BMW coupe drawn up behind it was also unoccupied. Kirov strolled past the lead vehicle and on through the courtyard of the low-level shopping precinct that fronted the Steigenberger. When he reached the main road, he turned right, headed toward the U-Bahn and descended the flight of steps to the concourse above the underground platforms, where he lingered for several minutes before exiting into Adenauer Allee.

No sign of a tail, but that didn't mean he was in the clear. He consulted the street map and looked around as though trying to get his bearings while he gave the area the once-over. Then suddenly aware that the armed policeman on duty outside the Bundes Kanzleramt was eyeing him suspiciously, he moved on past the official residence of the West German president, a huge villa set well back from the road and mostly hidden from view by a high wall topped with barbed wire. He noticed that there were remote-controlled TV cameras at strategic points that scanned the sidewalk and thought they were probably tracking his progress, first on one monitor screen, then on the next, until he was no longer in sight.

At the junction of Kaiser Friedrich Strasse and Adenauer Allee, Kirov turned right and walked to the far end of the cul-de-sac where the map showed there was a flight of steps to the riverside promenade below. He crossed over to the opposite pavement and strolled past a row of apartment houses that stretched as far as the iron railings enclosing the Gothic mansion occupied by the British army liaison staff in Bonn. At the bottom end of the cul-de-sac, he glanced around, saw only an empty street behind him, and went on down the steps.

The promenade and Stadt gardens reflected the onset of winter. The pontoons where pleasure steamers had moored in summer were deserted, and the colored lights strung between the streetlights hung limply in the cold night air. The grass was tufted, the neat flower beds were barren and choked with the fallen leaves of autumn, and high up on the bluff the alpine plants that clung tenaciously to the rock face had now been reduced to mere clumps of lifeless, gray-looking moss.

Out on the river, two coal barges from the Ruhr headed upstream, their diesel engines throbbing loudly as they battled against the current, and slowly overhauled the elderly couple taking their Alsatian for an evening walk along the promenade. Kirov thought they were the only people about, but as he neared the university library, the headlights of an oncoming vehicle suddenly illuminated the track-suited figure of a young woman jogging toward him on the foot-path. He saw the car pull over to give the cyclist who was pacing her more room, then the driver flashed his headlights twice in rapid succession and rammed his foot hard down on the accelerator.

A silver-green two-door BMW coupe, the same car he'd seen earlier parked outside the Steigenberger, boxed in behind a Mercedes. He glanced over his shoulder to see if the driver had been signaling to another vehicle, but there was nothing coming up behind. He'd been giving an all clear then, but to whom? The driver of the Mercedes? Maybe he'd followed him into Kaiser Friedrich Strasse and was now tagging along on foot? Whatever the explanation, the fact remained that the GRU had put a couple of rank amateurs on to him. He just hoped Joachim Abbetz was a lot more competent than they were.

The Zur Lese enjoyed a commanding view of the river from a promontory thirty feet above the road. A natural cave at ground level had been enlarged to make a small parking lot, and a service elevator had been installed linking it to the restaurant above. Leaving his overcoat with the hatcheck girl in the cloakroom, Kirov told the headwaiter that he was dining with Herr Joachim Abbetz and was shown to a table by the window.

The voice he had heard over the phone had sounded pompous and very smug, two characteristics that had immediately conjured up the image of a florid, overweight businessman in an expensive but tight-fitting suit. The reality was very different. Abbetz looked emaciated and reminded him of Moorcroft, except that he was at least thirty years older than the American and what was left of his hair had turned snow-white. When they shook hands, Kirov discovered that his index and little fingers had been severed below the knuckles.

"A souvenir of the last war, Mr. Kershaw." Abbetz stretched his bloodless lips in a fleeting smile. "A minor case of frostbite."

"I'm sorry to hear that," Kirov said, and sat down.

"You needn't be. I don't find it a handicap."

Kirov doubted if the Wehrmacht had thought so at the time. A man could learn to do most things with his left hand, but Abbetz would have found it a mite difficult to hold a Mauser rifle in the aim.

"Would you care for an aperitif before we order, Mr. Kershaw?"

"I wouldn't mind a brandy and ginger ale."

"And I'll have a vodka on crushed ice with a twist of lemon," Abbetz said, then repeated the order in German for the benefit of the waiter.

"Is that something else you acquired during the war?"

"What?"

"A taste for vodka," Kirov said.

"It kept some of us alive in the winter of '41 outside Leningrad."

The German was over sixty. Kirov tried to picture him as a young man, before he had lost two fingers and most of his hair, before his body had wasted away. A clear-eyed, blond, husky young tough? It was hard to tell now, but he would certainly have been arrogant; that was a trait that hadn't diminished with the years.

"I'd better give you this while I remember." Abbetz passed an oblong-shaped envelope across the table and gave him another of his wintry smiles. "My recommendations for minimizing corporation tax. There's no need to read them now, but I think your company will find I've given them sound advice."

Kirov took the hint and slipped the envelope into the

inside pocket of his jacket. "I'm sure you have," he said. "How long have you been a tax consultant? Twenty, twenty-five years?"

"Thirty." Abbetz paused while the waiter placed their drinks in front of them, then said, "I completed my articles in 1955 exactly three years after I returned from the war."

Abbetz had been a prisoner of war, then, and had remained in Soviet hands until 1952. An absolute minimum of seven years behind the wire, time enough to reeducate and turn him around. That was something he hadn't bargained for in those heady days of '41 when it had seemed that the city of Leningrad lay within the German grasp. A not unreasonable assumption in view of the scratch units that had opposed them, short of men, short of weapons, short of ammunition, short of everything except exhortations from the Committee for the Defense of Leningrad. "Personal for Colonel F. F. Kirov commanding 6th (Guards Volunteer) Division stop. Following reinforcements will join you 14 September: 35 Party workers and 120 Young Communists from the Vyborg District together with 10,000 rounds of rifle ammunition stop. On receipt of these reinforcements you are to launch an immediate counterattack with the object of recapturing the Duderhof Heights." Impossible orders to follow, but if his father had failed to retake the Duderhof Heights, at least he'd stopped the Thirty-sixth Motorized Division dead in their tracks. But at a terrible cost.

"Your good health," Kirov said and raised his glass, mocking him.

"*Prosit*," Abbetz murmured and looked up from the menu, "Shall we order? I can recommend the jugged hare, or would you prefer something else?" He pointed to the fish tank on his right where a dozen or so large trout were darting in and out of a mass of weed, kept alive by a tube that aerated the water. "A fresh trout grilled with almonds, for instance?"

"I think I'd like a Wiener schnitzel."

"And I'm going to start with an avocado vinaigrette. How about you?"

"French onion soup," Kirov said, determined to be awkward.

126

Abbetz chose a bottle of wine, gave their order to the waiter, and became the attentive host again. "Have you managed to do any sightseeing, Mr. Kershaw?"

"I haven't had much time for that sort of thing."

"Well, I wouldn't let it bother you; there's not a lot to Bonn, the university, the house where Beethoven lived; it's about as exciting as Weimar was in the twenties. Perhaps that's why it's now our capital and seat of government . . ."

Kirov tried to look interested, knowing that whether the evening proved long or short, it was going to seem interminable.

★   ★   ★

Natalia Rubanskaya examined the contents of her litter bin to satisfy herself that every scrap of paper had been torn up, then emptied the trash into the disposal sack that was labeled "For Secret Waste Only." Returning to her desk, she placed the litter bin upside down on the floor and in accordance with standing orders checked the filing trays again to make sure they were empty and that the sliding drawers had been locked. The other clerks had departed long ago, all of them slightly puzzled that she was staying on when there was no necessity for her to do so. Although either Natalia Rubanskaya or the chief archivist had to be on call during silent hours to deal with any signal classified Secret that had a minimum precedence of Op Immediate, they were aware that it was not her turn to be on duty.

One week on, one week off; the roster was no hardship for Natalia Rubanskaya, who had an apartment in the embassy compound, but it was a vastly different story for the chief archivist. Like other Soviet officials who were accompanied by their wives and children, he had been allocated a flat in Highgate, which meant that he had to live in whenever he was on duty. Toward the end of the day, Natalia had twice offered to stand in for him and had been politely but firmly rebuffed on each occasion. Moreover, the chief archivist had observed that there was obviously an ulterior motive to her offer and had hinted that he knew what it was. Just to underline the innuendo, he'd then jerked his head toward the corridor making it

127

clear that he'd also noticed that Denisenko was still in his office.

"Are you sure you don't want me to stand in for you?" Natalia asked him for the third time.

"Quite sure."

"I'll say goodnight then."

"Goodnight, Comrade Rubanskaya."

Natalia could feel his eyes boring into her back as she walked out of the registry. She wondered how long it would be before he finally voiced his suspicions to Captain Anatoli Zotov, the senior defense attaché. He couldn't do anything about it tonight but even though tomorrow was Saturday, Zotov would be at his desk first thing in the morning. She half-smiled to herself, thinking that matters were coming nicely to a head, and gravitated toward Denisenko's office.

Aleko Denisenko was poring over a large-scale map of the Underground and was slow to react when she walked through the door. Then, becoming aware of her presence, he looked up and leered at her like a small boy who'd just been told he could have all the ice cream he could eat. She thought it remarkable the difference twenty-four hours could make. The day after the chief archivist had interrupted their amorous groping, he'd been as nervous as a kitten, but now he'd bounced right back again. It wasn't difficult to guess why his confidence had returned. Had they been reported, Zotov would have called him into his office and delivered a formal rebuke. Since nothing of the kind had happened, Denisenko had assumed that he'd gotten away with it.

"Why are you still here, Aleko? I thought we'd had a pretty slack day." Natalia reached behind her back and gave the door a push, then moved up to the desk and perched herself on the edge, close to Denisenko. "I wonder, could it be you're in no hurry to go home?"

"I don't think you should have done that, Natalia," he said hoarsely.

"What are you talking about?"

"The door. It's against regulations to close it when the office is occupied."

"I thought I'd left it ajar."

Natalia twisted around to glance over her shoulder, seemingly unaware that she was showing a good deal of leg. The eye-catching exposure was all the encouragement Denisenko needed; she felt a sweaty palm come to rest on her knee. The amorous lover, Natalia thought, and marveled at his vanity. Aleko Denisenko was a dumpy little man with coarse features, bad teeth, and even fouler breath, yet he was conceited enough to delude himself that some women found him attractive. His hand slid furtively under the hem of her dress to stroke her thigh. As it moved inexorably upward, she opened her legs to make things easier for him and sighed audibly as if his touch excited her. Then, just as his fingertips encountered her panties, she reached down and grabbed hold of his wrist.

"Not now, Aleko," she breathed.

"What?" He gaped at her, his mouth open, eyes almost popping out of their sockets.

"It would be very embarrassing for both of us if somebody walked into the office at the wrong moment." Natalia inclined her head knowingly toward the corridor and saw the light dawn in his eyes.

"The chief archivist . . ." Denisenko swallowed and attempted to withdraw his hand, but she held on to his wrist with a grip of iron.

"We could go to my room," she murmured, "but one of the other girls might see us."

He nodded dumbly. His right hand was still between her legs and he could have sworn that she had moved it even higher. She was wearing tights instead of nylon stockings, but the sight of her dark blue slip trimmed with lace was electric and he couldn't stop trembling.

"I'm on night duty all next week," Natalia said in a low voice. "Perhaps you could arrange to work late one evening?"

"Which evening?" His mouth was so bone dry that his voice was reduced to a harsh croak.

"How about Tuesday? I'll hold some of your letters back until late in the afternoon, then you can phone your wife and tell her you've got to stay on at the office."

"Yes. Yes, I think I can make Raya believe that."

"Good." Natalia withdrew his hand, then stood up and adjusted her dress. "How do I look?" she asked.

"Marvelous."

"That's not what I meant." Natalia walked over to the door and opened it. "I don't look disheveled, do I?"

"Not in the least," Denisenko whispered.

"That's a relief." Natalia blew him a kiss and stepped out into the corridor. A niggling doubt that her voice might not have carried to the registry was dispelled when she glanced over her shoulder and saw the chief archivist standing in the doorway.

★   ★   ★

Kirov paid off the taxi outside the Steigenberger and walked up the short flight of steps to the front entrance. As he neared the plate-glass doors, a ground sensor automatically opened them and he passed through into the deserted lobby. He went over to reception, said good evening to the pert blonde behind the desk, and asked for the key to his room.

"Room 1208," the girl repeated and moved to collect the key from the pigeonholes on the far wall. "Ah, yes, Mr. Kershaw, we have a telex for you from New York."

"That'll be from my head office," he said laconically. "I wonder what they've got planned for me now?"

Kirov slipped the room key into his jacket pocket, picked up the telex, and started toward the elevators. The message was along the lines Nikishev had led him to expect. It said: "Understand Gamleys of London are heading for the rocks and are about to call in the Official Receiver. Essential you drop everything and get to London soonest. Contact their sales manager, Grisewood, at Regent 9319 tomorrow, Saturday, by midday latest and view stock before our competitors get wind of liquidation. Offer fifty cents on one pound sterling ex factory price." Still reading the telex, Kirov turned around and returned to the desk.

"Do you have a problem, Mr. Kershaw?" the girl asked him.

"Several." Kirov showed her the telex. "I have to be in London before noon tomorrow, and I'm just wondering who can give me some flight information at this time of night?"

"I can." The girl reached under the counter for a green-colored binder and flipped it open to the right page. "There's a Lufthansa flight departing Bonn/Cologne at 11:25 A.M., but that would be cutting it very fine, even though we're an hour ahead of London. Why don't I try to get you on an earlier flight from either Frankfurt or Düsseldorf?"

"Could you?"

"Certainly. Are you staying with friends in London, Mr. Kershaw, or should I also book you into a hotel?"

"I think we'd better go with a hotel," Kirov told her. "Any one will do so long as it's near the center."

"Okay, Mr. Kershaw, I'll call your room as soon as I've made the necessary reservations."

"That's very kind of you," he said.

"You're welcome."

It was a stock expression, but she gave him a warm smile and actually sounded as though she meant it. She was a nice girl, he thought, polite and attentive without being servile and representative of the postwar generation who were so very different from the likes of Joachim Abbetz. Or was she an Ausländer, one of the two million foreign workers who'd been welcomed with open arms when the economy was expanding, but who were now a source of resentment and fast becoming the Jewish problem of the eighties? Kirov entered the nearest elevator, turned around and gazed at her across the lobby. A typical Saxon, he decided, round face, cornflower blue eyes, blond hair, the kind of pure Aryan the Fascists had raved about. His face clouded. What the hell had gotten into him? After three hours in the company of Joachim Abbetz, he was even beginning to think like the late Doctor Goebbels. Angry with himself, he jabbed the button and rode up to the twelfth floor.

In the loneliness of his room, he fixed himself a brandy and ginger, recorded it on the mini-bar chit, and then examined the contents of the envelope Joachim Abbetz had passed to him at the Zur Lese. It contained a series of options for tax avoidance in the Federal Republic likely to be of interest to Nestor's Toy Emporiums and the open-ended return half of a TWA airline ticket New York–Frankfurt–New York purchased by George Kershaw. He would need to familiarize himself with the tax proposals, but right now he didn't have the stomach for it. Collecting the briefcase from the closet, he filed it with the rest of the junk that established the "legend" of George Kershaw, then started packing.

A few minutes later, the receptionist phoned to give him the news that he was booked on the 9:00 A.M. British Airways flight from Düsseldorf and would be staying at the Piccadilly Hotel.

CHAPTER X

"Can I get you a taxi, sir?"

Kirov hesitated, then nodded, smiling. The doorman had performed the same service for him on two previous occasions and obviously knew when he was on to a good thing. The pattern had been set that morning when Kirov had arrived from the airport in a taxi, and the weather had been against him ever since. The doorman had subtly conveyed to him with a raised eyebrow that the staff of the Piccadilly Hotel simply didn't expect its guests to wander around London in the rain.

Kirov walked toward the waiting taxi, slipped the doorman the usual pound note, and told the cabdriver to take him to the Globe Theater. Piccadilly Circus, around Eros and left onto Shaftesbury Avenue; he already knew the route backward and forward and could have found his way to the Globe Theater blindfolded. "Time spent on reconnaissance is seldom wasted" had been one of the first maxims he'd learned as a cadet at the Frunze Military Academy, and aided by an *A to Z Atlas of London*, he'd spent most of the morning and the entire afternoon familiarizing himself with the West End within a mile radius of the hotel. The Houses of Parliament, Nelson's Column, the National

Gallery, and the department stores on Oxford Street were strictly for tourists; his sole interest had been to pinpoint the location of every public telephone booth in the area.

"MARIA AITKEN, IAN OGILVY, and GARY BOND in Noel Coward's DESIGN FOR LIVING with ROLAND CURRAM. Gloriously sexy . . . Marvelously outrageous . . . Brilliantly stylized and quirky." The billboards outside the theater were facing him as he climbed out of the cab and parted with another pound.

"Good show, that," the cabdriver told him. "A giggle a minute."

"You've seen it?"

"No, but I picked up a fare last night who had. Said he laughed till it hurt."

You couldn't ask for a better recommendation than that, Kirov thought, and saw the cab move off before he could open his mouth. Fifty pence on the meter for a quarter-mile journey and the driver had kept the rest as a tip. He'd been warned about the excesses of a capitalist society, but if this was an example of free enterprise, they could keep it. Still hot under the collar, he crossed the avenue and strolled down Wardour Street, past a massage parlor and a porno bookshop to the junction with Gerrard Street, where he turned left. A slice of the Far East—Chinese restaurants, bars, exotic grocery stores, and pungent smells; he walked to the far end of the road and on around the corner into Newport Place where he knew there were a couple of phone booths near a parking lot.

Both of them were occupied, the nearest one by three young Chinese girls who looked as though they were there for the night, the other by a middle-aged man in a dark blue raincoat. As Kirov drew nearer, the man glanced over his shoulder and almost jumped out of his skin. A sickly smile made a brief appearance, then he slammed the phone down and left the booth to disappear into Lisle Street as fast as his legs could carry him without actually breaking into a sprint.

It didn't take Kirov long to find a plausible reason for his strange behavior. Scribbled on the back of an old envelope that had been left on top of the coin box were a couple of phone numbers in the London area. Below the second one, somebody with a shaky hand had written, "Denise, top flat next to Kempner's in Greek Street."

Smiling to himself, Kirov found a 10p coin among the loose change in his pocket, inserted it into the slot, then dialed the number in Highgate that Nikishev had given him during the final briefing at Mozhaysk. It rang only twice before the subscriber lifted the receiver and the dialing tone switched to a rapid blip. He pushed the coin home; when it dropped and the connection was complete, a voice that sounded breathless garbled the number.

Kirov said, "May I speak to Alec, please?"

"Who?"

"Alec Willets. You are Highgate 3041?"

"No. I'm afraid you've got the wrong number. This is 3042."

"I'm sorry," Kirov said. "I obviously misdialed."

He put the phone down and glanced at his wristwatch. Six forty-five; that meant he had three-quarters of an hour to kill before he called the second number. Whistling quietly, he left the phone booth to make his way to The Bunch of Grapes near the Garrick Theater on Charing Cross Road.

★   ★   ★

Konstantin Fomin and Mikhail Izveko were also killing time, but for a much longer period than Kirov. They had moved into the Aeroflot offices on Regent Street shortly before the staff had departed at one o'clock and a good six hours before they could expect to hear anything from the surveillance team assigned to Denisenko.

Fomin had decided to run the operation from the Aeroflot headquarters because, of all the Soviet agencies in London, he considered that the airline was the one least likely to be monitored by British Telecom on behalf of D15. This assumption was based on the knowledge that nothing of any security significance was ever communicated to or through Aeroflot, a fact British counterintelligence had obviously discovered for themselves long ago. However, Fomin was not the sort of man to leave anything to chance; experience had taught him that one should never take anything for granted and that every premise should be put to the test before it was accepted. On his instructions, a technician specializing in electronic countermeasures had spent the whole of Thursday afternoon checking the telephone in the manager's office to make sure it was "clean." Their early arrival was another example of Fomin's security awareness. Although it was possible to enter the office from the alleyway behind the building, he had preferred to arrive in daylight and at a time when they would not draw attention to themselves.

Patience was an essential prerequisite for every KGB officer, and both men possessed it in full measure. This characteristic was in fact one of the few things they had in common. Konstantin Fomin, the chief personnel security officer at the embassy, was a large, shaggy-looking man of forty-six whose ponderous manner and apparent lack of sparkle created the wholly false impression that he was not particularly bright and had no interests outside his job. Nothing could have been farther from the truth. Fomin was highly intelligent and incisive, and apart from being a keen philatelist, his other hobbies included chess, photography, and bird-watching.

If anyone had tunnel vision it was Mikhail Izveko. For him, the KGB was a calling and his dedication to the service was as devout and unquestioning as that of any priest of the Russian Orthodox Church. A former corporal in the militia, he had been one of the most ferocious middleweights ever to duck under the ropes and had won fifty-eight out of the fifty-nine bouts he'd had, most of them inside the distance. The one blot on his record had occurred in the semifinals of the amateur championships in 1970 when he'd been matched against a hard-punching southpaw who possessed a longer reach and considerably more skill than he. Unable to land a telling blow and continually on the receiving end of a straight right that had bloodied his nose, Izveko had eventually crowded his man into a corner and deliberately butted him in the face. Then, while he was still dazed, Izveko had punched him in the groin and had promptly been disqualified. Booed out of the ring, he had subsequently been carpeted by his commanding officer and reduced to the ranks for behaving in a manner likely to damage the reputation of his unit.

But other interested parties had been at the ringside that night, and they had formed a very different opinion of his conduct. In their opinion, his tenacity, ruthlessness, and determination to win at any cost were just the qualities the KGB looked for in an agent; following a detailed examination of his record of service, Izveko had been interviewed and accepted into the KGB. Graded outstanding on completion of the yearlong basic course, he had been selected for further training with the Special Executive Department of the First Chief Directorate. They had taught him the real meaning of self-discipline and patience and in the process had turned him into a highly lethal machine.

Izveko was twenty-nine years old, but a round cherub face conjuring up an image of childish innocence made him appear much younger. Before the evening was over, he would kill a man in cold blood. Looking at him now, Fomin thought the prospect didn't seem to bother him one bit.

"Did I tell you that Captain Zotov called me into his office this morning?" Fomin asked, breaking a lengthy silence.

"No. What did he want?"

"Apparently the GRU's chief archivist saw him first thing and said he thought the captain ought to know that Natalia Rubanskaya and Comrade Aleko Denisenko were having an affair. Zotov asked me if I knew anything about it. I told him no, but I'd look into it."

"He was covering himself," Izveko said flatly.

"Of course he was. Standing orders state that the chief of personnel security is to be informed forthwith of any occurrence that may have security implications, and Zotov wasn't going to keep that information to himself over the weekend." Fomin shook his head. "That Natalia Rubanskaya," he said, chuckling at the thought. "Somebody ought to give her a medal for services rendered above and beyond the call of duty."

The telephone cut in with a shrill jangle. Very calmly, very deliberately, Fomin lifted the receiver to say hello, then listened intently, his lips pursed. Observing him closely,

136

Izveko couldn't tell whether the news was good or bad and was still none the wiser when Fomin eventually put the phone down.

"Well?" Izveko demanded.

"It's started," Fomin said tersely. "The 'tourist' contacted Denisenko at six forty-five, then a few minutes later our fat friend left his apartment, drove to Highgate Underground station and parked his car in the yard. Right now he's heading into town on the Northern Line."

"No problems, then?"

"Not so far."

Fomin opened his briefcase, took out a diagram of the London Underground, and unfolded it. Contact had been established under the guise of a wrong number, a safeguard in case D15 had a wiretap on the apartment. That meant Denisenko would have to break his journey somewhere along the way and contact the "tourist" again in order to tell him where, when, and how they were going to meet up. It was a new development, one that Denisenko hadn't re-hearsed before, and a lot was going to depend on how well the surveillance team did their job. Even if they lost him, it wouldn't be a total catastrophe; in the end, Denisenko would return to Highgate station to collect his car and they could pick him up in the yard. But that was definitely a last resort and something to be avoided if humanly possible. No point worrying unnecessarily; half an hour or so from now and he'd know whether or not Denisenko would adhere to his original plan.

Fomin eyed the desk, wrinkled his nose fastidiously. Empty beer cans, the cellophane wrappings from ham sandwiches long since consumed, and two apple cores in the metal ashtray; the remains of the lousy snack lunch they'd brought with them in their briefcases.

"Let's get this mess cleared away," he growled in a moment of rare exasperation. "Damn place looks like a fucking pigsty."

★   ★   ★

Seven twenty-four. Kirov finished his beer and left the pub, only to discover that he needn't have hurried, because none of the phone booths opposite the Garrick Theater was occupied. Entering the nearest one, he sorted through his loose change and arranged a small pile of 10p coins on top of the box. Then, killing time, he ran his eye down the list of dialing codes and saw that 636 was the number of the Museum exchange. He wondered if the last four digits of the number Nikishev had given him would patch him through to a private subscriber or a phone booth. If it was the latter, he just hoped that the phone hadn't been vandalized, otherwise they would be well and truly in the shit. What would he do then? Go back to the beginning and try the Highgate number again? That would be like playing snakes and ladders except that nobody would be having a fun time.

Seven-thirty. He placed a coin in the slot, lifted the receiver, and dialed 636-9851. The number purred briefly, then a now familiar voice said hello, and he pushed the coin down.

"Hi, Alec," Kirov said. "It's me again—George Kershaw."

."Well, I never, what are you doing in London?"

"I'm here on business." Kirov closed his eyes, wondering how long Alec was prepared to keep up this pretense. The Museum number was supposed to be clean; if it wasn't, the link man ought to be locked up in a loony bin where he couldn't do any harm.

"Why don't we get together for a drink, George?"

"Let's do that."

"Good. Suppose you meet me outside the Embankment Underground at seven forty-five?"

"Fine." Kirov cleared his throat, then said, "Let's hope we recognize one another; it's been years since we met."

"Oh, I'm sure I'd know you anywhere, George. And I haven't changed all that much, just a little plumper and a little balder." Alec forced a laugh that sounded like a horse whinnying. "Swings and roundabouts, George. You win some, you lose some."

"Yes."

"Seven forty-five, then."

"Don't worry, I'll be there."

Kirov hung up, pocketed the rest of his change, and

backed out of the phone booth. A plump, balding man; it wasn't a lot to go on, but Alec had said he'd know him anywhere and he supposed that the GRU had sent the link man a photograph in the diplomatic bag. He glanced at his wristwatch, saw that he had twelve minutes to get there, and set off at a leisurely pace down Charing Cross Road, across Trafalgar Square, and onto Northumberland Avenue.

★   ★   ★

Fomin allowed the phone to ring several times before he answered it. Although the last fifty minutes had seemed like a lifetime, he resisted the temptation to snatch the receiver from the cradle. A flicker of the eyebrows told him that Izveko was impressed, but he hadn't been playing to the gallery. He'd merely been exercising a little self-discipline because good news or bad, he would need to have his wits about him, and few people could see things clearly when they were under stress. Face impassive, he waited until the caller had finished, then told him that they would stick to the original plan.

"I think it's going to be all right, Mikhail," Fomin said, smiling faintly. "Our fat friend got off at Tottenham Court Road and walked to a phone booth in Bedford Square where he must have received another call from the 'tourist.' Anyway, a little while later, he returned to the station and caught a southbound train on the Northern Line."

"He's back on course again?"

"Looks like it."

The surveillance team had shadowed Denisenko when he'd made a couple of dry runs during the previous fortnight. Unless he'd suddenly decided to vary the pattern, Fomin knew that he would switch to either the Circle or District Line at the Embankment and would get off at Gloucester Road. From there, he'd walk to Earls Court and double back to Leicester Square where he could pick up a Northern Line train to Highgate.

"Time we were moving, Mikhail."

"Right. What about our briefcases?"

"We'll leave them here and collect them on Monday. Have you got everything you need?"

"Of course." Izveko showed him the flat Haig whiskey bottle and a silver-plated cigarette case with lighter attached. "Just remember to hold your breath when I offer him a cigarette."

"I'm not likely to forget that in a hurry," Fomin said grimly.

He opened the back door and stepped out into the alleyway, leaving Izveko to switch off the lights before he joined him. He then locked the door and hurried after the younger man who'd gone on ahead; by the time he caught up with him on Regent Street, Izveko had already flagged down a passing cab.

"Grosvenor House," Fomin told the driver and scrambled inside.

Denisenko had a headstart of at least ten minutes on them, but there was very little traffic about on a Saturday evening and Fomin didn't anticipate any holdups. Regent Street, left onto Oxford Street, and left again at Marble Arch for the Grosvenor House on Park Lane, then cut through the pedestrian subway to the underground garage where they'd parked their car earlier that morning. If the park was still open to vehicular traffic, well and good; if not, they would have to circle Marble Arch and double back on Park Lane to pick up the A4 at Hyde Park Corner. Chances were they would be too late to intercept Denisenko at Gloucester Road station, but it was a good half-mile walk from there to Earls Court and, with any luck, they would beat him to it.

★　　★　　★

Kirov reached the bottom of Northumberland Avenue, turned left under Hungerford Bridge, and walked on past a small travel agency, a cafeteria, and a betting shop toward the gleam of light coming from the fish bar at the far end of the arcade. On the other side of the road, a colony of vagrants were sleeping rough on the pavement, feet stuffed inside cardboard boxes, their bodies enveloped in filthy quilts and blankets. Overhead, a southeast-bound train out of Charing Cross rumbled over the bridge, the noise from the bogie wheels reverberating through the steel girders.

Half-deafened by the grinding cacophony, he crossed the road and entered the Embankment Underground station.

There were only six people in the entrance hall, two lovers in a tight embrace, a young itinerant musician strumming a guitar, a couple of ticket collectors on the barriers, and a plump, balding man in a black trench coat who was loitering by the vending machines. After a moment's hesitation, the link man advanced toward Kirov, right hand outstretched, an uncertain smile on his lips.

"Hello, George. I must say it's good to see you again after all these years." He pumped his hand and clapped him on the shoulder as though they were long-lost brothers. "You haven't changed a bit."

"Neither have you, Alec," Kirov told him.

"Nonsense. Look at my waistline. Raya says I don't get enough exercise. Incidentally, she's dying to see you, George, but I'm afraid you're in her bad books."

"I am? Why's that?"

"Well, she feels you ought to have stayed with us."

Alec was hamming it up again. The nervousness he'd felt initially had worn off and his newfound confidence was reflected in a loud voice. His act was unnecessary, and dangerous too; up till now, nobody had taken any notice of them, but they soon would if he continued this charade much longer.

"Why didn't you give us a ring when you arrived in town? I know our flat on Gloucester Road is a bit on the small side but we do have a spare bedroom."

Kirov gritted his teeth, wondering how much longer this cretin intended to prolong their conversation. Then he looked at the fares displayed above the vending machines and realized why Alec had mentioned Gloucester Road. Digging some loose change out of his pocket, he fed a total of forty pence into the machine and got a pasteboard ticket in return.

"I didn't like to impose on you both. Besides, I didn't know I was coming to London until a telex arrived from New York last night." Kirov followed Alec through the barrier and caught up with him on the other side. "And since everything happened at the last minute, I got the hotel staff in Bonn to book me into the Piccadilly Hotel."

141

"Yes, well, I daresay Raya will forgive you."

Kirov found it impossible to tell whether anything was registering with Alec. If the link man didn't know where he was staying in London, how the hell could he get in touch with him again? Whether or not the necessity would arise before he took off for New York on Monday night was immaterial. Nikishev had been quite specific that any future contact would be initiated by the link man, yet Alec hadn't even so much as blinked when he'd mentioned the Piccadilly. If he'd been on the ball, he should have at least made some trite observation about the hotel to show he'd taken note of it.

"Do you think London has changed much since your last visit, George?"

"Some parts are seedier than I remember."

He could say that with conviction. He had seen things that would not be tolerated in Moscow: the porno book-shops, massage parlors, strip clubs, the litter in the back streets, the vagrants under Hungerford Bridge. Affluence on Oxford Street, poverty and degradation on the Embankment, visible proof of everything that was inherently wrong with the capitalist system.

"London's not as safe as it used to be either," Alec observed gloomily. "Every time you open a newspaper there's a report that somewhere some old person has been beaten up and robbed."

"It's the same in New York."

Kirov looked around. There were ten other passengers waiting on the platform, a man and a woman in their mid-thirties near the cigarette kiosk, the remaining eight to his right. None was within earshot, but Alec seemed to think it was necessary to continue making small talk. He looked up at the destination board: First—Ealing Broadway, Second—Circle, Third—Richmond.

"Any one will do us," Alec said as though reading his thoughts. "There's usually an interval of ten minutes between trains during off-peak hours."

Two pinpoints of light appeared in the tunnel and were preceded by a cold draft of air wafting down the platform. The spotlights grew steadily bigger, and presently Kirov could make out the blurred figure of the motorman in the cab. Reducing speed, the train rumbled out of the tunnel and slowly drew up alongside the platform, the brakes grinding as the motorman brought it to a halt. Then Alec moved forward, pressed a button to open the door, and led him into a "smoking" compartment.

"New rolling stock, George. The guard closes the door but you have to open it yourself."

"I'd never have guessed," Kirov said dryly.

There was just one other occupant in the compartment, an elderly man in a shabby duffel coat who was slumped in a corner seat and mumbling to himself. A drunk, Kirov decided, and pretty far gone at that. He could smell the beer on his breath as they moved past him to the far end of the coach. Outside, the platform attendant called out to mind the doors a split second after the guard had started to close them; as the train pulled out of the station, the drunk began to sing incomprehensible words to a tune that sounded way off-key.

"Do you ever run into Vera Willets these days?" Alec asked him softly.

"Haven't seen her in months."

"That doesn't surprise me. From what I hear, Vera's dropped most of her old friends and has become something of a recluse since her nervous breakdown."

"A recluse" was jargon for somebody who'd gone into hiding, but in stating that she had had a nervous breakdown, Alec was merely repeating the Party line. Like dissidents, defectors were simply mentally unbalanced people; as far as the State was concerned, there could be no other explanation for their conduct.

"The only news we've had of Vera came from a mutual friend." Alec reached inside his trench coat and produced a white envelope. "It's addressed to Raya but I know she won't mind you reading it."

The envelope had been mailed to a Mr. and Mrs. S. Caulfield, 29 Denby Road, Ealing, W13, and looked as though it had been rescued from a dustbin. Prising the slit apart with his thumb, Kirov saw that it contained several 100-dollar bills and a thin wad of traveler's checks.

143

"There's no need to read it now," Alec said hastily. "You can let me have it back anytime."

His voice, never much above a murmur, was made even less audible by the drunk. The song he'd been singing had given way to an equally discordant but slightly more recognizable version of "Two Lovely Black Eyes," which he was bellowing with gusto when the train pulled into Westminster. He was tone-deaf and raucous, but he was certainly a most effective deterrent, repulsing a very elderly couple about to board their coach.

"You ought to buy him a drink," Kirov said. "He's better than a guard dog."

Alec grunted, waited for the doors to close, then said, "I hear you're making quite a name for yourself with Nestor's, George."

"I am?"

"That's the word in the trade."

It was a veiled way of telling him that the GRU had been watching his back in Vienna and Bonn and had given him a clean bill of health. In the same oblique manner, Kirov learned exactly what kind of support would be available to him in New York and under what circumstances. He was also told whom to contact at Nestor's, and when, where, and how to go about it.

St. James's Park, Victoria, Sloane Square; Kirov checked their progress by the diagram of the District Line above the facing window and thought Alec was cutting it a bit fine if he intended to leave the train at Gloucester Road. The briefing had to be conducted in a roundabout fashion because of the venue, but he was suffering from a bad case of verbal diarrhea and was prolonging the whole business unnecessarily. It could be that Alec was the sort of man who couldn't resist using three words where one would do, or alternatively, he had been spinning things out to make it seem as if he was imparting much more information than he'd actually disclosed. There were, Kirov thought, two significant omissions; he hadn't received an updating on Vera Berggolts and there'd been nothing about the man who called himself Willets.

"It's been nice seeing you again, George," Alec said abruptly. "I'm glad we bumped into each other."

144

"What?" Kirov looked up and saw they were pulling into South Kensington. "Are you getting off here?"

"No." Alec smiled. "But you are."

"Thanks for telling me."

Kirov stood up and moved to the door. As soon as the train halted, he pressed the button and stepped out onto the platform. Ignoring the signs pointing to the exit, he turned left and walked briskly toward the interchange subway, then boarded the next-to-last coach seconds before the guard closed the doors. At Gloucester Road, he waited until the last possible moment before alighting and got the lucky break he'd been hoping for. The exit was roughly midway along the platform, almost in line with the smoking compartment, and he was just in time to catch a brief glimpse of Alec as he disappeared into the subway. Playing it safe, he waited until the train had pulled out before he went after him.

Emerging from the station, Kirov found that it was raining again, something it had been doing on and off all day. Apart from the fact that he was on a side street and had no idea where he was, there was also no sign of Alec. How long had he waited on the platform? A minute? Two minutes? Say three to be on the safe side. In that time Alec would have covered some two hundred and fifty yards at a normal walking pace, which meant he would still be in sight had he turned right outside the exit. Hesitating no longer, Kirov turned left and went on up to the main road. When he reached the T-junction, he saw that Alec had turned left again and heaved a sigh of relief.

The urban clearway looked familiar, but it wasn't until Kirov neared the West London Air Terminal that he realized that this was the route the cabdriver from Heathrow Airport had taken that morning. He also noticed that the couple he'd observed earlier on the platform at the Embankment was heading in the same direction but on the opposite side of the road. He wondered if they were following Alec too but eventually dismissed the idea when they carried on down the road after the link man had turned off to his left.

Staying well back, Kirov followed his quarry onto Knaresborough Place, discovered he'd lost him once more, and instinctively wheeled right onto Hogarth Road. Alec

145

was some three hundred yards ahead now, and as he approached the entrance to Earls Court station, two men stepped out of the shadows to greet him. Observing the trio from a distance, Kirov got the impression that the link man was surprised to see them, but as far as he could tell, Alec didn't seem very alarmed. There was a great deal of hand shaking, then all three moved off together and got into a car that was parked farther down the street.

They were embassy people. No doubt about that, and it was equally obvious to him that they'd met up with one another quite by chance. Then Kirov glanced over his shoulder, saw he had company, and knew he had been mistaken. The couple had doubled back on their tracks and had caught him red-handed. By following Alec he'd broken every rule in the book, and they'd report him for that as sure as there was going to be a tomorrow. Angry with himself for being so stupid, Kirov crossed the road, walked into Earls Court station, and caught the first train back to Piccadilly.

Chapter XI

Fomin reached up and adjusted the rearview mirror so that he could observe Denisenko out of the corner of his left eye. The GRU man was sitting in the back next to Izveko, bolt upright, legs close together, hands on knees. A pensive expression told him that Denisenko was having second thoughts and was beginning to doubt that he had run into them quite by chance as Fomin had claimed.

"What were you and Comrade Izveko doing in Earls Court?"

Although the question had obviously bothered him for some time, he seemed embarrassed to raise it.

"Waiting for you," Fomin told him calmly.

"Me?" Denisenko forced a laugh. "You must be joking. I mean, how on earth did you know where to meet me?"

"That's easy. You've been under surveillance since early this morning."

"Under surveillance?" Denisenko's voice rose a full octave in sheer disbelief. "Now I know you're joking."

Fomin didn't answer him. Silence was an effective weapon when it was used to keep a man in suspense. It would certainly make Denisenko look inward; and he had a lot to think about in the time it would take them to double back into London on the West Way and pick up the A1 to Highgate from The Angel, Islington.

"If this is a joke, Konstantin, I'm not amused."

"Neither was Captain Anatoli Zotov after your chief archivist saw him this morning." Fomin heard the sharp intake of breath and stepped up the pressure. "Funny thing is, you were the very last man I'd suspect of playing around." He shook his head. "That just shows you how wrong you can be."

"What are you implying?"

"Don't pretend with me, Comrade Denisenko. We've had a long talk with Natalia Rubanskaya and she really opened our eyes. Mind you, I still don't understand what she saw in you. After all, let's face it, you're no oil painting and Natalia's a very attractive woman, but there's no accounting for taste, is there?"

"I hardly know the lady," Denisenko said in a wooden voice.

"Oh, come on, you've been humping her for months."

"That's a damned lie."

"September the eleventh was the first time," Fomin continued unperturbed. "You were both on night duty and it happened to be your birthday. You'd brought a bottle of wine with you to celebrate the occasion, and when Natalia was called to the registry to deal with an Op Immediate signal, you invited her to have a drink with you after she'd deciphered the message."

"That's complete and utter rubbish."

"Are you saying you weren't on duty that night?"

"I really can't remember; it's so long ago now."

"Perhaps a copy of the duty roster would help to refresh your memory?"

"No, I'll take your word for it," Denisenko said huffily. "But it doesn't change anything; the fact remains I scarcely know the fucking woman."

"She was a lady a few moments ago," Izveko observed. "Now she's a fucking woman."

"An apt description," Fomin said. "Natalia Rubanskaya admits she's oversexed, something our friend here discovered for himself on his forty-fourth birthday. Tell me, Aleko, how many glasses of wine did it take before she was willing to get down on her back?"

"I don't have to listen to this filth," Denisenko said angrily.

"Two glasses? Three? No matter, after that first time she really had the hots for you. How did she put it, Mikhail? No man has ever satisfied me the way Aleko does."

Izveko nodded. "That's what she said, word for word."

"Natalia Rubanskaya?" Denisenko's voice was a high falsetto. He sounded incredulous, which Fomin allowed was understandable since the story was a complete fabrication from beginning to end, but he was also alarmed; the slight quaver was proof of that.

"You don't think we're making it up, do you?" Fomin said belligerently.

"I don't know what to think."

Observing the GRU officer out of the corner of his eye, Fomin saw him turn his head and look out of the window. They were driving east on the Hammersmith flyover toward the center of London at a steady sixty miles an hour, but it was evident he hadn't the faintest idea where they were, nor did he seem to care. He was lost in his own thoughts, oblivious to everything except perhaps the rhythmic click of the wiper blades and the swish of the tires on the wet surface.

"You don't really believe we were lovers, do you?" Denisenko asked after a lengthy silence.

"Natalia Rubanskaya was very convincing. Anyway, why would she lie about a thing like that?"

"Because the whole thing's a fantasy, something she dreamed up in the dark corners of her mind. Natalia Rubanskaya is clearly a highly neurotic and frustrated woman."

148

"That wasn't our impression," Fomin said. "As a matter of fact, she tried to brazen it out until we confronted her with the chief archivist and several other colleagues of hers who'd noticed how very friendly you were toward one another. Naturally, their evidence dented her composure and she became very upset, but there was nothing irrational about her behavior when she finally confessed. Everything Natalia told us checked out; the rosters showed you were on duty every night she claimed you'd made love to her."

"This is crazy, absolutely crazy. Why would I get involved with her? I'm a happily married man."

"We know you've got a wife and three children," Izveko said coldly, "but we've only your word for it that your marriage is happy."

Fomin smiled. You could rely on Mikhail to deliver a body blow at exactly the right moment, and he'd certainly winded him.

"It's my word against hers." Denisenko made fists of both hands and pounded his knees. "I want to hear the bitch repeat these monstrous allegations to my face. Furthermore, I demand the right to cross-examine her in the presence of a legally qualified officer. There's such a thing as slander and defamation of character, you know."

"I'm aware of that. And don't worry, you'll have an opportunity to question her."

"When?"

"Tonight," Fomin said. "As soon as we arrive at the embassy."

"But surely this isn't the way to Kensington Palace Gardens?"

"We're going to your place first. There are some questions we have to ask your wife."

"Raya?"

"Yes, Raya," Fomin said acidly. "How many wives have you got?"

"Oh, my God." It was a long, drawn-out cry of despair from a man for whom the Almighty was officially a non-person.

"You need a drink, Comrade." Izveko produced the

149

half-bottle of whiskey from his coat pocket, broke the seal, and then unscrewed the cap before passing it to Denisenko. "Take as much as you want; it'll do you good."

Fomin saw him hesitate for just a moment, then Denisenko raised the bottle to his mouth and took a large nip.

"Have another."

"Thank you, but no. One's enough for me."

There were two ways of persuading him to change his mind. Left to his own devices, Fomin knew his partner would undoubtedly resort to violence. He, on the other hand, preferred the more subtle method of psychological intimidation.

"Tell me, Aleko," he said casually, "whose idea was it to go across?"

"What?"

"Natalia Rubanskaya told us it was you who wanted to go to the British and ask for political asylum, but of course she would say that."

"She's mad," Denisenko said hoarsely, "stark, raving mad. Why would I defect to the British? Give me one good reason."

"Because you are living above your means and have got yourself into a financial mess."

"Rubbish. We live very frugally. If you don't believe me, take a good look at our apartment. You won't find any luxuries there, and unlike some people I could name, Raya doesn't have a closet full of expensive clothes. Nor does she have a sable coat."

"I'm not surprised; you've been spending all your money on Natalia Rubanskaya, buying her extravagant gifts. She showed me the emerald ring you bought her. It must have cost you the best part of a year's salary."

"An emerald ring? I bought her an emerald ring?"

Nobody had to press Denisenko to have another drink now. The more agitated he became, the more he needed to fortify himself.

"When has anybody seen that woman with an emerald on her finger?"

"Nobody has. It seems she was too frightened to wear the

ring and kept it hidden in the waste outlet of the washbasin in her room."

"If that woman does have an emerald, she didn't get it from me. You've only to check my personal account at the Narodny Bank for proof of that."

"Don't think we won't," Fomin told him. "However, I'm sure we'll find that everything is in order because you're cute enough to know that's the first place we'd look. Truth is, you probably borrowed the money from government funds."

"I presume you're referring to my incidental expense account?" Denisenko said in a dull voice.

"Right first time."

There was no way he could refute the allegation, and they both knew it. At the beginning of every financial year, a secret vote allocated Denisenko, in common with the other GRU officers, a sum of money that was automatically credited to a numbered account at the Narodny Bank. Checks drawn on these secret accounts were always made out to cash, and while each one had to be countersigned by Captain Anatoli Zotov, the senior defense attaché was not allowed to know the real name of the person who would eventually receive the money. The various transactions were recorded by the vote holder in an account book that was open to audit. However, since the whole purpose of the fund was to suborn new agents or reward others for services rendered, the recipient could hardly be expected to sign a receipt voucher. The necessary vouchers were therefore completed and certified by the account holder himself, which meant the system was open to fraud.

"We'll need to have a look at that secret bank account of yours, Aleko."

"Yes."

Fomin came to the end of the motorway and eased his foot on the accelerator to conform with the speed restriction of thirty miles an hour on Marylebone Road. "You sound depressed," he said cheerfully. "Don't tell me the account is showing a zero balance?"

"It's on the low side," Denisenko admitted. "I've had to fund one of our 'tourists.'"

151

"Naturally."

"What do you mean, naturally?"

"Well, in your shoes, that's exactly the kind of excuse I'd make, except that I can't ever see me having the nerve to go out on a limb for a woman the way you have. You're not an unintelligent man, Aleko, so you must have appreciated the appalling risks you were running when you photographed the GRU card index. That being the case, it beats me why you and Natalia didn't exercise a little more discretion."

"I don't believe this," Denisenko mumbled.

"Neither did we at first, but after what's happened this evening, we're beginning to think she may have been telling us the truth." Fomin cut across Gower Street before the lights changed to red and went on past Euston Station. "Incidentally," he continued, "did your friend tell you how much British Intelligence is willing to pay for the microfilm?"

"I know how it must look, but the man I saw tonight is a GRU officer. I don't know what he's doing over here or why he was sent, but there's nothing unusual or sinister about that, because they never tell you more than you need to know. Sometimes I wish they would, but in our business you do what you're told and no questions asked."

Fomin nodded. The same procedure was observed by the KGB and every other intelligence service worldwide. No one had told him why Denisenko had to be terminated, nor had Moscow Center seen fit to disclose what purpose would be served in destroying the entire GRU network in the United Kingdom. Even allowing for the bitter rivalry that had always existed between the two agencies, the operation simply didn't make sense to Fomin, but the orders he'd received by word of mouth had been authenticated at the highest level within the First Chief Directorate and he knew better than to question them.

"This 'tourist,'" Izveko said, snapping his fingers as though the point had just occurred to him. "Is there any way we can verify his ID, Aleko?"

"I know him as George Kershaw."

"That's a nice English-sounding name."

"I'm wasting my breath. It doesn't matter what I say

because you people have already made up your minds. If the facts are at odds with your preconceived ideas, you bend them around until they fit."

The whiskey was beginning to affect Denisenko, slurring his speech to the point where he found it difficult to get his tongue around some of the words. It was also making him garrulous, and he launched into a long, repetitive tirade against Natalia Rubanskaya. He was still ranting and raving about her when they reached The Angel, Islington, and turned left onto Upper Street to head north on the A1 trunk route.

There were very few people about, the oncoming traffic was light, and Fomin could see that the road behind was clear. It was, he decided, an opportune moment to wrap things up, and he lowered the offside window a fraction as a signal to Izveko. Slowly, almost lovingly, the younger man produced his silver cigarette case and offered a Pamir to Denisenko.

"Your favorite brand," he said, "specially imported."

"Thanks."

"Don't mention it."

Izveko drove an elbow into Denisenko's stomach hard enough to make him gasp for breath; then holding the lighter close to his face, he pressed the button to break the vial of hydrogen cyanide secreted inside. Denisenko dropped the half-bottle of whiskey he was still holding and clawed at his throat. It was the last thing he ever did, for the vapor density was such that death from massive cardiac arrest was almost instantaneous. Up front, Fomin continued to hold his breath for as long as was possible after he and Izveko had wound the windows down to ventilate the interior. Experts in the field of chemical warfare had assured both men that hydrogen cyanide was the most effective toxic agent in the Soviet armory; apart from its lethal qualities, it was non-persistent, considerably lighter than air, and highly volatile. Despite their assurances, Fomin leaned his head out of the window and filled his lungs with clean air before he gingerly tested the atmosphere. If the toxic agent was still present, he knew there would be a pungent odor of bitter almonds.

"Can you smell anything?"

153

"In this gale?" Izveko closed the window on his side, then leaned toward Denisenko and inhaled. "Whiskey," he said. "The stupid bastard is reeking of it. He must have emptied the rest of the bottle into his lap."

He could have taken a bath in the stuff for all Fomin cared. The vapor had dispersed and they weren't at risk; to his way of thinking, that was all that mattered. Closing the window, he lit a cigarette to help him relax while his partner donned a pair of cotton gloves before searching the dead man.

"Lighter, cigarettes, car keys, leather wallet." Izveko flipped it open and examined the contents with the aid of a pencil flashlight. "One five-pound note, six ones plus the return half of an Underground ticket issued at Highgate . . ."

"Get rid of it," Fomin told him.

"I already have."

"Good. What else is there?"

"Nothing. No ID, no embassy pass, no snapshots of the family, no driving permit. One thing you can say for Denisenko: he was a pro."

It was essential that British Intelligence knew it too. Reaching inside his jacket, Fomin produced a duplicate ID together with an envelope containing several strips of microfilm and then passed them over his shoulder to Izveko.

"Calling cards," he said laconically. "Put them in his wallet where the police will be sure to find them."

"Right. How are we doing for time?"

"We're not pressed. There's a fast train every half hour on the up line to St. Pancras."

"I meant how long before we reach Highgate station?"

"About ten minutes," Fomin said automatically, then checked his bearings.

Holloway Road. He spotted the sign in the glare from a streetlight opposite a corner bakery, and a short distance ahead there was a bridge spanning a railway cutting. Just over a mile to go, then, before he forked right at the bottom of Highgate Hill. Fomin had escorted enough visiting firemen to the cemetery where Karl Marx was buried to know the area like the back of his hand.

"Correction, make it five."

"Five or ten, it's all the same to me." Izveko juggled with Denisenko's car keys, tossing them into the air to catch them in the palm of his left hand. "From here on it's clear sailing."

Nothing was ever clear sailing. There was always the unforeseen hazard, the drunk driver who came out of a side road and rammed into you, the courting couple in the wrong place at the wrong time. If he had put his mind to it, Fomin could have reeled off a score of possibilities, but it would have been a fruitless exercise. Some jeopardies were unavoidable and it was best not to think about them.

"We're almost there."

"Yes?" Izveko transferred the car keys to his right hand and leaned forward.

"When we drive into the yard, keep your eyes open for a dark blue Lada with CD plates. The license number is 8831735 ZB."

"So you told me this morning."

"I'm just reminding you."

Fomin forked right into Archway Road. At the next set of traffic lights he turned right again, then filtered left into the station yard. The Lada was parked below the embankment between a Ford Granada and a BMW and was facing toward the entrance hall. Halting alongside, he switched the lights from main beam to side and shifted into neutral.

"Make it snappy."

"Don't worry, I will."

Izveko scrambled out of the car and closed the door behind him. By the time Fomin had completed a three-point turn at the top of the yard, he had already started the Lada and had eased it out of the parking slot. Fomin went on up to the lateral road, waited until the other vehicle was tucked in behind him, then doubled back onto the A1.

Fomin had spent more than four years in England, and for most of that time had been confined within a twenty-five-mile radius of London. Soviet diplomats who wanted to travel farther afield had to submit a detailed itinerary to the British Foreign Office and he couldn't afford to draw attention to himself. This self-imposed restriction meant that he had gotten to know London and its suburbs better than most of the indigenous population and had a very clear mental picture of the route he'd chosen. Highgate Golf Course, Lyttleton Playing Fields, and the North Circular Road were familiar landmarks for him and he knew to the precise minute how long it would take him to reach Elstree.

The copse he had in mind was roughly a mile and a half from the outskirts of Elstree and lay between Barnet Lane and the main line to St. Pancras. Although once a local beauty spot, the District Council had been obliged to fell and remove a large number of trees that had been attacked by Dutch elm disease, with the result that the wood was now easily accessible from the road. Approaching the wood, Fomin signaled for a turn to warn Izveko, then, shifting down to first, he doused the lights and turned off Barnet Lane onto a narrow track. A hundred yards farther on, and in a clearing that he'd noted on a previous visit to the area, he made a U-turn and pulled up. Cutting the engine, he got out of the car and showed Izveko exactly where he wanted him to park the Lada.

"So far so good." Izveko grinned. "Now we come to the difficult bit."

Fomin scowled. He didn't need Mikhail to remind him. Returning to his own vehicle, he opened the rear offside door, grabbed the dead man by the ankles, and hauled him out of the car. That done, he then removed Denisenko's shoes and wiped them on the grass.

"What's that for?"

"It's been raining all day."

"So?"

"So the ground is saturated and we don't want anybody wondering how our fat friend made it to the railway crossing without muddying his shoes." Fomin replaced the brogues and straightened up. "I've done my stuff, now you can do yours."

"I'm to provide the muscle power?"

"That's the general idea," Fomin said.

He was the stage director and it wasn't his job to move the scenery. In any case, the dead man weighed all of 175 pounds, and Fomin knew his own physical limitations. So he waited patiently while Izveko draped the corpse across

156

his shoulders in a fireman's carry, then moved off through the wood toward the crossing.

They were almost home and dry now, except dry was the wrong word when it was still raining. The weather could have been kinder to them, Fomin thought, but at least there was no moon and one had to be thankful for small mercies. He climbed the post-and-rail fence at the top of the embankment and went on down the steep incline, Izveko following close behind, agile and surefooted as a mountain goat.

Although in Fomin's experience suicides frequently resorted to the most bizarre methods to end their lives, he found it difficult to understand the thought processes that could lead a man to deliberately place his head on a railroad track. Would he face the oncoming train or would he lie there with his back toward it? What the hell did it matter? After the locomotive had run over Denisenko's head, nobody would know in which direction he had been facing.

"Where do you want him?" Izveko asked.

"Right here," Fomin said, "lying on his stomach with his neck over the line." Usually, it wasn't in his nature to look for a compromise solution, but it seemed the best one under the circumstances.

"How's that?" Izveko straightened up and stepped back a pace to admire his handiwork.

"Perfect. What have you done with his car keys?"

"I left them in the ignition."

"Good. That's it, then."

Fomin turned away and started back to the car. It had, he thought, been a long and tiring day.

*   *   *

"Can I get you a cab, sir?"

Kirov had been popping in and out of the Piccadilly Hotel all day and while the doorman had changed over, word had obviously gotten around that he was generous. This time, however, the doorman was going to be disappointed.

"No thanks." Kirov smiled. "I want to get a breath of fresh air before I turn in."

"Yes, sir." The doorman raised an eyebrow. "It's certainly fresh enough to blow the cobwebs away."

157

Kirov walked out into the street and found that the doorman wasn't exaggerating. It had stopped raining shortly
after ten o'clock, but now a stiff breeze had sprung up that
cut through his raincoat and raised goose bumps on his skin.
Hands thrust deep in his pockets, he waited for the pedestrian
lights to change to green, then hurried across the road and
made his way onto Lower Regent Street.

Kirov had dined alone, then retired to his room to watch
television. At least that had been his intention, but the
images on the screen had failed to hold his attention because
"Alec" had kept intruding. He had found himself thinking
about the link man and the scene he'd witnessed outside the
Underground station at Earls Court, which could be inter-
preted in two widely differing ways. It was, for instance,
quite conceivable that the GRU had had him under surveillance from the moment he'd arrived in London in order to
make sure he was still clean. That had certainly been the
pattern in Vienna and Bonn, and this contention was further
reinforced by the knowledge that, in following "Alec,"
he'd committed a gross breach of security.

On the other hand, the way the surveillance had been
conducted in the latter part of the evening was completely at
variance with all the recognized drills. You didn't shadow a
man by walking in front of him, yet the couple he'd first
observed on the platform at the Embankment station had
done just that. They could have been decoys for another,
more discreet, tail but Kirov didn't think so; decoys simply
wouldn't double back on their tracks. So it was logical to
conclude that they had been following "Alec." Why they
had been ordered to do so was beyond his ken, and right
now, it wasn't important. Right now, Kirov was far more
concerned to put the first part of his theory to the test.

He went on down Lower Regent Street, crossed Pall Mall
onto Wellington Place, and entered the phone booth near
the monument to the Duke of York. Digging a handful of
loose change out of his pocket, he inserted a 10p coin into
the slot and dialed the contact number in Highgate. The
woman who answered the call sounded hysterical and spoke
to him in Russian. It seemed a good idea to use the same
language.

158

"My name is Malakhov," Kirov said, choosing a common name. "Who am I speaking to?"

"Raya Denisenko." Her voice became even shriller. "Has something happened to my husband?"

A gamble that she was too distraught to pay much attention to the fictitious name had paid off. Kirov wondered if he should push his luck, then quickly decided he'd learned enough. Apologizing for having dialed the wrong number, he put the phone down before she had a chance to come back at him.

It was now 11:17; at the very latest he and Denisenko had parted company at 8:30, and with the best will in the world, he couldn't see how it would take him almost three hours to reach Highgate.

CHAPTER XII

Neil Edwards felt his head begin to nod and hurriedly opened the side window to let in a blast of fresh air. Two hours ago he'd been fast asleep in bed; two hours ago he and his wife, Jill, had been enjoying a "bargain break" at the Saracen's Head Hotel in Southwell. Then a phone call in the middle of the night had ruined the entire weekend. Worse still, Jill had been convinced the whole thing had been a put-up job. The long weekend had been her idea, something she had been planning ever since August, when Sara, their youngest of three, had gotten married. "Do you realize," Jill had said, "this will be the first time we've had a holiday on our own since the children were born?"

Southwell was a few miles north of Nottingham, and apart from the racecourse and the minster that dated back to the year one, he'd failed to see why Jill had been so keen to go there. However, Edwards hadn't lived with the same woman for thirty years without learning when it was unwise to voice his opinion, and somewhat to his agreeable surprise, he'd actually enjoyed the weekend right up to the moment the hall porter had knocked on their door to say he was wanted on the phone downstairs in the lobby. Thereafter, it had been a vastly different story.

Although couched in veiled speech, the message he'd received from the section duty officer had been sufficiently clear for Edwards to believe that his presence was urgently required in London, or to be more exact, at a lay-by on the A1 fourteen miles north of the capital. To say the least, Jill had not been amused. "You don't keep a dog and bark for it," she'd said, quoting a favorite saying of his. "And anyway, who are you trying to impress? You're not going any farther." Another quote, and one that was equally true, Edwards reflected wryly. He had reached his ceiling and had been told so officially, but even if he wasn't in the running for the appointment of director general when the present head of the Security Service retired, he was still in charge of the counterespionage desk and no matter how good one's subordinates might be, there were times when you needed to keep a firm hand on the tiller. And this was definitely one of them; he'd been sure of that the moment the duty officer had casually brought Jardine's name into the conversation. Jardine was a commander in the Special Branch and he wouldn't have put in an appearance unless something really big was in the wind, an argument that Jill had found singularly unconvincing. One couldn't blame her; a large part of his world was necessarily a closed book and it was unreasonable to expect her to appreciate the significance he attached to Len Jardine's involvement.

"Lay-by half a mile ahead." Edwards saw the sign by the roadside and slowed down. He had passed the turnoff to Cheshunt a mile or so back, and the duty officer had said to look out for a parking area just south of that. A few moments later, his headlights picked out a Ford Cortina on the hard shoulder and, pulling in behind it, he switched off the main beams, then greeted Jardine with a short honk before cutting the engine. The courtesy light that suddenly illuminated the interior of the Ford and a leisurely wave told him that the Special Branch officer intended to stay put. Muttering to himself, Edwards got out and went forward to join him in the other car.

160

"Sorry about that, Neil." Jardine pointed to a glowing bulb in the console and smiled apologetically. "But I thought I'd better stay by the radio."

"Busy, is it?"

"Not so far, and I want the Regional Crime Squad and the boys in blue to keep it that way. These fixed frequencies are all very well but they're not totally secure, and we don't want any radio hams eavesdropping on us. Next thing you know, every newspaper in town is carrying the story of the year."

"Right." Edwards glanced at the quartz clock in the facia and wondered just how many radio hams were up and about at 5:20 on a Sunday morning. Then another thought occurred to him. "How come the Regional Crime Squad is involved?" he asked. "I understood from my duty officer that we'd got ourselves an 'Ivan.'"

"So we have," Jardine said. "Trouble is he happens to be a dead one. His name was Aleko Denisenko."

"Foul play?"

It wasn't so much a question as a logical assumption. If Denisenko had died from natural causes, he would still be in Soviet hands. Unless, of course, he'd walked into a police station and had a heart attack when he realized the magnitude of what he was doing.

"No, it looks as though the silly bastard committed suicide."

"It looks?" Edwards repeated with heavy emphasis. "That means you aren't sure."

"The driver of the train from Leicester made an unofficial stop at Hendon to report he'd hit an obstruction on the line a mile south of Elstree and believed it might have been a body. The train was doing over eighty at the moment of impact and the driver didn't see the obstruction until he was right on top of it. I think he thought it was a sleeper, closed his eyes, and hoped for the best. There are loads of mindless vandals about these days, some degenerate enough to think derailing a train is one hell of a giggle."

"Yes, I know," Edwards said, impatient for him to get to the point.

"Anyway, the Hertfordshire police were pretty quick off

161

the mark and they had a patrol car in the vicinity within minutes of the call from the stationmaster. The two constables who found Denisenko threw up when they saw what the locomotive had done to his head. Ninety tons of diesel engine traveling at speed is one hell of a garden roller and it made a right pancake of Denisenko when it sideswiped him out of the way. Neither man fancied searching the body, so they tossed a coin and the winner returned to the patrol car to call for an ambulance."

The police constable who'd subsequently found the wallet had shown commendable presence of mind. Appreciating the significance of the ID card, he'd told the ambulance crew that there was no means of identification on the body. Then, having learned the ultimate destination of the corpse, he'd returned to the patrol car and contacted the duty inspector at Police Headquarters.

"Who else knows about Denisenko?" Edwards asked.

"Every senior officer in the chain of command up to and including the chief constable, plus the detective chief superintendent in charge of the Regional Crime Squad." Jardine smiled. "And me of course. I was briefed by the commissioner of the Metropolitan Police soon after the chief constable had spoken to him. I then got in touch with your duty officer. That makes a total of eight including the two police officers who found him."

"Where's the body now, Len?"

"In the morgue of the County Hospital at Barnet. I've already seen it. Apart from the head and neck injuries, there are no other marks, and the cause of death seems consistent with the facts as we know them."

The inherent caution of a good police officer who wasn't prepared to accept anything at face value. That quality had always been present in him even as a young man back in '54, when Jardine had been doing his National Service as a sergeant in the Royal Military Police in Berlin. Edwards had been employed by the British Security Service Organization in those days, a job he'd wangled just before his short service commission in the Intelligence Corps was due to expire, and they'd worked together on several refugee cases before Jardine was demobbed. The younger man

162

had joined the police force on his release, and when next they'd met sixteen years later in London, Edwards had been the deputy head of counterintelligence while Jardine had risen to the rank of detective inspector in the Special Branch. Tweedledum and Tweedledee: their careers had followed a similar pattern and they even looked alike, medium height, medium build, sharp features, and dark hair with varying shades of gray. But there were differences; Jardine had been promoted four times since 1970 and was probably still on the way up, while Edwards had advanced but one step and was going nowhere. He was also conscious that Jardine was only forty-eight and his junior by ten years.

"He'd been drinking," Jardine continued after a lengthy pause. "His trousers reeked of whiskey."

"Dutch courage?"

"Maybe. I had the morgue attendant draw off a sample of blood for analysis." He smiled lopsidedly. "Somehow I don't think there'll be a postmortem."

Jardine was right. The Russians would claim Denisenko's body as soon as they were notified of his death by the Foreign and Commonwealth Office. "What about the press?" Edwards asked, pursuing a train of thought. "How long can we keep them out of it?"

"The local newspaper is part of the East Anglian Publishing Corporation and the editor is unlikely to give us any trouble. The chief constable and the proprietor are close friends, members of the same golf club and all that. A word in his ear and he'll ensure that the story ends up on the spike. The national dailies are a different matter."

The low background mush from the rebroadcast unit below the dashboard suddenly cut out, then a measured, neutral voice called up control to report that a Lada saloon, registration number 8831735ZB, had been found abandoned in Boreham Copse with the keys still in the ignition.

"That'll save them the trouble of bypassing the switch," Jardine said.

"They're going to bring it in?"

"That's the general idea, Neil. Question is, do we put the car under a microscope?"

"It depends on what you've already got for me."

Jardine reached across, opened the glove compartment, and took out a small envelope. "Besides the ID card, we found this in his wallet. It contains five strips of microfilm."

The microfilm suggested that Denisenko had intended to defect; then for some reason he'd apparently lost his nerve and had taken the hard way out. The only thing Edwards was certain of was that if the Soviet Embassy wasn't already aware that one of their comrades was missing, they soon would be.

"The longer we sit on the news, the more suspicious it will look." He glanced at Jardine, seeking confirmation, but it wasn't forthcoming. Clearly, the younger man felt it was Edward's decision and his alone. "Does the Home Office know about Denisenko?"

"Not yet."

"All right, Len, you'd better get on to the commissioner and ask him to pass the good word along, but give me an hour to contact and brief my director general before you do."

"Okay. What do we do about the car?"

"Nothing. It's probably clean anyway." Edwards opened the passenger door. "I'd like to know the results of the blood test though."

"It may take a little time. Where can I reach you?"

"My office, where else?"

Edwards got out, closed the door behind him, and returned to his own car. The Home Office would convey the news of Denisenko's death to the resident clerk at the Foreign and Commonwealth and he in turn would get in touch with the Soviet Embassy. That was the recognized procedure, but it would do no harm to have a word with the FCO security people; in a situation like this there was no telling how the professional diplomats would react, and it might be a good idea to have a few friends at court who talked the same language. However, finding someone to develop and enlarge the microfilm was his first priority, and that would have to be done pretty damn quick because the director general would be breathing down his neck, wanting to know what they had as soon as he heard the news.

After that, he could look forward to one conference after another with just about everybody who was anybody putting his oar in as they tried to decide how much credence should be attached to the information on the film. He'd have to phone Jill sometime to let her know when she could expect to see him again, but there was no point doing that until he could see how things were shaping up. Whether the conferences were long or short, Jill would probably have to make her own way home, and she was going to love that. Some bargain break, Edwards thought as he started the engine and pulled out of the lay-by to drive to his office on Curzon Street.

★   ★   ★

Fomin pulled on his overcoat, left his quarters in the embassy compound, and walked over to the GRU residency in the main building. He hadn't bothered to shave, his hair was uncombed, and the suit he was wearing under the overcoat needed a good pressing. In short, Fomin looked as though he'd leaped out of bed and put on the first things at hand, which was exactly the impression he wanted to create when he strolled into Captain Anatoli Zotov's office. A hunch that the senior defense attaché would conduct their conversation in front of witnesses was confirmed by the presence of Major Yerokhin, the branch duty officer, and the chief archivist.

"You wanted to see me, Comrade Captain?" he said.

"Yes, I do." Zotov usually acted the part of the bluff, confident sailor turned reluctant diplomat who couldn't wait for the day when he was given another seagoing appointment. This morning, he looked worried and decidedly on edge as though Defense Minister Ustinov had taken him at his word. "I believe you're aware that Mrs. Denisenko phoned the embassy at two o'clock this morning to report that she hadn't seen her husband since he left their apartment at six-fifty yesterday evening?"

"Yes. Major Yerokhin must have called me seconds after she'd put the receiver down. He also told me that Raya Denisenko had said she'd had a mysterious telephone call around eleven-fifteen last night and wondered if somebody from the embassy had been trying to contact her. I asked the major here if Denisenko had anything going and he said he thought he had." Fomin gazed at Yerokhin. "That's more or less what you told me, isn't it?" he asked and got a reluctant nod from the Air Force major.

"I've already questioned Comrade Yerokhin at some length," Zotov said irritably. "Now I want to know what action you took after the branch duty officer phoned you."

"I went back to bed," Fomin said.

"You did what?"

"I went back to bed. What did you expect me to do? I'd no reason to think anything was wrong."

"I see. It didn't occur to you that his disappearance might be connected with another member of this department?"

"Don't tell me somebody else has gone astray?"

"Are you trying to be impertinent?" Zotov demanded.

"Not in the least."

In fact, Fomin was doing his level best to be insolent. There were quicksands ahead and he wanted to provoke Zotov to the point where the naval attaché lost his temper and made some indiscreet reference to Natalia Rubanskaya. A dark flush spreading up from Zotov's neck told him he was succeeding.

"Obtuse, then?"

"I'm not with you."

"I'm referring to the information I gave you about the alleged relationship between Natalia Rubanskaya and Aleksandrovich Denisenko."

"I wasn't aware that was public knowledge," Fomin said, then glanced pointedly in Yerokhin's direction. "Correct me if I'm wrong, but I was given to understand that apart from myself, only you and the chief archivist were in the know?"

"The branch duty officer would have to know sooner or later," Zotov said lamely.

"Quite. But I can't see that it's any business of his how I reacted to the information."

"You're absolutely right." Zotov turned to the Air Force officer and smiled bleakly. "I don't think we need detain you any longer, Major Yerokhin."

One witness down, one to go. Fomin waited until the major had left the room, then said, "For your ears only, Natalia Rubanskaya has been under surveillance since noon yesterday and I can assure you that she hasn't left her quarters in the embassy compound from the time she came off duty at two. I checked with my people before I went to bed, after your branch duty officer phoned me, and again when I was summoned here. Now, before we go any farther, I'd like to know whether or not Denisenko was running an operation last night?"

"He must have been." Zotov frowned. "I've certainly countersigned quite a number of checks for him in the last two months."

"Do you have any idea of the total sum involved?"

"In sterling?"

"Why not?"

"About two thousand pounds."

"That's a lot of money," Fomin said.

"I gathered it was a big operation and several people were involved. Naturally I didn't question him too closely." A nervous smile made a brief appearance. "After all, one has to observe the basic principles, the need to know and so on."

"Right. All the same, two thousand pounds is a tidy old sum, and it could be that our erstwhile comrade regarded it as a terminal grant for services rendered. Still, we shouldn't jump to conclusions. In a situation like this, we should start at the bottom and work our way up." Fomin rubbed his jaw, a gesture that was intended to convey the impression that he was uncertain where they should begin. "Why don't we take a look at Denisenko's safe?" he said brightly, as though he'd suddenly had a flash of inspiration. "I presume one of you will know the combination?"

"It's kept in a sealed envelope held by the chief archivist," Zotov told him.

"Good. What are we waiting for?"

From a seemingly disadvantageous position, Fomin had succeeded in imposing his will on the others. He had only to snap his fingers now and they would jump through a hoop for him like performing dogs. He was the circus ringmaster, totally in control of the situation, and no one was more aware of it than the hearty sailor turned reluctant diplomat.

"You may feel I've been lax," Zotov said, the moment they were alone together. "But even with the benefit of hindsight, I don't see how I could have supervised Aleko Denisenko more closely than I did."

"I think you did everything that could reasonably be expected of a senior officer in your position, and I shall say so in my report." Fomin contrived a wry smile. "Unfortunately, Moscow is apt to take a hard line when there is a defection, and somehow I don't think I'm going to come out of this affair too well either."

"How can they possibly blame you for being negligent, Konstantin? You didn't sit on the information I gave you."

It was a case of you scratch my back and I'll scratch yours, which was exactly the kind of attitude Fomin had wanted him to adopt. From now on, Zotov would be an ally instead of a potential antagonist. In his anxiety to save his own skin, he would agree to anything Fomin suggested and there would be no awkward questions.

"I imagine your chief archivist must be waiting for us, Anatoli."

"Quite so."

Fomin noted the relieved expression on Zotov's face and thought it amazing how the casual use of his first name had restored his morale. Hiding a triumphant smile, he followed him out of the room and along the transverse corridor to the office formerly occupied by Denisenko.

The chief archivist was already there, sealed envelope in one hand, penknife at the ready. Fomin assumed he wanted him to see that it hadn't been tampered with before he slit the flap open and extracted the combination to the safe. His apparent faith in their basic security measures was quite touching and incredibly naïve when there wasn't an envelope on the market that was safe from a flap–and–seal artist like Natalia Rubanskaya. In a craft dominated by women who alone possessed the necessary patience and deftness of touch with the specially adapted crochet needles, it was a comfort to know that she was regarded as one of the best in the business.

168

The chief archivist went through the sequence of numbers demanded by the combination and yanked the handle down; then, having opened the safe, he stood to one side to enable them to see the contents. There were eight Top Secret case files on the shelf that divided the interior, together with a register of classified documents. Below the shelf, the cipher books and one-time pads had been neatly arranged in two separate piles. Slowly and very deliberately, Zotov emptied the safe and stacked everything on the desk.

"What exactly are we looking for, Konstantin?"

"I really don't know." Fomin crouched down and peered inside, then ran his fingers under the shelf. "Seems to be some kind of obstruction," he muttered, "right at the back."

"What?"

"Feels like a small oblong box, except that it's a Minox camera. Well, what do you know, there are a couple of magnets set in the base."

"So I see," Zotov said grimly.

"Very simple but very ingenious. You'd never spot it anchored under the shelf, would you? I mean, a safe is the last place you'd expect Denisenko to hide a camera."

"Is it loaded?"

Fomin peered at the aperture and made a face. "Unfortunately it is. Furthermore, he's taken twelve exposures. Question is, what did he photograph?"

"We may know the answer to that when the film is developed," Zotov said.

"Oh, it'll give us a lead, but it won't necessarily indicate the whole range of Denisenko's activities. I wonder, what would you go for if you were in his shoes and thinking of defecting to the British?"

"The card index."

The question had been addressed to Zotov, but it was the chief archivist who'd answered it.

"But it would be very difficult," he added.

"Why?"

"Because of the way the GRU residency is organized and the fact that each officer is responsible for maintaining his own card index. These in turn are kept in separate safety deposit boxes, which are then lodged in the registry safe during silent hours. As a further safeguard, the keys to the boxes are held in my combination safe."

"So whenever an officer wants to open his own safety deposit box, he has to get the keys from you?"

"Yes."

"Suppose you were off sick or on leave," Fomin said innocently. "What happens then?"

"They would have to ask my assistant, Natalia Rubanskaya. She knows the combination."

Fomin nodded sagely. It had taken them a long time to reach the crunch point, but with a good deal of subtle bear-leading by him, they'd finally made it.

"You'll want to interrogate Natalia Rubanskaya," Zotov said, drawing the obvious conclusion.

"With the assistance of Mikhail Izveko. You may sit in on the interrogation if you wish, Anatoli."

"Yes, well, I'd like to be present. After all, she is one of my subordinates."

"Quite."

Fomin was confident there would be no slipups. He had been assured that Natalia Rubanskaya had been told what to expect and had committed her confession to memory long before the operation had started. However, for the sake of appearances, it would be necessary to take a firm line and perhaps even rough her up a little.

"What time do you propose to start, Konstantin?"

Fomin consulted his wristwatch. "Seven-thirty," he said, "after we've had a bite to eat. Meanwhile, we'll place her under close arrest."

He couldn't help feeling sorry for Natalia Rubanskaya. One way or another, she was about to get a raw deal, yet it was largely due to her work behind the scenes that the operation was proceeding even more smoothly than he'd dared to hope. No doubt she believed she would be suitably rewarded upon her return to Moscow, allegedly under arrest, but if they had a mind to, there was nothing to stop the KGB from charging her with treason. He certainly couldn't think of a better solution to the problem of ensuring that she kept her mouth permanently shut.

Later, much later, it occurred to Fomin that by the same token, Moscow Center could also put him on trial for dereliction of duty.

★   ★   ★

Sunday the seventh of November, the sixty-fifth anniversary of the October Revolution, the day Lenin and the Bolsheviks had consolidated their hold on Petrograd after the Red Guards had stormed the Winter Palace the night before. Sunday the seventh of November, the day the Russian calendar had finally conformed with the Julian, the first of many reforms introduced by the Council of People's Commissars. In Moscow, the military parade would be assembling on the inner-ring motorway, ready to march through Red Square.

In London, Kirov was sitting alone in the compartment of an Underground train northbound to Highgate. He had no idea where the diplomatic staff was quartered; information such as that had not been included in the basic intelligence course he'd attended in 1976, and Nikishev had not seen fit to enlighten him. But he had a copy of the *A to Z* street guide of London and he was sure the Soviet Embassy would be holding an official reception to celebrate the October Revolution. Even the lowliest clerk would be required to attend, which meant there would be more activity in the Highgate area than was usual for a Sunday morning in winter.

It was the one concrete fact Kirov had to go on and although the chances of finding the right block of flats were slim, he had to try. The memory of Raya Denisenko's voice on the phone last night was imprinted on his mind and would stay with him as long as he lived. "Has something happened to my husband?" she'd asked, her voice hysterical because the man he knew as "Alec" was three hours overdue. The question had kept him awake most of the night and had finally drawn him to Highgate. For once in his life, though, Kirov hoped he was on a wild goose chase.

Chapter XIII

The Security Service had been created in 1909 by Vernon Kell, a captain in the South Staffordshire Regiment. Apart from the fact that Kell spoke fluent German, French, Italian, Russian, and passable Cantonese, his qualifications for the job were not readily apparent, and it was generally agreed that he'd been chosen because he'd just completed a report on the Russo-Japanese war for the Imperial Committee on Defense and had happened to be available when the government of the day had decided to do something about the growing threat posed by the German Intelligence Service. The embryo organization was tacked onto the Director General of Military Operations Department and was known as the Secret Bureau, possibly because nobody had a very clear idea as to how it was going to function. Located on Victoria Street, the establishment consisted of Kell, one civilian clerical officer, and a retired detective inspector of the Metropolitan Police who expressed a strong aversion to working on surveillance duty after normal office hours.

Kell was fortunate in one respect; since his political and military masters had failed to lay down any guidelines, he was left in peace to get on with the job. The basic problem as he saw it was very simple; Britain's immigration laws at the turn of the century were so liberal that the authorities had no idea how many aliens were living in their midst. Kell therefore had made it his business to visit every chief constable and police authority in the country in order to persuade them to inaugurate an aliens register, a task that had taken him all of eighteen months to accomplish.

Once the scheme got under way, the trickle of information coming in from the provinces rapidly gathered momentum until it reached the point where the clerical officer, a Mr. Westmacott, was unable to cope with the inflow. An assistant was obviously required to deal with the highly sensitive information reaching Victoria Street, but in those days no vetting system existed for screening potential applicants. Kell solved the problem by engaging Mr. Westmacott's daughter, followed by his two nephews, after she too found herself snowed under.

By the outbreak of World War I, the bureau's unofficial card index contained the names of thirty thousand aliens, of whom more than eleven thousand were German or of German extraction. Among this latter group, discreet in-depth inquiries had succeeded in identifying practically every enemy agent who'd been infiltrated into the country, so that, at the outbreak of hostilities, Kell was able to deal the German Intelligence Service a blow from which it never recovered.

Mobilized in 1914 as MO5, the bureau changed its designation again on the formation of the Directorate of Military Intelligence two years later, when it then became MI5, a title that has clung to it ever since despite the fact that the organization ceased to be part of the army in October 1931, when it was civilianized and reconstituted as the Security Service. From one captain, an elderly clerk, and a retired detective, the service had grown to a small army of analysts, technicians, typists, accountants, and scientists; from a small back room on Victoria Street, it had acquired a dozen offices spread across London. In 1909 the princely sum of three pounds ten shillings was spent on purchasing a camera for surveillance purposes; by 1982 the budget ran to several million a year, and the service was equipped with a wide range of sophisticated electronic devices.

Although of course he and Kell had never met, Edwards had a great admiration for the first director general. The D.G.'s portrait in service dress uniform and Sam Browne was the only painting to grace his office and it was hung in a prominent position facing his desk, where it caught his eye every time he looked up. Kell was a visible reminder to him that his subdivision was still the backbone of the Security Service; comparative newcomers like the counterterrorist, subversive, and Irish desks were but limbs that had grown out of the trunk. If ever he believed himself to be drifting helplessly in a backwater, Edwards had only to look up at the sharp-featured man on the wall to be reassured. This morning, however, he didn't need to be reassured of his own importance in the scheme of things; this morning he was convinced that by a stroke of good fortune, he'd been presented with the biggest intelligence coup since Colonel Oleg Penkovsky had offered his services to the SIS.

The first strip of microfilm had been developed and enlarged by 0930 hours, which was no mean achievement considering that the standby photographer lived in the outer suburb of Ruislip and had been sound asleep when he'd called him. Edwards hadn't been so concerned about the two Russian linguists who resided even farther afield, because they couldn't do anything until the raw material was produced, but, they too had made the office in double-quick time. It was a good thing they had; there was a wealth of information on the microfilm, far in excess of what he'd anticipated; and somewhat rashly, he'd promised the D.G. that the Cabinet Office would have an outline assessment of the haul by five o'clock that evening.

Translation wasn't the problem. Although a little rusty, Edwards had passed the first-class interpreter's examination when he'd been stationed in Berlin and, between the linguists and him, he figured that that part of the task would be completed by mid-afternoon at the latest. It was the subsequent cross-checking of the individual names on the GRU card index with the department's own records that was likely to prove a time-consuming business. The fact that he was constantly being interrupted by the telephone didn't help either; it had been ringing all morning and now the damn thing was trilling at him again. Answering it, he found he had Jardine on the line. The Special Branch officer had already called him twice, once to report that the Home Office had contacted the resident clerk at the Foreign and Commonwealth about Denisenko and then, barely five minutes later, to suggest that they put a surveillance team on the Russian enclave at Highgate to observe the comings and goings. This was something Edwards should have thought of himself, and he wondered if Jardine was about to remind him of some other point he'd overlooked. At

174

Jardine's request, he activated the secure speech facility, then told him to go ahead.

Jardine said, "Something funny's going on. It seems we're not the only ones watching the Highgate enclave. My lads have just reported an intruder, a good-looking guy around five foot eleven weighing approximately one seventy-five with dark brown hair and strong angular features. He's wearing a dark gray raincoat unbuttoned over a tweed sports jacket and slacks. He couldn't be one of yours, could he, Neil?"

"Absolutely not."

"I didn't think he was." Jardine clucked his tongue. "He's not a reporter either."

"How do you know?"

"Because my lads can tell them a mile off. Besides, he's on his ownsome."

"Did they photograph him?"

"Full frontal and profile. I'll have a set of prints run off for you as soon as we get hold of the film."

"Good. Do you have anything else for me?" Edwards didn't mean to sound impatient, but he couldn't afford to waste time chatting on the telephone.

"I've got the results of the blood-alcohol test we ran on Denisenko. The medics say he was well over the limit."

"He obviously needed a lot of Dutch courage."

"We didn't find a whiskey bottle in the Lada saloon," Jardine continued remorselessly. "There wasn't a whiff of the stuff either, yet his trousers reeked of it. Of course the smell could have dispersed had one of the windows been left open, but none of them had. I also had a word with the police constable who drove the Lada back to police head-quarters, and he's positive he didn't smell anything when he opened the door."

"What are you suggesting?" Edwards asked.

"I don't know. I just have this feeling that something's wrong. I mean, what if somebody else drove the Lada out to Boreham Wood and Denisenko was traveling in another car?"

"Alive or dead?"

"How about unconscious?" Jardine said, hedging.

"Either way, that would make him a plant."

"Yes, that's what I thought, but of course the whole idea's crazy, isn't it?"

Edwards heard him put the phone down and slowly replaced the receiver. Jardine was right; it was a crazy hypothesis. He looked up at Kell's portrait, recalled that Churchill had sacked him in 1940 largely because he had lacked the imagination to reorganize the Security Service to meet the changing circumstances of the day, and began to have second thoughts.

★　　★　　★

Fomin went through the motions of searching the room Denisenko had used as a study in his apartment in Highgate. He rolled back the carpet and underpad, tested the floorboards to see if any of them was loose, then took the external and internal measurements of the small writing table in the window. Much to his annoyance, Zotov had insisted on accompanying him to the flat, and having the defense attaché constantly looking over his shoulder was an inhibiting factor he could have done without. Moscow had been very insistent that further incriminating evidence should be planted inside the apartment, and it was impossible to do that when the hearty sailor was breathing down his neck.

"Looking for something?"

Fomin grunted. The man had a talent for stating the blindingly obvious in a judicious manner, as though, after years of patient research, he'd suddenly discovered some profound truth. He wished the gallant captain would take himself off to the sitting room across the hall and assist his wife with the comforting of Raya Denisenko. The children, three chubby-faced, round-eyed little girls between the ages of six and nine, had quietened down but their mother was still wailing away.

"That writing table looks like a cheap reproduction to me," Zotov went on. "The drawers are very shallow and there's no depth to them. You'd have to be a highly skilled carpenter to build a secret compartment in the available space."

"You're probably right."

"And somehow I find it hard to believe Denisenko was a handyman. He always struck me as being particularly clumsy."

"Is that so?" Fomin pressed a button on the drum magazine to retract the flexible steel ruler, then slipped it into his jacket pocket. "Well, there's nothing irregular about this item of furniture; the measurements tally inside and out."

"I'm not surprised, Konstantin. I could see at a glance that it couldn't be adapted."

Fomin would have been staggered if he had found anything. There were no secret hiding places in the Denisenko household and there never had been, but it was necessary to search the apartment from top to bottom for the sake of appearances. The whole operation was one vast confidence trick, and conviction was the essence of all successful deceptions. Even though Natalia Rubanskaya had proved a better actress than he'd allowed for, the interrogation had lacked real authenticity until Izveko had struck her across the face with the flat of his hand, then with a forearm backhander. Her bottom lip had been split open and she'd bled from the nose, but it wasn't so much the violent assault itself that had unnerved her as the fact that she hadn't been prepared for it. From then on, Natalia Rubanskaya hadn't been acting; her fear had been real, not contrived. A feeling that perhaps she too was being set up had become a near-certainty in her mind when Fomin had heard from the minister-counselor that the British Foreign Office had just contacted the embassy to inform the ambassador that the body of a Russian diplomat, believed to be Aleko Denisenko, had been found on the railway line near Elstree. Her subsequent confession had therefore been utterly convincing and, not surprisingly, Zotov had believed every word.

"Beautiful."

"What is?" Zotov asked him.

"That picture," Fomin said hastily and pointed to a watercolor of a nondescript landscape above the free-standing bookcase inside the door.

"I don't see anything remarkable about it; seems to me it could be any river anywhere in Europe."

"It's the size of the painting that appeals to me." Fomin crossed the room to view the watercolor close up, then unhooked it and examined the back. "According to Denisenko's accounts, most of the two thousand pounds he drew from the secret bank account were converted into traveler's checks."

"Yes," Zotov eyed the picture. "I suppose he could have concealed them inside the frame, but I doubt if they're still there."

"The British police are adamant that his wallet contained only one five-pound note and six ones."

"The officers who found Denisenko probably stole the checks."

"They'd have a hard time cashing them. The bank teller would require proof of identity and they would have to forge Denisenko's signature in front of him."

Fomin produced a penknife and cut around the frame to remove the cardboard backing that had been sealed with black adhesive tape. Then he took the picture apart.

"Nothing, absolutely nothing." Fomin scratched his head and contrived to look bewildered. "I suppose we'd better search the bathroom next. It's about the only place in the apartment where he could be sure of being alone."

"I still think the police stole them."

"No, it's more likely he threw them away after Natalia Rubanskaya told him that she was concerned for her elderly parents and couldn't go through with it. If you want my opinion, it was her last-minute refusal to defect that precipitated his eventual suicide. Denisenko was afraid she would report him, if only to protect herself, and he couldn't face the consequences. Chances are he got quietly drunk before he went out and killed himself."

"Do you think Moscow will believe that?" Zotov asked dubiously.

The irony of the question appealed to Fomin's warped sense of humor, and he found it hard to resist a smile. The whole scenario had been written by the First Chief Directorate, for reasons best known to them, and it was unlikely they would suddenly do a *volte-face*—at least he certainly hoped they wouldn't.

"Your guess is as good as mine, Anatoli. Personally, I would have thought the money will be the least of their problems."

"Then why are we searching high and low for it?" Zotov demanded.

"Because I like to see things neat and tidy. When I tell Moscow we were unable to find the checks, I want to be quite sure we've covered all the angles."

Fomin reached into his jacket pocket and felt the bill of sale for the emerald ring Denisenko was supposed to have given Natalia Rubanskaya. The purchase price exceeded the two thousand pounds he'd recently drawn from the secret bank account, but that was immaterial. Given the circumstances of his death, Zotov would assume that Denisenko had been milking the fund for months. Unfortunately, the way things were going, he was unlikely to have an opportunity to plant the final damning piece of evidence.

"Perhaps Raya Denisenko may know something?" Zotov perched himself on the writing table and sat there, gazing down at the street below, arms folded across his chest. "Not that she will be in a fit state to answer any questions if she's required to identify her husband."

"It's not our intention to expose her to such an ordeal," Fomin told him. "The minister-counselor and I will do all that's necessary as soon as the body arrives from the mortuary. If there's any doubt in our minds, we'll call in the resident physician to identify the corpse with the aid of Denisenko's medical and dental records."

"What else have you arranged, Konstantin?"

"It's been agreed the family will return to Moscow on the scheduled Aeroflot tomorrow morning. In the meantime, the ambassador feels that they should move into the embassy compound."

"A very sensible idea."

Fomin thought so too, since it had been his suggestion. The Denisenko affair was a potential time bomb, and it was essential to isolate the family from their neighbors before

179

somebody inadvertently set the fuse ticking with a chance remark.

"What about their household effects?"

"The administrative officer will have somebody take care of that," Fomin said.

"Good."

"Raya seems to have calmed down a bit."

"Yes," Zotov said absently.

"Perhaps we should get her into the car before she breaks down again?"

"What about the opposition? I presume it doesn't matter if they see the Denisenkos leaving?"

"Whom are you referring to?" Fomin asked and joined him at the window.

"That man over there standing at the bus stop, the one in the dark gray raincoat. I noticed him earlier on when we drew up outside the apartment block."

The British would have alerted their Security Service, and while they would undoubtedly have the immediate area under surveillance, Fomin couldn't accept that they would be quite so open about it.

"If they weren't aware that Denisenko was a GRU officer, they are now," Zotov said bitterly. "And of course you were right, Konstantin, I shouldn't have come with you. As the naval attaché, my face is too well known."

Tall, well built, and very sure of himself. The sort of cool character you didn't want to tangle with, unless the odds were very much in your favor. Fomin was certain he'd seen the man at the bus stop somewhere before.

"Your cover is still intact," Zotov continued. "So far as the British are concerned, you're listed as the administrative officer."

"It's too late for regrets now," Fomin said bluntly.

Where had he seen the stranger before? The question nagged at Fomin; then suddenly the images came together and he was able to place him. He'd been there hovering in the background when they'd picked up Denisenko outside the Underground station in Earls Court yesterday evening. The mysterious George Kershaw, the "tourist" he wasn't supposed to know about? If his assumption was correct, and offhand he couldn't see why it shouldn't be, George Kershaw had broken every rule in the book by following his contact after the meet had been terminated.

"Are you going on with the search?" Zotov asked.

"In a limited fashion. Give me five minutes to check out the bathroom and we'll call it a day." Fomin turned away from the window and walked over to the door. "Meanwhile, you might tell Raya Denisenko that she had better get herself ready to leave," he added, then left the room.

The main bedroom was next to the bathroom at the other end of the hallway. The Denisenkos, mother and three small daughters, were in the sitting room along with Mrs. Zotov, the minister-counselor, and the first secretary, of commerce—who, according to the staff list submitted to the Foreign and Commonwealth Office, was the deceased's superior officer. It took Fomin less than a minute to enter the bedroom and plant the bill of sale in one of the suits hanging in the closet. Then he went into the bathroom and spent the remaining time searching through the medicine cabinet. Inevitably, his thoughts returned to the man at the bus stop.

The deduction he'd made raised two further questions. First, what had prompted Kershaw to deliberately commit a major breach of security? And second, how did you warn Moscow that the "tourist" might be about to throw a spanner in the works when officially you weren't supposed to know he existed? He was still trying to work out the answers when Zotov informed him that the Denisenkos were ready to leave.

★   ★   ★

Kirov watched them leave the apartment house; three solemn little girls, two women, and four embassy officials, one of whom was carrying a small suitcase. From the moment they appeared in view, there was no doubt in his mind as to who was "Alec's" wife, and what had happened was equally obvious to him. Although a good head shorter than "Alec," Raya Denisenko was, if anything, even plumper than her late husband, and the other woman, a trim brunette, clearly found it difficult to support her weight as she leaned against her. One of the embassy officials was holding Raya's other arm under the elbow, but it was evident that he was more concerned to steer her toward the nearer of the two Zil limousines parked in the forecourt than to offer any practical comfort to the bereaved woman.

None of the men seemed predisposed to help her into the car, and the chauffeur was too busy putting the suitcase into the trunk to do any more than open the rear door. Somehow the brunette managed to get her into the back and then, having shown the three little girls where they should sit, she joined Raya and closed the door. After some discussion among themselves, one of the embassy officials got in beside the driver while the remaining three made off toward the second limousine. The last Kirov saw of Raya Denisenko, she was dabbing her eyes with a handkerchief.

"I don't know what we've done to offend them."

"Sorry?" Kirov turned to the elderly woman standing next to him at the bus stop and smiled politely. "I didn't catch what you said."

"I was talking about them Russians who've just driven off. One of the men looked very peeved, gave us a real dirty look."

"He probably got out of bed on the wrong side this morning."

"Ugly great bear," the woman said and sniffed.

It was an apt description. The seemingly bad-tempered diplomat was a big, shambling man whose hands and feet were almost as broad as they were long. He'd reminded Kirov of a bear the first time he'd seen him outside the Underground station at Earls Court.

"How long have you been waiting for a bus, young man?"

"Far too long," Kirov said.

"There's supposed to be a bus every twenty minutes on a Sunday," the woman complained. "But that's London Transport for you. Sometimes I think they run the buses for the benefit of the drivers."

"Yes, well, I don't intend to hang around here any longer."

182

"I should give it another minute or two if I was you. You mark my words, a bus'll turn up moments after you've left. It always happens."

"It wouldn't make any difference now," Kirov told her. "My date's obviously giving me the brush-off."

"Stood you up, has she?"

"Looks like it."

"I can't understand young women these days, they don't know when they're well off. Where are you from? New York?"

"Vancouver. Canada." Kirov began to edge away. "It's been nice talking to you," he said, then added, "Have a nice day."

"And you, love," the woman called after him.

Kirov went on up the hill, turned left at the top by the village green, and started on down the High Street looking for a pub that was open; he found one almost opposite the entrance to Waterlow Park. Entering it, he asked the barmaid for a lager and ploughman's lunch, then sat down at a table to think things out.

Denisenko, the man he knew as "Alec," was dead. Not long after they had parted company at Gloucester Road last night, the "Bear" and his youngish-looking companion had murdered him. Although the precise motive for the killing was unclear, Kirov was convinced it was directly connected with his own assignment. Brezhnev was a dying man and two rival factions within the Politburo were already engaged in a bitter struggle for power. Denisenko and possibly the American, Russell Moorcroft, were the first casualties, but there would be others before the issue was settled. In a situation where it was impossible for most of the combatants to know who was on whose side, Kirov was fortunate to a degree in that he at least could recognize the faces of two of his enemies. Just how he could exploit that advantage was something he was still pondering when the pub closed at three o'clock.

★   ★   ★

Edwards spent some minutes examining the large glossy prints, then arranged them face up on his desk as though he and Jardine were partners in a game of bridge and he was dummy.

"There are some old familiar faces here, Len," he murmured.

"Then you're well on the way to answering the four basic questions. I know where and when the pictures were taken and you say you can put a name to the faces. All we've got to do now is decide the reason each man was there."

"Right." Edwards picked up a photograph and showed it to him. "Savelev, the minister-counselor and the number two man in the embassy. He would take it upon himself to convey the ambassador's sympathies to the widow. Agreed?"

"You're the expert on protocol, Neil."

"So people tell me." Edwards discarded Savelev's photograph in favor of the next. "Oskin, first secretary, commerce, and Denisenko's boss according to the Foreign Office staff list. He'd have been stuck with the job of telling Mrs. Denisenko that her husband was dead. That brings us to the Zotovs, Anatoli and wife. If I were in charge of security at the Soviet Embassy they would be the last people I'd want around, because their presence would tell the British that Denisenko was a GRU officer."

"They may have assumed we already know that," Jardine said.

"A woman would be much better at comforting the widow than a man," Edwards continued unperturbed, "but the Zotovs and the Denisenkos have never been seen in each other's company. Furthermore, both Savelev and Oskin are married."

"Does it matter why the Zotovs were there?"

It probably didn't. There was ample proof on the microfilm that Zotov had attempted to recruit several informants among naval dockyard workers. There was nothing at all unusual about that; defense attachés the world over engaged in espionage, but with the evidence now in their possession, the government could expel him whenever it suited their purpose to make a political point.

"Konstantin Fomin, administrative officer, the embassy's

184

Mr. Fix-It." Edwards rubbed his jaw. "What's he staring at?"

"There's a bus stop across the road from the apartment block." Jardine leaned across the desk and pointed to one of the remaining photographs. "For my money, he was interested in this guy."

"The intruder your people were on about this morning?"

"Yes. He was wandering around like a lost sheep when they first saw him, then he spotted the CD plates on the vehicles parked in the forecourt and went over to the bus stop."

"Before or after the embassy crowd arrived?"

"Before. My lads figure he was watching the apartment block as though he was half-expecting them to show up."

"You think somebody had tipped him off about Denisenko?"

"Maybe."

"Could he be a reporter?"

"I doubt it. A pressman would have known exactly where the Soviet diplomats lived. This man didn't; he had to nose around." Jardine lit a cigarette and leaned back in his chair. "I'll tell you something else, Neil. The guy you said was Fomin—I think he knows our friend at the bus stop and couldn't figure out what the hell he was doing there."

"Your people didn't follow him, by any chance?"

"You've got to be joking. They were down a manhole allegedly carrying out emergency repairs to the telephone cables. They could hardly drop what they were doing and clamber aboard their bright yellow truck the moment he walked off."

"No, I guess not." Edwards sorted through the half-dozen photographs the Special Branch had taken of the one man he couldn't identify and selected a full frontal. "How many prints would you need to cover all the exits?" he asked.

"About a couple of hundred," Jardine told him. "Or even more if you're thinking of covering every tinpot airfield and port of embarkation. Running them off won't take any time at all; it's getting them out to the people on the ground that's the problem."

"I'd like Immigration at Gatwick and Heathrow to have them as soon as possible. How long would that take?"

Jardine glanced at his wristwatch. "It's now twenty past five; barring any unforeseen snarl-ups, I think we can guarantee they will have a print in their hot little hands by nine."

"Good. All I want is his name and destination."

"This whole thing is a bit of a long shot, isn't it, Neil? Or do you know something I don't?"

"I'm as much in the dark as you are." Edwards looked up at the portrait on the wall behind Jardine. "But I don't intend to make the same mistake General Kell did back in 1940."

"Oh? What was that?"

"Failing to use his imagination," Edwards said.

★   ★   ★

The color was poor and distorted as it invariably was when the picture was received via satellite. The camera, which Kirov assumed was positioned somewhere near the GUM store in Red Square, lingered briefly on St. Basil's Cathedral with its eight unmatched and riotously colored onion domes, then panned to the 220-foot-high Spassky Tower before zooming in on the reviewing stand outside the Kremlin Wall. General Aleksei Yepishev, chief of the Armed Forces Political Directorate; Marshal Viktor Kulikov, commander in chief of the Warsaw Pact; Marshal Nikolai Ogarkov, chief of the General Staff; despite the fuzziness of the picture and their orange-colored faces, Kirov recognized them instantly. Defense Minister Marshal Dimitri Ustinov, Leonid Brezhnev, Prime Minister Nikolai Tikhonov, Party Secretary Konstantin Chernenko and finally, Yuri Andropov, the former head of the KGB. He wondered if there was any significance to be read into the respective postitions on the dais vis-à-vis Leonid Brezhnev, then decided there wasn't. Although Marshal Ustinov was a possible contender for the leadership, Prime Minister Tikhonov was just too much of a nonentity to be numbered even among the rank outsiders that Fedor Fedorovich had mentioned.

The camera drew back and showed the massed ranks of

the Guards Division marching past the dais in review order, each file twenty abreast and perfectly in line. Behind them came the tracked armored personnel carriers, the SS20 nuclear missiles and T72 main battle tanks. And there was Brezhnev again, standing rigidly to attention at the salute, seemingly indestructible yet about as animated and real as a tailor's dummy in a shop window. Whoever succeeded him would inherit the Red Army, arguably the most formidable fighting machine the world had ever seen. It was a sobering thought for a man reluctantly involved in the jockeying for position.

Kirov got up, crossed the room, and switched off the television. He wished he could blank out his mind at the touch of a button as he had the screen, but the images indelibly remained. The Kremlin walls, the towering cathedrals of the Annunciation and the Assumption, and the Moskva River; but above all, he saw the people he loved, Fedor Fedorovich, the raging bull who licked his wounds and did the best he could for his family, and Irena, half sister, friend, confidante, and the surrogate mother who'd brought him up. All his life they had cherished and protected him; now it was his turn to look after them.

Ustinov, Chernenko, Andropov, or Grigory Romanov, the Party boss of Leningrad? Kirov didn't care who came to power, but he had been drafted into Romanov's camp; if he failed to carry out his assignment or bungled it, then Irena, Fedor Fedorovich, Lydia, and her twin daughters would be the ones to suffer the consequences.

Nikishev had told him to remain in London until Monday evening in case the link man found it necessary to get in touch with him again, but this instruction was no longer relevant. Denisenko was dead, and it was a cast-iron certainty that the men who'd killed him would now be very anxious to liquidate George Kershaw. It didn't enter his head to question either assumption. The popular serial on Moscow television that depicted the KGB as dedicated but friendly neighborhood policemen was a fanciful piece of brainwashing. When the stakes were high enough, Kirov knew the KGB could be just as ruthless as they had been in Stalin's day, and it certainly wouldn't bother the hit men of the Executive Action Department if they were ordered to eliminate a GRU officer like Denisenko. Merely to survive and stay in the game, Kirov would need to break the mold and do the unexpected.

He checked his wallet. There were the three thousand dollars in traveler's checks allegedly purchased by George Kershaw while in London. The signature Denisenko had forged on each check bore a passing resemblance to the one in the Canadian passport delivered to him in Budapest, and he didn't think it would be difficult to copy. He also had the balance of the 1,500 Deutschmarks he'd received from Abbetz, plus the transfer value of the return half of the TWA round trip ticket from New York to Frankfurt. All told, Kirov figured he had a little over four thousand dollars to play with, enough to make him independent of the contact at Nestor's Toy Emporiums in New York. No problem, then; first thing tomorrow he would check out of the Piccadilly and start laying a false trail.

Chapter XIV

Nine to five, Monday to Friday, was the norm for the vast majority of civil servants. Edwards, however, was rarely so fortunate; he was lucky if he left the office at seven and, except for occasional weekends, he worked most Saturday mornings. By way of a change, this particular week had started in the early hours of Sunday, which had made him decidedly unpopular with one particular person. According to the forecast, the rest of the country could expect bright intervals between intermittent rain showers with temperatures rising above the seasonal average to eleven degrees Centigrade, fifty-two Fahrenheit. At 26 Riverside Way in Chiswick, where he and Jill lived, he wouldn't have been surprised if it was registering thirty below zero, with every sign that it would fall even lower.

The localized arctic weather conditions had set in late on

Sunday night. Edwards had stayed on in London much longer than he'd anticipated, largely because the Cabinet Office worked all the hours God made and expected no less from other government departments whenever there was a crisis. Whether or not the Denisenko affair could be regarded as a crisis was a debatable point, but he'd thought it only politic to remain on call until the director general had finished briefing the Prime Minister's staff. The briefing had started at 5:10 P.M.; three hours later, the D.G. had called him from Downing Street to say that there would be a conference for all department heads at 8:30 A.M. on Monday. Even though he'd left it to the branch duty officer to warn the others and had driven back to Southwell like a bat out of hell, it had been getting on to 11:00 P.M. by the time he'd arrived at the Saracen's Head. The conference had meant an early start on an empty stomach, and the two-and-a-half hour journey had taken place in an atmosphere of frosty silence from beginning to end.

Edwards had left the car in Chiswick and doubled back into London on the Underground to avoid the usual rush-hour traffic. However, by a quirk of fate, a signal failure at Hammersmith had produced the same kind of snarl-up, and he'd arrived at Curzon Street some ten minutes after the meeting had started, which hadn't gone down too well with the D.G. Matters hadn't been improved either when, having apologized profusely, he'd then been asked to give his views on a signal intercept from the Soviet Embassy that he hadn't seen because he'd gone straight into the conference room without stopping at his office.

In fact, it transpired that there were grounds for thinking there had been two signals, one sent in clear, the other in cipher. The latter had been squirted at ultrahigh speed via a communication satellite, and only the tail end of the message had been captured. The clear text transmission had been addressed to the Foreign Ministry and had informed Moscow of the death of Aleko Denisenko under unusual circumstances. It had also stated that arrangements were being made for the next of kin to return home on the next Aeroflot scheduled flight and that a full report would follow in the diplomatic bag.

189

Most of the experts around the table had been of the opinion that the clear and ultrahigh-speed transmissions were connected. Just what should be read into this had produced widely different views, but at the end of a two-hour discussion, there had been a considerable body of support for the view of the Foreign and Commonwealth representative that the information on the microfilm should be treated with caution. Nobody had gone so far as to imply that it was possibly bogus, but Edwards had been left with the impression that the director general no longer regarded the haul with quite the same degree of enthusiasm as he'd shown on Sunday evening.

Returning to his office, he found that his secretary had placed a photocopy of the unclassified signal to Moscow on his desk. Attached to the photocopy was a brief handwritten note that said, "This was received by our new clerical assistant shortly after she came on duty at eight o'clock. My apologies for the hiccup, but unfortunately she didn't appreciate its significance and your meeting had already started by the time I saw it. Mr. Jardine phoned twice while you were in conference, but declined to leave a message. He asked if you would call him when you had a free moment."

Edwards screwed up the note, dropped it into the wastepaper bin, then dialed Jardine's number and got a busy signal. A few minutes later, he tried again and had better luck.

Jardine said, "That stranger you're interested in; his name is George Kershaw. He was on the 0925 Aer Lingus flight to Dublin this morning, a last-minute booking."

"Anything else?"

"He has a Canadian passport," Jardine told him. "Describes himself as a businessman."

"I see." Edwards had gotten what he'd originally asked for, but it was no longer enough. The Canadian had come to his notice because Fomin appeared to know him, and now Special Branch had established an Irish connection. "I think you'd better talk to your friends in The Garda and see if they have a trace on him. If Kershaw hasn't come to their notice, ask them if they can find out where he's staying in Dublin."

"Right."

"One more thing," Edwards continued. "If Kershaw should leave the Emerald Isle, I'd like to know where he's going."

"You want The Garda to put him under surveillance?"

"That's the general idea."

"What do I tell them if they ask me why?"

"You tell them we think he may be a Soviet agent," Edwards said.

★   ★   ★

Nikishev marched into the general's office, halted in front of the desk and saluted, then removed his peaked cap and tucked it under his left arm. He had not been told why Petr Ivanovich Ivashutin had sent for him; he had been about to deliver a lecture at the training school when he was picked up in a staff car by an aide who had been singularly uncommunicative throughout the short journey to the GRU Headquarters on Znamenskaja. The general didn't seem in a hurry to enlighten him either; he was too busy reading a teletype in an attitude of total concentration, his elbows on the desk, head lowered, his chin cupped in both palms. When finally he did look up, there was a faraway expression in his eyes, as though he had never met Nikishev before.

"Refresh my memory about Aleko Denisenko," he said in an equally distant voice. "When did he graduate from training school?"

"Nineteen seventy-one. He was a late entrant, Comrade General. He has a master's degree in mechanical engineering from Volgagrad Institute of Technology, and we began to take an interest in him when he was working for the Industrial Planning Unit at the Ministry of Internal Affairs."

"This would be after Denisenko had completed his military service?"

"Yes." Nikishev sensed trouble. Ivashutin might be an ex-KGB man, but he had been in the chair long enough to know that if he wanted a potted biography, he had only to send for his chief of personnel.

"The Foreign Ministry expressed no reservations about him?"

191

It wouldn't have made a jot of difference had the Foreign Ministry raised all kinds of objections. They were not in a position to veto the appointment of any GRU candidate for the diplomatic service, as the general well knew.

"There's nothing in his security file that would indicate they were reluctant to accept him," Nikishev said, choosing his words with care. "Of course, I wouldn't know about his personal file; that's held by the personnel branch, and the chief of staff decided there was no need for me to see it." He thought it prudent to remind the general that his headquarters staff knew more about Denisenko than he did, especially as they had constant access to the relevant documents. If something had gone wrong, it was advisable to get the record straight before the shit started flying.

"Are you implying that certain information was deliberately withheld from you?" Ivashutin demanded icily.

It was a heads you win, tails I lose situation. A yes answer would be tantamount to admitting that the selection process had been conducted in a slipshod manner; a no answer and he wouldn't have a leg to stand on should events prove that Denisenko had been less than competent. Somehow he had to steer a middle course, and that wasn't going to be easy.

"Everyone was extremely cooperative," Nikishev assured him in the oily manner he had perfected over the years. "And the confidential assessments I saw were very reassuring. While none of his superiors had ever regarded him as an outstanding officer, they all agreed that Denisenko is loyal, discreet, hardworking, and reliable. You could not wish for a more conscientious subordinate, Comrade General."

"And you considered he was undoubtedly the best candidate for the assignment?"

Something had gone wrong in London, and Ivashutin had received a preliminary report in the teletype. Had he been a gambling man, Nikishev would have bet a month's pay on it.

"One was faced with a limited choice," he said, temporizing. "There are several more able officers currently serving in London, but they are the official military attachés and their faces are obviously known to the British Security Service. This meant I had to confine myself to the covert element accredited to the embassy and our permanent trade delegation. Of the officers in this category, Denisenko appeared to be the best on paper. Naturally, it wasn't possible to interview him or any of the other eligible candidates in person."

"You examined his medical documents?"

"Yes, Comrade General. Denisenko underwent a rigorous physical examination before he was posted abroad and was given a clean bill of health. The director of psychiatry also stated that he was not suffering from any personality disorders."

It was difficult to see the purpose of the present line of questioning, but he thought Ivashutin could hardly fail to be impressed by the depth of his knowledge. The gratuitous information might also convince him that he had not overlooked anything that could have affected his final choice.

"What about the reports he has submitted? Did you see any of those?"

"I read them all," Nikishev told him eagerly, "including the ones he sent when he was attached to our embassy in Delhi. Incidentally, Comrade General, I noticed that Denisenko had received a special commendation for his work in India."

"I presume you were equally impressed by his more recent performance in London?"

"Yes." Nikishev hesitated, then said, "The chief of staff indicated that he thought Denisenko was going from strength to strength."

"His reports on the Falklands crisis didn't strike you as being a little odd?"

"In what respect, Comrade General?"

"Don't be obtuse with me, Colonel." As Ivashutin worked himself into a rage, his voice rose accordingly. "Did you or did you not get the impression that he was becoming pro-British?"

Denisenko had gone across; the explanation hit Nikishev with the force of a bullet and he could feel himself buckling at the knees. "That bastard Kirov was behind it," he said hoarsely.

"What on earth are you talking about?"

"Denisenko and Kirov—they've both defected, haven't they?"

"Denisenko is dead." Ivashutin picked up the telephone on his desk and waved it at him. "This signal is ambiguous but it looks as though he may have committed suicide."

"Suicide?" Nikishev repeated in a hollow voice.

"The British police found his body by a railroad track on the northern outskirts of London."

"His whole world was coming apart at the seams. From a long way off, Nikishev heard himself ask when it had happened.

"Sometime on Saturday evening," Ivashutin informed him.

And now it was two-thirty on Monday afternoon. The occurrence had probably been reported to the Foreign Ministry in the first instance but, even allowing for the subsequent delay and the fact that Moscow was three hours ahead of Greenwich mean time, it was ludicrous to suppose that Ivashutin had only just heard the news.

"Do we know if he met Kirov?" Nikishev raised the question only to see what kind of reaction it would produce.

"Why do you keep mentioning his name? What has he got to do with Denisenko?"

For all his bluster, the general was nervous; it showed in the brittle tone of voice and in the slight tremor of his hand as he continued to wave the teletype at him. His tactics were equally clear; in a very crude and transparent way he was attempting to dissociate himself from the whole enterprise. But he could never get away with that—or could he? Nikishev tried to recall one single event that would implicate the general and drew a complete blank. Right from the very beginning every aspect had been handled by the chief of staff. True, Ivashutin had wandered into the office on at least two occasions when Nikishev and the chief of staff had been conferring, but the general had never contributed anything to their discussions and had acted as though he was merely passing the time of day.

194

"I asked you a question," Ivashutin said. "I'm still waiting for an answer."

The general was busy digging a pit for him. He had evidently made up his mind that the coup was going to fail and was determined to save his own skin come what may. The whole interview had been carefully stage-managed, and throughout he had acted the part of the bewildered superior anxious to discover just what had been going on behind his back.

"I find your continued silence very puzzling. I wonder, could it be that you have something to hide?"

"I was only following orders . . ." Nikishev found himself floundering and took a deep breath. This wouldn't do at all; he was responding like a guilty man about to confess. "The truth is," he went on, "I'm as much in the dark as you are, Comrade General."

"No matter, it will soon be dawn."

"What?"

"I'm informed that a full report on the Denisenko affair will arrive in the diplomatic bag later this afternoon." Ivashutin laid the teletype aside, then gazed at him as though he were an object to be pitied. "Let us hope for your sake that it doesn't contain anything to indicate that he was thinking of defecting to the British."

*   *   *

The doughnut arrived with the midafternoon cup of tea. It was shaped like a small cannonball, looked heavy enough to be one, and something unappetizing that was supposed to be strawberry jam was oozing out of a shallow hole in the top. Edwards had asked the clerical assistant to get him a Danish pastry or whatever, because the two ham sandwiches he'd consumed at lunchtime had failed to placate his stomach, which was still rumbling with pangs of hunger. The "whatever" had resulted in a sticky doughnut that appeared to have glued itself to the paper handkerchief the assistant had thoughtfully provided. Gingerly separating it from the tissue, Edwards tried an exploratory bite and found the doughnut to be just as indigestible as he'd surmised. He also discovered that it lodged in his throat when he attempted to swallow a mouthful and answer the phone at the same time.

Jardine made some observation about a bad connection, then said, "Our Canadian friend is one very busy business-man."

"Are you telling me he's left Dublin?"

"By Aer Lingus to Paris after spending less than two hours in the city."

"That's interesting."

"It gets better," Jardine said. "He arrived at Orly at 1405 local time and departed from Charles de Gaulle on a TWA flight to New York at 1620 hours."

Edwards grabbed a pencil and made a note of the departure time on his scratch pad, added the estimated flying time, then deducted the zone difference to arrive at an ETA. "That means he'll be landing at Kennedy around 1800 hours."

"Around 1700," Jardine corrected him. "The French are an hour ahead of us."

"We shall have to get a move on."

"Less of the 'we'; he's your pigeon from now on, Neil."

"Of course he is; I was just thinking out loud. Rest assured, either the director general or I will talk to the FBI."

"Yes? Well, before you do, I think there's something you should know. George Kershaw may be hopping about like a demented cricket but he's no chameleon. He hasn't changed his name or switched passports. So okay, Kershaw may be a courier, but if he is, he's one hell of a fast worker."

The same observation could well apply to a legitimate entrepreneur. Unless the people Kershaw was doing business with had met him at both airports, there was no way he could have put a deal together in so short a time.

"Did Kershaw see anyone in Dublin or Paris?" Edwards asked, pursuing this train of thought.

"You've got to be joking. He was in and out so fast that neither the Garda nor the Direction Surveillance Territoire had a chance to get on to him."

Kershaw was on the run; there could be no other explanation. A man didn't travel to New York by way of Dublin and Paris unless he was trying to lay a false trail.

196

"Let's go back to the beginning," Edwards said. "Were there any security men from the Soviet Embassy around when Kershaw left Heathrow this morning?"

"There was a whole gaggle of officials at Number Three Terminal to see Mrs. Denisenko and her children off on the Aeroflot flight to Moscow, but our boy left from Number One."

"Those terminal buildings are no distance apart. Fomin could have doubled from one to the other."

"I wouldn't know, Neil. You asked us to keep an eye out for Kershaw and that's what we did. You didn't express an interest in Fomin as I recall."

"I am now," Edwards said. "It may be a little late in the day, but I'd like you to show his photograph around. Okay?"

"So long as you don't want an answer instanter. We do have other commitments."

"There's no rush, Len."

"Fine, I'll get back to you as soon as I can. By the way, my lads tell me there were two other members of the embassy staff on the Moscow flight besides the Denisenko family. A young guy with a face like a choirboy and a woman in her late thirties or early forties with a better than average figure. She was wearing dark sunglasses and had her coat collar turned up so that nobody could see too much of her face, but they thought she seemed pretty upset about something. Anyway, according to Immigration, their names are Mikhail Izveko and Natalia Rubanskaya. They haven't come to our notice before, but you could try matching them against your card index."

One of Jardine's less endearing traits was a tendency to teach his grandmother to suck eggs. Edwards managed to hold back the obvious retort and even remembered to thank him for being so helpful before he put the phone down.

A quick check showed that both Russians featured in the card index, but their respective files merely contained the original information supplied by the Foreign and Commonwealth Office when they'd first joined the embassy. According to the profile "handirefs," Mikhail Izveko was employed as a chauffeur, while Natalia Rubanskaya was listed as a clerical officer in the section controlled by Oskin, the first secretary, commerce. In Edward's view, this tied her in with Aleko Denisenko and he noted too that both Izveko and Rubanskaya were not due to be relieved of their posts until late '83. He wondered if Rubanskaya had blotted her copy book. If she had, and the offense was serious enough to warrant it, they would send her home under escort; that could explain the presence of one of the embassy chauffeurs on board the plane.

Fomin, Denisenko, Rubanskaya, Izveko, and Kershaw: the connecting thread was somewhat tenuous but it could hardly be ignored. Edwards compiled a brief aide-mémoire on his scratch pad, then rang the director general's personal assistant and arranged to see him.

The TWA flight from Paris was just over an hour from touchdown at Kennedy airport by the time he finally persuaded the D.G. that it would be advisable to give the FBI what little they had on George Kershaw.

★   ★   ★

The second postmortem on the Denisenko affair began at 1730 hours, some considerable time after the detailed report from London had arrived in the diplomatic bag, and it was conducted by Ivashutin in a manner that was more in keeping with a summary trial than a preliminary inquiry. It differed from Nikishev's first session with him in that the general had decided that his chief of staff should be present, a development Nikishev regarded with mixed feelings. From the moment Ivashutin began to read the report aloud, it was evident that he was going to be judge, jury, and prosecuting counsel all rolled into one. The chief of staff appeared to have a more ambiguous role and Nikishev wasn't sure whether it was as codefendant, defense counsel, or simply the court usher. There was, however, no doubt in his mind as to who was the accused. The hectoring tone of voice and the sly innuendos Ivashutin made at every opportunity were clear indications that Nikishev was going to be the scapegoat for everything that had happened in London. Even more incredible, it seemed that he was to blame for failing to ensure that Denisenko was whiter than white.

"You do me an injustice, Comrade General," Nikishev

interjected. "How was I to know he was having an affair with this Natalia Rubanskaya?"

"You should have asked for an up-to-date assessment of his character."

It was an absurd proposition. The operation was ultra-sensitive, and he had been specifically told by the chief of staff that he was not to contact Captain Anatoli Zotov or any other intelligence officer attached to the embassy in London. For similar security reasons, Denisenko had been briefed in the utmost secrecy by a special courier from Moscow, but only the deputy chief of the GRU was in a position to confirm these instructions, and Nikishev could see that he wasn't going to be drawn. In the circumstances, there was only one thing he could do.

"I don't understand why our people in London didn't submit a change-of-circumstance report on Denisenko," he said tentatively. "The report would seem to indicate that they had been lovers for some time. No matter how discreet they might have been, you'd have thought there would have been a certain amount of gossip."

"Nikishev has a point," the chief of staff said quietly. "To say the least, Denisenko's colleagues were less than observant."

"You think there was a lack of security awareness?" Ivashutin asked.

"Definitely. If it hadn't been for the chief archivist, we'd never have known anything about it. As it is, we've no idea just how much damage has been done to our intelligence network in England."

"Natalia Rubanskaya will tell us," Ivashutin said grimly.

"She was taken straight to Dzerzhinsky Square from the airport. I doubt if the KGB will release her to our custody."

"Nonsense. We have the right to question her. She belongs to us."

"So did Penkovsky," the chief of staff reminded him, "but they still handled the investigation. State security is their province, not ours, though I daresay they wouldn't object if we asked for an observer to be present during the interrogation. I could have a word with Vatutin if you like?"

"Do that," Ivashutin growled.

"On the other hand, we don't want to give them the impression that we are seeking to control their investigation. Thanks to Vatutin we've received a lot of help from the KGB, but he's made a number of enemies in the process and we don't want to make his life any more difficult than it is at present."

It was, Nikishev realized, the nearest either man had come to mentioning Kirov's assignment, and their reluctance to come to grips with the situation worried him. He could not forget that it was the chief of staff who had pushed Kirov to the fore and made light of Nikishev's reservations. The man was devious and too clever by half; despite the fact that he had interceded with Ivashutin on his behalf, Nikishev didn't altogether trust him.

"I take your point," Ivashutin said presently, "but we can't just sit back and do nothing."

"With respect, Comrade General, there's no reason we shouldn't conduct our own parallel investigation. We could send somebody over to London to question Zotov and the other military attachés. One has to assume the British Security Service will be on full alert, which means we'll have to provide our man with an adequate 'legend.' I suggest he should be sent as a temporary replacement for one of our officials at the trade delegation who's had to return home at short notice for compassionate reasons. We could shuffle the pack, transferring people from one embassy to another to simulate the kind of domino effect that usually occurs whenever a stopgap replacement has to be found. The German Democratic Republic would be a good jumping-off point for our man."

"How long do you need to set it up?" Ivashutin asked.

"With a little cooperation from the Foreign Ministry, he could fly to East Berlin the day after tomorrow and be in London by Friday at the latest."

"Good. Whom do you have in mind for the job?"

"Nikishev, Comrade General."

"Nikishev?"

"Why not? He knows more about Denisenko than any other officer on the staff. Besides, he also has a personal ax to grind."

Even for somebody who wasn't familiar with Ivashutin's mannerisms, the occasional but emphatic nod made his intentions transparently clear. Nikishev heaved a sigh of relief, recognizing that the temporary assignment had more plus factors going for it than adverse. Among other things, he could handle the investigation in such a way that he came out of the affair with his reputation intact, and it would also afford him an opportunity to discover just what Kirov had been up to in London. There was, however, one small problem area, and he thought it advisable to mention that his English was not all that good before the general questioned him about it and decided he was unsuitable. He need not have worried. Before Ivashutin had a chance to come back at him, the chief of staff pointed out that he wouldn't be questioning Zotov in English.

Shortly after that, the meeting broke up and Nikishev returned to the training school. Although it was after eight, he stopped in at his office to clear the in-tray before going home. Apart from a batch of training notes issued by the commandant, he found a brief memo from Moscow Military District Headquarters that was attached to a transport requisition apparently signed by him. The requisition was dated the twenty-seventh of October and required the motor pool to provide a Zil truck to collect personnel and baggage from the airport. The memo asked him to explain why the vehicle in question had clocked 100 miles when the round trip was only 34.

Nikishev opened his desk diary, saw that 27 October was the day Kirov had arrived in Moscow after leaving Colonel Leonid Paskar's intelligence unit near the Afghan border, and assumed the motor pool had sent a Zil truck instead of a staff car to collect him from the airport. Wasting no further time on what he regarded as a typical foul-up by district headquarters, Nikishev drafted an equally brief reply. In it he stated that the vehicle had obviously been misused by Major Kirov, who would be required to account for the excess journey as soon as he returned to Moscow.

Nikishev could not have anticipated that this memo would prove to be the biggest mistake he'd ever made. It would be a major cause of his own destruction in a way that even Vatutin had not foreseen when he'd baited the trap for him.

★   ★   ★

Kirov checked into the Travel Lodge on West 42nd Street, carried his bags up to the single room on the fourth floor, and started unpacking. There had been a few anxious moments at Kennedy airport when an Immigration official had asked to see his work permit, but the forged document, like his passport, had been accepted without comment. From Kennedy he'd taken the IND subway to the Avenue of the Americas, where he'd flagged down a cab to complete the final leg of his journey. London to New York via Dublin and Paris: he wondered if the long detour had been worth all the effort. If his assumption was correct and the men who'd killed Denisenko had been waiting for him at Heathrow, then his unexpected diversion to Ireland could well have given them a nasty surprise. It would be nice to think that it had also caused them to distrust the information they'd extracted from their victim, but that was too much to hope for.

As far as Kirov could tell, nobody had followed him from the airport and until he'd picked up one of their leaflets from a travel agency in Dublin, he'd never heard of the Travel Lodge hotel chain. That didn't mean he was safe; to cash some of the traveler's checks, he'd had to register as George Kershaw, and if the opposition was looking for him, they'd start calling all the hotels in town. To assume a new identity was easier said than done. It wasn't just a question of using a different name; hard evidence was needed to support a "legend," and he didn't have either the time or the necessary backup to produce a new Social Security card, driver's license, and the like. Under the circumstances, his only recourse was to ensure that he was always one move ahead of the anti-Romanov faction in the KGB.

Kirov opened his briefcase, took out the Michelin guide to New England that he'd purchased in Dublin, and carefully plotted a route to New Haven. That done, he then checked the telephone directory for Manhattan.

"I have two sisters, one older than me, one younger," Moorcroft had told him. "Helen's the elder; she's married to a geologist, has four kids, and lives in San Francisco. We still write to each other occasionally, but Liz is the one I really get on with. She's twenty-five going on twenty-six and is very bright. She majored in English Lit at N.Y.U. and was an editor with Putnam's before she became a literary agent with Samuels and Stein."

Moorcroft E.L. 71 East 59th Street. Kirov stared at the entry for some moments, then slowly lifted the receiver from the bedside phone and punched out her number. It rang half a dozen times before the girl with a cheerful voice answered the call.

"Miss Elizabeth Moorcroft?" he asked politely.

"Yes. Who's this?"

"My name's George Kershaw," Kirov told her. "We haven't met, but I got to know your brother, Russell, pretty well when I was working in Pakistan."

"You know Russell?" Her voice a mixture of delight and incredulity.

"We ran into each other in a little place called Miram Shah. That's in the Waziristan Province up on the northwest frontier."

"How is he?"

"Suntanned, fit, and healthy," Kirov said, and hated himself for the lie.

"When did you last see Russell? Why hasn't he written?"

The questions came thick and fast and he fielded them all, drawing on the reservoir of knowledge he'd acquired from the interrogation. Anxious not to force the pace, Kirov waited patiently for an opportune moment to make a tenuous contact a shade closer. It came when Elizabeth Moorcroft asked him if Russell had mentioned when he might be coming home.

"I doubt if you'll see him before the New Year," Kirov said, and once more squirmed inwardly. "As a matter of fact, when Russell heard I expected to be home in time for Christmas he asked if I had room for a small present he'd bought you."

"A present? Now I feel awful. I haven't given Christmas

a thought yet. But that's typical of Russell; he always did spoil me. I wonder what it can be?"

"Russell didn't say, except that it was fragile and would I deliver it in person."

There was a long pause and Kirov pictured her frowning and feverishly thinking of a place where they could have the briefest and most public of meetings.

"I realize it may not be convenient," he added hastily, "but it so happens I'm going to be in New York tomorrow evening. Perhaps we could meet somewhere?"

This time there was an even longer pause, and he could hear Elizabeth Moorcroft sucking her teeth as she considered his suggestion. Then finally she asked him if he knew the Top of the Sixes.

"Who doesn't?" Kirov said.

"Well, okay, suppose we meet in the cocktail lounge around six?"

"I'll look forward to it, Miss Moorcroft."

"So shall I," she said and sounded as though she meant it.

Kirov heard a faint click followed by a continuous burr and slowly replaced the receiver. He had cleared the first hurdle, but there were others in his path that were even more formidable.

Finding a Yellow Pages on the shelf beneath the bedside table, he searched the entries looking for an Indian gift shop that was still open.

CHAPTER XV

The Ford sedan was described as a compact, though it didn't seem particularly small to Kirov. From the Hertz rental agency on West 42nd Street, he had gingerly picked his way uptown on Tenth Avenue, Amsterdam, and Broadway, and on across the George Washington Bridge in a state of hyper-tension, worried that at each intersection he was either going to ram the car in front or somebody was going to shunt into him. He'd begun to feel a little more confident by the time he'd cleared the Cross Bronx Expressway and was heading out of New York on Interstate 95, and it wasn't only because the traffic was correspondingly lighter. There was, he thought, an air of brooding malevolence about Upper Manhattan and the Bronx that was decidedly intimidating. Originally, he'd thought that Tudin, the American defector who'd briefed him at Mozhaysk, had simply been making political capital with his cautionary tales of crime and violence in the inner cities, but now, having seen the decaying tenements at firsthand, he'd rapidly altered his opinion.

The feeling of unease had vanished as soon as he'd started driving through Fairfield County. There was a sense of freedom, of space to live, and an absence of the fear that prevailed in the concrete jungle of the city. It wasn't difficult to understand the attraction a small town like Greenwich would have for those who could afford to commute back and forth to New York. Why live in Manhattan when the sandy beaches of Long Island Sound, the oak, hickory, maple, and white pine woods around the villages of New Canaan and Ridgefield were less than an hour from the metropolis? On such a bright sunny day, he couldn't help thinking that it was going to take a lot more than what he had to offer to lure Vera Berggolts away from her new homeland.

Kirov wondered how he could raise the offer should the lady prove to be sales-resistant. Show your face in Moscow for a year, then quietly slip away again if America still means that much to you? Even a person like Vera Berggolts, who was used to being spoiled, might find that proposition a bit hard to swallow, but he doubted if she would reject his overtures out of hand. The gold ring with three rubies set in a triangle that Nikishev had given him the night before he'd left for Budapest would at least persuade her that there was no harm in phoning Helsinki. The rest would then be up to her father-in-law; if Grigory Romanov really wanted to move into the Kremlin, he might well have to promise her the moon and the stars above.

Norwalk, Fairfield, Stratford, and on across the mouth

of the Housatonic River; Kirov drove steadily toward an uncertain rendezvous, one eye constantly checking the speedometer to ensure that he didn't exceed the fifty-five-mile-an-hour restriction. He passed the connecting link to the Wilbur Cross Parkway, then Exit 39 to Milford, and instinctively eased his foot on the accelerator, knowing that around the next bend he would be approaching the outskirts of West Haven.

The key landmarks he'd noted from the Michelin guide started coming up: the turnoff for Route 122, a large cemetery on the left-hand side of the road, the bridge over First Avenue. A half-mile beyond West River, Kirov left Interstate 95 and headed into New Haven on Howard Avenue. Shortly after turning right onto Spring Street, he parked next to a phone booth to call the number he'd been given.

The woman he spoke to had a brisk, almost aggressive manner and was extremely fluent, as though English were her native tongue. Later, when he checked the directory, Kirov discovered that the Willets were not listed, nor could he find any other subscriber residing on Constitution Avenue, which suggested the address, like her surname, was equally fictitious. Only the fact that she'd made the correct responses after he'd apologized for having mistaken her for somebody else persuaded him that he'd been talking to the former Vera Berggolts. Returning to his car, he drove on to Church Street, went past the cylindrical-towered Knights of Columbus building, and parked alongside The Green.

Romanov was a scientist specializing in metallurgy and had been in charge of a research team at the Izhorsky factory in Leningrad before he'd defected. Although it was likely he'd obtained the appointment largely through nepotism, Kirov assumed that he must have possessed the necessary qualifications for the job. Of course, as the son of a prominent figure in the Soviet hierarchy, he would have been welcomed with open arms by the Americans, but there was a limit even to their generosity, and Romanov could never have become a faculty member at Yale unless he had something to offer. The state of Connecticut had a thriving arms industry; the Colt revolver and Winchester rifle were manufactured in Hartford, and the world's first nuclear-powered submarine had been built by the Electric Boat Division of General Dynamics at Groton. Whether or not Romanov was engaged in defense research was immaterial; what mattered was the fact that the FBI had given him a new identity and was obviously still responsible for his protection. Viewing the situation dispassionately, Kirov figured that he was threatened on two fronts; by the agents who were guarding Romanov in New Haven and by the highly placed source in Washington who had blown his cover to Soviet Intelligence.

The operation was a setup engineered by the KGB. Kirov had suspected something of the kind right from the very beginning when he'd allegedly broken Moorcroft. The KGB people weren't in Grigory Romanov's camp; their aim was to destroy the Party boss of Leningrad before he became a serious contender for the leadership. In furtherance of this objective, they had killed Denisenko and now they were about to move in on him, or rather the FBI was. "Russian Spy Arrested in New Haven," "FBI Grabs Red Agent on Yale Campus"; he could visualize the banner headlines in the quality newspapers and the tabloids. By the time the Sundays were going to press, investigative journalists would have dug up enough additional material for one of their in-depth authoritative exposés that usually raised more questions than they answered:

In New Haven on Tuesday, November 9, at 10:45 A.M., FBI agents swooped on Church Street and apprehended Georgi Kirov alias George Kershaw. Kirov, a thirty-two-year-old major in the GRU, was sitting in a Ford compact he'd rented in New York earlier that day from a Hertz rental agency on West 42nd Street. The sedan was parked a short distance from the ivy-covered Connecticut Hall, Yale's oldest structure, and several eyewitnesses who saw the arrest swear that Kirov had been there for only ten or fifteen mi   s when the FBI closed in on him. The incident raise   o intriguing questions. Who was Kirov waiting for ?   now was it the FBI was able to apprehend him less tha   venty-four hours after he'd arrived from Paris by TV   ?"

A Chrysler Imperial turned onto Church Street from the direction of Whitney Avenue and cruised slowly past him. There had been a steady procession of vehicles during the time Kirov had been waiting, but this particular limousine happened to be unique. It was dark blue, the license number tallied with the details Nikishev had given him, and the driver and sole occupant was a dark-haired young woman whose face, even in profile, was instantly recognizable. Vera Berggolts, right on time and heading toward the prearranged rendezvous. Kirov checked that the road behind was clear and pulled out from the curb.

The second level of the parking lot on Water Street was hardly the most original rendezvous and was a typical example of Moscow playing it safe. The biggest parking lot in town was the kind of landmark a complete stranger could easily find; anything less obvious and there was a risk they would have been waiting for each other at two separate locations.

Kirov reversed the compact into a vacant slot to the right of the ramp, then walked over to the Chrysler, which was parked across the way, its nose facing the external parapet. Vera Berggolts had moved along the bench seat and was peering into the vanity mirror in the glove compartment, busily repairing her makeup. He walked down the left side of the limousine, opened the door, and got in. Slowly and very deliberately, Kirov crooked his right elbow and showed her the gold ring on his little finger.

"You recognize this, don't you?" he asked her quietly.

"Of course I do. It belongs to my father-in-law." Vera Berggolts turned away from him and peered into the vanity mirror again to inspect the lipstick she'd applied to her mouth. "I presume you have a message from him."

"He'd like you to come home," Kirov said.

"So what's new about that?"

"The difference is that Romanov's all set to move into the Kremlin."

"If that's what Grigory wants, then I'm happy for him." Vera Berggolts exchanged the lipstick for a comb, which she ran through her short dark hair a few times before putting it away in her handbag. "But it isn't for us. We like it here," she added.

"I heard different," Kirov told her coldly. "The American way of life might suit you, but your husband wants to go back."

"Nonsense. Mischa is perfectly happy so long as he's with me."

"It was another way of saying that she had Mischa Romanov under her thumb, though for the life of him, Kirov couldn't see why. Vera Berggolts was attractive but far from beautiful; she was on the small side and beginning to lose her athletic figure. Beauty was said to be only skin-deep, but if she possessed an inner warmth and vitality it wasn't reflected in her face, which looked sulky. In the end, though, it didn't matter what he thought of her; to Mischa Romanov she was the entire universe and he'd do well to remember that.

"You may think you have a good life here," Kirov said slowly, "but Grigory Romanov could give you a better one."

"I bet."

"All you have to do is talk to him."

"I'm not interested in anything he has to say."

"Then what are you doing here?" he snapped.

It would have given Kirov a great deal of satisfaction if he'd been able to grab Vera Berggolts by the collar and shake her until her teeth rattled. He couldn't, because he had Irena and Fedor Fedorovich to consider; their safety ultimately depended on his being nice to this selfish little bitch.

"I'm sorry," he said contritely. "I didn't mean to shout my mouth off, but I just couldn't understand why you'd bothered to come if that was the way you felt. I still can't, as a matter of fact."

"I came because I have a message for Grigory Romanov."

"A message?"

"Yes. I want you to tell him to leave me alone."

"Oh, no. He'll have to hear it from you. Romanov won't buy it secondhand from me."

"That's your problem, not mine."

209

"You're wrong there. Can't you see he'll keep on pestering you unless he's convinced it's a waste of time?" Kirov forced a smile. It wasn't an easy thing to do when he was more inclined to grit his teeth in anger, and his face felt as though it was about to crack in two. "Look, it's no big deal, Vera. All you have to do is phone the Inter-Continental Hotel in Helsinki the day after tomorrow and ask for Mr. Willetowski. Where's the harm in that?"

"Are you threatening me?"

"Come again?"

"I think you are trying to intimidate me."

She wasn't just saying it for his benefit. Her speech was a shade too deliberate, as though she were anxious that a third party should catch every word. The mike was somewhere in front of her, possibly inside the glove compartment and no bigger than a pinhead. He looked down, saw that the key was still in the ignition, and switched on the auxiliary circuit.

"Don't be silly; what good would that do? I can't force you to talk to Grigory." Kirov switched on the car radio and began to search up and down the wave band. In the process, he produced a high-decibel oscillating noise that was guaranteed to drive any would-be eavesdropper nuts. "But somebody else might," he continued softly.

"Get out. Get out of my car."

"And if I refuse? What will you do, call for help?"

"I'd be wasting my breath. Who's going to hear me?"

There was a gray Dodge pickup parked nose first into a bay twenty feet to his left. Kirov had noticed the vehicle as he'd approached the Chrysler, but hadn't paid much attention to it then. Now, it had begun to look decidedly ominous.

"Your friends lurking in the gray van over there," he told her. "You holler loud enough and they'll come running."

"You're crazy."

"And you're a lousy actress, Vera. You may know your lines, but you're wooden and lack emotion. And that's odd, because I know the FBI has a wiretap on your phone and you should have been apprehensive in case they'd followed you here."

"I learned to control my emotions when I was an athlete."

210

"Bullshit. You've kept the FBI informed ever since our people first made contact. They knew where the rendezvous was going to be long before I arrived on the scene, and you kept me waiting on The Green until they'd moved their van into position."

Vera Berggolts didn't have to say anything; her silence was eloquent in itself. A station wagon cruised past them and went on up to the third level, its tires screeching as the driver made a tight right-hand turn into the ramp.

"The next move is up to you," Kirov said quietly. "The FBI could put me away but, if I were you, I wouldn't be in too much of a hurry to call them over. Moscow will only send another courier, and he won't be quite so reasonable. You've made yourself a lot of enemies, Vera, and some of them prefer action to negotiation. To put it another way, you've been likened to a malignant tumor on Romanov's brain; the physicians among us have prescribed a course of radium treatment, the surgeons want to reach for the knife. However, both parties are agreed on the diagnosis; provided the tumor is neutralized, Mischa Romanov will make a complete recovery and come to his senses."

"What are you trying to tell me?"

Kirov wondered why he should be surprised the allusion had escaped her. Vera Berggolts might be lucid where her own narrow field of athletics was concerned, but she was not overly bright about anything else.

"Leonid Ilyich Brezhnev is a very sick man," Kirov said, spelling it out. "His life expectancy is uncertain, but it could be you'll make it to the grave before he does. Naturally, Mischa will be heartbroken, but he won't suspect anything, nor will anyone else. Your death will be attributed to natural causes."

Kirov was unaware of any such contingency plan and doubted if one existed. However, although the projected scenario was a figment of his imagination, thanks to their germ warfare specialists, the GRU possessed the technical know-how and the bacteriological means to liquidate her. Whether it would ever come to that was irrelevant; he had set out to convince Vera Berggolts that her life was in real danger and had succeeded in doing so.

"I don't have much choice, do I?" she said wearily.

"Not a lot."

"So what do I say to Grigory?"

Vera Berggolts revealed a childlike impetuosity, wanting to run before she had learned to walk. In a few terse sentences, Kirov laid down the guidelines she was to follow when the FBI grilled her about their meeting, then told her where, when, and how she was to contact Grigory Romanov.

"You make it sound so easy," she complained, "but suppose they try to prevent me from going to New York? What happens then?"

"You'll think of something, Vera. If worse comes to worst, you could tell them that your father's life will be at risk if they stop you. The Americans may not believe it but they won't take any chances."

"And if they have me followed?"

"You let me worry about that," Kirov said grimly. "You just be at Grand Central the day after tomorrow at twelve noon."

Kirov cranked the engine into life, released the hand brake, and shifted the gear lever into reverse. Backing out of the slot, he put the wheel hard over to the left and kept on reversing until the tail end of the Chrysler was dead in line with the Dodge pickup. Then, satisfied that he'd boxed in the other vehicle and that nobody in the back could get out, he applied the hand brake again, selected forward drive, and deliberately stalled the engine. With the gearshift in drive and the hand brake still on, he restarted the car and put his foot down on the accelerator. Like a startled kangaroo, the car jumped forward and stalled.

"You get the idea?" Kirov said. "I want you to keep doing that until I've got a head start on your friends."

Kirov opened the door, scrambled out of the Chrysler, and made it to the Ford in double-quick time. By now, Vera Berggolts had taken his place behind the wheel, and as he pulled out to head for the exit ramp he caught a final glimpse of her in his rearview mirror, her small, heart-shaped face wearing an anxious expression that reflected his own feelings. Down on the first level, he tucked in behind a battered-looking Volkswagen that had suddenly nipped out of a parking bay, but they eventually parted company at the intersection of Whitney and Congress avenues.

He took a different route back to New York, a decision largely influenced by a supposition that by going on back roads he was unlikely to encounter too many patrol cars belonging to the State Police. It had also been drummed into him when he was an infantryman that you didn't retrace your steps in enemy country, and old maxims tend to linger in the mind. Avoiding Interstate 95, he made a wide detour taking in Derby, Danbury, Ridgefield, the foothills of the Appalachians, and the Saw Mill River Parkway. If he was being shadowed by the FBI, he wasn't aware of it. He did, however, get himself hopelessly lost coming into New York and somehow managed to end up in Brooklyn.

★   ★   ★

Aaron Hines was a mild, inoffensive little man of fifty-six who, had he been an actor, would have gone through life forever being typecast in the role of a small-town draper. He was in fact a small-town lawyer from Iowa whose appearance was completely at odds with the clean-cut image most people had of a typical law enforcement officer in the Federal Bureau of Investigation. Hines had joined the bureau in 1952 during the halcyon days of McCarthyism and had been involved in peripheral work for the Senate sub-committee on un-American activities chaired by the senator from Wisconsin. As a newcomer, he had investigated the lesser fry, the bit players as opposed to the movie stars, university lecturers rather than the heads of departments, and in so doing had gained a reputation for being thorough, open-minded, and scrupulously fair.

Despite these sterling qualities, Hines had never been regarded as a flyer and, as a result, promotion had come slowly. When, after seventeen years' service, he'd been sent to Hartford to fill the number two slot in the bureau's Connecticut office, everybody had agreed that he'd reached his ceiling. Eight months later, the bureau chief had been killed in a traffic accident and Hines had stepped into his shoes. Although at the time Washington had made it very clear that this was purely a temporary arrangement until a suitable replacement could be found, they never had gotten around to nominating a successor. Instead, they'd waited until 1975 before confirming him in the appointment, which Hines, with characteristic good humor, attributed to embarrassment on their part rather than a belated recognition of his abilities.

In the major crime league, the state of Connecticut was near the bottom of the table and the job of bureau chief was not therefore a particularly challenging one, which had suited him down to a tee. Things had heated up on a different front during the Nixon administration, but with consummate tact and not inconsiderable skill, Hines had managed to circumvent the more outrageous demands emanating from the White House. Consequently, there had been no widespread use of phone taps, and in the campaign against subversives, antiwar demonstrators, pinkos, and liberals whom Nixon had been determined to expose, the program for recruiting informers among the students at Yale had been quietly shelved. Although Hines hadn't advertised it, the faculty had been able to put two and two together and had developed a high regard for him. Years later, this was to make his job of protecting the Willetses considerably easier than it might have been.

Vera and Matthew Willets had been in his care since the fall of 1979. In common with other defectors, they had been provided with new identities, and Washington had deliberately withheld details of their former lives from Hines in the interests of security. His knowledge of them was therefore confined to the "legends" concocted by the State Department in conjunction with the FBI, and while these offered a number of clues to their respective backgrounds, none was sufficiently revealing for him to guess who they really were. Vera had obviously been an athlete at some time or other and Matthew was a scientist, but their achievements had not attracted the kind of publicity that would have brought them international recognition. The fact that the FBI had placed them in the low-risk category was another reason he'd assumed the Willetses had been relatively obscure people in their native country.

Until recently, he'd had no cause to revise this assessment

of them. It was true that in the early spring of '81 Matthew Willets had been a little depressed on occasions, and one of the counselors had reported that he'd spoken wistfully of his native land, but his mood had rapidly changed and he'd appeared to snap out of it. Then, six months ago, life had begun to get hectic. On Monday the tenth of May, Vera had gone to New York on one of her regular shopping sprees and had picked up a free offer outside Gimbels from a complete stranger who had put a name to her. Hines hadn't liked that; neither had Carl Landers, the link man in Washington. Between them, they'd decided there would be no more jaunts to the big city, but it hadn't made any difference. The opposition had gotten their hooks into Vera and knew her too well—her habits, where she went, how she spent her time. And they'd started bombarding her with messages until the whole of New Haven had become one goddamned dead-letter box.

There were recognized procedures for dealing with such an emergency, but Washington had ignored his advice and decided to play a waiting game. "We have our reasons," Landers had told him loftily, "and Vera's a cool enough lady to handle the situation." After what had happened in the parking lot, Hines was beginning to doubt it. Returning to Hartford and his office in Constitution Plaza, he called Washington on the scrambler and briefed Landers. Without wasting words, Hines told him just why he was unhappy about the way Vera had behaved.

"I think she tipped the guy off," Hines said, winding up. "One moment we could hear them perfectly, then he starts fiddling with the radio and we end up catching one word in five."

"This was after Vera said she thought he was trying to intimidate her?" Landers asked.

"Right."

"And was he?"

"According to Vera he was. She claims that he said her life would be at risk if she refused to cooperate. I guess he must have scared the pants off her because she certainly helped him make a clean getaway. We could have grabbed him but for her."

215

"That was never the intention, Aaron."

He didn't need Landers to remind him. "I'm aware of that," he said calmly. "Question is, Carl, how do we play it from now on?"

"This courier," Landers said, ducking the issue. "Let's have his description again."

"What for? I already told you we're developing a batch of photographs."

"Just do as I ask, Aaron. Okay?"

"Well, okay, if that's how you want it. He's fairly tall, between five-eleven and six foot, weighs around one-seventy, has dark brown hair and carries himself erect like a Marine."

"Sounds as if he could be the mysterious George Kershaw."

"Who?"

"George Kershaw. A guy by the name of Edwards called us from London yesterday evening hinting he could be a Soviet agent. Edwards was pretty cagey and he told us kind of late; by the time our New York office got onto it, Kershaw had already cleared Immigration."

"Terrific. I knew we should have grabbed him when we had the chance."

"Nothing's changed, Aaron. He's still there for the taking."

It was some moments before the implication sank in. When it did, Hines wondered if the people in Washington knew what they were doing. "Are you proposing that Vera should meet Kershaw again?" he asked incredulously.

"She has to."

"Why?"

"I can't tell you that."

"I'm responsible for her safety, Carl," Hines reminded him. "I've a right to know."

"The decision was taken at the highest level. If you don't like it, Aaron, take the matter up with the director."

"Don't worry, I will."

"That's your privilege," Landers said and hung up on him.

Hines broke the connection, started to dial the director's

number, then had second thoughts. Telephone conversations were often omitted from the record, and he wanted his reservations placed in the file. When confronted with the almost certain probability that the Soviets had access to a highly placed source within the FBI, it was only prudent to state the case in writing.

Chapter XVI

She arrived alone, a fairly tall, slender girl with ash blond hair that stopped just short of being shoulder length. Her eyes were set well apart in a face notable for its prominent cheekbones, classic Roman nose, and firm jaw. Despite the slightly defiant tilt of her chin as she gazed around the room, an otherwise severe image was softened by a gentle mouth on which there was a tentative smile. Observing her closely, Kirov thought he detected a family resemblance; the fact that she'd also arrived more or less on time and was clearly hoping that somewhere in the crowded bar at the Top of the Sixes someone would recognize her clinched it as far as he was concerned, and he moved purposefully toward her.

"Miss Elizabeth Moorcroft?" he inquired politely.

"Yes."

"My name's George Kershaw," Kirov told her.

The smile was no longer uncertain and she shook his outstretched hand with something approaching relief, as though she'd feared his phone call the previous evening might have been a cruel hoax.

"How clever of you to recognize me," she said.

"Not really. Russell gave me a very full description and I can see the family likeness." Kirov gently steered her toward the spot he'd been occupying at the bar and pulled out a stool. "But he wasn't quite so forthcoming about your likes and dislikes." He grinned at her and said, "In other words, what can I get you to drink?"

"The same as you, please, a Scotch on the rocks."

Kirov signaled the bartender, pointed to his half-empty glass, and told him to make it two of the same with plenty of ice. Then, delving into his jacket pocket, he produced the small box containing the jade brooch he'd purchased the previous evening.

"Before I forget," he said, "here's the little something Russell asked me to deliver in person."

She unfastened the tiny clasp and opened the jewel box. A small frown appeared the instant she saw the name of the Fifth Avenue Indian gift shop inside the lid. "I don't understand . . ." she began.

"Well, it's really very simple, Miss Moorcroft," Kirov said, cutting her short. "Russell asked me if I'd get you that brooch, or something very similar, next time I was in New York. He didn't trust the mail, figured the brooch would become missing long before it left Pakistan. I'm afraid I told you a small lie when I phoned you last evening."

"You're forgiven," she said quietly.

"That's a relief."

"I hope my brother remembered to give you the money for it."

"Cash in advance," Kirov told her, then raised his glass and said, "Cheers."

"Cheers."

"I hope our choice meets with your approval?"

"It's beautiful, just what I wanted." She placed her glass on the bar and carefully pinned the brooch onto a lapel of the green dress she was wearing under a showerproof raincoat. "Where did you say you ran into Russ?" she asked, still examining the jade.

"In Miram Shah, a flea-ridden dump in Waziristan near the Afghan border. You name it, Miram Shah had it—heat, dirt, flies, dysentery, scrub typhus. I tell you it's no place for a tourist."

"Yet Russ is suntanned, fit, and healthy."

She quoted his words back at him and looked up, her cool gray eyes searching his face quizzically. Yesterday's lie was now a booby trap that would have to be carefully defused if he was going to use this girl as a means of protecting Irena and Fedor Fedorovich.

"You can hardly fail to acquire a suntan when the average temperature is a hundred and three in the shade."

Kirov was talking on one plane, thinking on another. To his younger sister, Moorcroft had been Russ; he wondered if anybody outside the family circle had called him that. His close friends, perhaps? No matter how long an interrogation lasted, there were always some fine points of detail that got overlooked, especially when the prime object was to obtain military intelligence.

"But he was definitely fit?" she persisted.

"I guess he was much thinner than when you last saw him," Kirov said, squirming inwardly.

"And how did the climate affect you, Mr. Kershaw?"

"It didn't." Kirov glanced about him and instinctively lowered his voice. "You see, I fought my war behind a desk in an air-conditioned office I shared with George Lamar."

"George Lamar?"

"Yes, an itty-bitty fella, about five foot six, fat as a barrel and in his mid-forties."

"Oh?"

Elizabeth's tone of voice was a clear indication that she had never heard of him. Kirov thought that there were two possibilities: either Moorcroft had deliberately misled him and there was no such person, or else he'd never mentioned him in any of his letters.

"Your brother didn't care much for him," he continued softly. "As a matter of fact, Lamar wasn't exactly popular with his two sergeants either. I don't recall Silverman or Opalko ever having a good word to say for him."

"Henry Silverman?"

From Chicago, Kirov told her, and knew by her reaction that he was on surer ground. Silverman, quick-witted and hard-nosed, so very different from the slow-speaking Jerry Opalko from Omaha, Nebraska. With growing confidence, he doled out the background information Moorcroft had given him and in the telling of it gave Elizabeth the impression that he knew them well.

"Russ is dead, isn't he?"

Kirov avoided her gaze and stared at the pinpoints of light from the continuous stream of traffic moving south on Fifth

Avenue four hundred feet below the plate-glass window. It wasn't so much a question as a quiet acceptance of the truth as she saw it, and he didn't know what to say to her.

"What have you been told officially?" he asked, hedging.

"Nothing."

It figured. Had the Pentagon previously informed Elizabeth that her brother was missing in action, her reaction to his phone call last night would have been very different. She certainly wouldn't have asked him why Russell hadn't written to her; on the contrary, she would have been anxious to know if the army had now learned that he was safe and well.

"Then I don't think we should jump to any conclusions," he said, still feeling his way.

"I know you mean well, Mr. Kershaw, but why pretend? Russ nominated me as his next of kin, and I don't think you'd be here unless something bad had happened to him."

"The army didn't send me. I got in touch because I knew your brother and liked him." That much happened to be true, even though he did have an ulterior motive for contacting Elizabeth Moorcroft.

"You mean you don't have official permission to see me?" Elizabeth shook her head as if she found the whole idea incredible. "You obviously believe in living dangerously, Mr. Kershaw," she added dryly.

Kirov reached for his glass, the alarm bells ringing in his head. There was only one explanation for her cryptic remark that he could think of. When letters from her brother had stopped coming, Elizabeth had tried to discover what had happened to him and had run into trouble.

"Have those people in Washington been giving you a hard time?" he asked casually.

"You could say that."

"You want to tell me about it?"

"There's not a lot to tell. Russ wrote to me back in April hinting between the lines that he'd been given a job to do and that I wasn't to worry if I didn't hear from him for a few weeks or so. When September came around and there was still no word from him, I called the Pentagon and got nowhere fast. Every officer I spoke to denied all knowledge of Russ and referred me to another department. I even went down to Washington to see my Congressman, but he too was singularly unhelpful. Finally, in sheer desperation, I called the CIA, and one evening a week later somebody from the National Security Agency or the FBI came to my apartment to warn me that I could find myself in all kinds of difficulties if I persisted in making waves."

Kirov wasn't surprised to learn that the authorities had tried to lean on her. He'd never supposed that the KGB was the only institution that resorted to intimidation when it was a question of safeguarding the interests of the state. The essential difference between the Soviet Union and the United States was the fact that the American government had to contend with a free press. *Pravda* was merely the propaganda mouthpiece for the Politburo; newspapers like the *Washington Post* could, and had, changed the course of history. If dissidents like Solzhenitsyn owed their freedom to such newspapers, then, with the right kind of publicity, it was not inconceivable that the foreign press could make the people at the Kremlin think twice before they turned on Irena and Fedor Fedorovich.

"What exactly is the Worldwide Famine Relief Team, Mr. Kershaw?"

"My friends call me George." Kirov smiled. "And I think you already know the answer to that question."

"Please. I'd still like to hear it from you."

"Well, okay, it's the cover name for the 2028th Special Forces Advisery Group."

"The Pentagon claims there is no such unit. So does the CIA. In fact, they claim that Russ, Jerry Opalko, and Henry Silverman are mercenaries. The CIA also said they had evidence that my brother was making a nice thing out of running guns into Afghanistan."

"That's a load of rubbish. Your brother is an army officer; his serial number is JA 614003."

"And what are you, George?" she asked him quietly.

"The same." He was also a hypocritical liar who was finding it increasingly difficult to live with the fact.

"Russ carried a lot of life insurance, a hundred thousand dollars all risks."

And naturally the insurance company would refuse to pay up until they were satisfied that Moorcroft was dead. He wondered how long Elizabeth would have to wait if she couldn't prove it. Five years? Seven?

"I know what you're thinking, George, but it isn't like that."

"You don't have to explain anything to me," he said tersely.

"Oh, but I do." She paused, then said, "I don't suppose Russ told you he had a child, did he?"

"No." Kirov felt his jaw drop and closed it hurriedly.

"I'm not surprised. In many ways, my brother was a very private person."

Moorcroft had begun a disastrous marriage shortly after he'd been commissioned into the infantry. His bride had been four months pregnant at the time, and in March 1977 she had given birth to a baby daughter. Less than a year later she had walked out on him, unable to face the fact that their child was a Mongol.

"Her name's Victoria," Elizabeth continued, "and she lives with my parents over on Staten Island. However, Victoria is now five years old and the time is fast approaching when, to realize her full potential, it's essential we send her to a special school for Down's syndrome children."

And that would cost a lot of money, Kirov thought. But he was only partially right; in the next breath Elizabeth told him that Victoria's education was not a problem because the whole family was prepared to contribute, and that included her brother-in-law, the geologist in San Francisco, who had four children of his own to provide for. No, it was the long-term future she was concerned about, the time when inevitably Victoria would find herself alone in the world.

"Properly invested, a hundred thousand dollars could provide a trust fund that would yield a comfortable income for the rest of her life."

"I guess it would," Kirov murmured.

"Unfortunately, the premiums on the insurance policy are paid by standing order twice a year, in June and December. I know the June installment was met, but the policy will lapse if the bank terminates the standing order, which could happen next month. Now perhaps you can understand why I have to know what's happened to Russ. The question is, can you help me, George?"

"How?"

"That's for you to answer."

Kirov had two options; either he could pretend that he hadn't the faintest idea what had happened to Moorcroft in Afghanistan or else he could give Elizabeth the basic facts and leave her to draw her own conclusions. It took him less than a minute to make up his mind.

"All right," he said, "I'll tell you what I know, but not here."

"Where, then?"

His hotel? He'd checked into the Claredon on East 31st Street that afternoon, but neither the bar nor the restaurant was likely to offer the kind of privacy they needed. He toyed with the idea of inviting her up to his room, then rejected it out of hand.

"My office is only a few minutes from here," Elizabeth suggested quietly.

"So what are we waiting for?" he said.

The literary agency of Samuels and Stein was located on the third floor of a narrow graystone at 32 East 50th Street, one block beyond Saks and facing the Irish Consulate. Somewhat low down in the pecking order, Elizabeth had to make do with a small office at the back of the building that overlooked an equally small courtyard. The room, oblong in shape, measured roughly twelve feet by eight but seemed narrower because of a floor-to-ceiling bookshelf that took up the whole of one wall. To create a sense of space, Elizabeth had positioned her desk diagonally across the bottom right-hand corner, but the desired effect was spoiled by four filing trays overflowing with typescripts. Opposite the desk there was a club chair, and next to it a low coffee table that was also buried under a pile of manuscripts.

"It is kind of crowded," Elizabeth admitted, "but I like it." She waved a hand at the crammed bookshelves. "Of course, not all those authors are on my list; it's just that Herbie doesn't have room for them in his office."

"Herbie?" Kirov lowered himself into the club chair.

"Herbie Stein." Elizabeth moved around the desk, opened a drawer, and took out a battery-powered Sony tape recorder. "Would you mind if we used this, George?" she asked.

Kirov hesitated fractionally, then slowly shook his head.

"You're a good man, George. Not too many people in your position would go out on a limb for a complete stranger."

A good man? Kirov wanted to scream the truth aloud and tell her who and what he was, then see if she still thought he was marvelous. Shit. Shit. Shit.

"Whenever you're ready, George," Elizabeth said in a quiet voice. She was crouching by the low coffee table now, holding the mike toward him. "Just press this little button when you want to speak."

"Sure." He reached for the mike and touched her hand briefly. You're beautiful, he thought, and looked hurriedly away, unnerved by a sudden tight feeling in his chest. "Well, okay," he said hoarsely, "here goes," then rattled off her brother's name, rank, and serial number and took a deep breath.

"Russell left Miram Shah on the nineteenth of April and crossed over into Afghanistan. George Lamar, the resident CIA officer, had given him a twofold mission: to link up with Daoud Khan, the leader of the Paghman faction, and to generally make life hell for the Soviet-backed forces operating in the Khinjan Valley. We've good reason to believe he did just that."

The rest came easy; he described the ambush that had taken place on the seventh of June eight miles from the village of Doshi. His narrative was based on the report submitted by the Soviet ground force commander, leavened by what Moorcroft had eventually told him, and he didn't find it at all difficult to strike the right attitude. In Pata Kasai, he'd been very angry about the nineteen Russian soldiers who'd been killed and wounded in action, but now the memory of a skeletal figure in hospital fatigues whose right leg had been amputated above the knee weighed far more heavily on his conscience.

"He should have made tracks before the Russians had a

224

chance to react," Kirov said in the same dispassionate voice, "but I guess that's easier said than done. The guerrilla band Russell was attached to are a pretty wild bunch and they don't take kindly to discipline, especially when a foreigner is trying to impose it. Anyway, it seems that they were still in the area when a company of Soviet paratroopers arrived by helicopter. According to Sergeants Henry Silverman and Jerry Opalko, Captain Moorcroft took it upon himself to organize and lead a small rear guard force to cover the withdrawal of the remainder. I regret to say the tribesmen under his command abandoned him after he was hit in the ankle by a high-velocity bullet."

"Could he have been taken prisoner by the Russians, George?"

Kirov lit two cigarettes, gave one to Elizabeth, then picked up the mike again. "Anything's possible," he said, "but I don't think you should bank on it. If the Russians had taken him, they'd have made a big production out of it long before now. Russell would have provided visible proof that the American government is actively supporting the anti-Babrak Karmal rebels."

It suddenly occurred to him that her brother had realized he would never see his homeland again. "Will there be a show trial?" the American had asked him with pathetic eagerness and, like a stupid idiot, Kirov had drawn the wrong conclusion. Moorcroft didn't give a damn how much it would embarrass his government; he'd wanted a show trial with all its attendant publicity, because it was the only way he could let his people know he was still alive.

"Thank you, George." Her voice was very quiet, very dignified.

"For what?"

"For being so honest with me."

Kirov drew on his cigarette and inhaled the smoke, half wishing it would choke him. Perhaps one day she would know the whole unadulterated truth, but right now he was obliged to sit there taking the credit for something he hadn't done and looking suitably modest about it.

"I wonder if I could ask you one more favor?"

"You've only to name it," Kirov told her and meant it.

225

"I'd like to transcribe your statement and have it authenticated by a notary public." Elizabeth found an ashtray among the piles of manuscripts on the coffee table and nervously stubbed out her cigarette. "I won't use it unless the bank terminates the standing order, and even then, I'll show it only to the insurance company. If they won't accept the affidavit, you have my promise that I won't go to court without first obtaining your permission."

The next installment was due at the beginning of December, and if he agreed to Elizabeth's request, there was no telling what might happen. All being well, he would be back in the USSR long before the first of December, but what if she became sufficiently desperate to resort to legal action? The case was bound to attract a lot of publicity and the Soviet Embassy in Washington would get to hear about it. Then Kirov remembered that Fedor Fedorovich had said that he doubted if Leonid Brezhnev would live through the winter with his heart condition.

"When will this transcript of yours be ready?" he asked.

"Tomorrow lunchtime?"

Kirov stubbed out his cigarette. "Okay, you've got yourself a deal. I'll meet you here around twelve-thirty."

She started crying then, and it seemed only natural to take Elizabeth into his arms and comfort her.

★   ★   ★

The most important man in the Soviet Union sat on the edge of the single bed, one sock on, one sock off, his pajama jacket unbuttoned to the waist. The parade on Sunday had taxed his strength more than he cared to admit and it was an effort to bend down and put the other sock on, when there was this terrible pain in his chest. Gritting his teeth, he crossed one leg over the other and leaned forward. Suddenly the pain became a knife that plunged into his heart, and he toppled forward to lie still on the carpet, his eyes wide open and sightless.

Outside his modest apartment in the Kremlin, the Spassky chimes began to toll the hour of eight.

Chapter XVII

Vatutin got out of the chauffeur-driven Zil limousine, showed his ID card to the sentry guarding the rear entrance to the KGB Headquarters of Dzerzhinsky Square, and walked into the ocher-colored rococo building where he was met by General Fedorchuk's aide. Despite his seemingly impassive expression, Vatutin was apprehensive. The phone call he'd received less than half an hour ago had been terse, unfriendly, and singularly uninformative. Instead of the usual pleasantries, Fedorchuk had merely informed him that a chauffeur-driven car would arrive shortly at the First Chief Directorate and that he expected to see Vatutin in his office by 11:15 at the latest.

Vatutin could think of only one possible reason for the urgent summons. During the silent hours of Tuesday night, the directorate had received a flash signal from the KGB resident in Washington stating that Kirov's "legend" had undoubtedly been blown. The information had come from a highly placed source within the FBI, who'd informed his Soviet control that the British Security Service had been in touch with the bureau to warn them about a Mr. George Kershaw whom they suspected could be a Russian agent. The flash signal hadn't explained how or why Kershaw had been spotted by the British, nor had it indicated whether or not Kirov had been apprehended by the FBI. Apart from these two unanswered questions, Vatutin was also at a loss to understand how the chairman had gotten to hear about it, assuming he had. Flash messages were automatically referred to the appropriate deputy controller of the First Chief Directorate, no matter what hour of the day or night they arrived, and with the agreement of his superior, Vatutin had decided that no further action should be taken until the full report arrived in the diplomatic bag. Although his chief might have subsequently informed Fedorchuk, he thought it unlikely. Still uneasy as to why the chairman wanted to see him, he stepped out of the elevator on the ninth floor and followed the aide down the corridor.

Fedorchuk greeted him with a perfunctory nod, then pointed to the chair positioned in front of his desk.

"Better prepare yourself for a shock," he said tersely. "Leonid Ilyich Brezhnev is dead."

"When did he die?" Vatutin heard himself ask in a voice that sounded a long way off.

"Between eight and nine this morning; his valet found him lying unconscious on the floor. Of course, he was rushed to the Novaja Clinic, where the doctors did their best to stimulate his heart, but he was already dead on arrival."

And the time was now 11:15 exactly. A lot could happen in two and a quarter hours, Vatutin thought. The emergency resuscitation would have been a mere formality; no physician had yet succeeded in raising the dead, but for the sake of appearances, it was essential to have some neutral body certify that Brezhnev had died of natural causes.

"Comrade Yuri Andropov has been unanimously appointed chairman of the twenty-five-strong committee for the funeral arrangements. The other offices of state are as good as his." Fedorchuk allowed himself a bleak smile as gray as the wintry sky outside the window. "Defense Minister Ustinov was one of the first to declare his support for Comrade Andropov, and one can understand why. Ever since the Denisenko affair blew up in their faces, General Ivashutin and those idiots at GRU headquarters have been running around like a bunch of headless chickens, trying to assess the damage. The crisis could not have occurred at a more inopportune moment so far as the armed forces are concerned."

That had been the whole object of the operation, and a few words of appreciation would not have come amiss. Comrade Vitaly Fedorchuk was not, however, a man noted for being lavish with his praise.

"The news that Leonid Ilyich Brezhnev is dead will be announced on Moscow Radio at 1100 hours tomorrow,

Thursday November eleventh," the chairman continued. "You therefore have twenty-four hours in which to tidy things up. Do I make myself clear?"

"Perfectly," Vatutin said.

"Good. I need hardly point out that the present favorable situation would rapidly deteriorate were the GRU able to prove that we had engineered the Denisenko affair."

The observation raised a doubt in Vatutin's mind where none had previously existed. The Kirov mission had always consisted of two separate and quite distinct phases, but now Fedorchuk seemed to be implying that he was required to sanitize only the first.

"May I inquire how this sudden development affects our plans for Grigory Romanov?" he asked tactfully.

"Nothing's changed as far as he's concerned. Romanov will have no reason to alter his plans at the last minute because steps have already been taken to ensure that there is a complete breakdown of communications between Moscow and Leningrad for the next twenty-four hours. So he'll go to Helsinki where, all being well, Vera Berggolts will phone him."

"All being well" was the key proviso and an uncomfortable reminder that the chairman had been deliberately kept in the dark about Kirov. With so little time to play with, it was no longer advisable to wait until a full report reached them in the diplomatic bag before breaking the news to him.

"There's something I think you should know," Vatutin began, then gave him the bald facts in a few nerve-racking sentences.

"Let's take the worst case," Fedorchuk said after a lengthy silence. "Let's assume the FBI has got Kirov and he tells them why the GRU sent him to America. Where's the harm in that? Those cretins in Znamensky Street end up even deeper in the shit, and the Americans destroy Grigory Romanov before he can become a political figure to be reckoned with."

"They may put Kirov on trial."

"So?"

"Well, what if his defense counsel decides to put him on

the witness stand and he tells the court about Moorcroft? No matter how much it embarrasses the U.S. government, the allegation will be widely reported on the radio, in the newspapers, and on television. The whole of our embassy staff in Washington will inevitably read or hear about it, and there's no way we can effectively muzzle them. In the end, the story will reach Moscow by word of mouth, and too many senior officers in the army are aware that Moorcroft was handed over to the KGB when he was discharged from the base hospital."

It wasn't necessary for Vatutin to state the obvious. A worried frown told him that the chairman was quite capable of assessing the possible repercussions.

"The Americans will interrogate Kirov in depth," Fedorchuk said eventually. "It will be months, possibly as much as a year from now before they put him on trial. By then, Comrade Andropov will be firmly established in power."

"Yes." Vatutin cleared his throat, then said, "I wonder if we could examine the situation from a more favorable aspect? Suppose the FBI hasn't arrested Kirov yet? Would it not be in our interest to deal with the problem before it becomes a nuisance?"

"Certainly."

"Then I have your authority to take whatever action is necessary?"

"I know we can rely on you to find a satisfactory means of resolving the problem, Lyosha."

It wasn't quite the unequivocal answer Vatutin had hoped for, but it was good enough.

"Are there any other points you wish to discuss with me?" Fedorchuk asked him.

"None that I can think of right now."

"Then I needn't detain you any longer. Time, I might add, is not a commodity we can afford to squander."

The same aide was waiting for Vatutin in the corridor, summoned by the buzzer Fedorchuk had pressed as their discussion ended. He escorted Vatutin to the elevator and on down to the ground floor, making innocuous small talk the way aides are prone to do the world over. As they emerged from the building, the driver of the Zil limousine switched on the engine and, leaving it running, scrambled out of the car and ran to open the left-hand rear door for Vatutin. With a faint grunt that was meant to express his appreciation, he climbed inside and settled himself in the back. Moments later, the driver pulled out of the narrow alleyway between the KGB Headquarters and the Lubyanka prison and headed for the twelve-lane outer-ring motorway. Oblivious to the swishing noise made by the tires on the slush-covered road, Vatutin considered what action had to be taken in order to comply with Fedorchuk's instructions.

Colonel Dmitri Nikishev posed the greatest threat. He was the case officer for the Kirov mission and was the only person who knew the extent to which the KGB had supposedly agreed to support the operation. Although he didn't think he was intelligent enough to realize there was a connection between the foul-up in London and the power struggle within the Kremlin, there were plenty of GRU officers who would see the link, were they to question him. Having said that, Vatutin couldn't have wished for a better scapegoat than this sleek pussy cat of a lieutenant colonel.

However, it was vital that Nikishev should be persuaded to make a full and voluntary confession that would stand up in court. Ordinarily this would be extracted by subjecting him to unrelenting psychological intimidation, but this method was time-consuming and time was one thing Vatutin didn't have. The interrogators would therefore have to adopt a less sophisticated approach, a job that was tailor made for Captain Viktor Petrovich Ignatchenko and the NCOs of 26 Counterintelligence and Interrogation Team. Ignatchenko would be only too anxious to obtain a confession, because he was the man who'd put his signature to a sworn deposition that implied that the GRU still had Moorcroft in their custody.

Vatutin quickly turned his mind to the other KGB bit players whom it might be necessary to isolate. Fomin was one of the old guard and could be trusted to keep his mouth shut. In any case, he was already effectively quarantined in

London and it would be a comparatively simple matter to extend his tour at the embassy should the leadership issue show signs of becoming a protracted struggle. There was no need to do anything about Mikhail Izveko either. The man was a proven killer, committed beyond the point of no return by the murder of Aleko Denisenko. He would make an additional and very useful member of Captain Ignatchenko's team. That left Natalia Rubanskaya, Warrant Officers Lavrenti Litvinov and Nikolai Bukharin who had buried Moorcroft behind the dacha belonging to General F. F. Kirov, plus the driver who had delivered the corpse. All four would have to be posted to some of the more remote townships in Siberia and it would be necessary to provide a new identity for Natalia Rubanskaya, after she had been tried and sentenced to a term of imprisonment that of course she would never serve.

Vatutin reached for the radio telephone that was positioned below the glass partition separating him from the driver and put through a call to the chief of staff at GRU Headquarters. He didn't want Ivashutin making a nuisance of himself when he learned that one of his officers had been arrested, and the chief of staff was just the person to calm him down. He was the man who had posted Kirov to Blagoveshchensk as a favor to the aging Deputy Minister of Defense who'd wanted to bed Tania Abalakinova and had been paying for his mistake ever since.

An arrogant belief that he had the situation firmly under control rapidly evaporated soon after he'd spoken to the chief of staff and discovered that his chosen scapegoat was about to depart on a GDR flight to East Berlin. Thereafter, Vatutin spent the rest of the journey back to the First Chief Directorate phoning one number after another to arrange for Nikishev to be detained at the airport on some pretext.

★   ★   ★

Nikishev stared at the flight information screen in the departure lounge, vexed to know why GDR flight 2544 to East Berlin had been delayed at the last minute. Had the plane left on schedule, he and the other passengers would have been halfway to the intermediate stop at Warsaw by now, but less than ten minutes before the estimated time of departure, there had been a bald announcement on the loudspeaker that flight 2544 was subject to an indefinite delay. There had been no apology and no explanation, and in the absence of any information, he could only assume that the aircraft had developed some sort of technical fault or else that the Polish Solidarity reactionaries had taken to the streets again and General Jaruzelski had been forced to close the Warsaw airport. One thing was certain, the delay hadn't been occasioned by the weather. Although it had started snowing again, visibility was still reasonably good, the runways were clear, and furthermore, the Aeroflot domestic flight to Volgagrad was about to take off.

Bored to distraction, Nikishev sank back in his chair, picked up the magazine he'd purchased from a newsstand in the terminal building, and leafed through it again, looking for some feature he hadn't read the first time around. A discreet cough interrupted his perusal and he slowly looked up to find he had company. The stranger blocking his view was a good head shorter than he and was wearing a gray pinstripe suit that was at least one size too big and badly needed pressing. His most arresting features were a round cherub face that conjured up an image of childish innocence and a friendly smile that was guaranteed to put most people at their ease.

"Colonel Nikishev?" the stranger inquired politely.

"Yes. Do I know you?"

The plump, gray-haired female loitering in the background who'd checked his papers earlier on had obviously pointed him out to the stranger, but Nikishev was traveling under a different name and couldn't understand how either of them could possibly know who he really was.

"Comrade General Vatutin presents his compliments and asks if you could spare him a few minutes." An ID card, discreetly cupped in the palm of his hand, revealed his identity.

Mikhail Izveko, Nikishev read, and immediately compared the photograph with the real-life figure. "I'm not sure I can," he said. "I mean, it'll take us a good half hour to reach his office and my flight may be called forward at any moment—"

"He's here at the airport," Izveko said, interrupting him.

"Oh, well, that's different."

Nikishev stuffed the magazine into his briefcase, picked up his topcoat from the adjoining seat and draped it over his left arm, then followed the KGB man toward the exit. He assumed Vatutin would be waiting for him in the VIP lounge but as they entered the main concourse, Izveko turned sharply right and made for a door marked "Airport staff only." Beyond it, a concrete staircase spiraled down to the ground floor.

"Are you sure this is the way?" Nikishev asked dubiously.

"Quite sure." Izveko reached the bottom of the staircase, opened a swinging door to his right, and ushered Nikishev into a narrow passageway that led to the baggage handling area. "The Comrade General decided the VIP lounge wasn't sufficiently private. That's why he's waiting for you in his limousine."

Nikishev didn't question the explanation, because he had other more important things on his mind. Vatutin had undoubtedly arranged for his flight to be delayed which could only mean that further adverse factors relating to the Denisenko affair had suddenly come to light. It was only when Nikishev reached the deserted baggage area and saw two burly men standing by a closed van that he began to have an inkling of just how adverse the situation had undoubtedly become for him.

"Where's the general's car?"

"I wouldn't know," Izveko told him.

Thoroughly alarmed, Nikishev spun around to face the younger man and took a vicious short arm jab under the heart. Winded by the blow, he dropped his briefcase and topcoat and doubled up in pain. Before he had a chance to recover, Izveko grabbed his left arm, twisted it around behind his back, and ran him into the wall. Somebody whom Izvenko referred to as Dishukin seized his other arm and manacled his wrists together with a pair of handcuffs. Then, between them, they dragged him over to the van and heaved him into the back as though he were a sack of potatoes.

234

Landing head first, he hit the metal floor with a sickening crunch and felt himself sliding down into what seemed to be a dark, bottomless void.

★   ★   ★

A chink of gray light slowly swam into focus before Nikishev's eyes and was accompanied by other sensory perceptions: the deep-throated purr from a combustion engine, the pungent aroma of a cigarette, and a tingling sensation in his hands and left arm.

Then somebody prodded him with his foot and Izveko said, "Well, what do you know, I do believe our pussycat is waking up at last."

"In that case, you'd better get him ready. We can't have much farther to go now."

Nikishev couldn't place the second voice, but it had to be either Dishukin or the other burly figure who'd been hovering near the truck. Not that names were relevant; what mattered was how long had he been unconscious, where were they taking him, and what had prompted Vatutin to have him arrested? He could only guess the answers to the first and third questions, but the way the driver kept varying their speed and the increasing volume of noise from other vehicles on the road suggested they were heading into Moscow, which meant he was destined for the Lubyanka. The thought sent a cold shiver down his spine.

"Easy does it," Izveko said and crouched beside him.

Nikishev raised his head, saw what the KGB man was holding in his hands, and realized he was going to hood him. Panic-stricken, he thrashed this way and that, but it was an uneven match and he didn't stand a chance. With almost contemptuous ease, Izveko encased his head in the canvas sack, pulled the drawstrings tight around his neck and knotted them. Despite the air hole, Nikishev found it difficult to breathe properly and within seconds had convinced himself he was going to suffocate. Totally disoriented, totally demoralized, he was no longer capable of thinking in a rational manner. He wasn't even aware that the van had stopped until Izveko and Dishukin hauled him out of the back and forced him to march at the double.

235

They had covered roughly twenty yards when he heard a harsh grating noise, then a heavy steel door clanged behind them and their footsteps echoed briefly in a narrow corridor. A few seconds later, they wheeled right, and he was ordered to mark time. One of the KGB men then opened another door and he was shoved across the threshold. When the hood was finally removed, Nikishev found himself in an office slightly bigger than a double bedroom with a frosted glass window set high up on the facing wall, well above eye level. A thin, sallow-complexioned man sat behind a counter spanning the entire width of the room.

"Name?" he rasped.

"You've got a choice," Izveko said before Nikishev could answer. "The one he's traveling under or his own. Personally, I'd stick him down as A. N. Other because he isn't going to be here long enough to become an administrative problem."

"Been a bad boy, has he?"

"Theft, forgery, bribery, corruption, illegal possession of official documents, currency speculation, espionage; you name it, he's done it."

"I'm an officer in the GRU," Nikishev said with as much dignity as he could muster, then gave his name, rank, and serial number.

"You're an asshole in anybody's language," Dishukin told him as he removed the handcuffs. "Now strip."

"What?"

"You heard the man," Izveko roared. "Put your clothes on the counter. We want you stark, bare assed naked."

Nikishev removed his jacket and tie. His fingers lacked a sense of touch and were still tingling with the aftereffects of cramp, so that a simple task like unbuttoning his shirt was almost beyond him. His clumsiness drew a torrent of abuse and when he bent down to unlace his shoes, Izveko kicked him in the rump and sent him sprawling onto the floor.

"You stupid bastard," Dishukin shouted. "Who gave you permission to lie down on the floor? What do you think this place is—a rest house?"

Nikishev pulled off his shoes and socks, got to his feet and hastily shed his string vest, trousers, and shorts. The sallow-faced clerk swept his things into a linen bag, then produced a few basic items of clothing from under the counter.

"One regulation issue denim jacket," he intoned. "Likewise one pair of trousers and one pair of shoes, rope soles, medium size."

"Well, what are you waiting for?" Izevko demanded. "Pick them up. I'm not your fucking servant."

"Yes, of course." Nikishev licked his lips. "Do I put them on now?" he asked, eager to appear cooperative.

"Not yet," Dishukin told him. "You've got to see the quack first. We want to be sure you're free from infection."

The medical inspection room was only next door, but they made him run up and down the corridor until he was out of breath before they wheeled him inside. Despite the white smock and the stethoscope around his neck, which he wore like a badge of office, the doctor was the most unlikely looking physician Nikishev had ever encountered. He had lank hair, bad breath, coarse features, and an equally coarse tongue, which he used to good effect throughout a long and unnecessarily humiliating physical. Finally he donned a pair of surgical gloves and ordered him to turn around and bend over, observing that it was something Nikishev should be used to. Then he began to probe his anus.

"You're a regular little bum boy, aren't you?" he said.

"You can't talk to him like that," Dishukin protested in mock indignation. "He's a lieutenant colonel."

"Yes? Well, now we know how he got his promotion."

The medical officer cackled hilariously at his own joke, then gave Nikishev a playful slap on the buttocks and told him to get dressed. Even before he put it on, he knew the uniform was the wrong size and that it was intentional. They were determined he should look and feel ridiculous; it was all part of their campaign to crush what little remained of his spirit, and they were succeeding. How could a man retain a vestige of self-respect in a pair of trousers that barely reached his shins, in a jacket that was tight across the chest and rode above his stomach? Nikishev stared at his reflection in the full-length mirror, at the lump on his forehead, and swallowed hard, fighting off tears of self-pity.

237

"Time we were moving on," Izveko said. "You've got a lot of explaining to do."

They put the handcuffs on again, led him out of the medical center and along the corridor to an interview room at the far end. It didn't come as any surprise to Nikishev to find that two KGB officers were already there waiting for him—the driver whom he'd seen at the airport and a man with reddish hair who was seated at a table. The latter was busy examining the contents of Nikishev's briefcase and wallet, which had obviously been taken from him when he was lying unconscious in the van.

"I'm Captain Ignatchenko," he said without looking up.

"And I'm Colonel Nikishev." He tried to sound defiant, but the quaver in his voice let him down.

"Really?" Ignatchenko raised his eyes and looked right through him. "Then perhaps you can tell me how a passport belonging to Viktor Spichkin came to be in your possession?"

"It was issued to me for a special assignment." Nikishev bit his lip. The explanation sounded feeble, even to his ears, but the truth often was. "It was made up from one of the blanks allocated to the GRU for undercover operations," he added desperately.

"That's only partially correct." Ignatchenko's tone was surprisingly mild, dangerously so. "This passport did indeed belong to the batch issued to the GRU, but it was reported to have been stolen five weeks ago. As a routine precaution, the serial number was circulated to the Immigration Department and their officers were advised that it had been canceled. So when a Mr. Viktor Spichkin presented his passport for inspection at Moscow airport this morning, the Immigration official checked it against the listings, saw that serial number 903225A had surfaced, and unobtrusively alerted the chief security officer."

"That's a complete pack of lies," Nikishev said wildly. "The exit visa was issued by the Foreign Ministry."

"There is a special printing section on the establishment of the GRU Training School." Ignatchenko continued in the same deadly calm voice. "They are responsible for the production of course programs, pamphlets, exercise papers,

238

and certain training aids. I am informed that some of these training aids consist of replicas such as the identity card issued to officers in the British army. The printing section also has an operational commitment, in which role it is frequently called upon to reproduce whatever papers and documents are required to support an agent in the field. In this and other matters, you are responsible to the commandant of the training school for the day-to-day supervision of this highly specialized department."

"What are you implying? That I forged the visa?"

"You had the means, the technical know-how, and the opportunity."

"That's absolute nonsense."

"Compared to your other crimes, I'm inclined to agree that the forged passport is just a nonsense."

"What other crimes?" Nikishev asked in a hoarse whisper.

"Murder. The victim was Captain Russell Moorcroft, an officer in the United States Army who was captured in Afghanistan while operating with the terrorists."

"I've never laid eyes on the man—"

"He was handed over to the GRU for questioning."

"By Major Kirov—"

"And was last seen alive at the Aleksandr Nevsky Air Force Base outside Moscow on the afternoon of Wednesday the twenty-seventh of October—"

"What has this got to do with me?" Nikishev demanded shrilly. "It's Kirov you should be questioning. I always said he—" Nikishev gasped, suddenly unable to finish the sentence as he doubled up in agony from a low blow to the groin.

"It's bad manners to interrupt the comrade captain when he's talking," Izveko said, wagging an admonishing finger under his nose.

The pain was excruciating and his bowels felt as though they were literally dropping out of him. The room was revolving, and there was a loud rushing noise in his ears that affected his hearing.

"Acting on information received . . ." A different voice—the driver reading from a notebook in what seemed a low murmur—". . . body found in a shallow grave . . .

239

dacha . . . General F. F. Kirov . . . victim shot . . . Makarov automatic . . ."

". . . evidence to secure a conviction . . ." Ignatchenko again, his voice gradually becoming clearer, ". . . best to make a full statement. That's what I would do in your position."

"Never," Nikishev said vehemently, and shook his head.

"You've got an hour to think about it," Ignatchenko informed him calmly.

The interview was over, but others would follow because they would keep on at him until he agreed to make a full and voluntary confession. Izveko and Dishukin told him so repeatedly as they hustled him out of the room and into an elevator in the transverse corridor to begin a long, slow descent to the cells below ground.

"You'll find this is a high-class establishment," Izveko said, grinning. "All the modern conveniences. Nobody, to our knowledge, has ever complained about the accommodation."

The accommodation measured some ten by seven feet, and the only item of furniture was a wooden board on which there were a couple of threadbare blankets. A revolting stench came from a small hole in the concrete floor that served as a latrine.

"The comrade colonel doesn't look too good," Dishukin observed with mock solicitude. "Do you think he's going to faint?"

"Don't ask me," Izveko said. "Maybe you'd better give him a snort."

"Right." Dishukin produced a small bottle and unscrewed the cap. "Here," he said gruffly, "drink this. It will do you a power of good."

Nikishev didn't want to, but his hands were still manacled behind his back and he was in no position to decline the offer once they'd forced the neck of the bottle into his mouth. The liquid was oily, tasted foul, and made him gag. Within minutes of their closing and locking the cell door, the castor oil produced the desired effect and his bowels exploded.

★   ★   ★

Kirov opened the door off the dining alcove and found himself in a tiny cubbyhole that was even smaller than the kitchen in Irena's flat in Moscow. Outside the sash-cord window, a fire escape led to the alleyway below.

"I admit it's kind of small," the real estate agent said, beating him to it, "but everything's conveniently at hand—refrigerator, stove."

"I can see that," Kirov said.

"And you couldn't wish to live in a nicer neighborhood."

The apartment was on Waverly Place, two blocks west of Washington Square Park and close to Seventh Avenue. An old brownstone, it was one of the few properties in the area that hadn't been taken over by various offshoots of New York University.

"How much did you say the rent was?"

"One sixty-five a week, Mr. Kingsland." The real estate agent eyed Kirov thoughtfully, recalled that he hadn't shown him any references, then added. "The minimum lease is one year, and the owner wants three months' rent in advance, preferably in cash."

Kirov did a rapid piece of mental arithmetic and frowned at the idea of having to shell out close to $2,000. It wouldn't leave him much to play with by the time he'd settled his hotel bill at the Claredon, but he didn't have much choice. George Kershaw was becoming too well known, especially with the FBI, and it was essential that he drop out of sight while the going was still good. He also needed somewhere private to bring Vera Berggolts after he met her at Grand Central, and apartments weren't all that easy to come by.

"I'll take it," he said abruptly, "but only on condition that you guarantee to have a telephone installed before tomorrow morning."

The real estate agent stifled a sigh of relief. "No problem, Mr. Kingsland," he told him. "The previous tenant had one, and the jacks are still in position. You name the time and the man from the phone company will be here if I have to lead him around by the nose."

Kirov glanced at his wristwatch, saw that it was later than

241

he'd thought, and realized he was due to meet Elizabeth Moorcroft in less than an hour's time.

"How about four o'clock this afternoon?" he asked and got an affirmative nod.

Chapter XVIII

The switchboard operator-cum-receptionist at Samuels and Stein was a pleasant though formidable-looking woman in her late forties or early fifties. She had been with the literary agency for more years than she cared to remember and knew every author by sight and could put a name to the majority of them. Consequently, the moment Kirov crossed the threshold, he was intercepted with a polite but firm "Can I help you?"

"My name's George Kershaw," he told her. "Miss Moorcroft is expecting me."

A faint smile conveyed the impression that she'd heard that one before and wasn't about to take his word for it. Her eyes went to a large desk diary and did a rapid double take; then she buzzed Elizabeth to tell her that a Mr. George Kershaw was waiting in the outer office. When, after several "uh huhs," she eventually put the phone down, there was a suitably apologetic expression on her face.

"I'm afraid Liz is still closeted with one of her authors. She asked me to give you her profuse apologies."

"That's okay." Kirov smiled. "As a matter of fact, I'm a few minutes early."

"I can see why Liz would like you," the woman told him. "Anyway, she'll be with you just as soon as she can. Meantime, can I get you a cup of coffee or something?"

Kirov politely declined the offer, sat down in one of the vinyl easy chairs set aside for visitors, and browsed through the back numbers of the *New Yorker, Time* magazine and *Publishers' Weekly*. Twelve-thirty came and went, then one o'clock. By one-fifteen he'd read everything there was to read and was getting a little restless. At one-twenty, the door to Elizabeth's office suddenly opened and she appeared accompanied by a slim, dark-haired man who wore built-up shoes, walked with a bounce, and was inordinately full of himself. Watching him surreptitiously while pretending to be immersed in *Newsweek*, Kirov took it as a personal affront when God's greatest gift to the literary world kissed her goodbye. "You idiot," he told himself and raised the magazine, retreating behind it.

"Hi there."

Kirov lowered the magazine and looked up, his eyes slowly taking in the brown velvet pants suit worn over a frilly-necked blouse. Aware of a tight feeling in his chest again, he wondered how it was that a girl he hardly knew could have such a disturbing effect on him.

"I'm so sorry, George. I did my best to shoo him out on time, but he refused to budge."

"Some people are like that. He was probably hoping you'd invite him to lunch."

"Yes. Well, I finally told him I already had a lunch date with you."

"Oh." Kirov got to his feet, followed Elizabeth into her office, and closed the door behind him. "Did he believe you?"

"I don't see why not. It happens to be true."

It was news to him, but he let it pass and sat down to read the affidavit Elizabeth had given him. It was neatly typed and contained no errors that he could see.

"Is this all your own work?" he asked cautiously.

The statement could prove lethal in the wrong hands, and the fewer people who knew of its existence the better it would be for all concerned. He trusted Elizabeth, and the notary public would take his instructions from her, but a third party would be under no such constraint.

"You don't have to worry, George," she said, as if reading his thoughts. "My secretary hasn't seen it. I came in early and typed it myself."

"In that case, I owe you an apology."

"How come?"

"I thought you might have broken a confidence. I should have known better."

"No need for apologies, George. If our positions were reversed, I'd be just as cagey."

Somehow Kirov doubted it. Elizabeth was a lot more open and trusting than he was, but of course she hadn't had the benefit of his training. By the time the GRU had finished their schooling, you weren't inclined to take your own family on trust, let alone a comparative stranger.

"Where do I sign?" he asked, conscious that she was gazing at him thoughtfully.

"In front of a notary," Elizabeth said, "and after we've had lunch. I've booked a table at the Four Seasons. Okay?"

"Provided there's a quid pro quo."

"What?"

"If lunch is on you, then dinner tonight is on me."

A warning voice inside his head told him he'd taken leave of his senses, but there was nothing new about that. His behavior had been schizophrenic ever since he'd contacted Elizabeth Moorcroft soon after he'd checked into the Travel Lodge on Monday evening. At first he'd tried to justify his actions by kidding himself that he was going to use her as a means of protecting Irena and Fedor Fedorovich, but that purpose had become secondary the instant she'd walked into the bar at the Top of the Sixes. Right there and then, he'd wanted her for himself, and the ghost of Tania had finally been laid to rest. It had been, and still was, as simple and crazy as that.

"Okay, George, it's a deal."

"Good." Kirov smiled. "I'll pick you up at your place at eight."

The warning voice censured him again, but he was in no mood to heed it.

★   ★   ★

There was nothing General Kirov enjoyed more than putting his feet up and having a quiet snooze in his study, particularly after a very heavy and satisfying lunch. Conversely, nothing irritated him more than being rudely awakened just as he'd gotten himself comfortably settled in his favorite armchair and was about to drop off. The unwarranted intrusion began with a low murmur of voices in the hall and culminated with his wife Lydia opening the door to announce that two gentlemen wanted to see him.

Inspecting his visitors with a jaundiced but professional eye, Fedor Fedorovich decided that only the younger of the two could be regarded as a gentleman. Although he looked wet behind the ears in his gray flannel suit and horn-rimmed glasses, he, at least, had had the grace to stand aside in order to allow Lydia to enter the room first. His companion, an unprepossessing individual whose sharp features reminded the general of a rodent, had displayed the manners of a pig in elbowing past her.

"Who are these people?" Fedor Fedorovich asked in a voice that sounded like a volcano about to erupt.

"This gentleman is Boris, dear." Lydia stopped wringing her hands long enough to point out the rodent-featured man. "He's one of Igor's friends."

"He's come to the wrong address then." Igor Gusovsky, the poisonous toad of a son-in-law. The very mention of his name sent his blood pressure soaring.

"And this is Sergei—"

"I'm not interested in their first names. What do they want?"

"It's to do with Georgi." Lydia saw the dangerous glint in her husband's eyes and swallowed nervously. "They'd like to see the letter he wrote to you from Mozhaysk."

"A matter of state security," Boris informed him. "Where will I find it? In the writing desk over there?"

The KGB man went to the bureau near the window, turned the key and folded back the roll top, then began to rifle through the drawers. Breathing heavily, Fedor Fedorovich pushed the footstool out of the way, got up and lurched toward him.

"Just what the hell do you think you're doing?" he roared.

"Don't get uppity with me, old man. Your son, the gallant major, has skipped the country. Now why don't you sit down again and take the weight off your feet?"

Boris placed a restraining hand on the general's shoulder and tried to push him out of the way. The assault, whether

245

or not it had been intentional, drew a reproving frown from the younger KGB officer. In Sergei's opinion, his colleague's behavior was bringing the service into disrepute and was thereby ruining the favorable TV image created by the drama series, "Seventeen Moments in Spring." Furthermore, it was all very well treating the Gusovskys with scant respect, but the old man was a full general and a Hero of the Soviet Union twice over, who still had influential friends in high places. Both considerations weighed heavily with him, but as an ex-university entrant and comparative newcomer who was still on probation, he was reluctant to reprimand Boris.

Fedor Fedorovich suffered from no such inhibitions and was sufficiently angry not to care about the consequences. Looking around for a suitable weapon, he picked up the heavy glass paperweight lying on top of the bureau and whacked it against Boris's head, knocking him senseless. He then turned around, took aim, and let fly at the younger officer. Sergei had all the time in the world to avoid the missile but was simply too flabbergasted to duck. As a result, the paperweight struck him flush in the mouth, dislodging two front teeth while drawing a fountain of blood from his nose. Staggering backward, he fell over the general's footstool, cracked his head on the hard wooden floor, and lay there gazing blankly up at the ceiling. There was a brief moment of silence, then Lydia asked Fedor Fedorovich if he'd taken leave of his senses in a voice that was little more than a whisper.

"You're the one who's half-witted. I can't think what came over you, Lydia. What the hell made you invite these two petty sneak thieves into the house? We could have been beaten up and robbed."

"But they're KGB," she said faintly.

"You didn't tell me," Fedor Fedorovich said innocently. "I distinctly remember your saying they were gentlemen."

"What are we going to do, Fedor?" A fist went to her mouth and she began to chew at the knuckles.

"Do?" he repeated. "Well, for a start you can stop gnawing your fist and answer a few questions. Did they show you their warrant cards?"

"I don't remember."

"Did you ask to see them?"

"No." Lydia shook her head. "No, I don't think so."

"Good. Just don't change your tune when the police arrive."

"The police?"

"Of course," Fedor Fedorovich said irritably. "Isn't it the duty of every law-abiding citizen to assist the police? I'm about to report a case of attempted robbery with violence."

He turned his back on Lydia and stepped over the prostrate Boris; then, having calculated the angle of contact with the desk, he deliberately smashed his head against a sharp corner and inflicted a wound above the left eyebrow. After that, he made two phone calls, the first to the precinct station on Kalinina Prospekt, the second to the office of his former comrade-in-arms, Defense Minister Marshal Ustinov.

★　　★　　★

To obtain a private telephone was a long and arduous business for the ordinary Muscovite. Prising the requisite forms out of a reluctant Post and Telecommunications Ministry was in itself a major achievement, but this difficulty was merely the tip of the iceberg. The application form was not the sort of thing that could be completed in a few minutes, since it required the would-be subscriber to furnish what amounted to a detailed autobiography. The Ministry of Telecommunications then referred this document to the KGB for their scrutiny and approval before adding the applicant's name to the waiting list. Thereafter, there was usually a delay of a year to a year and a half before the telephone was finally installed.

Despite the confident assurance Kirov had received from the American real estate agent, he'd still thought it something of a miracle when he'd answered the door to his apartment on Waverly Place to find that the man from the phone company had arrived dead on time. Within half an hour a slimline phone had been installed in an otherwise empty living room. Even more importantly, the instrument was in perfect working order, which was not always the case back in Moscow. There had been other differences too. Nobody had asked him any awkward questions, nor had they thought it peculiar that he should want a telephone before the apartment was furnished. In fact, his refusal to use a credit card to settle future bills was the only instance where the odd eyebrow had been raised but, in the end, the people concerned had accepted that he was just one of those eccentrics who preferred to pay his way with hard-earned cash.

Kirov lifted the receiver once more to satisfy himself that the phone really was in working order, then unwrapped the small tape recorder and two cassettes he'd purchased earlier that afternoon. After reading the instructions carefully, he inserted a cassette and carried out a voice test prior to reading from the notes he'd jotted down on the back of an envelope. The statement he proposed to record was concise and extremely dangerous; in the wrong hands there was no telling what forces it could unleash but, like the nuclear deterrent, he hoped the occasion would never arise when it would have to be used.

Kirov hesitated, wondered momentarily if he should go through with it, then told himself that if Irena and Fedor Fedorovich meant that much to him, he had no alternative. Setting the tape running, he picked up the mike and said, "My name is Georgi Kirov; I am thirty-two years old and a major in the GRU. On Monday November eighth 1982, I arrived at Kennedy airport on TWA flight 1620 from Paris. The airline, Immigration authorities, the Travel Lodge on West 42nd Street, the Hertz rental agency, and the Claredon Hotel all know me as George Kershaw. My visa, work permit, driver's license, and Social Security cards were supplied by Lieutenant Colonel Dmitri Nikishev of the GRU Training School on Militia Street. Leonid Ilyich Brezhnev has a chronic heart condition and could die at any moment. That's why I was sent to America to negotiate with the daughter-in-law of the man who may succeed him. Her name is Vera Berggolts . . ."

*   *   *

Ignatchenko placed the case folder to one side and lit a cigarette. Of all the interrogations he'd conducted, this one was undoubtedly the most difficult to handle and

248

potentially the most dangerous. It was difficult to handle because the preliminary briefing he'd received from the colonel in charge of Department 13 at the First Chief Directorate had been notable for its brevity, paucity of information, and ill-defined parameters. In fact, he'd departed for the Lubyanka knowing only that Moorcroft, the United States Army captain whom he had personally questioned at length soon after he'd been captured, was now dead and that he was required to obtain a statement from Lieutenant Colonel Dmitri Nikishev that would absolve the KGB of any blame.

The interrogation was potentially dangerous because nobody had seen fit to tell him why the American had subsequently been handed over to the GRU for further questioning, when he'd already disclosed everything there was to know about his involvement with the Afghan terrorists. In his own mind, Ignatchenko was certain that this vital piece of information had been deliberately withheld from him and he'd been very careful not to press Nikishev on this point, in case he inadvertently learned something he shouldn't know.

There was another inhibiting factor that exercised Ignatchenko, a gut feeling that the head of Department 13 was simply a go-between for someone much higher up in the chain of command who was determined to control the interrogation from a distance. The two phone calls from the chief of Department 13, the first shortly after he'd arrived at the Lubyanka, the second minutes before he was about to interview Nikishev, tended to support this contention. On both occasions, the department chief's general demeanor and hesitant speech had led Ignatchenko to believe that the colonel was looking over his shoulder seeking approval for every word he said. Then there was the way the evidence was being delivered piecemeal, as though the material was being vetted before he was allowed to see it. Finally, there was the case file itself, which had only just arrived. Apart from fleshing out the information Ignatchenko had received at the initial briefing, it also laid down exactly what inducements he was permitted to offer Nikishev in order to obtain his confession.

Ignatchenko stubbed out his cigarette, reached under the table, and pressed a small button. Outside in the corridor the red light above the door went out and the green one came on. Moments later, Izveko and Dishukin marched their prisoner into the interview room.

If Nikishev had presented a sorry spectacle before he was taken down to the cells, he was now the picture of misery and degradation. In the space of one hour he'd aged ten years and looked as though he'd spent a lifetime in the Gulag Archipelago. Naked except for the towel around his waist that was no bigger than a loincloth, he stood in front of Ignatchenko, head bowed, shoulders hunched, numb with cold, and shivering like a man with a bad case of malaria.

"Why isn't this prisoner in uniform?"

Ignatchenko wasn't being solicitous. He already knew the answer to his question and merely raised it to add to Nikishev's humiliation.

"He soiled it, Comrade Captain," Dishukin said, responding to the cue in a loud voice.

"Diarrhea?"

"It's more likely he was scared shitless."

"So would you be in his shoes, Sergeant Major." Ignatchenko flipped open the case folder, extracted a dun-colored form, and held it out for Nikishev to see. "Do you recognize this?" he demanded.

"Yes, it's a transport requisition."

"Right first time. It's addressed to Moscow Military District Headquarters and requires the officer in charge of the motor pool to provide one Zil truck to collect personnel and baggage from the airport on Wednesday the twenty-seventh of October."

"I'll take your word for it," Nikishev said wearily.
"That is your signature at the bottom, isn't it?"

"It's very similar, but I don't remember signing the requisition."

"Then your memory is obviously at fault. On the eighth of November, the transport officer sent a note asking you to explain why the work ticket showed that the vehicle had clocked up a hundred miles when the round trip should have been no more than thirty-four. You replied that only Major Kirov was in a position to answer the query and that the matter should be referred to him on his return from temporary duty overseas."

Ignatchenko produced photocopies of both letters from the folder and presented them to Nikishev for his inspection. He didn't need to ask the colonel for an explanation; the look of consternation on his face said it all. Nevertheless, he reminded Nikishev that the date in question was the day Kirov had returned to Moscow from Uzbekistan.

"I made a terrible mistake."

"You certainly did," Ignatchenko agreed.

"No, you don't understand. I was tired and it was late at night when I drafted my reply and I genuinely thought the transport officer was referring to the staff car that collected Major Kirov from the airport."

"There were two requisitions, one for a staff car, the other for a Zil truck. You signed them both."

"I can't have—"

"Let's talk about Tania Abalakinova," Ignatchenko said, cutting him short.

"Who?"

Nikishev's air of bewilderment didn't fool him. It was contrived, the instinctive defense mechanism of a man who had much to hide. It would do no harm, though, to disclose just how much the KGB knew.

"Kirov's late wife, the young woman who was knocked down and killed in Samolocny Lane by a drunken cabdriver. This was back in April of last year when Kirov was serving in Blagoveshchensk. Don't pretend you've never heard of her; she made you a rich man."

"Me? Rich?" Nikishev forced a nervous laugh. "You should see my bank statements."

"We have, but I'm talking about the numbered account in Basel and the two hundred thousand Swiss francs you received for smuggling Kirov out of the country."

"You're mad, all of you—"

The brief spark of defiance from Nikishev ended in a whimper, the result of a sharp jab in the kidneys and a warning from Izveko not to interrupt the officer.

"Kirov wouldn't accept the police version of the accident," Ignatchenko continued. "He refused to believe that his wife was a common little tart, and he was right. Tania Abalakinova was simply a beautiful, naïve, and rather vain young woman; she really thought her elderly admirer on the Central Committee just enjoyed being in her company and wasn't interested in her body. Well, Tania knew different when the old goat tried to rape her. She was half-naked when she ran out of that house in Samolocny Lane straight into the path of an oncoming vehicle. Anyway, it would seem Kirov is no fool. He sensed that someone had pulled a few strings to make sure the truth never came out and he raised all kinds of hell."

"He would," Nikishev said with feeling. "Kirov's a born troublemaker."

"GRU Headquarters must have thought so too. They posted him to Colonel Paskar's intelligence unit in Uzbekistan, hoping the move would shut him up, but even in that remote outpost, there was no silencing Kirov. And that's when you were drawn into the affair. Of course, Mr. Big didn't contact you directly; he sent an emissary, a man called Vladimir Rozlovsky."

"I've never heard of him."

"Oh, really?" Ignatchenko picked up the summary of evidence, found the passage he wanted, then said, "This is what Comrade Rozlovsky will state in court. Quote: 'After some discussion, Colonel Nikishev said Kirov could be gotten out of the country provided he was recalled to Moscow and attached to the training school. For this to happen, it was essential to restore his somewhat tarnished image with the high command. One way of doing this was to ensure he got the credit for breaking the American. I asked Colonel Nikishev whom he meant and he said my friend, the Deputy Minister, would know and that it was up to him to fix it.' Unquote."

Ignatchenko looked up and waited patiently for Nikishev to say something. That he eventually denied all knowledge of Rozlovsky was no great surprise.

"It's possible you aren't lying for once. Rozlovsky could well have used an alias in his dealings with you, but the fact remains that his evidence contains more than a grain of truth, does it not? Kirov did interrogate Moorcroft, and on the strength of the information he allegedly obtained from the American, he was subsequently recalled to Moscow and promoted to major."

"Yes, but—"

"He arrived on October the twenty-seventh. The following morning you collected him from General Kirov's residence and drove him out to the safe house at Mozhaysk. You had persuaded your superiors that the training school should take cognizance of the techniques he'd used to break the American and they'd agreed that you could debrief him with a view to rewriting the instructional handbook on methods of interrogation. In reality, you wanted Kirov tucked away while his new identity papers were being prepared by your own printing section, who were under the impression that the Canadian passport and other documents relating to George Kershaw were simply required for exercise purposes. You also gave Alexandra Podgorny and Nikolai Tudin the same story when you needed their help."

"No, that's a monstrous distortion of the truth." Nikishev shifted his weight from one foot to the other and looked everywhere but at Ignatchenko. "Kirov had been selected for a special mission, and it was my job to ensure that he was properly equipped to carry it out."

"I'm disappointed in you, Colonel." Ignatchenko sighed. "I expected a more original story."

"You don't have to take my word for it. Call the chief of staff at GRU Headquarters—he'll confirm everything I've told you."

"I don't think so. Both he and General Ivashutin have already stated quite categorically that it has never been their intention to send Kirov into the field. In fact, he's been posted as a deserter with effect from roll call this morning." Ignatchenko paused for effect, then delivered the final knife thrust. "Their sworn depositions are in this folder, if you would care to see them?"

The slow headshake said it all. The two people whom Nikishev had been counting on had pulled the rug out from under his feet, and he knew he was finished. However, it would be necessary for Ignatchenko to give the knife another twist before Nikishev would be willing to confess.

"Everyone's got it in for you, haven't they?" Ignatchenko said disarmingly. "Especially Rozlovsky—he'd have us believe that you killed Moorcroft. Personally, I'm not entirely sure you did, but his evidence is very convincing and it certainly fits the facts as we know them."

By and large, the case against Nikishev looked solid on paper, and while some of the evidence was obviously hearsay and pure conjecture, Ignatchenko had no difficulty in persuading himself that the colonel had committed most of the offenses set out in the indictment. The only thing he found hard to swallow was the allegation that Nikishev had murdered the American in cold blood. A man who was capable of such a crime would be a tough nut to crack, and this one was made of jelly. If the large question marks in the margin were anything to go by, the officer who'd transcribed Rozlovsky's statement had evidently shared his doubts. So had the chief investigator, whoever he was. Attached to the summary of evidence was a brief unsigned note that said, "No matter how much pressure is brought to bear, Nikishev is unlikely to confess to this crime. However, he might admit to being an accessory after the fact." The suggestion was decidedly tentative, but Ignatchenko seized on it, knowing he was running out of time and had a deadline to meet.

"Of course, Rozlovsky may be trying to save his own skin," Ignatchenko continued. "After all, we've only his word for what happened on Wednesday October the twenty-seventh, and the driver of the Zil truck who'd been detailed to collect personnel and baggage from the airfield is unable to tell us very much. All he knows is that shortly after arriving at the Aleksandr Nevsky Air Force Base, he was called to the telephone in the guardroom and was told by an officer claiming to be Colonel Nikishev to hand over his vehicle to the duty sergeant. Now, although Rozlovsky admits you didn't collect the American from the air force base, he claims that you intercepted the truck when it was on its way to the GRU detention center at Sezhodyna, seventeen miles northwest of Moscow. He says that you had borrowed a staff car for the journey, probably the same one that had met Kirov off Aeroflot flight 265 at Moscow airport. You then shot Moorcroft in the head and calmly told the mysterious sergeant to look after the staff car while you disposed of the body."

Anyone else would have denied the allegations vehemently, but not Dmitri Nikishev. Abject fear had reduced him to a comatose state of mind, and he stood there mewling helplessly like a stray kitten who'd lost its mother.

"Actually, I happen to think the American was already dead when you rendezvoused with the truck. Up till then, it had never entered your head that the people who wanted Kirov out of the way would double-cross you, but when they did, you were determined to pay them back in kind. That's why you drove out to Molzaninovka and buried the American behind the dacha belonging to General Fedor Fedorovich Kirov."

The suggestion aroused a faint spark of interest, discernible in the way Nikishev slowly raised his head as if to say, "All right, I'll buy that, but what's in it for me?"

"Do yourself a favor," Ignatchenko told him. "Plead guilty to the lesser charges. It's the Deputy Minister of Defense we're after, not you."

"I didn't kill Moorcroft."

"I believe you."

"And I didn't bury him either."

"I'm pretty sure you did, but we'll let that pass. I doubt that the prosecution will want the world and his wife to know that an officer in the Red Army was a party to the murder of an American citizen."

"Supposing I did make a voluntary statement," Nikishev said hesitantly, "what's the worst that can happen to me?"

"You'll be stripped of your rank, dismissed from the service, and will forfeit all pension rights. Depending on how the judge feels, you'll draw a five-to-ten stretch in a labor camp. But that's infinitely preferable to a rendezvous with a firing squad in the yard of the Lubyanka one cold morning, isn't it?"

Nikishev thought it over, then nodded. "I may need some help with my statement," he mumbled.

"I'll guide your hand," Ignatchenko assured him.

A battle of wills had been fought and won, but in truth it had never been much of a contest.

Chapter XIX

Vatutin picked up the penknife, held it like a dagger in his right hand, and, venting his spleen on the desk, drove the blade deep into the leather-covered surface. The display of anger was completely out of character for someone whom the diplomatic community regarded as urbane, charming, witty, and cultured. It was, however, symptomatic of the increasing sense of frustration and feeling of impotence that had been steadily building up inside him ever since the full report of the "Kershaw" episode had arrived in the diplomatic bag from Washington.

Fedor Fedorovich and Georgi Kirov—he wasn't sure whom he hated and feared the most, the father or the son. Both men were living proof that, to borrow an English expression, there was such a thing as Sod's Law—what did the Americans call it? Murphy's Law—the imponderable human element that was guaranteed to send a computer haywire and bring any operation to a grinding halt just when everything appeared to be going smoothly.

The son was more intelligent than the father, preferring subtlety of purpose to brute force, but the old man possessed a low animal cunning that made him a dangerous adversary. Fedor Fedorovich had demonstrated that quality in full shortly after he'd assaulted the two KGB officers who'd called on him at his house on the corner of Arbatskaja Square and Kalinina Prospekt. It wasn't the general's phone call to the police that worried Vatutin. His excuse that he'd genuinely thought his visitors were going to mug him had been so transparently absurd as to be laughable, but his subsequent conversation with Defense Minister Marshal Ustinov was no joking matter. Although Vatutin had no idea what they had said to each other, it was a certainty that Fedor Fedorovich hadn't contacted his former comrade-in-arms merely to exchange a few social pleasantries. If that had been the case, Marshal Ustinov would never have telephoned the chairman of the KGB and, in his turn, Fedorchuk wouldn't have been at him demanding to know what Vatutin and the First Chief Directorate thought they were playing at.

The chairman's instructions, though couched in veiled language, had been very clear. General Fedor Fedorovich Kirov was one of the great untouchables; he was to receive a full apology and the two KGB officers were to be disciplined for exceeding their authority. In his anxiety to ensure that nobody rocked the boat, Fedorchuk had effectively torpedoed the scenario that Vatutin had painstakingly constructed, and Nikishev's confession was no longer worth the paper it had been written on. As a direct result of the general's immunity, every reference to Moorcroft would have to be expunged from the statement and the same stricture would apply to the evidence concerning Tania Abalakinova. Once that had been done, the prosecution would be left without a motive for the crimes Nikishev was alleged to have committed. Nikishev's voluntary statement was therefore useless in the present context. Later on, when things had quieted down a bit, it could always be resurrected to form the basis of a fresh confession wherein he would admit to fraud, embezzlement, misuse of government funds, and currency speculation. Meanwhile, Nikishev would remain where he was, out of sight and out of mind in solitary confinement.

The general may have fought and won a local skirmish for personal reasons, and on grounds of his own choosing, but his victory, though irritating, represented only a minor setback and in the broader scheme of things could be dismissed as an encounter of no great consequence. His son, however, was now in a position to provide the old man with the sort of ammunition that could blow them all away—Fedorchuk, Vatutin, and Andropov together with his supporters in the Politburo. That made Georgi Kirov exceedingly dangerous, and there were ominous signs that he'd guessed what was at stake.

It was all there in the follow-up report to yesterday's flash signal, provided one read between the lines. Of course, Kirov had carried out his instructions up to a point; he had contacted Vera Berggolts in the prescribed manner and he had arranged to meet her again at noon eastern standard time on Thursday the eleventh of November, but he'd failed to check in with his link man at Nestor's Toy Emporiums. The KGB resident in Washington was inclined to attribute this omission to the best of all possible motives. "It's possible," he'd argued, "that something happened to make Kirov suspect that his cover had been blown and he is therefore attempting to shield his link man."

Vatutin did not agree with him. Until he'd arrived in London, Kirov had stuck faithfully to his brief; thereafter he'd gone completely off the rails. Despite a reputation for being difficult, he would never have done that without a good reason, and Vatutin was certain he knew what it was. Denisenko must have aroused his suspicions in some way and he'd followed the link man and had been present when Fomin and Izveko had abducted him. Then, on Sunday morning, Kirov had probably gone to Highgate and kept the Denisenkos' apartment under surveillance, which would explain how the British Security Service had gotten on to him. But even more disturbing from Vatutin's point of view was the speed with which, having witnessed the arrival of the embassy staff and their subsequent departure with the widow, Kirov had put two and two together. Maybe he didn't have all the answers, but he knew enough to topple Yuri Andropov from power.

"I know we can rely on you to find a satisfactory means of resolving the problem, Lyosha." Vatutin recalled the chairman's words and smiled grimly. The only satisfactory solution was to have Kirov eliminated, and he'd already set the wheels in motion. All he needed now was confirmation from Washington that his cablegram had been received and understood. A feeling that a reply was long overdue set him on edge again to the point where only the timely arrival of his personal assistant stopped him from inflicting further damage on the desk. One look at her puzzled expression and

258

the flimsy she was holding was enough to release the inner tension and leave him visibly relaxed.

"I'm not sure this cable is meant for us . . ." she began.

"Who's it addressed to?"

"It looks as though it was intended for Uddenholm Investments in Stockholm, but it has our indicator number on it."

"Then it's come to the right place," Vatutin said and took the cable from her.

Like the one he'd sent, the cable had been composed around a simple commercial code that made sense only to the originator and recipient. It said: "Your desire to unload Bluechip stock understood and will act accordingly. Present indications are that trading will start quietly in New York before moving sharply upward toward midday. Therefore propose to sell when market is most buoyant."

"Should I send an acknowledgment?" his PA asked.

"Thank you, but that won't be necessary," Vatutin said politely.

Although a reputable firm of stockbrokers with a proven track record for shrewd trading, Uddenholm Investments was in fact a business front for the KGB. Its primary function was to obtain hard currency for the First Chief Directorate, but in this instance, Uddenholm Investments was acting as an alternative means of communication with the Soviet Embassy in Washington via the New York head office of Nestor's Toy Emporiums. In commercial terms, Bluechip stock referred to Kirov; the rest of the cable told Vatutin that a hit man would pick him off at the first suitable opportunity.

Vatutin's profound sense of relief at the satisfactory outcome lasted as long as it took him to read the cable again; then he suddenly realized that one vital factor had been overlooked. Moscow was three hours ahead of Greenwich mean time, while eastern standard was five hours behind; when the news of Brezhnev's death was broadcast on Moscow Radio, it would therefore be 3.00 A.M. in New York. He didn't have to worry about Vera Berggolts—come what may, the FBI source would ensure that she kept her appointment at Grand Central—but there was no such guarantee where Kirov was concerned.

If Kirov gave her a wide berth, where would he go, what would he do? He was completely alone in New York and had no one to turn to for help. Unless . . . Vatutin left his desk, opened the combination safe, and sorted through the neat stack of cassettes on the top shelf to find the one he wanted. Returning to the desk, he loaded the cassette into a tape recorder and played it back, listening to odd snatches of conversation, then winding forward until he located the relevant passage.

A voice from the grave said, "Liz is the one I really get on with. She's twenty-five going on twenty-six and is very bright. She majored in English Lit at N.Y.U. and was an editor with Putnam's before she became a literary agent with Samuels and Stein. That was about the time she moved out of the family home on Staten Island into an apartment on 59th Street."

Vatutin couldn't think of one logical reason Kirov should take it into his head to contact Moorcroft's sister. To do so would run counter to everything the GRU had taught him, but with so much at stake, Vatutin decided it was too dangerous to leave even the smallest possibility to chance. Moving the tape recorder to one side, he picked up his scratch pad and began to draft a cable, the contents of which would ultimately reach the FBI source in Washington via Uddenholm Investments and Nestor's Toy Emporiums. That done, he lifted the phone and called Stockholm.

★   ★   ★

They dined in the Rose Room at the Algonquin on West 44th Street, a venue chosen by Kirov because, in fleshing out the "legend" the GRU had put together, Tudin had told him that the cuisine was good and that the place had character and atmosphere. The Algonquin, the American defector had said, had been the home of the Round Table and was one of Manhattan's cherished landmarks.

But for Kirov, all the atmosphere and all the character that evening stemmed from Elizabeth Moorcroft. The more he saw of her, the more he enjoyed being in her company. Well read, intelligent, and amusing, she was, he thought, one of the easiest of persons to converse with. The only awkward moments had come early on, when she had been reminiscing about her childhood and how she and Russ had always been close, but he'd quickly switched their conversation around to the safer topic of her job.

"I've been very lucky since I graduated from N.Y.U." she told him. "Most girls who want to get into publishing have to work their way up from the ground floor, but I guess Putnam's thought I'd make a better copy editor than a typist. It wasn't very exciting, though, and I was beginning to think I'd gotten myself into a rut, when the assistant to the executive editor upped and left for California and they let me have the job."

Elizabeth had gradually been given responsibility for a few of the lesser-known authors, some of whom had been inclined to get very uptight about her suggestions for improving their manuscripts. In most cases it had simply been a matter of ruffled feathers, and once she'd smoothed them down, they'd invariably come around to her point of view.

She attributed the move to the literary agency to another stroke of luck. One of the authors whom Elizabeth had looked after when she was with Putnam's had been a client of Samuels and Stein, a writer with a string of entertaining novels to his credit, none of which had ever really taken off. His fourteenth manuscript had therefore been received with the usual, "Here's one more solid book from good old Harry—it won't set the Hudson on fire but we won't lose any money on it." Elizabeth had taken a more positive attitude toward the book and had batted hard for it, lobbying her boss, the sales and subsidiary rights people, and the vice-president and editor-in-chief until they finally agreed to put a little muscle behind the novel. It hadn't turned out to be a second *Gone with the Wind*, as she'd claimed in one of her wilder moments, but a good paperback deal and several strong reviews had helped it onto the *New York Times* best seller list for a period of two weeks.

"It never went higher than number fourteen, but the author had never had anything like that happen to him before."

"And it brought you to the notice of Samuels and Stein?"

"Well, I guess that's when Herbie Stein began to keep an

eye on me." Her face clouded. "Poor Russ, why couldn't he have had some of my luck?" she said wistfully.

"Luck isn't something you can spread around, Elizabeth. Some people have it, some don't, and that's all there is to it. Anyway, I think you're doing yourself an injustice; the opportunity was there, you recognized it and took a calculated risk."

"Do you always weigh the odds before you make a decision, George?"

"I like to think so," Kirov said. But, on reflection, he had to admit to himself that the tape-recorded statement he was carrying with him, along with the duplicate cassette hidden behind the toilet tank in the rented apartment, was about the one calculated thing he'd done in the past few days.

"I'm not that logical. My reasons for leaving Putnam's were entirely personal. If Herbie hadn't invited me to join the agency, I'd have looked around for another job."

Office bickering or a love affair that had gone sour? The way Elizabeth emphasized that her motives had been wholly personal convinced him it had been the latter. Kirov also decided that the man had probably been married, and that in the fullness of time Elizabeth had realized he'd no intention of divorcing his wife. Good-looking and very sure of himself, no doubt, an engaging personality with a smooth line in sincerity and a dazzling smile made even more gleaming by a mouthful of capped teeth. He found himself hating the image of the unknown lover his own fertile imagination had created. It was, of course, absurd and irrational to become emotionally entangled with a girl he hardly knew and would never see again after tonight, but he was afflicted with a kind of autism that blinded him to the realities of life. He knew that if he spent the rest of his life looking for a substitute, he would never find another Elizabeth.

"But you've no regrets?" Kirov said, retreating from making a commitment to her that he couldn't possibly keep.

"None whatever, George. I love what I'm doing."

They were back on safe ground now, and thereafter he steered their conversation in the direction he wanted it to go. The more they discussed their likes and dislikes, the more he discovered how much they had in common, so that every second, every minute, every hour he spent in her company became precious, something to be remembered and treasured for the rest of time.

★   ★   ★

Seven fifty-five. The fir trees screening the First Chief Directorate from the twelve-lane outer-ring motorway were just visible in the first gray light of day. Three hours to go before it was officially announced that Leonid Ilyich Brezhnev was dead, and it was still only midnight in New York. Vatutin wondered if the news flash would make the later editions and rapidly came to the conclusion that, in the end, it wouldn't make a scrap of difference. If the newspapers didn't carry the story, the radio and TV stations would, and it was both futile and dangerous to hope that Kirov would remain in ignorance. Nobody could read his mind and predict with any degree of certainty how he would react to the news; the only answer was for Vatutin to spread the net as wide as possible and keep his fingers crossed that Kirov would walk into it.

The telephone pinged once as though, having dialed his number, somebody at the other end of the line had suddenly hung up before it could ring out. Probably Fedorchuk, he thought, a not unreasonable assumption since the chairman had been calling him on and off through the small hours of the night, wanting to know if he had the situation under control. The phone gave another anticipatory ping, then started trilling in earnest. Wearily, he lifted the receiver, fully expecting to find it was Fedorchuk. Instead a tired voice informed him that the signals centre had just received a cable from Stockholm.

"Read it to me," Vatutin said and felt his pulse quicken.

"Originator's reference—"

"Just give me the text."

"Yes, sir."

There was a brief pause and he had a mental picture of a flustered signalman mouthing four-letter words to himself.

"The text reads, quote: 'In event market is depressed will

263

check out Bluechip link with Moorcroft as you suggest. Stop. Signed Uddenholm.' Unquote."

"Thank you. Thank you very much."

Vatutin put the phone down, stretched his arms above his head and gave way to a yawn. "That's it," he said aloud. "There's nothing to worry about, you're home free." But somehow the words lacked conviction.

★   ★   ★

They walked back to her apartment on East 59th Street, two lovers arm in arm leaning into a gusting wind that swept down Fifth Avenue. Fifteen city blocks, past landmarks that had become familiar to him—Rockefeller Center, Saks, St. Patrick's Cathedral, and Tiffany's. Setting the pace, Kirov ambled along, trying to stretch every second into a minute, the leaden feeling in his stomach becoming heavier with every step that brought them nearer to the General Motors building.

"Not much farther now," she said, echoing his thoughts in a voice that sounded flat.

A prowl car cruised slowly past, the patrolman nearest the curbside eyeing them suspiciously. For a moment it looked as though they were going to stop, but then the driver picked up speed again and the taillights disappeared into the night.

"I wonder what that was all about?" he muttered.

"Who knows?" Elizabeth shrugged her shoulders. "Maybe they took me for a hooker."

"You, a hooker? They've got to be out of their tiny minds.

"Don't get mad, George. They're only doing their job."

"They should have their eyes examined," Kirov grumbled.

"You're beginning to sound like a native," Elizabeth said and hugged his arm closer.

They turned the corner into East 59th, crossed over to the north side of the street and continued on toward Madison Avenue. Twenty-five, twenty-seven, twenty-nine, thirty-one; Kirov checked the house numbers, dreading the moment when they would reach her apartment.

"I've really enjoyed this evening, George."

"Me too," he said.

A pause, then, "How long are you staying over in New York?"

"I don't know," he said vaguely. "A day, two days, a week. It depends on how things work out."

"Oh."

There was, he thought, no more expressive word in the English language. Depending on the tone of voice, it covered every emotion from surprise and joy to disappointment and sadness.

"It's not like you think it is," he blurted out. "I'd give my right arm to see you again."

"You don't have to do anything as drastic as that, George." Elizabeth stopped outside her apartment building and turned to face him. "Just give me a call sometime."

"Tomorrow?" he heard himself ask.

"Fine. I'll be working at home all day. I've got a lot of manuscripts to read." She moved nearer to him, stood on tiptoe, and planted a swift kiss on his mouth. "That's a little something to be going on with," she murmured.

Then, before he knew what was happening, she slipped out of his arms and ran up the short flight of steps to disappear inside the building. He watched the street door close behind her. It seemed like history repeating itself.

Chapter XX

Kirov woke up a few minutes after seven with a crick in his neck and feeling stiff all over from lying on the hard floor. A chill nip in the air told him that the central heating wasn't operating efficiently, and it was with some reluctance that he unzipped the sleeping bag he'd purchased the previous afternoon from a store on Third Avenue. With even greater reluctance he reached out, grabbed the pair of socks he'd left on top of his suitcase, and pulled them on. Then, like a robot responding to a computerized program, he got to his feet and did a few loosening-up exercises, bending, stretching, and rotating his trunk until the stiffness had worn off. Still functioning by rote, he went into the bathroom, filled the sink with hot water, and began to shave.

The next few hours were going to be critical, yet at a time when he needed to have all his wits about him, Elizabeth occupied his thoughts to the exclusion of everything else. Ever since he'd entered the Suvorov Military Academy at the age of ten he had given unswerving loyalty to the army and the fatherland, yet now he was thinking of defecting. The notion had crystallized only that instant, but Kirov supposed it must have been there at the back of his mind, steadily taking root from the moment she had walked into the bar on Tuesday evening. Just thirty-six hours—that was all it had taken to destroy a pattern of behavior the army had spent twenty-two years in the molding. The enormity of what he was contemplating, of the people whom he would be betraying, suddenly came home to him and he stared at his reflection in the bathroom mirror with loathing.

"You bastard," he said aloud. "You contemptible bastard."

Kirov sluiced his face with water, hastily brushed his teeth, then retrieved the duplicate cassette he'd concealed behind the toilet tank and returned to the bedroom. Apart from the tweed sports jacket and slacks, there were two suits hanging on the rail in the closet, a dark blue pinstripe and a plum-colored two-piece with a faint check. The former wouldn't go too well with his last remaining clean shirt, but it didn't have too many creases and undoubtedly looked the more presentable. He stripped off his pajamas, stuffed them into the suitcase on top of the other dirty clothes, and got dressed.

Passport, work permit, driver's license, loose change, billfold, door keys, and the two cassettes; he checked the items one by one to make sure he hadn't overlooked anything. The billfold was a lot thinner now and contained just $468. It would be enough to keep him going for several days, but it was a long way short of a plane ticket to Rome and the subsequent train fare to Vienna, assuming he decided to follow Nikishev's instructions for the return journey. In fact, by the time he'd rented a safe deposit box and had settled certain legal expenses, it was doubtful if he would have enough even to make it to the Canadian border by Greyhound bus. But there was no point looking that far ahead. If he got through today in one piece, he would think of a way to screw some money out of the contact at Nestor's Toy Emporiums.

Kirov checked the items a second time before distributing them about his person, then packed the rest of his things and hid the suitcase in the closet together with the sleeping bag. That done, he unfolded Hagstrom's map of the New York subways to recheck the route he planned to take after Vera Berggolts had met him at Grand Central. Finally, he went into the living room and lifted the receiver to satisfy himself that the phone was still in working order.

At eight-fifteen, Kirov left his apartment on Waverly Place and walked toward a cafeteria he'd observed near Washington Square that boasted a twenty-four-hour service. He was not particularly hungry, but the army had taught him that on operations you ate where you could and when you could, in the certain knowledge that sooner or later there was bound to be a foul-up in the resupply system. There were only two other diners present when he entered the cafeteria, neither of whom took the slightest notice of him. Passing them, he went to the far end of the counter, perched himself on a stool, and reached for a menu. The bill of fare was somewhat limited, but the service was prompt.

"What'll you have?" the counterman asked him.

"A cup of coffee and two bacon sandwiches."

The counterman nodded, moved to the service hatch and repeated the order in a parade ground bellow, then poured him a large cup of coffee. "You heard the news?" he asked, making conversation.

"What news?"

"Brezhnev's dead. I heard it on the radio this morning."

Kirov absently began to pour sugar into his coffee. Brezhnev dead? It didn't seem possible; the man had been around so long it was hard to believe he'd left the stage.

Fedor Fedorovich had said he was unlikely to live through the winter, but he'd looked pretty durable taking the salute at the big parade in Red Square last Sunday.

"I can see you've got a sweet tooth."

"Yeah." Kirov looked up. "Did they say who his successor is?" he asked.

"Some guy by the name of Andopov."

"You mean Yuri Andropov?"

"Yeah, that's it, Yuri Andropov. He's the one in charge of the funeral arrangements."

The power struggle was over before it had begun, and Grigory Romanov had been left waiting at the bus stop. So what was the point of going on when the situation had changed out of all recognition? Or had it? Irena and Fedor Fedorovich were still vulnerable, and Andropov's supporters wouldn't rest easy until they had dealt with Major Georgi Kirov. There was no necessity to change his plans, then; he would leave one of the cassettes in a safe deposit box and arrange for some attorney to be a custodian. From there on he'd have to play it by ear, tackling each problem as it arose, beginning with Vera Berggolts.

"Are you feeling okay, mister?"

"I'm fine," Kirov said. "Somebody just walked over my grave, that's all."

"It happens to us all," the counterman said philosophically.

★　　　★　　　★

Aaron Hines, the bureau chief in Hartford, Connecticut, had just sat down to breakfast when he heard the news about Brezhnev. Tarrying only long enough to swallow a glass of orange juice, he left his house on the double, scrambled into his car and drove like a bat out of hell to the FBI office on Constitution Plaza. At exactly 7:29 A.M. eastern standard time, he put through a call to Washington, got Carl Landers on the line, and curtly told him to activate the scrambler at his end.

"I assume you've heard the news?" he said, following a brief pause.

"Of course I have," Landers told him. "And I know what

you're going to say, Aaron. But nothing's changed; we still want Vera to keep her appointment with Kershaw."

"You guys must be crazy. The way things are, she could end up with a hole in her head."

"That's not the view of the State Department."

"State? What the hell have those people got to do with it?"

"Everything," Landers snapped. "This is a political shenanigan; it always has been."

"I don't buy that. Physical protection is our business, not theirs."

"For Chrissakes, Aaron, just do as you're told and see she gets there. Okay?"

"No, it's not okay," Hines said obstinately.

"Look, I don't have time to argue with you," Landers growled. "I'm supposed to be in New York by nine and I've got a plane to catch. If you don't like the setup, go cry on the director's shoulder. You know how to reach him. But I'm telling you this whole business has been authorized at the highest level."

"You're not snowing me, are you, Carl?"

"Aw, shit." Landers sighed, then said, "I was summoned to the office at four this morning shortly after the news had been announced on Moscow Radio. Ever since then, there's been a constant stream of visitors from the State Department and the CIA wanting to see the director. It doesn't matter what you, or I, or the director thinks, the State Department is calling the shots and they've got the White House on their side. As far as I can gather, some of our Kremlinologists think it would be no bad thing if we created a little dissension among the Soviets, and they look upon Vera as the ace up their sleeve. You get the picture?"

Hines wasn't sure he did, but Landers seemed to know what he was talking about and he didn't want to make a fool of himself. "Listen, Carl," he said earnestly, "forget what I just said, okay? I mean, I wasn't aware of all the facts when I started to pitch into you."

"Sure."

"And don't worry about Vera. I'll wire her for sound and get her to Grand Central if it's the last thing I do."

"I knew I could rely on you, Aaron. There is just one thing—your responsibility ends the moment she arrives in New York. From there on, we'll keep her under surveillance, so don't go messing up the cover. If you do and Kershaw is frightened off, we'll have your ass in a sling."

Hines wanted to know who Landers meant by "we," but before he could ask, Carl had hung up on him. He sat there staring at the phone, uneasy in his mind about Landers and not at all sure what he was going to do. Ever since Soviet Intelligence had gotten in touch with Vera, it had been evident to him that their information was coming from a highly placed source within the bureau. For a number of good reasons, Landers seemed the most likely candidate, but if Hines could figure that out, so could a lot of other people.

"This is a political shenanigan, it always has been." Hines thought that all kinds of things could be read into that statement, including the possibility that the FBI had set Carl up as a double agent. There was only one way to test the hypothesis. Lifting the receiver again, Hines called the director's personal assistant and told her he'd been trying to contact Mr. Landers for the past two hours and did she know where he was?

The PA was noted for being ultradiscreet and what little information he did manage to squeeze out of her tended to support Carl's story and erase the doubts in his mind.

★   ★   ★

Aldo Rozzi was a junior partner in the law firm of Brooks, Levy and Pheiffer. As he was fond of pointing out to his clients, he was everybody's idea of what the proprietor of an Italian restaurant should look like—short, dark, olive-skinned, cheerful, and several pounds overweight from eating too many of his own pizzas. The first to admit that his casual appearance suggested he was disorganized, with an equally untidy mind, he was in fact as sharp as a razor, an attribute that courtroom opponents who made the mistake of taking him at face value soon learned to their dismay.

Kirov knew nothing of his reputation at the bar. Rozzi was merely a name on a frosted glass door, and he had chosen the lawyer simply because his office happened to be in the same building and on the same floor as the notary public Elizabeth had used. As it happened, he couldn't have made a better choice; Rozzi listened attentively, made a few notes on his scratch pad, and didn't ask any questions until Kirov had finished briefing him.

"Let's see if I've got this straight," Rozzi said, glancing at his pad. "You have made some kind of oral statement that is now lodged in a safe deposit box at an unnamed bank somewhere in Manhattan. You want me to act as a custodian, and in this connection you propose to give me the key to the box. Every month between the first and the seventh, I will receive a telephone call from you during normal office hours. Should I not hear from you, I am to wait until the following month, then if there's still no word from you, I'm expected to locate the bank, take possession of the safe deposit box, and dispose of the contents?"

"You've got it," Kirov said. "The statement has been sealed in a jiffy bag addressed to the chief of Army G2, the Pentagon, Washington."

"Yeah?" Rozzi stared at him blankly, then gave a slight shrug and went back to his notes. "This arrangement is to continue for the foreseeable future or until such time as you terminate it in person." He looked up from his pad again. "How long is the foreseeable future?" he asked.

"Ten to fifteen years." Fedor Fedorovich was sixty-nine and Andropov only a year or so younger. Chances were that one or both of them would be dead long before the mid-1990s. In any event, the deterrent value of the cassette would be gradually eroded with the passage of time. There was nothing more fossilized than yesterday's headlines.

"I'm forty-seven and overweight," Rozzi said. "Suppose I had a fatal heart attack?"

"I was going to suggest that you nominate one of your partners to answer for you." Kirov smiled fleetingly. "That may sound a little callous, but on the other hand, you can't plan your vacations around my telephone calls."

"You've got it all figured out, haven't you, Mr. Kingsland?"

"I hope so."

"You want to tell me how I obtain possession of the deposit box, should the necessity arise?"

"I imagine you'll obtain a court order, then find the bank by a process of elimination."

"With a little help from the NYPD."

Kirov frowned. No briefing was ever 100 percent, and the initials temporarily floored him. "Is that likely to be a problem?" he asked, feeling his way.

"It depends on what's in the jiffy bag. I don't want any trouble from the cops."

"They won't give you any. There's nothing in the jiffy bag that could incriminate you."

"And that's all you're prepared to tell me?"

Kirov nodded. He was unwilling to confide in Rozzi, in case the lawyer was tempted to obtain a court order the moment his back was turned. He was also concerned about protecting Rozzi from Andropov's supporters, and the less he knew, the safer he would be. The judicial process would be his safeguard, and if the KGB did get on to him, he could always plead it was impossible to short-circuit the system.

"I'm supposed to take you on trust?"

"It works both ways, Mr. Rozzi."

"I guess it does." Rozzi opened a drawer in his desk, took out several sheets of letterhead notepaper. "All right, Mr. Kingsland, you may be a nut case for all I know, but you've got yourself a lawyer." He looked up, brown eyes twinkling. "It is Mr. Kingsland, isn't it?"

"That's what my billfold says," Kirov told him.

"In that case, my initial retainer will be two hundred dollars. Thereafter, it's a hundred and fifty a month, payable in arrears. I don't know if that sounds kind of steep to you, but you won't get a better deal in New York."

"You won't hear me querying the fees."

"Good. Now all I want are your instructions in writing." Rozzi selected a ballpoint from the cluster he kept in a pewter tankard on the desk and gave it to Kirov, then pushed the headed notepaper toward him. "It might save

272

us both a lot of time if I dictated the terms of reference," he said disarmingly.

★ ★ ★

Vera Berggolts glanced at her wristwatch, saw that it was a few minutes after twelve, and hurriedly stubbed out the cigarette she had been smoking. Leaving the coffee shop in the main concourse of Grand Central, she walked toward Gate 5, her eyes darting everywhere in the hope of seeing a familiar face in the noonday crowd. She remembered what Aaron Hines had told her before they'd parted and tried to console herself with the thought that Carl Landers and the others were there somewhere, watching her every move and listening to her heart beat. She had only to open her mouth and they would come running, provided, of course, that everything was in working order. Instinctively, she fingered the roll neck of the brown cashmere sweater she was wearing under the tan two-piece and felt the throat mike nestling in the hollow between her collarbones. From the mike, two thin wires passed beneath her bra to the flat miniaturized transmitter held rigidly in place below her navel with a strip of adhesive. Somewhat reassured, she wondered what sort of effect a loud cough would have on the bystanders, then a hand tapped her on the shoulder and she spun around, stomach suddenly churning.

"Hi, Vera." Kirov smiled, tried to embrace her, and felt a restraining hand on his chest. "Don't be stupid," he muttered angrily. "I don't care for this any more than you do."

He kissed Vera and continued to hold her close while he scanned the concourse. If the FBI was going to lift him, this was the moment when they would close in, but nobody in the immediate vicinity showed any signs of doing so. They were playing it cool, then, content to keep him under surveillance until she had made the phone call to Helsinki. It was pure guesswork, of course, but no matter what their intentions might be, he was fully committed now and there was no turning back. Releasing Vera, he seized her left hand and led her toward the IRT subway.

An itchy feeling between his shoulder blades prompted Kirov to check his back at the token booth and again after they'd passed through the turnstiles, but nobody appeared to be following them. Still wary, he started to follow the directional signs for the shuttle service to Times Square, then doubled back on his tracks to make for the Flushing line. It was the oldest trick in the book and the only reaction it produced was a sarcastic question from Vera Berggolts, who asked him if he knew where he was going.

"I know what I'm doing," Kirov told her. "Just be thankful for that."

He led her on down to the platform and joined the small crowd who'd gotten there ahead of them. Although there was safety in numbers, it worked both ways, providing cover for the hunted and the hunters alike. In an attempt to flush them out, Kirov gave the first train a miss and boarded the express that pulled in five minutes later.

At Forty-ninth Avenue, he got off and, holding Vera tightly by the elbow, steered her toward the exit, then stopped just short of it to read a billboard. The only other passenger equally reluctant to leave the platform was a thin, wiry-haired man wearing a jacket over a pair of faded jeans, who took time out to light a cigarette before he finally called it quits and shuffled past them.

Catching the next train, they went on up to Queensboro Plaza and switched to the Broadway local on the BMT line. One glance at the route map in their car was enough to give Vera Berggolts a fair idea of what he had in mind, and it didn't meet with her approval.

"I'm getting awfully tired of this charade," she snapped. "You keep this up much longer and we'll be back where we started."

"So?"

"So I want to know where we're going, Mr. Kershaw."

"Yes? Well, strictly between ourselves, I'm taking you to somewhere nice and private where there's a telephone."

"Where?"

"That's a trade secret," Kirov said.

"It'd better not be unless you want me to get off at the next stop."

"You're bluffing."

"You just wait and see if I am." Her voice rose in anger

274

and she rounded on him, eyes glinting spitefully. "You know how I feel about my father-in-law. I agreed to speak to him only because of the threats you made, but there's a limit to how far I can be pushed and you've gone beyond it."

Vera Berggolts's high, penetrating voice made itself heard above the grinding clatter of the train as it hurtled toward Lexington Avenue. From the interested expression on their faces, Kirov could tell that the elderly couple across the aisle was listening to every word she said. So was the transit cop who was standing in front of the communicating door to the adjoining car.

"For God's sake, keep your voice down." Kirov forced a smile for the benefit of the elderly couple. "Do you want everyone to overhear our conversation?"

"I just want to know where we're going."

It was the last thing Kirov wanted to tell her, but the transit cop was beginning to eye him suspiciously and he had no choice. "I've rented an apartment on Waverly Place," he told her quietly.

"Prove it."

"What?"

"You heard me—prove it. Seeing is believing."

Kirov hesitated, saw that the cop had moved a pace nearer, and reluctantly produced his billfold to show her the receipt he'd obtained from the real estate agent. "Here," he said, "maybe this will convince you."

"Apartment 8A, 117 Waverly Place," she intoned, then looked up and smiled. "Looks like I owe you an apology."

The mini-transmitter the FBI had provided for Vera Berggolts had an operating range in excess of one and half miles. The associated microphone was so ultrasensitive that it was capable of reproducing the noise made by the saliva in her mouth whenever she swallowed. Had she spoken in a whisper, her voice would still have carried to the FBI agents in the front and rearmost cars of the train. As it was, she almost deafened them.

The address of the apartment on Waverly Place was therefore heard by a young, attractive black girl in the front car who gave the impression that she was absorbed in the

275

music on her portable radio and by a thickset Irish-American wearing a patrolman's uniform who sat next to Carl Landers in the rearmost car. There was also one unauthorized listener, a mild-looking, sandy-haired man who wore rimless glasses and a hearing aid. His silent presence on the surveillance net was a direct result of the cable Vatutin had sent to the FBI source via Uddenholm and the head office of Nestor's Toy Emporiums. Known to Landers only as "the deaf Ukrainian," he left the train at Fifth Avenue, hailed a cab outside the subway station, and headed downtown to Washington Square.

As far as the State Department was concerned, the deaf Ukrainian was an interpreter with the Soviet delegation to the United Nations, whereas in reality he was a dormant member of the First Chief Directorate's Special Executive Department. He was a marksman with both rifle and hand-gun, but in common with other agents of the elite Special Executive Department, he had been taught a secondary trade during the two-year-long basic course. In his case, it had been that of a highly skilled locksmith.

CHAPTER XXI

Kirov made one more switch, changing to the IRT division's Lexington Avenue–Pelham local at 14th Street, then got off at Astor Place and started walking toward Washington Square. Vera Berggolts had ceased carping at him and had been in a much more conciliatory mood ever since he'd given her the address of his apartment on Waverly Place. In fact, she had become a little too friendly for his liking. The almost sunny disposition was out of character, and it was obvious to him that Vera was working at it. In his own mind, Kirov was convinced she had set him up for the FBI; the only unknown factor was just when they would arrest him.

Kirov stopped by a curbside street vendor, bought two

hot dogs, gave one to Berggolts and lingered by the stand, giving the square the once-over while he ate the soft roll and frankfurter. There was nothing to arouse his suspicion, but then he figured that the FBI could afford to play it cool. Chances were they had Vera wired for sound and, thanks to her, they already knew where they could find him.

Short of searching her, there was no way of proving his theory, but it was not an unreasonable assumption, and it certainly explained how they would be able to keep him under surveillance without showing themselves. He thought it likely they would grab him after she had phoned Helsinki and not before. Assuming he was right, then it followed that the U.S. State Department was not averse to lending Grigory Romanov a helping hand in his bid to succeed Brezhnev. Taking it a step farther, Kirov figured that the Reagan administration would be seriously embarrassed if the media got hold of that story. Vera Berggolts was there-fore his trump card, and he would make damn sure they left the apartment house together. Then, if the FBI did try to grab him on the street, he would do everything in his power to ensure that the incident got maximum publicity.

"Time we were moving on," Kirov said.

Vera nodded, dumped the remains of her hot dog in a trash bin, and wiped her fingers on a handkerchief. "I'm ready when you are," she told him.

Waverly Place was a five-minute walk from the east side of Washington Square. Nothing untoward happened in that time, nor did he see any unusual activity within the immediate area of the apartment house that suggested they were lying in wait for him. Cautiously, he ushered Vera into the hallway, then led her up to his flat on the fourth floor.

"End of the line." Kirov smiled. "From here on the rest is easy."

"I sincerely hope you're right, Mr. Kershaw."

It was the last intelligible thing she said. Unlocking the door, Kirov pushed it open, then stood to one side and gestured for her to lead the way. As she stepped across the threshold his left coat sleeve was splattered with brain tissue and small fragments of bone. A split second later, he heard

277

the distinctive noise made by a silencer followed by a small, animallike grunt from Vera Berggolts, who cannoned into the door frame, then collapsed like a rag doll, her legs folding beneath her at different angles.

Hugging the nearside wall to screen himself from the line of fire, Kirov crabbed his way down the staircase to the next landing as fast as he could, then broke cover and made a dash for the hallway two floors below. Once there, he paused just long enough to wipe the worst of the mess from his coat sleeve, then went on out into the street, turned right, and walked toward Sixth Avenue. He steeled himself to appear cool, calm, and collected, even though his every inclination was to break into a run.

★   ★   ★

Landers was approaching the intersection of MacDougal Street and Waverly Place when he heard the animallike grunt in his earpiece. Moments later the surveillance net exploded into life.

"Did you hear that, Dee?" a voice with an Irish brogue asked.

"I surely did, Carey," the girl confirmed, then fired a question at Landers. "What do you make of it, Carl?"

"I think Vera may have bumped into a piece of furniture."

"It didn't sound like that to me." Carey paused, then added, "You don't suppose he took a swing at her, do you, Carl?"

"Why would he do that?" Dee asked.

"Let's cut the idle chatter," Landers told them coldly.

Something was very wrong. The Ukrainian wasn't supposed to hit Kershaw while Vera Berggolts was still with him, but now it was beginning to look as though the idiot had jumped the gun. With Carey watching the back of the apartment house from MacDougal and Dee covering the other flank on Sixth Avenue, there was no way the Ukrainian could leave the place without being spotted unless Landers redeployed the surveillance team. He was still wondering how he could do this without arousing their suspicion, when he saw a familiar figure leave the building.

"Holy shit, it's Kershaw."

The words were out of his mouth before he knew it and they produced the inevitable reaction from the surveillance team. "Where's he going? What's he doing? Is Vera with him?" The questions came thick and fast, stretching his nerves to the limit.

"He's coming your way," Landers said hoarsely.

"Whose way?" two voices demanded almost simultaneously.

"Kershaw is heading toward Sixth Avenue." Landers took a deep breath, then continued in a much calmer voice. "Stay with him, Dee, but no heroics. Just keep me informed of his movements."

"Do you want me to back her up, Carl?"

"No, you get around here on the double," Landers told him. "We're going up to the apartment."

The cover was off now, leaving the Ukrainian a clear field, but he wasn't out of the woods yet. Full of apprehension, Landers stopped outside 117 Waverly Place, waited for Carey to join him, then entered the apartment house and went on up to the fourth floor.

The door to 8A was shut, but the key was still in the lock. Without saying a word, Carey unholstered his .38 revolver, moved to the left side of the door and took position, his back against the wall. Slowly and very gingerly, Landers turned the key, heard the lug disengage above the noise of a TV quiz program coming from the apartment across the landing, and gave the door a shove. It moved a bare six inches, then encountered an obstruction and refused to budge any farther. Backing off a pace, Landers hit the paneling with his right shoulder and forced the door open far enough for Carey to squeeze through the gap.

Vera Berggolts was lying flat on her back inside the small hallway, her feet surrounded by shards of glass and pointing toward the living room, her head close enough to the door to prevent it from opening fully. There was a neat round hole above the bridge of her nose and a lot of blood, slimy tissue, and brain fluid on the vinyl-tiled floor. But it was her eyes more than anything else that affected Landers; though blank and sightless, he felt they were accusing him. Mesmerized by the body at his feet, he stood there rooted to the spot while Carey went through the apartment checking out each room in turn.

"For Chrissakes, Carl, what the hell do you think you're playing at? Do you want the neighbors to see her lying there?"

Landers flinched as though Carey had struck him and hurriedly closed the door. "I was trying to figure things out," he mumbled.

"I would have thought it was pretty obvious. Kershaw knew Vera was going to be shot when he brought her to his apartment, but the hit didn't happen the way he'd been told it would and he thought the killer was gunning for him too. That's why he got the hell out of it so fast and left his key in the lock."

Landers nodded as though he agreed with everything the younger man was saying, but his mind was working on an altogether different track. The Ukrainian had bungled it and a golden opportunity to eliminate Kershaw had been lost. Worse still, Kershaw now knew that his own people were after him, and there was no telling how he would react. If Kershaw decided to ask for political asylum, his FBI interrogators would rapidly discover that Soviet Intelligence had a double agent in the bureau, and it wouldn't take them long to figure out who he was.

"The killer went after him but when he reached the landing, Kershaw was nowhere in sight. So he moved Vera's body, closed the door, and went out the back way. I figure he came down the fire escape soon after you'd pulled me off MacDougal."

The implication wasn't lost on Landers. In a roundabout fashion, Carey was saying that he'd goofed. It was an allegation that he'd undoubtedly voice more openly when the bureau held an inquiry. The Irisher was full of bullshit, but at least his half-baked theory had given him an idea.

"We're all going to end up with egg on our faces," Landers said testily. "You, me, the bureau, but most of all the State Department. They were hoping to put a dove into the Kremlin, but the people they were dealing with double-crossed them. The only thing we can do now is sweep the mess under the carpet."

"I don't see how."

"That's my problem. You seen a phone in your travels?"

"There's one in the next room."

"Good." Landers reached inside his jacket for a small notebook. "You want to check the number for me?" he asked.

"Sure." Carey moved past him into the living room and walked over to the phone, which was plugged into a socket near the window overlooking the street. "It's 212-9071," he called out, then lifted the receiver and held it to his ear. "It's in working order too."

"Thank God for small mercies." Landers jotted the number down and put his notebook away. "Okay," he said casually, "I want you to stay here by the phone while I go uptown and talk to Washington on a secure line. Once I know how they want to play it, I'll make the necessary arrangements for Vera's disposal, then call you on this number. Meantime, you'd better go through the apartment with a fine-tooth comb. You can never tell; Kershaw may have left something behind that will give us a lead. If the killer used an automatic, I doubt whether he'd have hung around to pick up the empty shells either. You got it?"

"Yeah." Carey removed his peaked cap, pushed a hand through his jet-black hair. "What about Dee?" he asked.

Landers frowned. He'd completely forgotten her in the heat of the moment. "Did you get all that, Dee?" he said loudly.

"Except for the phone number." Her voice kept fading and there was a lot of background mush, a sign of a faulty connection between her mike and the transmitter.

"Okay—it's 212-9071."

"Roger."

"Where are you now, Dee?"

"Approaching the intersection Sixth Avenue and 14th. It looks as though he's making for the subway."

"Keep us posted," Landers told her. "I'll get you some help soon as I can. Over and out."

Landers left the house on Waverly Place, made his way onto Sixth Avenue, and headed north. Entering the first pay phone he came to, he undid his coat and jacket, then unbuttoned his shirt at the waist and disconnected the lead from the throat mike to the transmitter.

He didn't need to look up Elizabeth Moorcroft in the directory. She had first come to the notice of the FBI back in September, when she had started making inquiries about her brother. Once State had decided Vera Berggolts should be encouraged to talk to her father-in-law, the FBI had automatically gone to their computer records and pulled a list of subversives whom Kershaw might turn to for assistance. The subversives were classified by age, sex, occupation, degree of risk, and geographic area. Elizabeth Moorcroft was a category five minimal-security risk living in Manhattan. Landers doubted very much if Moscow Center was aware that the FBI had her on file, and it was indicative of the kind of turmoil they were in over there that the briefing he'd received from them via Nestor's Toy Emporiums had been wholly inadequate. Without the computer printout to fall back on, he would have had no idea whom they were talking about.

Without disclosing his identity, he phoned Samuels and Stein, asked to speak to Elizabeth Moorcroft, and learned from her secretary that she was working at home.

Landers fed another coin into the slot and dialed his contact at the head office of Nestor's Toy Emporiums. He said, "I'm afraid we didn't clinch the deal."

"So I've heard."

The voice was cool, unruffled, and pleasant, qualities one would expect of a mature career woman who was undoubtedly very efficient. The image was pure conjecture; Landers had never met the lady, nor was he ever likely to.

"There's a chance we can get together for another meeting," he continued, "probably at Moorcroft's place at 71 East 59th Street. It could be we'll have to move on from there, and I think we should also beef up our sales team."

"We've already taken care of that," the woman told him.

"Fine. How quickly can you get in touch with your chief sales executive?"

"In no time at all. Mr. Quaker is standing by at the other end of the telephone."

Landers made a mental note that Quaker was the cover

name for the Ukrainian and told the contact he'd get back to her as soon as he'd prepared the ground. Then he put the phone down, reconnected the transmitter, and left the booth. The fact that the Ukrainian would ice Elizabeth Moorcroft along with Kershaw didn't bother him one bit. Ultimately, his survival depended on it.

*   *   *

Kirov entered the IND subway station on 14th Street, purchased a token at the booth and passed through the turnstile. He'd spotted the girl the first time he'd checked his back less than a city block from Waverly Place. She hadn't done anything to claim his attention, nor was she remarkably conspicuous. Indeed, he'd told himself that knickerbocker suits were all the rage, that young people did walk the streets of Manhattan listening to their portable radios, and that there were thousands of attractive black girls in New York, but a feeling that there was something vaguely familiar about her had persisted. Then suddenly, everything had jelled and he'd recalled catching a glimpse of her walking toward the exit as the train had pulled out of 23rd Street. She was obviously a Cuban, but there was nothing very surprising about that. The KGB frequently used a satellite intelligence service whenever they were faced with a particularly messy problem. The Poles, the Czechs, and the Bulgarians had all been given various "wet jobs" in the past, and no doubt the people in Moscow had reminded Castro that he still owed them the odd favor.

Kirov moved down the platform and stopped on the far side of a pillar to screen himself from the entrance. The girl had been roughly sixty yards behind him before he'd dived into the subway, and he calculated that he had a good one-minute head start on her, but less than forty seconds later, she ambled past him, seemingly unaware of his existence. Distancing herself from him, she gradually came to a halt and turned to face the track. The way her shoulders gradually relaxed was an indication of just how relieved she was to find that he hadn't given her the slip after all.

The girl was out on a limb without anyone to back her

up because he had caught the opposition on the hop. They hadn't expected him to walk away from the ambush, and their surveillance team had been too widely dispersed to react to the situation. It was her job to keep them posted while they regrouped before having another go at him, but right now her throat mike was about as much use as a bell without a clapper. There was a lot of concrete between her and the sky above, which would screen the emissions from her transmitter, reducing the signal strength to the point where there would be a virtual blackout.

The girl would have told them that he was making for the subway, but they had no idea where he was heading. By intelligent use of the system, he could switch from the IND to the BMT to the IRT and surface anywhere in Manhattan, Brooklyn, Queens, or the Bronx. He was safe, then, so long as he stayed below ground, but it would be a different story once he broke cover. He would have to shake her off but fast, then phone Nestor's Toy Emporiums to advise the contact that he or she was about to receive a very enlightening package. Thereafter, it was just a question of staying alive in the hope that the KGB would eventually decide to call off the hunt.

A distant rumble accompanied by an increasingly strong gust of warm air warned Kirov that a train was coming. As it clattered out of the tunnel and drew into the station, he instinctively glanced over his shoulder to see if anybody was standing directly behind him. One good shove at the right moment and the motorman would do the job for them, but the only person within striking distance was a very stout woman whose high color suggested she had high blood pressure. Boarding the train, he went on up to East 42nd, caught the shuttle and got out at Times Square.

The girl was a good thirty paces behind him when he exited onto Broadway and lost further ground in the lunchtime press on the sidewalk. In no apparent hurry, Kirov strolled past the Rialto, turned right onto West 42nd Street, and then broke into a loping run. The girl was still approaching the intersection when he dived into a porno movie theater, bought a ticket, and passed through the doors into the dark auditorium.

284

He stopped at a seat five rows down near the centre aisle, made sure no one was watching him, then got up, moved to the far end of the row and went out through one of the emergency exits into an alleyway. Turning left outside, Kirov followed the alleyway into West 43rd Street and flagged down a cab.

* * *

Elizabeth turned the page, found that she had come to the end of a chapter, and wondered if it was really worth going on to the next. The story line didn't make for compulsive reading and, being realistic about it, she knew she could never place the manuscript with a publisher. But the author was not without talent; given the right sort of encouragement, there was always the possibility that he would persevere and go on to produce something that was marketable. Still undecided what to do about the manuscript, she reached for a ham sandwich and found herself answering the phone instead.

"Miss Elizabeth Moorcroft?" The voice sounded well educated and belonged to a man who seemed very sure of himself.

"Yes. Who is this?" she asked, frowning.

"My name is Landers, Carl Landers. I'm with the FBI."

"Oh." She was about to add, "Hooray for you," but held it back. She had crossed swords with the bureau a month or two back and they were not her favorite people.

"We have reason to believe a man calling himself George Kershaw may have contacted you," Landers continued.

"What makes you say that?"

"Has he been in touch?"

It was another way of saying, "Just answer the question," and it made her hackles rise. "What is this?" Elizabeth demanded. "The Spanish Inquisition?"

"Please, Miss Moorcroft, this is important."

"Why?"

"Because George Kershaw is a Russian intelligence officer."

"If this is your idea of a practical joke, Mr. Landers, you've got to be sick."

285

"This is not a joking matter. I've never been more serious in my life."

"Why should I believe you, Mr. Landers? I don't know you from Adam; you're just a voice on the telephone. As a matter of fact, I think I'm going to put the phone down right now."

"Would you please do something for me?" Landers said, before she could hang up. "Would you look up the number of the FBI office in the Manhattan directory and call me back? I'm at extension 028."

"I'll think about it, Mr. Landers."

Elizabeth hung up and sat there staring at the phone. George a Russian spy? It didn't seem possible. Except . . . except, come to think of it, he'd never really told her anything about himself. Reluctantly, she looked up the number in the directory, then slowly punched it out, and asked the FBI switchboard operator for extension 028.

Landers said, "Thank you for returning my call, Miss Moorcroft. Believe me, you won't regret it."

But she did, the moment he began to tell her about the double life George Kershaw had been leading. Hurt, angry, and bewildered in turn, Elizabeth listened to him with only half an ear until he told her she could be in danger.

"From George?" she asked incredulously.

"He's on the run, Miss Moorcroft, and you may be the only person he can turn to for help. That's why we feel you need some protection. I'd like to handle it myself, but Mr. Quaker is a very experienced agent."

"Who?"

"Mr. Quaker."

"Oh." Elizabeth bit her lip, then said, "When can I expect him?"

"Ten, maybe fifteen minutes from now."

"I see."

"One other thing," Landers continued. "Kershaw may try to call you, so I don't think you should answer the phone from here on."

"Of course," Elizabeth said in a voice that sounded utterly dispirited.

"Thank you."

"For what?" she asked.

"For making my job that much easier," Landers told her.

Chapter XXII

The Ukrainian stared at the quartz clock in the dashboard, becoming more and more tense as the minutes ticked inexorably by. Ninth Avenue onto Columbus, a right turn onto West 65th and on across Central Park to Fifth Avenue, then south to East 59th; the driver had chosen the worst of all possible routes from the bar where he'd received the vital phone call from the woman at Nestor's Toy Emporiums. They should have arrived at the girl's apartment by one-thirty, yet here they were at a quarter of two stuck in a traffic jam on the transverse road through the park, and crawling toward Fifth Avenue.

It was just one more fiasco in a whole string of fiascos. He still couldn't understand how he'd missed Kershaw and killed the woman instead. Admittedly, he'd been on the other side of the interior door and the frosted glass had blurred the target in the hallway, but his brain should have registered the fact that the visible mass had suddenly contracted. He'd aimed dead center because a head shot was too chancy, and since he'd already taken up the first pressure on the trigger before Kershaw had stepped to one side, you could say the rest had simply happened by pure reflex. He'd assumed the same target would reappear and the index finger of his right hand had responded accordingly. Moscow, however, would never accept that his brain had been slow to register that the foresight was centered on the head instead of the chest; they would say he'd lost his nerve and panicked.

Not that he was the only one. Carl Landers sounded as though he too was in a panic; he could hear him on his hearing aid talking on the phone to a man named Carey from an office somewhere in Manhattan. Although he could hear only one side of the conversation, it seemed that Carey was still stuck in the apartment house on Waverly Place and was demanding to know what had happened to the ambulance that was supposed to be collecting the body.

The driver filtered into the traffic on Fifth Avenue and started to edge his way across the traffic flow toward the left-hand lane, muttering to himself in Russian. Like the morose Leningrader in the back seat, his command of the English language was limited and was yet another example of the kind of reverses that had bedeviled him all day. The idiots had only to open their mouths and the girl would know they weren't from the FBI.

The Ukrainian sighed; the operation had become a colossal gamble. There was no guarantee that Kershaw would show up at her apartment, and he would have preferred to keep the house under discreet surveillance, but Landers had committed him. The girl was expecting him and he would have to remain with her in the apartment while the other two stayed in the Chevrolet and watched the street. If Kershaw did put in an appearance, the Leningrader had strict instructions that he was to wait exactly five minutes before following him into the building. Although the plan had the virtue of being simple, it made him uneasy. Too many things could go wrong; one of the neighbors might notice the Chevrolet and phone the police to report that the occupants were behaving suspiciously, and there was no telling how the Moorcroft girl would react when he invited her to accompany him. It would be so much easier to shoot them both on the spot, but he'd been told that she and Kershaw had to disappear without leaving any trace.

The driver turned into East 59th and started checking the house numbers on the north side as they approached Madison Avenue. Finding a vacant spot at the curbside wasn't easy, and they had to settle for one outside number 83, which was some distance beyond the apartment house where the Moorcroft girl was living. Still muttering to himself in Russian, the driver reversed into the parking space and cut the engine.

Leaving them to it, the Ukrainian got out, walked back to the house, looked for her name among the list of tenants, and pressed the appropriate button. A buzzing noise told him she'd tripped the lock and, pushing the door open, he entered the building and climbed the staircase to her apartment on the second floor. He barely had time to ring the bell before the door was opened as far as the security chain would permit, a sign that she had been watching him through the peephole.

"My name is Quaker," he informed her politely. "I believe you're expecting me?"

"Yes. I had a phone call from Mr. Landers."

She fiddled with the security chain and finally managed to unlatch it. Distracted by the hearing aid, on which she kept her eyes fixed the whole time, this simple task seemed twice as difficult.

"It's a two-way radio," he told her.

"Oh, I'm sorry, Mr. Quaker, I didn't mean to stare at you." An apologetic smile made a brief appearance and softened her angular face. "Come in, won't you?"

He stepped inside a small hallway, waited until she had closed the door behind him, then followed her into a fairly large room with a dining area to his right. A three-piece suite that had seen better days was arranged in a semi-circle around the TV set, with a low coffee table in front of the settee. Four upright ladder-back chairs were positioned haphazardly about the room, divorced from the dining table, which had been pushed up against the far wall to serve as a desk. The telephone was partially concealed by an array of manuscripts.

"Has anyone called you since you spoke to Mr. Landers?" he asked.

"No." She shook her head, seemingly for emphasis.

"Are you expecting anyone at the office to phone?"

"Not unless there's something my secretary can't handle, and that's unlikely."

"Well, if it should ring, I recommend you don't answer it."

"Your Mr. Landers gave me the same advice," she told him.

"It bears repeating, Miss Moorcroft," he said mildly. "You can't be too careful when you're up against someone as ruthless as George Kershaw."

"If you say so." She shrugged her shoulders. "But from what little I know of George, I would never have guessed he was dangerous. Matter of fact, I still can't believe he's a spy."

"I wouldn't be here if he weren't."

"You have a point, Mr. Quaker. Of course, all this is way above my head. I mean, I don't understand how you knew he'd gotten in touch with me."

Her apparent bewilderment didn't fool him. It was just an act to catch him off guard, and he knew he was dealing with a very bright lady.

"It was a shot in the dark," he said casually. "Kershaw had to leave his apartment on Waverly Place in a hurry, and we found an address book amongst the personal effects he left behind. Your name was in it."

"George had an apartment downtown? That's funny; he led me to believe he was spending only a few days in New York?"

"Really? What else did he tell you, Miss Moorcroft?" It was vital he discover exactly what story Kershaw had given her, then he'd play it by ear from there.

"He claimed he'd met my brother when he was in Pakistan. He seemed to know an awful lot about Russ, where he was stationed, what he was doing, whom he worked for and the names of various noncoms. I got the impression he was either a Green Beret like Russ or with the CIA."

"He is—he just happens to be working for the other side. So, okay, Kershaw gave you a few names, but that doesn't mean anything. He was probably checking one source against another to verify the information he'd already obtained elsewhere. Take it from me, Kershaw didn't get in touch with you out of friendship. He had an ulterior motive."

"He certainly fooled me."

290

Her voice was brittle with anger, and it was also notice-able that in the last few minutes she had stopped referring to Kershaw as George. There was, he hoped, only one explanation for the sudden change of mood. Somewhere in the back of her mind she must have had a niggling doubt about Kershaw, and the Ukrainian had been lucky enough to confirm it.

"The whys and wherefores aren't important," the Ukrainian continued. "Right now, the one thing that matters is the fact that Kershaw is out there on the street in just the clothes he stands up in and he knows his Soviet control won't lift a finger to help him."

"And that's why you think he'll turn to me?"

"Well, if he does, we're going to be ready for him, Miss Moorcroft." The Ukrainian walked over to the window and beckoned Elizabeth to join him. "You see that blue Chevy a little way up the street? As soon as you let Kershaw into the building, one of my colleagues will get out of the car and follow him inside. When Kershaw rings the bell to your apartment, I'd like you to meet him at the door and show him into this room. Would you do that for me?"

"It'll be a pleasure, Mr. Quaker."

"Could you also try to look as though you're pleased to see him?"

"Don't worry," Elizabeth said grimly, "I won't frighten him off."

*　　*　　*

"Messenger, huh?" The counter clerk looked at the address Kirov had printed on the jiffy bag and pursed his lips. "I hate to see people wasting their money—211 West 34th Street is only a couple of blocks from here and Nestor's Toy Emporiums would get this package a whole lot quicker if you delivered it in person."

"I don't have the time," Kirov said.

"Well, I guess it's your dough." The clerk weighed the jiffy bag, his tongue clacking. "Let's hope your Ms. Damaris Roth doesn't leave the office before five, otherwise she won't get the package tonight."

There was no danger of that, Kirov thought. Once he'd acquainted her with the facts, it would be more than her life was worth. Pocketing his change, he left the messenger service office to make his way to Penn Station and the bank of pay phones outside the main concourse.

Damaris Roth had hung up on him the first time he'd called her, one of several mistakes she'd made from the moment she'd lifted the receiver. Most people either say "hello" or give their number when they answer the phone, but she had identified herself in a brisk, businesslike manner. That had been her first error; numbers two and three had been a sharp intake of breath followed by what had seemed a lengthy silence after he'd given her the code word. "I don't know anyone called Troika," she'd told him and then slammed the phone down. Nikishev had given him only a number; had Damaris Roth kept her head and bluffed it out, the identity of the contact at Nestor's would have remained in doubt and he would have been compelled to deliver the cassette in person.

Kirov entered the nearest phone booth, fed a coin into the slot, and punched out the number.

When Damaris Roth answered, he said, "This is Troika again, and this time don't hang up until I've finished. You're about to receive a package. It's marked 'Personal For' and will arrive before close of business today. The cassette inside the jiffy bag contains material of a highly sensitive nature. In the wrong hands, it could precipitate an international crisis the likes of which you and I have not seen in our lifetime. You get the picture?"

"I haven't the faintest idea what you're talking about."

"Then I'll spell it out for you," Kirov said grimly. "There are two identical cassettes. If anything happens to me or any member of my family, there is no way you can prevent the duplicate from reaching the U.S. Defense Intelligence Agency. Your only alternative is to ensure that the original gets to the right person in the shortest possible time."

"And just who is that?" she asked tartly.

"Whoever it is you're allowed to contact in an emergency."

"You don't know what you're asking."

292

"Oh, but I do. I'll call you again on this number at six and you'd better be there with some answers."

"Are you giving me an ultimatum?" she snapped.

"In the American vernacular, you bet your sweet ass I am," Kirov said, and hung up.

For the first time in weeks he felt he was in control of events instead of the other way around. The euphoria lasted all of a minute and was abruptly terminated by a montage of vivid recollections. In a fleeting kaleidoscope, he saw the hutted camp near the Afghan border at Pata Kasai, the Mi–24 hovering above the helicopter landing pad in the compound, and the stretcher bearers emerging from the side door, their heads unnecessarily lowered in the mistaken belief they were likely to be decapitated by the whirling rotor blades. Then Moorcroft, a skeletal figure in hospital fatigues, talking to him as though they were old friends who hadn't seen one another in years, while in the adjoining room a Signals NCO watched the spools slowly revolving on the tape recorder.

"Liz is the one I really get on with." Kirov stopped dead in his tracks, ice water in the pit of his stomach. Elizabeth was no stranger to the men in Moscow; it was all there on the tape—her name, address, and occupation. She couldn't hurt Andropov, but his supporters had already demonstrated they weren't the kind of people who left things to chance. Although she was a mere pawn in the game, the power struggle had started with Moorcroft and anybody who'd known him was now in danger, no matter how remote the connection. And Elizabeth was hardly in that category, for she had gained a reputation as a troublemaker by demanding to know what had happened to her brother. It didn't matter whether or not the highly placed source within the FBI had passed that item of information on to Moscow; the possibility existed and he couldn't afford to ignore it.

Kirov started to retrace his steps toward the bank of pay phones, then thought better of it. What could he say to Elizabeth over the phone that would make any sense to her? Leave town, your life in danger? Hell, Elizabeth would think he'd flipped out, especially if he told her he was an officer in the GRU and knew what he was talking about. But face to face, she might just believe him.

Kirov turned around, walked out into the street, and started looking for a cab.

★   ★   ★

The heroine, who was unbelievably attractive and a very talented copywriter, couldn't make up her mind whether she wanted to settle down and marry the nice but unexciting accountant from her hometown in Indiana or stay on in the big city and pursue her career. Her problem was further complicated by a growing awareness that she was falling in love with her boss, an older, more sophisticated woman who seemed to find her equally desirable. Her thoughts preoccupied with George Kershaw, Elizabeth really didn't give a damn what happened to the heroine of the manuscript she was trying to read, or her lesbian admirer either.

George Kershaw. There weren't enough four-letter words in even the most progressive of dictionaries to describe how she felt about him now. The gallant intelligence officer who was prepared to put his career on the line for the sake of Russell's handicapped daughter. To think he'd actually let her draw up an affidavit that he'd then sworn to in front of a notary public. Quaker had said he was probably out to verify the information he'd gotten from another source, but did he really have to prolong the charade? What purpose had it served other than to give him a sadistic kind of pleasure? Building people up only to let them down—maybe that was how Kershaw got his kicks?

"Well, well," Quaker said quietly. "It seems we guessed right."

"You mean Kershaw's arrived?" she asked.

"Yeah, he's just paying off the cab."

"Good," Elizabeth said venomously, "I can't wait to see his face."

★   ★   ★

Kirov tipped the cabdriver a dollar and gave the street a quick once-over. Then, satisfied that nobody appeared to be keeping the apartment house under surveillance, he

294

walked up the front steps to the porch and pressed the button alongside Elizabeth's name. Her voice sounded harsh when she came through the speaker to ask who was there.

"It's me." Kirov put his mouth close to the mike and tried again. "It's George," he said.

"What a nice surprise. Come on up, George."

There was a short buzzing noise followed by a click as she tripped the lock. Pushing the door open, he entered the hallway and went on up to her apartment on the second floor to find Elizabeth waiting for him at the top of the staircase. Her smile as she greeted him was dazzling, but it wasn't reflected in her eyes.

"I haven't come at an inopportune moment, have I?" he asked.

"Good heavens, no."

"I mean, if you're busy I can always come back later."

"I'm glad of a break. Come in, George. I'll make us a cup of coffee."

Although the affection she had shown him the previous evening was missing, Elizabeth seemed friendly enough. But he couldn't have been more wrong; as he followed her into the living room, Elizabeth suddenly whirled around and slapped his face with every ounce of strength in her body.

"You bastard. You lying, hypocritical bastard."

He saw the next swing coming and raised his left arm to block it. As he did so, a voice behind him said, "Freeze. Hold it right there."

Kirov glanced over his left shoulder. The man had his back to the wall and was standing a few paces to the right of the doorway into the hall. Anemic-looking and apparently hard of hearing, the one thing that impressed him was the automatic pistol leveled at his back.

"Who are you?" he asked.

"Quaker, FBI."

"I'm in no position to argue with you," Kirov said.

The automatic was fitted with a silencer, the kind of refinement a law enforcement officer was unlikely to require in the course of his duties. Furthermore, the attachment doubled the length of the barrel, making it too large for a

295

hip or shoulder holster. That meant Quaker had assembled the weapon while Elizabeth was letting Kirov in.

"What happens now?"

"You lie face down on the floor," Quaker told him, "arms and legs spread wide apart."

"Whatever you say." Kirov licked his lips. "Just take it easy, I don't want to end up dead on the carpet."

He was facing the wrong way and wasn't close enough to jump Quaker. Somehow he had to get within striking distance, and that wasn't going to be easy without some kind of diversion. Elizabeth had backed off and was nursing her wrist, which had evidently been bruised when he'd blocked her second swing at him. Glaring at her, Kirov went out of his way to provoke her. "You bitch," he mouthed silently, "you bitch."

She came at him fast, hatred in her eyes, fingers spread to rake his face with her nails. Grabbing her wrists, he gave ground, then swung Elizabeth around so that he presented a slimmer target for Quaker to aim at as he edged nearer.

"I said freeze," Quaker shouted.

"Then tell this hellcat to cut it out." Kirov shoved Elizabeth out of the line of fire and whipped around to face him. "The goddam bitch nearly clawed my eyes out."

"Why don't you shut your mouth and get down on the floor?"

"All right, all right."

Kirov folded at the waist, hands spread before him, right leg extended to the rear, the left bent at the knee. Quaker still had one eye on Elizabeth and the automatic had wandered to the right and was off target when he launched himself at him. Diving head first, Kirov butted him in the stomach and simultaneously knocked his right hand aside so that the pistol was pointing toward the far wall when it went off, shattering the china mug on the table where Elizabeth had been working. Quaker gasped for breath, staggered back into the wall, cracked his head, and went down. Landing on top of him, Kirov grabbed a handful of his hair and battered his skull against the wall until he was unconscious, then scrambled after the automatic that had fallen from his grasp and picked it up before Elizabeth could reach it.

"Okay," he said breathlessly. "I want some quick answers. Who else is with Quaker?"

"Go to hell."

"Take a good look at this pistol. It's fitted with a silencer."

"So?"

"So why does an FBI agent need one? And I'll tell you something else; this weapon is a Stechkin 9mm machine pistol with a twenty-round magazine and the capacity to fire single shot or in bursts. If the FBI is buying small arms from the USSR, it's news to me."

"Are you implying that Quaker is a Russian?"

Anger was slowly being replaced by doubt, but there was still a long way to go before she was prepared to trust him.

"He's not an American, that's for sure." Kirov held her eyes, silently pleading with Elizabeth to help him. "Now, how many others are there beside Quaker?" he asked quietly.

"There's a blue Chevrolet parked down the street," Elizabeth said, then stopped abruptly, taken aback by the sudden warning note from the buzzer. "That'll be one of his colleagues," she continued. "I'm supposed to let him in."

"All right, go ahead and do it. I'll take him when he comes through the door."

A momentary hesitation seemed agonizingly interminable, but finally Elizabeth went out into the hall and tripped the lock. Kirov followed her, checked which side the door was hinged on, then flattened himself against the wall a couple of feet or so beyond the opposing frame. When the door opened inward, he didn't want to be in a position where he was trapped behind it.

"I don't know why I'm doing this," Elizabeth said.

"I'll tell you later when there's more time."

"It isn't going to work, you know. One look at my face and he'll smell a rat."

"No, he'll expect you to look tense and shaken. After all, you've just been through a very harrowing experience."

Kirov heard the measured tread of footsteps on the staircase and froze. After what seemed an incredibly long time, the bell in the hallway finally rang. Bracing herself, Elizabeth opened the door, told Quaker's partner that he was waiting for him in the living room, and invited him to go on through. Then the unexpected happened, the way it often does. Instead of moving past Elizabeth when she stepped aside, the stranger paused to wipe his feet on the mat, glanced to his left, and saw Kirov.

"*Proizoshla Avariya.*" Kirov smiled, delivered a vicious jab to the stomach with his left and poleaxed him with the Stechkin machine pistol as he doubled up. "There's nothing like catching a man off guard," he observed.

"What did you say to him?"

"I said, there's been an accident."

"And he didn't understand."

"I spoke to him in his native tongue."

"Yes?" Elizabeth couldn't have sounded more skeptical if she'd tried.

"Perhaps I should have given him a chance to reply, but it didn't seem a good idea at the time." Kirov crouched over the unconscious Russian, searched him quickly, and found a Makarov in a shoulder holster under his left arm. "You've got to admit one thing," he said. "If Quaker and this man are FBI agents, the small arms manufacturers of America aren't making a fat living out of them."

"You're wasting your breath," Elizabeth told him. "I don't know a damn thing about firearms."

"And we're wasting precious time. You'd better get your coat and handbag."

"Why?"

"Because we're getting out of here and I'm practically flat broke."

"Oh, no." Elizabeth shook her head vigorously. "I'll give you what cash I have, but I'm not going with you."

"Listen, if you stay here, these people are going to kill you."

"We could go to the police."

Kirov straightened up, shoved both automatics into his coat pockets, then grabbed hold of Elizabeth and steered her into the living room. He liked the "we," but her suggestion was a nonstarter. As soon as the police learned about the Russian connection, they would hand them over to the FBI, and there were too many indications that the opposition had a highly placed source within the bureau for him to have any faith in the degree of protection the law enforcement agency would be able to afford them.

"No more arguments," he said. "Just grab your handbag, okay?"

Quaker was still unconscious and lay on his back staring blankly up at the ceiling with his mouth open. Bending over him, Kirov removed the hearing aid to inspect it more closely.

"It's a two-way radio," Elizabeth informed him. "At least, that's what Quaker said."

She had been deliberately misinformed; the module could receive but not transmit. At that particular moment, it was picking up one side of what appeared to be a telephone conversation.

"You ever heard this man before?" He held the miniature receiver to her ear and saw her eyes widen.

"It's Carl Landers," she said, "the FBI agent who sent Quaker here."

"Now you know why I don't trust them."

"I'm finding it difficult to know whom to trust lately. Everyone seems to have his own ax to grind."

The innuendo wasn't lost on him, but he noticed Elizabeth had collected her handbag and had put a coat on over the cardigan suit she was wearing. In the short space of time between leaving her apartment and reaching the street, he told her what he had in mind and what he'd like her to do. The occasional "uh huh" he got in return was singularly noncommittal and he could only hope she'd agreed to cooperate.

The blue Chevrolet was twenty yards or so to their left, a gray Mercedes in front of it, a Buick Electra behind. Kirov figured that the driver would have the interior mirror angled toward the house and would expect to see three men and a woman emerge from the building. There was no reason for him to suppose things hadn't gone quite the way Quaker had planned, and if Elizabeth was the first person to appear in view, there was a chance he'd assume everything was still okay and would take his eye off her momentarily to start the engine, ready for a quick getaway. By the time he looked into his mirror again, they would be outside the angle of vision.

As they approached the Chevrolet, the vapor from the exhaust pipe told him that at least one of his assumptions had been fulfilled. Still keeping well away from the curbside to minimize the risk of being seen, Kirov waited until they were level with the rear fender before he darted toward the car, yanked the rear door open and scrambled into the back. When the driver glanced over his shoulder, he found himself looking into the barrel of the Stechkin.

Kirov said, "Face front and switch off the engine. Then keep both hands on the wheel where I can see them and don't make another move unless I tell you to."

The driver gaped at him, eyes blank and uncomprehending until he repeated the order in Russian, when the message sank in. Sliding across the seat, Kirov positioned himself behind the driver, transferred the automatic to his left hand and pressed the silencer into the Russian's neck while he told him exactly how he was to surrender his pistol.

"Nice and slow, butt first over your right shoulder. You get the idea?"

"Yes."

"Good. Just remember this Stechkin's loaded, the safety catch is off, and my finger's taken up the slack on the trigger."

The driver gingerly removed a 9mm Makarov from his shoulder holster and passed the weapon back to Kirov. "What now?" he asked.

Kirov placed the spare automatic on the seat beside him, glanced toward the curb and saw that Elizabeth was standing by the nearside door, which meant that no one on the sidewalk could see what was happening inside the Chevrolet.

"You remove the keys from the ignition," Kirov told him. "Then you throw them at the window to your left."

"I do what?"

"When the lady gets in, you get out and wait for your friends."

"You're letting me go?"

300

"That's the general idea," Kirov said.

The keys hit the window and dropped back onto the seat almost before the words were out of his mouth. Responding to the signal, Elizabeth opened the door and got in.

"Say goodbye to the lady," Kirov told him.

"Goodbye."

"In Russian."

"*Do svidanya*." The driver opened the door on his side, scrambled out of the car, and hurried away.

"What was all that about?" Elizabeth asked.

"I was trying to make a point. Evidently you didn't get it."

"Yes, well, since I met you it's become increasingly difficult to tell the good guys from the bad guys."

"Come on, let's get out of here."

"Okay." Elizabeth moved in behind the wheel, inserted the ignition key, and started the engine. "Where do you want to go?"

"Anywhere, provided it's a long way from New York."

"You're the boss." Elizabeth pulled out from the curb, went on to Park Avenue and turned left. "Do you mind if I ask a question?" she said presently.

"Why not? It's supposed to be a free country."

"Just who the hell are you, Mr. Kershaw?"

"My real name's Kirov," he said, "Georgi Kirov. I'm a major in the Glavnoe Razvedyvatelnoe Upravlenie, commonly known as the GRU."

"What does that make you? A spy or a defector?"

"Neither. I'm a special envoy. I was sent over here to persuade a spoiled young woman that it was time she returned home to Leningrad. Unfortunately, I wasn't successful."

"She turned you down?"

"The lady's dead," Kirov said flatly. "Quaker shot her."

Elizabeth reared back, inadvertently steered toward the inside lane, and got a blast on the horn from an irate taxi driver as she hastily put the wheel over to the left.

"Of course it was a mistake," he continued in the same expressionless voice. "Quaker was gunning for me and hit the wrong target. Some of the high-powered men in the

301

Politburo and the KGB are going to be very unhappy about that. They thought they had a foolproof scenario. Then Brezhnev died sooner than expected and I started to make a nuisance of myself, so they had to unscramble everything fast."

"You're not making an awful lot of sense, Kirov."

"Well, that's politics for you. In your country, you have the executive, the legislative and the judiciary; in mine, we have a troika consisting of the Politburo, the KGB, and the armed forces, which in effect means the Red Army."

It was difficult, he said, for an outsider to understand the machinations of the Politburo in their desire to keep both the Red Army and the KGB in check and why Stalin and his successors had always played them off against each other. The thing she had to grasp was the ever-present fear in their minds that both organizations might become powerful enough to supplant them. It was this secret dread that had led Stalin to unleash the Secret Police and decimate the entire officer corps in 1937 when Marshal M. N. Tukhachevsky had let it be known abroad that the Red Army was there to defend Russia, not the Politburo. Sixteen years later, Khrushchev and the Politburo had used the Red Army to pen the Secret Police in their barracks while they liquidated Beria. From then on, the army's star had been in the ascendancy; they had made Khrushchev, survived the Cuban debacle, and consolidated their position under Brezhnev.

"The Politburo couldn't allow the situation to continue; the army had to be cut down to size while Brezhnev was still alive, otherwise the generals would be choosing his successor. So they set out to discredit the GRU because we're the eyes and ears of the armed forces. We had to be caught red-handed, dabbling in politics at the behest of the high command. Their concept was bold, original, and ingenious, but if the smear was going to stick, they needed a creditable envoy, someone who would point a finger at the five-star generals."

"And they chose you," Elizabeth said tersely.

"I had the necessary credentials."

Even now, he could only guess the rest of the scenario.

The KGB had probably photographed him when he'd met Vera Berggolts in New Haven, and there would have been other candid camera shots of her and Mischa Romanov returning home via some clandestine route like Halifax, Reykjavik, Helsinki, and the border crossing point at Vyborg. The Denisenko episode in London had obviously been a curtain raiser designed to make people think the people at the GRU were a bunch of incompetent assholes who were capable of committing every blunder under the sun. Two major scandals, one following hard on the heels of the other, would persuade the generals to stay on the sidelines and effectively kill any political aspirations Grigory Romanov may have had.

"What about my brother, Kirov? Was he part of your credentials?"

The question came like a bolt out of the blue and left him unnerved. "He restored my somewhat tarnished reputation," Kirov said, carefully feeling his way.

"How?"

"Russell gave me certain highly classified information that other interrogators had allegedly been unable to obtain."

"I see."

She put a wealth of meaning into two little words, and he writhed inwardly as though she'd just cut him with a whiplash. "I see" implied he'd tortured Moorcroft, subjecting him to every kind of bestial treatment until his spirit had been completely and utterly broken.

"I didn't lay a finger on your brother," he told her, "nor did any of the NCOs under my command. Russell told me everything he knew because the KGB had already broken him. The whole thing was a put-up job to make me look good in the eyes of my superiors. Your brother participated in that deception because the KGB had led him to believe that he would be exchanged for one of our agents if he cooperated."

"You don't really expect me to believe all that garbage, do you, Kirov?"

He didn't answer her, just sat there like a stone man. Park Avenue merged with Harlem River Drive and gradually her foot went down on the accelerator, building speed until

303

they were doing close to sixty. The George Washington Bridge was the one landmark he recognized from the trip to New Haven, but thereafter he hadn't the faintest idea where they were, and Elizabeth didn't enlighten him. Highbridge Park, Dyckman Street, and the Henry Hudson Parkway: the directional signs left him none the wiser.

"Did you kill Russ?" Elizabeth asked, breaking a long silence.

"No. I've already told you I never laid a finger on him."

"He was alive and well when you last saw him. Is that what you'd have me believe, Kirov?"

"He was alive. His right leg had been amputated above the knee and he'd lost a lot of weight."

"How much weight?"

"I'd say he was down to a hundred and ten pounds." Kirov cleared his throat with a dry nervous cough. "Russell was taken prisoner on the seventh of June; I saw him for the first time on Saturday the twenty-third of October."

"And that's your alibi, is it?"

The cold front that had built up between them plummeted to zero and enveloped them in an icy cocoon of silence. Grim-faced, they went on up the Henry Hudson Parkway past Inwood Hill Park and crossed the toll bridge over the Harlem River.

"It's time we ditched this car and got another," Kirov said abruptly.

"Are you thinking of adding auto theft to your list of crimes?"

"No. I figured we'd rent one. You've got a credit card, haven't you?"

"My God, Kirov, you've got a nerve."

"I'm glad you think so," he said dryly. "I'm going to be in need of it if we're to make a deal with the KGB."

"You're proposing to do what?" Elizabeth snapped.

"Make a deal—it's in everyone's interests."

"No way. If you didn't kill Russ, those people did."

"And you're crying out for justice. You want the whole world to know what happened to your brother."

"Yes."

"The U.S. State Department won't like it. They'll deny

the whole story, because they're not going to admit to an American involvement in Afghanistan."

"Then I'll give the story to the *New York Times*."

"That's a terrific idea," he said caustically. "If they print it, you could well become a footnote in history books, like the assassin at Sarajevo. Except there may not be any more history books by the time you've finished stirring things up. Right now, there are some very nervous men in the Kremlin and, equally, there are quite a few hawks knocking around Washington who are not averse to meddling with the internal affairs of my country. You put the two factions into juxtaposition and you've got a very explosive situation. Surely you can see that?"

Elizabeth made no comment and what little he could see of her face in the rearview mirror was just as uncommunicative. If there was a more persuasive argument that would make her see reason, Kirov wished it would come to him in a blinding flash of inspiration. Truth was, he was tired, so tired he could hardly keep his eyes open, much less think straight. He peered at his wristwatch and was amazed to see that it was only a quarter of four. Bloody thing must have stopped, he mumbled to himself, and stared at the second hand, lids drooping, then closing altogether.

He came to less than ten minutes later, his subconscious suddenly registering the fact that the rolling motion had stopped and it was singularly quiet. A Cadillac parked in front of them . . . a precinct across the street . . . drugstore, Jewish bakery, and a delicatessen . . . His heart started thumping.

"There's an Avis rental agency a little way back." Elizabeth twisted around to face him. "You'd better stay here while I do the necessary."

Kirov gazed at her uncomprehendingly, like a boxer who'd taken one punch too many.

"You still want to ditch the Chevrolet, don't you?" she said.

"Why don't I come with you?"

"Don't you think it would look a little odd, me renting a car on my credit card, you just standing there watching me?"

Elizabeth had a point but he felt vaguely uneasy and wondered what had suddenly prompted her to be so helpful.

"I guess you're right," Kirov conceded reluctantly. "Give me a toot on the horn when you drive past, then I'll pull out and follow you. Three short and one long blast is your signal to pull over to the side and stop. It would only arouse people's curiosity if we made the switch here."

"Right."

Elizabeth opened the door and stepped out onto the sidewalk. Changing places, Kirov got in behind the wheel and watched her walk away in the rearview mirror. His stomach began to churn the moment she reached the intersection and turned the corner to disappear from sight.

One emergency phone call and it would all be over. She knew the license number of the Chevrolet and could tell the cops exactly where it was parked. And when they searched him, they would find three automatics on him, one of them a murder weapon. The FBI would receive him, gift wrapped like a present on Thanksgiving Day. He was the ideal scapegoat, the jealous lover who'd taken Vera Berggolts to an empty apartment and blown her brains out. The perfect solution to a vexing problem, one that would certainly get Landers off the hook and would undoubtedly be greeted in Moscow with a huge sigh of relief.

A horn blasted and made him jump out of his skin. Then a two-door Ford glided past with a familiar figure at the wheel and he let out a joyous whoop, started the engine, and shifted the automatic transmission into drive. A mile farther on, he signaled Elizabeth to pull over to the curb, overtook the Ford and turned right into West 252nd Street. Then he parked the Chevrolet, locked the doors, and walked back to the main road. Any wishful thinking that everything had been forgiven and forgotten was quickly dispelled when he got into the Ford.

"I don't know how to thank you," he began.

"Don't even try," she said coolly. "Just tell me where you want to go."

"Where are we now?"

"Riverdale."

"Come again?"

306

"It's in the Bronx."

Kirov nodded, made a mental note of the location. "All right," he said, "keep heading north."

Elizabeth drove on, made a series of incomprehensible turns and, more by luck than judgment, managed to get back on the Henry Hudson Parkway. The road veered eastward, led them into Van Cortland Park and a maze of spaghetti loops. By the time Elizabeth got herself sorted out, they were traveling due south on a slip road to the Major Deegan Expressway.

"Sorry about that," she said. "The directional signs confused me, but I know where we are now."

They headed north again into Yonkers, found themselves on Interstate 87 and crossed the Hudson by the Tappan Zee Bridge. Leaving the toll road, Elizabeth swung onto Route 9W and drove through Nyack. Exactly six miles beyond the outskirts of town, Kirov asked her to pull off the road and stop.

"You mind telling me why?"

"I want to get rid of this arsenal I'm carrying around."

"And leave yourself defenseless?" She shook her head. "You must be nuts."

"Please, just do as I ask."

"Well, okay, it's your funeral." Elizabeth eased her foot on the accelerator, steered onto the hard shoulder, and applied the brakes. "There," she said. "Does that suit you?"

Kirov ignored the question and checked the odometer; then he got out of the Ford and looked around. From the hard shoulder, a narrow rough verge fronted a strip of dense woodland beyond which lay the Hudson. Away to his right in the direction of Nyack, Hook Mountain rose precipitously from the river's edge on the west bank to a height of eight hundred feet.

He walked slowly forward toward the tree line following a manmade track that meandered through the coarse grass, his eyes searching the ground for a distinguishable landmark that Quaker would be able to recognize without too much difficulty. Fortune smiled on him; some twenty yards inside the wood and just off the path, he found the classic drop, an oak tree with a hollow trunk. Bending down, he unloaded

307

his coat pockets, stuffed both Makarovs and the Stechkin inside the hollow and covered them with dead leaves. That done, he returned to the Ford, counting off the number of paces to himself.

"Where did you dump them?" Elizabeth asked him. "In the river?"

"No, I found a suitable cache that Quaker should be able to locate."

"Now I know you're crazy."

"It's all part of the deal," he said vaguely.

"You know something, Kirov? You could make a fortune if you took up poker. The way you play things close to the chest, no one would ever know what cards you were holding."

"You're wrong there," he told her. "At least one other person in this game knows exactly what I have in my hand. However, I do have one surprise in store for them."

"I'm glad to hear it." Elizabeth switched on the ignition and started the engine. "Where to now?" she asked.

"Someplace off the beaten track where I can make a phone call."

"How about the Catskill Mountains? They're roughly a forty-minute drive from here."

Kirov glanced at the clock in the dashboard, saw that it was close to 5.20, and said, "Why not?"

Checking to make sure the road behind was clear, Elizabeth pulled off the hard shoulder and drove on to Kingston, the light fading rapidly.

*　　*　　*

The Mobil filling station was situated midway between Kingston and Phoenicia on Route 28 and was just the sort of place Kirov had had in mind. Totally isolated, it lay back from the road on a level, crescent-shaped piece of ground below the wooded slopes of Slide Mountain. The only sign of life was a light burning in the office on the forecourt where, in addition to the usual toilet facilities, he'd noticed there was a pay phone. As they turned off the road and drove toward the pumps, a cable stretched across the gravel summoned a friendly-looking attendant from the office.

Alighting from the car, Kirov waited while Elizabeth told the man to fill the tank, check the oil, and clean the windshield, then steered her toward the pay phone.

"This is the moment of truth, is it?" she said.

"Now's as good a time as any to start praying."

He closed the door behind them, lifted the phone off the hook, fed thirty cents into the slot, and dialed the office number of the contact at Nestor's. It rang just twice before she answered the call in a breathless voice. Beckoning Elizabeth to draw nearer, Kirov held the receiver between them so that she could overhear the conversation.

He said, "This is Troika again. I assume you've received the package I sent you?"

"About two hours ago," she told him.

"And?"

"Everybody's been told to cool it for the time being."

"Yes? Well, since our mutual friends are obviously thinking it over, you can tell them to add Elizabeth Moorcroft to the list of untouchables. And while you're at it, you can also inform them that I want a hundred thousand dollars in cash."

"A hundred thousand dollars?" she repeated in a voice that had risen an octave. "Are you mad?"

Kirov said he'd never been saner and that she was the one who was being stupid. What he was asking was a small price to pay for his silence, and the embassy would have no difficulty in raising the money. She forgot that in his line of business he knew precisely how much petty cash they had in the contingency fund for just such an emergency. Then he told her where he'd left the Chevrolet and how Quaker could find the missing hardware in the hollow of an oak tree 6.4 miles north of Nyack on Route 9W.

"Have you got all that?" he asked.

"There's nothing wrong with my shorthand."

"There'd better not be." Kirov glanced at the dial, read out the phone number, then said, "I'll be here on Monday at 10:00 A.M. eastern standard waiting for a call from our mutual friends in a different time zone. There will be no last-minute haggling. If they find the terms unacceptable, they needn't bother to phone me."

309

"You're being very high-handed, aren't you?" she said.

"I can afford to be; it's a seller's market."

Kirov hung up before she had a chance to come back at him. He thought he'd sounded like a man who was very sure of himself, but despite the confident tone, his palms were slippery and tiny beads of perspiration were oozing from his forehead.

He wiped his brow with the back of his hand. "It's a little stuffy in here," he said, smiling weakly.

"Yes."

He could tell there was a question on the tip of her tongue, but she didn't know how to put it. "Something bothering you?" he asked.

"In a way." A pause, then, "Why do you want a hundred thousand dollars?"

"I don't. It's for your niece. Russell just cashed in his insurance policy."

"I don't think you should have gone out on a limb for Victoria. To browbeat them like that can only make things worse for you."

It wasn't quite the reaction he'd expected, and her attitude left him feeling deflated. Pushing the door open for Elizabeth, he followed her out of the booth and paid the attendant for the gas with his last ten-dollar bill. When he turned around, he saw that she had changed places with him.

"I thought you'd like to drive," she told him as he got in behind the wheel.

They drove on to Phoenicia, checked into a motel on the outskirts, then dined at a restaurant in town. They ate, making desultory but polite conversation like two strangers obliged to share the same table. Elizabeth said she would have to phone Samuels and Stein first thing in the morning to explain her absence, though right now she couldn't think of a convincing excuse. Kirov suggested that a virus infection allied to a sore throat might do the trick, but it appeared that her secretary would know she wasn't calling from home. Toward the end of the meal, Elizabeth slipped him forty dollars to pay the bill while she went to the powder room. After he'd settled up, they walked around the town looking for a drugstore that was still open and bought a couple of toothbrushes and sundry other items. Then they made their way back to the motel and watched TV for a while before retiring early to the twin beds separated only by a narrow locker that might just as well have been a high partition.

It was only after he'd put the lights out that she suddenly confessed what he'd suspected all along.

"There's something you should know, Kirov," she said quietly. "When I walked into that Avis rental agency back in Riverdale, I had every intention of asking the receptionist to call the cops."

"Why didn't you?"

"That's a difficult question to answer. I can give you two very good reasons why I should have done so—you're a Russian intelligence officer and an eyewitness to a homicide—but somehow I couldn't bring myself to do it. Oh, I wanted to hurt you all right—Quaker had destroyed all my illusions and I was angry that I'd allowed myself to be taken in by you. I know it sounds crazy, but I really thought that meeting you was one of the best things that had ever happened to me. I liked, admired, respected, and even loved you for the way you were prepared to put your whole future at risk. Then Landers told me you had been using me as a sounding board and I felt betrayed."

"I did intend to use you," Kirov said. "I wasn't exactly sure how you could help me protect the people I loved, but there was no one else I could turn to."

He told her about Fedor Fedorovich and Irena, half sister and surrogate mother, and why they both meant so much to him. He talked about Tania Abalakinova and why he'd gone off the rails after she had been killed and how his erratic behavior had rebounded on the entire family and made life difficult for them. With that kind of background, he was the perfect foil the KGB was looking for, a man with the right connections and a chip on his shoulder, someone they could later prove was a psychological mess.

"Even before things started to go wrong in London, I knew there was a bad smell about this assignment, but there was no way I could duck out of it. I had to go on and do the best I could for Irena and Fedor Fedorovich. Then I met

311

you, and almost at once you became the most important person in my life. I'll tell you why I made that statement and agreed to have it notarized: because it gave me an excuse to see you again. Can you believe that?"

"Yes." Her voice was no more than a sigh, like the wind in the fir trees outside their cabin.

"Russell never meant to involve you," he went on, "but every word that passed between us was on tape, and when it occurred to me that the KGB might go after you, that was another situation I couldn't walk away from."

"You're a fine man, Kirov. It would be very easy to fall in love with you."

"Don't," he said. "There's no future in it."

"Then let's not waste what little time we have," Elizabeth said and came to him in the dark, warm and loving and tender.

★   ★   ★

It snowed on Monday, brief flurries from a gray sky that was exactly in keeping with Kirov's somber mood as he stood there in the booth, one eye on the phone, the other on his wristwatch. It was 9:59 A.M. eastern standard time, 5:59 P.M. Moscow time; the second hand moving inexorably toward zero. Minus thirty seconds: he swallowed nervously, his mouth suddenly dry. Minus fifteen: what if there was no word from Moscow? Did he defect? Minus ten—nine— eight—seven—six—five—he found himself holding his breath. Four—three—two—one—the phone rang and slowly he lifted the receiver.

"Troika." Kirov closed his eyes. "This is Troika," he repeated in a harsh whisper.

And then a cool voice a long way off said, "Well, now, Georgi don't you think it's time you came home?"

Chapter XXIII

The pilot lost altitude and took the Mi-24 around again, affording Kirov a bird's-eye view of the camp below. Nothing had changed: same dreary barrack huts in the middle of nowhere surrounded by a barbed-wire perimeter fence, same H-pad in the center of the compound, a smoke pot indicating a moderate cross wind. The usual fire-fighting party was there at the ready, a junior NCO and two private soldiers standing off to one flank equipped with hand-held foam extinguishers that couldn't put a decent bonfire out, let alone a major conflagration. Behind them stood the rescue team, two fatigue men dragged from the cookhouse and issued axes (felling) for the occasion. Up front and out of sight at the moment would be the man who was supposed to guide the pilot down once the helicopter went into the hover above the H-pad. His presence, however, was largely superfluous; few pilots took much notice of his hand signals, preferring instead to rely on their own judgment.

The helicopter made another tight turn. As it did so, Kirov caught a fleeting glimpse of a familiar dumpy figure striding across the compound from his office. A Zil six-by-four truck appeared in view, its tailboard lowered ready to receive the miscellaneous stores and fresh rations surrounding him in the cargo hold. Then the Mi-24 lost altitude rapidly and went into the hover, the NCO crewman in the cargo hold prematurely opening the sliding door a few moments before the pilot set the helicopter down on the H-pad.

Kirov unfastened the seat belt, picked up his suitcase in his left hand, and alighted from the helicopter. Holding onto his peaked cap to prevent it being swept off his head by the downwash from the whirling rotor blades, he walked toward Colonel Leonid Paskar. When level with the fire-fighting party, he let go of his cap and started marching, head up, shoulders back, right arm swinging. He halted

313

several paces in front of the colonel, grounded the suitcase, snapped to attention, and saluted.

"Major Kirov reporting for duty," he said formally and just about made himself heard above the dying whine from the turbine engines.

Paskar returned his salute, then stepped forward and embraced him. "It's good to have you back, Georgi. How long have you been away? Four months?"

"I left here on the twenty-seventh of October," Kirov said. "Eleven weeks ago tomorrow."

"Funny." Paskar shook his head. "I could have sworn it was longer than that."

"So could I."

The last seven weeks in Moscow had seemed a lifetime. "My name's Viktor Ignatchenko," his interrogator had said, introducing himself, "and this is Mikhail Dishukin. We're KGB." Then it had started, an endless stream of questions and accusations. How well did the comrade major know Dmitri Nikishev? Was he aware that this former officer was now under arrest pending trial on charges of fraud, theft of official documents, and currency speculation? Would he be surprised to learn that Nikishev had made a voluntary statement that implicated him? Question and accusation, question and answer; two sessions a day, seven days a week for a solid month. And always it had been Nikishev they'd wanted to talk about, never Vera Berggolts. There was no such person as far as Ignatchenko and Dishukin were concerned, and by the time they'd finished brainwashing him, he'd almost begun to think she'd never existed either.

"I don't see what you've got to look so disgruntled about," Paskar told him. "I only wish I were in your shoes."

"Do you?"

"I should say so. What wouldn't I give to spend a week in Moscow every month? How did you wangle it, Georgi?"

"Influence," Kirov said.

"I thought so." Paskar waited until he'd picked up his suitcase, then steered him toward the officers' quarters on the far side of the compound. "How is General Fedor Fedorovich these days?"

"As well as can be expected at his age."

But he wasn't. His father had changed out of all recognition since he'd been away. His color was bad, his skin blotchy, and his chest wheezed every time he drew breath. Lydia had told him that Fedor Fedorovich had already had one severe attack of bronchitis since the onset of winter, but despite what his doctor had said to him about smoking and drinking too much, he'd refused to cut down on either habit.

"Does he get out and about?" Paskar asked.

"Not as much as he used to."

"The general won't like that, he was always a very active man. Still, I expect he has plenty of visitors, old comrades like Defense Minister Ustinov?"

Kirov wondered who'd told him that. His father certainly hadn't. Although Paskar liked to pretend that he and Fedor Fedorovich were old friends, they weren't even on nodding terms. The only time they'd served together had been during the latter stages of the Great Patriotic War when Fedor Fedorovich had been a major general of artillery on Zhukov's staff while Paskar had been commanding a rifle company in the Third Shock Army.

"Well, here we are." Paskar stopped outside one of the wooden huts, opened the door, and ushered Kirov inside. "Same old room, I'm afraid, but the quartermaster has done his best to make it more comfortable for you."

The quarters had been furnished originally with a single bed, combination closet and chest of drawers, a bedside locker, a wooden upright chair, and a trestle table. As far as Kirov could see, the fireside chair and a small rug were the only improvements that had been made in his absence.

"It's very nice," he said, trying to sound as though he meant it.

"I thought it would meet with your approval." Paskar glanced at the potbellied stove, unbuttoned his greatcoat, and sat down on the bed. "Better close the damper after I've gone," he said. "Damned fire has been on the draw since first thing this morning."

"Right."

Kirov removed his greatcoat and opened the closet to hang it up, only to find there was very little room. Most of

315

the available space was already taken up by his mess kit and spare winter field uniforms, all of them recently pressed and neatly arranged on coat hangers. It was the same with the chest of drawers; his shirts and underwear had been freshly laundered and carefully put away.

"Your trunk arrived a couple of days ago," Paskar told him. "I got my orderly to unpack it."

"That was very kind of you, Comrade Colonel."

He'd packed the trunk the night before he'd left for Moscow. According to his movement order, the Military Communications Service was supposed to send it on by rail, but in all probability the trunk had never left the freight depot at Tashkent.

"To tell you the truth, Georgi, I didn't expect to see you back in the unit, and I'm not sure what we're going to do with you. GRU Headquarters sent us a replacement officer at the beginning of December and he's taken over your old job. It's been suggested that we should establish a special section to process the raw intelligence we're getting from Kabul, and that could be right up your alley. Still, that's something we can discuss over dinner tonight." Paskar stood up and buttoned his greatcoat. "Seven o'clock, my quarters. All right?"

"I'll look forward to it."

"Me too. We can compare notes; from what I've heard, Moscow is awash with rumors these days. There's even a buzz going the rounds that Grigory Romanov is in line for a top job."

"Really?" Kirov raised his eyebrows, seemingly astonished. "That's news to me."

But it wasn't. He'd heard the same story from Fedor Fedorovich the night before last, when he'd dined with his father and Lydia. "I don't believe it," he'd said. "His son, Mischa, lives in America; he followed Vera Berggolts into exile after she defected." Then in his inimitable way Fedor Fedorovich had told him he knew fuck-all about it and, as usual, had got it wrong again; Mischa happened to be Romanov's nephew, not his son, and, far from defecting, had gone to Yale on an exchange fellowship. Furthermore, he was still single.

316

"Do you think there's anything to the rumor, Georgi?" Paskar asked.

"I don't know, Comrade Colonel."

"Leonid." Paskar smiled, revealing dentures stained with nicotine. "You may call me by my first name, Georgi. We're not on duty now."

Kirov gulped. "I'll try to remember that—Leonid," he said faintly.

"Good." Paskar nodded approval, then said, "Actually, I heard it from General Petr Ivanovich Ivashutin when he paid us a surprise visit ten days ago."

It was true, then, what his father had said. For all that he was in power, Yuri Andropov had one eye over his shoulder and was busy building bridges. Fedor Fedorovich had also intimated that Andropov was a very sick man and was unlikely to make old bones. Perhaps that was why the Politburo had prepared a sanitized biography that would appear in *Pravda* the day after Grigory Romanov was promoted and joined the hierarchy in Moscow. Kirov smiled bitterly, thinking how ironic it was that in a perverse way he had opened the door for him.

"Are you going to share the joke, Georgi?"

"What?"

"You were smiling at something."

"Oh, well, I was just recalling some rather impractical advice my father gave me when he told me to keep my head well down."

"I don't follow."

"He thinks I should see service in a more active theater. In his view, no one really knows a thing about soldiering until they've been shot at."

"He has a point," Paskar said gravely.

"Oh, quite, but there's a fat chance I'll be sent to Afghanistan."

"I wouldn't be too sure of that if I were you." Paskar opened the door, went down the steps, then turned around. "You know the army, Georgi; anything's possible," he said and closed the door.

Kirov picked up his suitcase, dumped it on the bed, then moved silently to the window and watched Paskar striding across the compound. Was that how it was going to be? A bullet in the back and a telegram to Fedor Fedorovich informing him that his only son had been killed in action? That would be a neat solution to a vexing problem. But it was unlikely to happen for a while; the men in the Politburo were realists, they knew he could reach them from the grave, and Andropov would wait until he was very sure of his position before he gave the word. Meanwhile, they would continue to allow him to phone New York every month and talk to Aldo Rozzi, the cheerful Italian lawyer at Brooks, Levy and Pheiffer. And Elizabeth—that was another concession he'd wrung out of them.

Elizabeth: he closed his eyes, tried to ignore the lump in his throat. She was a part of him and always would be; she was his Achilles' heel and the KGB knew it. They'd demonstrated that the second time he'd called her from Moscow; less than a minute after the switchboard operator at Samuels and Stein had connected them and they'd wished each other a Happy New Year, the line had suddenly gone dead before he'd had a chance to tell her how much he loved and missed her.

Kirov told himself that he had to stop thinking about Elizabeth and do something positive, otherwise he would go crazy. Hands shaking, he opened his suitcase and began to unpack. Shirts, socks, underwear in the chest of drawers, a pair of pajamas on the bed, and remember to hang the dressing gown on the hook behind the door. That's the style—now put your walking shoes and slippers away. Responding to the inner voice, he crouched in front of the bedside locker, opened the door and saw the bottle of Soviet brandy he'd left behind. It seemed a little fuller than he remembered.

"Surprise, surprise," Kirov said aloud, then reached inside the locker again, knowing he would find the photograph of Tania Abalakinova sunning herself on the beach at Sochi.

A bullet in the back wasn't the only way the KGB could destroy a man. They could ensure he was sent to a remote outpost without a proper job to do and all day to do it in. They could put him under a commanding officer like Colonel Leonid Paskar, a hardened drinker who would encourage him to hit the bottle and become a confirmed alcoholic.

That was it, then. They meant to turn him into a befuddled drunk long before Andropov gave the word to terminate his existence and long before Fedor Fedorovich died. Kirov forced himself to consider the strong possibility that his father wouldn't be alive when the snow thawed in Moscow, and wondered what he would do. Naturally, he would still have to protect Irena, but it wasn't necessary to remain in the Soviet Union to do that. He would see his half sister the next time he was in Moscow and tell her just how she was to distance herself from him and make the KGB believe that their relationship had gone sour. A little playacting, that was all it would take, and Igor Gusovsky would do the rest. Then he would suck up to Paskar, get himself attached to a combat unit in Afghanistan, and go over the hill at the first opportunity. It would take time, of course, and he would need to stay trim if he was going to survive all those drinking bouts with Paskar that stood between him and freedom and Elizabeth.

Kirov raised his eyes and stared at the snowcapped mountains in the distance. "I'm coming back," he whispered. "You hear me, I'm coming back."

Then he stripped to the waist, got down on the floor, and started on 100 push-ups.